The Water Company

A Novel by

Bull Marquette

BRAVE NEW GENRE, INC.

Fresno, CA

THE WATER COMPANY
© 2015 Bull Marquette

Marquette, Bull
The Water Company
ISBN: 978-9820474-9-1
Cover Art by Randi Smith

BRAVE NEW GENRE, INC.
Publishers of Books, Music & Films
6535 N Palm Ave. #101
Fresno, CA 93704
www.bravenewgenre.com

For Monika

CHAPTER 1
THE GIRL IN THE LAUNDROMAT

Organ grinder music floating acrss the Brazos heralded the start of the annual River Festival. The difference this year was a screeching guitar lick being played by a virtuoso who sounded like Bob Dylan. "It's not Dylan."

"Of course it is, no one else's voice sounds that bad."

Keith Clayton didn't believe in conspiracy theories. But on the afternoon when he ran out of beer, and his brother Larry called out of the blue to say there would be no more loans, it was like the Universe had gathered its armies against him.

"I can't talk, Larry. On my way to do my laundry with the last five quarters to my name." He yelled the words into the phone.

"Not kidding, big brother. I've got a girl friend, now, and I'll never be able to take Jenny to Dallas without saving my pennies. Six months is enough. People are starting to think you're strange, Dude."

"It hasn't been any six months. Why do you want to go to Dallas? Sironia's got movies. A minor league team. Take her out to eat at the Water Company. Ol' Ben'll give you his regular discount. Same one he never offered me."

"He wasn't in your grade, asshole. I mean it, Keith. And speaking of the restaurant, why haven't you gone down there all this time? Ben said he'd take care of you. Hell, a job waiting tables is better than starving. Which is what you're going to do now. That, or move back with mom and dad."

In the laundromat down on Fifth, by Sironia State, the afternoon sun and the steamy Brazos made outside almost as humid as in by the dryers. Keith sat in a plastic chair, *War and Peace* in his lap, too stunned to read a word.

The place was empty. Usually was in the afternoons, though sometimes he was tortured by the arrival of a coed. All the State girls were knockouts. Or maybe it had just been too long. Didn't matter. If a girl was using these washers, it usually meant she was living off campus and married. The only times he'd had the nerve to chat one of them up, he'd been put down.

And today, there was insult to injury. The only other humans in the place were a couple of smart-ass guys. Each of them drinking a forty-ounce beer. In clear violation of the signs plastered all over the walls. In the old days, Keith would have marched across to the Seven Eleven, bought one for himself, come back, and there would've been a party.

But that took money.

He tried to read. Couldn't. The jerks were laughing. College boys, of course. Jokes spoken in whispers. Insipid smiles. He remembered being that age. Not really that long ago. Classes he didn't always have to go to. Enough pocket change for booze. Girlfriends. My God, girlfriends weren't so – so *final* – when you were in college.

A weird feeling crawled up his spine. Hair standing up on his neck. He reached back and rubbed the back of his head, scratching an itch that wasn't really there – and that was when he saw her. There, outside the plate glass window. A woman was standing. Staring at him just as sure as he'd been watching the jerks. Another shiver seized him. She'd been there for some time. Did she have some wash in one of the machines?

It happened too fast – she dodged his gaze. Made for the door. Stepped in, and walked straight for the wall of dryers. Long black hair. A powerful nose, but delicate. Dark, full eyebrows. Medium-tall, but he would bet she could take either of the jerks.

"Hi," one of them said as she passed.

Of course she was here to pick up her laundry. But only Keith's and the punks' still tossed in the windows. She didn't open any of the other machines. Just stopped and watched his clothes for a moment. Then moved down three machines, and watched the college boys' clothes. The whispering and laughing started again. And belching from the beer.

Keith ignored them and studied at her strange attire. A long, full skirt, white blouse, black garters on the sleeves. He'd seen that sort of attire before – in the movies and – where else?

There was no time to search his memory, because she wheeled, looked straight into his eyes, and walked over and sat down right next to him.

"Hi," Keith managed to say. "Do you know those guys? Go to school with them?"

She was staring straight ahead. Turned now. Her black eyes were like whirlpools, pulling him in. A smell of magnolia. Or roses – no, honeysuckle. Yes, it *had* been too long. Of course he'd had endless fantasies, sitting at home on the couch, watching Triple-X movies, but he'd forgotten how much electricity could be generated by just sitting next to a female.

"You're the only one here with any energy," she said.

It was like a body blow. A beautiful woman, laying a line on *him*. Even if it was something a hippie might say. Larry always accused Keith of falling in love with space cadets.

"Thanks. I'm Keith. What's your name?"

The guys across the way burst into laughter. Elbowed each other, like Keith had delivered the funniest joke in history. But it had really been only seconds since she came in, and she turned in the seat, looking like a woman on a mission.

"You go to college here at State?"

He barely got the question out when she leaned over and kissed him. Long and hard. Too stunned to move, he let her tongue – cold, like she'd just swallowed a mouthful of ice – play with his. Shivering, like he'd stuck his finger in a wall socket.

She pulled away before he even opened his eyes. Stood there for a second, gave him a strange, dark look. Then she was gone, through the door, a shadow in the grimy plate glass window. Gone.

He stood up, shaking. It was more than a fantasy. Keith felt like he'd been thrust into some weird movie. Outside, he looked both directions, couldn't remember which way she went. He swallowed, and turned on the college boys.

"Excuse me. Do you guys know that lady who just left?"

"We work with her." The blond one recoiled. "You mean you don't know her?"

The pair of them seemed vastly unsettled, so she must not act this way with everyone. The tall one had rolled a copy of *Playboy* into a tight cylinder, as if that should be concealed instead of the alcohol. He snickered, and nudged the other one. "Never saw Carlotta give anyone the time of day. Much less suck face with him." They both collapsed in giggles. Again.

"You ass. She's not Carlotta."

"Well, she looks like her." They were enjoying their inside joke so much.

"C'mon, give me a break here. Do you know her? Where do you work?"

"Huh?" They looked at each other. Like Keith was the dullest tool in the shed. "Three guesses," the tall one said. "Didn't you see how she was dressed? Gay Nineties. You know, all the waitresses at the Water Company wear that get-up. The guys wear railroad overalls."

"The restaurant?"

The blond one raised his bottle. "The man's a genius. But don't tell her we spilled the beans. Nobody messes with Carlotta."

"Carlotta? Is that her name or not? She married?"

They laughed again. Bumping shoulders. Slapping backs. "Feel sorry for her husband if she is. She's an ice queen. That is, until now."

"Maybe this guy awakened the slut within," Blondie said, and they both stumbled to the dryer, laughing so hard Keith couldn't get a word in edgewise.

"We gotta get our clothes and go, Mister," the tall one said when Keith kept sidling up.

"What, you said she's a waitress? Hostess?" Keith ambled after them, but they lugged their basket between them, set their empty bottles delicately on chairs, and hustled out, mumbling to each other, Keith following them in slow motion.

The blond one paused in the doorway.

"Come see us. We'll buy you a drink," he said.

From the parking lot, the tall one bellowed, "Yeah. You might get lucky."

Obscene gestures, until doors slammed and their car peeled out of the lot.

Still reeling, Keith opened his own dryer, pulled pants and underwear out, then tried to still his shaking hands.

Linda said he was never spontaneous. Maybe so. But as he stuffed his laundry basket into the car's trunk, that was about to change. Larry had been hounding him to go get a waiter's job at the Water Company for months. His brother's best friend, Ben, was the manager there. A broken-down, hundred-year old brick mausoleum had been converted by five millionaires into Sironia's biggest eating attraction, complete with antique farm implements on the wall and a famous chef from Chicago, New Orleans, and – and now this – this girl who works there shows up, strikes like lightning, and – what the hell happened, anyway?

Out on River Drive, the car seemed to know exactly where it was going. Keith took deep gulps of the hot, humid afternoon air, trying to coax his heart to beat slower. Looking for excuses to just go home and forget the dark eyes, the sizzling touch. The cold tongue. Airconditioner in his car still broken. He wasn't ready for this. Months of inaction – then, all of a sudden, the heavens opened up. A woman like her couldn't possibly be real. Could she?

Logical explanations buzzed in his head like bees. But this was far beyond logic. He'd always heard of love at first sight. Even thought it happened to him a dozen times in junior high. This time, it was the real thing. Forget what Larry and his college buds might say about a girl who kisses you the first time you meet her. They were louts. And they had never met...Carlotta.

CHAPTER 2
INTRODUCTION

"Well, my brother finally talked me into it." Keith shook Ben's hand and sat down across on the opposite side of a ponderous, scratched-up desk in a cluttered office up on the second floor. "So this is behind the scenes of a major restaurant, eh?" The air conditioner worked up here, in stark contrast to the steamy kitchen he had just been escorted through.

"A world class restaurant, Bucko. Chef Thomas has been the head honcho at so many--"

"I know, Ben. Save it. I've read the articles about him. You know I'm desperate, so I won't try to scam an old friend. I need money. I need to get my life back on track. I need to meet some of these beautiful waitresses I hear so much about." No – too early to tell Ben he already had one picked out.

The manager chuckled, coloring. He seemed relaxed, an adult, all of a sudden. Little Ben – the punk kid he and Larry used to dunk in the pool, running an eatery with six dozen employees. "Great," Ben said. "Good to see you again, man." He seized a stapler off of the desk and began scratching his head with it, not really looking in Keith's direction.

"Look, I can start anytime. Hell, tomorrow, if necessary. I know I need to learn a few things, like which wines go with what, that sort of thing. But, you know me, I can play the elegant part. I can open a damned bottle of wine without busting the cork."

"Damn, Keith." Ben held his hand up. "I'm in a spot. The normal thing is to start as a bus person, then work your way up. Thomas — he's the big boss — is a stickler for promoting from within. I mean, that's how he came up. Started as a little kid at the Plaza in New York."

"No shit?" Keith felt the ground shifting. "Well? How long would I have to do that? Sorry, I guess I was believing Larry's bullshit about how much pull you had — " Oops. That was the wrong way to put it. Even to Ben. "I mean--"

"I know. I know." The stapler came open and closed in nervous spasms. "It's not his fault. I thought I could get around the rules. Then, when you never showed up, I just gave away the last bus-person opening." Ben sat back, his gaze scanning the ceiling. "I mean, we have turnover. Hell, this is the restaurant business. It won't be two weeks, I bet, until..." His voice faded out. Face still red. Stupid, Keith wanted to shout. You're the one doing the hiring. You don't have to be under pressure.

"Great." So much for omens. It looked like the only way he would meet Carlotta would be to come in and buy a dinner with money he did not have.

"There is one thing." The stapler waved hopefully in the air. "You could start out where I did. In the kitchen. I just had a cook quit on me. She got spooked upstairs. Oh--" He chuckled. Even more embarrassment. "Forgot to tell you. The place is haunted. But, hell, we've all heard the stories."

"I haven't. What do you mean, starting as a cook? Working down in that sweaty hell-hole I just came through?"

Ben leaned forward. "It's the ace up our sleeve. I told you, I started there, too. Give it a few months behind the Line, and you won't ever have to bus. I can jump you into a waiter's slot. Thomas'll swallow that."

No way. Keith sat back. The one speech he hadn't composed was one telling Ben no thanks for the big favor.

"Excuse me." A voice behind startled him. A scantily clad cocktail waitress brushed past Keith's arm. Mid-length black hair, brown eyes, impeccably applied make-up, and graceful fingers that flexed along the edge of the tray she carried.

"Ben, could you check this? Happy hour is about to start."

"Sure." Ben took the small metal box off of her tray. "Keith, Andrea. She waits down in the bar. Keith wants to work with us." He pulled out a stack of bills and began counting.

"Oh." When she shook hands, Keith did not want to let go of such softness. The smell of some expensive perfume. "Are you replacing Brenda?" she asked, but turned away before he could answer, leaving him to a view of the back seams of her black-net nylons.

"Trying to talk him into it," Ben answered for him.

Keith felt his blood rise. "Is that the cook who quit?"

"Yes." Andrea sighed. "Gosh, she was here for five or ten years, a long time." Keith imagined what those long fingers could do. If he got nowhere with Carlotta, this would be a nice fallback.

"What was that you said, Ben?" Perhaps talking would make her stay. "The place is haunted? Do you believe that, Andrea?"

She shrugged. "I hear weird sounds, but this is an old building. We sort of talk it up. Keeps the customers coming back."

Ben snapped the box shut. "It's all there."

"Thanks." A smile. "Well, nice to meet you," she said. Silky voice. She even patted Keith's shoulder on her way out.

"Yeah," Keith croaked, then cleared his throat. "Likewise."

Ben laid his head on the desk, stifling a guffaw. "Don't let your eyes glaze over like that, you horn-dog."

"I'll take it."

"What?"

"Well, all the ad agencies in town are on hiring freeze. I hate the thought of that kitchen, but if it lets me meet creatures like her—"

"No kidding?" Ben smiled. "The way you looked before, I thought you were going to tell me to shove it. Hey, it's just a little more than minimum wage."

Keith took a breath. "Look, this puts me back in circulation, that's all. I've been a hermit too long, and Larry won't lend me any more dough. If you can't work me into waiter in a couple of months, I'll start looking. Fair enough?" First, his love life. Financial health would follow. That formula had already failed him once. So what?

Ben stood. "Of course. We're all looking. Always."

"And can you introduce me to Carlotta?"

Ben looked puzzled. "Did Larry tell you about them?"

"Them? It's a she, old pal. One of the most striking she's I've ever seen. Oh, God, don't tell me she has a boyfriend."

Ben chuckled. "Not that I know of. You're so full of shit. Come on. The guy who will train you isn't on duty yet. I'll introduce you to Thomas." He set a fast pace down the hall.

"The big boss?"

A nod. "Owner and head chef." He slowed. "Well, the other four guys are still in the picture, but he's buying them out."

The upstairs alcove opened into both dining rooms, as well as the stairs leading down to the kitchen. In one corner, though, a darkened doorway led to smaller stairs that went up. Ben rushed ahead.

"This place has a third floor?" Cautiously, Keith put his foot onto the bottom of a rickety spiral staircase that climbed into blackness.

"Just Thomas's office. Plus a storeroom. Don't worry about the stairs. They're new. I helped rebuild them."

"Now I know we're screwed."

After two turns, the roof opened above them, slanting upwards for another story--maybe two--toward the apex of the huge ceiling. Keith's fingers tightened on the rough wooden railing.

The ceiling above them was black, giving one the illusion of standing under a vault of night, except for the opaque skylights through which blinding shafts of sunlight glared. The storm must have passed. Galaxies of dust specks floated in the empty space. A deep breath, to keep his knees from buckling.

"God, I hope I don't have to come up here very often."
Ben just chuckled.

They emerged onto a wide landing, and the old
mausoleum's ambiance became even more bizarre. To the left,
a narrow catwalk stretched over a chasm toward a small shed-
like room that appeared tacked on to the inner wall of the
building.

"Upper storage room. What's the matter?" Ben seemed
amused.

Keith gasped for breath. "Sorry. Months with my ass
on the couch."

"That's Thomas's office." A wave toward what looked
like a one-room shack with windows. Above the door, a single
floodlight burned. "This was the supervisor's office back in the
old days of the Sironia Water Company. We call it the
Lookout." He wrung his hands together, Boris Karloff-style.
"Where ze boss plans vich waitress he vill bed next."

"So that's how it is?"

Ben only smiled. "But, since you're such an eager
beaver, you gotta meet our mascots --"

Keith followed him cautiously across the landing,
which wobbled just enough to give a sensation of floating. Ben
stopped and waved his hand. "Voila."

Two huge antique wooden Indians towered above Ben
in the dim light. Between them, a rope had been stretched, and
from that, three largish wooden marionettes hung in the
shadows, quivering faintly from the rumble of sizeable air
conditioners that made a sort of wall on the landing's far side.

"They--they're puppets," Keith blurted.

"Sure. Larry told you, or you wouldn't have brought it
up." Besides the three hanging, another one lay crumpled at
the base of one of the Indians. "These guys have been at The
Water Company longer than any of us." Ben swept his hand
like a carnival barker. "Decades."

He pointed to the wooden Indian on the left. "This is
Cochise, the big one. The mean-looking one is Geronimo.
Supposedly, they stood outside two tobacco stores on Main

Street, opposite each other for years. Mr. Payton--you know, Jennifer Payton's grandfather?"

"Of course, you idiot. I dated her."

"He bought the Indians in the thirties, from the Terrace estate, across the street. Been here ever since."

"I wonder how old they were when he got them." The faces of the marionettes were unsettling, too real in the shadows and the vibrations from the big fans. Larger than children's toys, they made Keith remember stories his grandparents used to tell about Sunday socials down in River Park.

The craftsmanship was faultless and detailed, harking back to a time when a woodcarver could make a living. The one nearest Ben had a roundish face with large dots on the cheeks and a pointy wooden nose. He was dressed in black tie and wore a short top hat. Each of them had moveable wooden eyes. Heavy lashes lined lids that could open and shut. The round-faced man stared straight ahead, almost accusingly.

"Do they have names?" Keith asked.

Ben pulled on the little man's strings. An arm worked up and down. "Thomas calls this one Hercule. I kind of like Poindexter better."

He pointed to the middle puppet, a beautifully fashioned light-green dragon, larger than the others. A purplish cape fell from its neck, held by a tarnished chain. The mouth hung open, dingy-white teeth bared, the lacquer finish pocked with gashes. "That's just *Dragon*. The one down on the floor is a leprechaun, ro something." A small pipe stuck out from a grimacing face.

"And her?"

Keith's gaze had not been able to leave her for long. The face resembled a beautiful gypsy woman. She had long, dark hair and a red sequined dress that fell full length over her dangling legs. Her features had been rendered remarkably smooth except for a prominent nose and sweeping painted eyebrows. Ben gave her strings a feeble shove, and her eyelids fluttered, as if trying to open.

"Hey," Keith said and jumped back.

Ben bent over laughing. "Yeah. Spooky as hell up here, isn't it?"

Keith gasped, waiting for his heartbeat to calm. "So? What's her name?"

"Huh?" A sneering chuckle. It was Little Ben from junior high, looking down on the masses who wanted to copy his math homework. "It's the one you said you wanted to see, dumbass. This is Carlotta."

CHAPTER 3
LIONEL

He waited until after the others left to call her from the dead. In the shadows of the huge air conditioning ducts, in the attic of the great building, Lionel sat, listening to the voices below, catching the occasional word in English. The loud-mouthed *Norte Americanos* were loud enough to be heard this high up. The Mexicans spoke much more quietly.

His own countrymen—they were the ones he could not trust. He saw their damning glances, caught them smirking in the corners among themselves. A person's story follows him when he crosses the river. Would they be so holier-than-thou if they knew what he was about to do?

Cars scraped gravel, rumbling out of the back parking lot and onto the smooth road by the river.

He had been in the *Estados Unidos* barely three months, and had hated every minute—until this one. How he longed to walk in the field beside his uncle again, listen to his funny stories. Yet, he could not think of the kind old man too much, for the images of that last night would come back to his head.

"All things happen for a reason," Uncle used to say. That seemed a cruel lie. Until now.

He did not care what the others said about him, nor that they despised him for not drinking *cerveza*. Beer cluttered their minds and kept them stupid. Sure, they claimed to be loyal, and pure, and forever *Mexicano*, but he watched them sink slowly into American slovenliness. All the talk about family, then cheap excuses when they quit sending money home.

But maybe it would be the same at home. Not one of these poor *cabrones* could see the treasure in front of their noses: the wooden lady, Carlotta, was possessed by the spirit of a beautiful princess. Back in Guadalajara, they would say it was devil worship.

Lionel concentrated, then whispered the chant—the dangerous one that Uncle had warned him to use only at the most extreme moment. This was such a moment. If the old man's teachings had stayed with him, it must happen tonight.

A last car rumbled out of the lot, leaving silence and the wind. None of the Mexicans had come looking for him. So much the better. He knew all the places to hide.

He stealthed down the staircases, through the dining rooms, and moved the heavy table to open the way to the basement. Dank and stale, the tiny concrete cells seemed to grow from the river clay itself. He found his sacred spot, lit the candle, and took deep breaths, listening for the barely audible rush of the river.

The flickering light hurt his eyes, so he closed them. On the inside of his eyelids, shadows of the crazed townspeople began to play, dancing, laughing at the way the helpless old man strained against the ropes. The candle became Uncle's shack, then the fencepost where they bound him, a yellow and white stain in the pitch night of the Mexican prairie. The old man never cried out, except with his eyes. Of course he was a magician, but could never have done what the Aguilar girl said.

Finally, the candle burned steady, and the chant began by itself, words rising and falling as if Lionel's tongue belonged to someone else. Concentrate--the words, the void, surrender to the flame. The wish floated to the top of his consciousness, and the cubicle fell silent.

Exhausted, he fell back, the concrete wall cool against his head. He reached for the magic blanket and pulled it over him. A great clap of thunder shook the building, heralding another rush of rain. Noises like that were confirmations: he had touched a nerve in the cosmos.

From behind the long dying rumbles, he thought he heard a scraping. Vague at first, then unmistakable. Footsteps. Far away, up the stairs.

Heart beating. A new day – he could reach the other side without Uncle! Maybe the first time was an accident, but this--Lionel imagined the wizened face of his teacher, shrouded on the dark farmhouse porch. Smiling.

Now the wooden floor above his head groaned lightly, charting a slow, easy movement, all the way to the basement stairs. "Please, my Savior, let it be her," he whispered.

At last the folds of her dress appeared, rich red color muted in the candlelight, its hem long enough to brush her bare feet. Fingers reached around the wall, indistinguishable from their own shadows. Black Gypsy hair fell over the arms, almost to her waist.

The shine of her eyes. Faint at first, like the soft birth of stars in the twilight sky, as if her soul had to travel far to fill her phantom's body.

He began power-breathing. Entities from beyond would bite like a snake if they felt you slipping. *Dios mio*, what was his request? A spirit such as she could grant a wish. The boldness to ask, Uncle had explained, separated ordinary men from true magicians.

"Your power grows." Her whisper froze him in mid-thought. She closed her eyes and stretched, a movement that oozed a wild freedom. His hand moved to touch her shoulder, but stopped when her eyes came open again.

"Who are you? What is your name?" he blurted in choppy English. But he was wasting his chances -- "Take me to your world," he whispered.

A thief's audacity rippled across her countenance. Was she, too, fighting for control? After a moment, she moved around the room, seeming fascinated by the empty walls, ignoring him. She flexed her hands, as if they were a novelty, and suddenly turned. Lionel fought not to be consumed by that gaze.

"He is with the Children," she said quietly. Perhaps an intense whisper, maybe only a loud thought. "You are in danger as long as I remain here with you. I must return, or he will discover you."

"Not afraid, " he blurted, though, of course, that was a lie. Could she possibly have feelings for him? And what could a soul cast into wood have to fear? "I will protect you from anyone."

He pushed his shaking fingers through empty space. She watched them intertwine with her own. Lionel gasped at the iciness of her hands. He had almost forgotten. The same as the first time.

"They will capture someone. Very soon. I do not want it to be you." Softer, infinite softness. Closer, and her gaze bore into him, raking through his mind.

"Can your power stop them?"

"Stop who?"

She pulled one hand free and led him into the blackness of the hall. Lionel strained to see, and when he blinked, was astonished to find they had emerged into fresh air. Not only had the basement vanished, but the entire building with it. He looked at each cardinal point. The rolling landscape, somehow familiar. The grassy rise, smooth and empty — the Water Company should be standing here, all around them. The river lay in its expected place, even the old mansion across the street, but no telephone poles, and River Drive had been replaced by a worn dirt road.

Fog crept up from the water, making it hard to see where his feet were landing. She was standing above him. Stared deep into his eyes, until he felt naked, ultimately embarrassed. She pulled him to his feet, then along a narrow path into the Terrace grounds, through a strange stone fence. The old house looked different, somehow more clean. Raw.

A push sent him stumbling through the front door. She stayed close, but would not meet his eyes. Lightly, her fingers traced his backbone until they interlaced behind his neck. She pulled him down and kissed him, her tongue a shaft of fire between lips of ice. Lionel struggled to catch his breath.

"My love, what are you doing?" he cried out between gasps of air. His body shook. He must keep his thoughts pure.

She tugged again, pulling him up the stairs, then into a bedroom where eerie orange light flickered through the windows. When she closed the door, smoke engulfed their feet.

They were not alone. Another man – strange, with thick, curly hair – sat only a foot away from them, on the edge of a bed. Flames slashed in, shattering the windows. A woman's voice screamed somewhere. Yet, the young man sat peacefully, seeming resigned to a wretched, burning death.

Carlotta's chilly fingers slipped from Lionel's and she was suddenly perched on the bed, next to the young man, whispering into his ear. Lionel could not make out the words, but the man was hypnotized, resigned to listen to her commands above any urge to save himself. Carlotta asked the lonely man to stay calm, accept his fate. In velvet tones, she was begging him to join her in the world of the dead.

Smoke poured in furiously now, stinging Lionel's eyes until his view of the couple warped and slid away.

Lionel rubbed his face and blinked. Stale earth and mildew. He was back. The candle burned serenely now, shorter. His shirt was soaked with chilly sweat. A shiver rose from the center of his soul. The man's face – he had seen it before, somewhere. From his own childhood? Or in a dream. The events he witnessed must have happened long ago.

He commanded the horrible crime to leave his mind – if it was a crime. But that last look, the pain on Carlotta's beautiful face remained. Another memory came to the fore: one that couldn't possibly have occurred. They stood out on the grass again – he and Carlotta. Together. Holding hands. Her stare, icy.

"You are not ready," she said.

He awoke. This time, for real. Thunder chuckled, high, high above, welcoming him back.

Yes, he was ready. She was underestimating him. Forgivable, because she couldn't possibly realize how pure his heart was.

As Lionel folded the magic blanket, then put out the candle, an impossible scheme began to take shape in his mind. A tour de force, the exercise that would demonstrate his power to her. She deserved a better eternity than this. Her spirit was noble, perfect; of that he was sure. How long had it been since her body walked the earth?

There was a way to bring her back to this life. Not easy, certainly, but his uncle had done just that. It was said.

Now the thunder gods spoke a warning. Much closer. Unhappy with his thoughts? The old foundation seemed to sway, as if the ancient building had set sail on the wide Brazos. Yes, there was a way. Even a small mistake with Uncle's teachings could mean disaster, but there was a way.

He groped through blackness, felt the walls of the hall, crossed the large, empty dank-smellng cubicle, until his feet hit the concrete steps. Through the trapdoor above, the dining room exit lights cast a calm red glow, broken by flashes of lightning through the restaurant's leaded-glass windows. Like a neon sign, the flashing declared that he had found it – the reason for coming to this land. His destiny was here. And his destiny was Carlotta. Lionel placed his foot on the bottom step and climbed toward that promise.

CHAPTER 4
THE KISS

"Goddam it, I told you. A bunch of the waitresses have dark hair." Ben brandished the application form Keith had just handed him.

"Not dark. Black. Raven black, almost down to her waist."

The manager seemed to think, but only for an instant. "Look. You said she used the name Carlotta. Well, that's the goddam puppet up there. There's never been a waitress with that name. So somebody's pulling your leg. Maybe she *is* a waitress here, but she was wearing a black wig. Or--" Now he frowned, and it felt like they were back in high school. "-- you and Larry are trying to set me up for a prank."

"I don't pull gags," Keith corrected. "That's *you* and my brother, not me. Remember?"

Ben stared at the form. "Look, if I was a dame, and some creepy guy – no offense, but it *was* in a Laundromat, for God's sake – I wouldn't give my right name, either. So come on, Keith. You want this job or not?"

If they were not old friends, this would be a good time to stop the whole thing. He had spent a rough night, filled out the application, and now Ben was sending him on another unexpected errand, plus still being coy about the identity of the real "Carlotta."

"If I don't get the job, I'll have to move back in with my parents. I'll be around long enough to learn it, Ben, but my finances are worse than I thought. You should know that I'll be hitting up the ad agencies whenever I can."

"I told you, we're all looking." Ben sat back. "What about Dallas?"

Keith shrugged. "Perhaps. That's funny. If I had just gone to Dallas, Linda might have stayed with me. That's all she ever talked about. 'Sironia's dying. Sironia's dying.' You know."

"Shit, it is dying. Here." He handed over a different, shorter form. "Take that down to the health department — Fourth street, you know? They keep it, then they'll send us the health card. Can you start tomorrow?"

Keith stood. "Morning?"

"Eight o'clock. Prep time. Saturday brunch starts at eleven." They shook hands.

In the hallway, Keith turned. "I figured it out. Those two waiters were being smart asses, giving her the puppet's name. There is a resemblance, though. Just wait 'til I see one of those guys down in the kitchen."

"Ignore the bastards, whoever they are." Ben's grimace turned into a sly smile. "Once we get you behind the line, your mystery lady will come prancing down with a dinner order, and it will be love at first sight."

"Second sight."

Ben dug a pencil into Keith's chest, holding him in place. "Just you behave when you do see her. We've got sexual harassment rules, you know."

"God, Ben. You talk like I'm in heat or something."

"You are. Can't think of any other reason you'd want to work here, for God's sake."

In the alcove, Keith paused in front of the dark stairway. Was there really a resemblance? Folding the health form carefully, he decided to take one more look at the lady puppet, and mounted the shuddering stairs. Ben was right. He had to get hold of himself. She was just one girl, and anything he felt in the Laundromat had to be magnified by the fact that women had been absent from his life — too long. That would change, he resolved, and felt a rush of excitement at the thought.

As he climbed, though, the darkness seemed to eat into his resolve. How could Thomas stand to work up here every day, alone in this spooky attic? He had seemed so affable at their meeting yesterday. Carefree. Why not? The town gossips claimed he was worth a million by now.

As Ben said, the man had paid his dues, years as a cook, then head chef at headliner restaurants in New York, Chicago, New Orleans. He had an almost childish penchant for little hand-held games. Not video games, the old ones, like the ball-and-jack he fidgeted with throughout the interview.

At the top of the stairs, Keith stood panting, squinting. The puppets were nowhere to be seen. A rumble overhead — another storm approaching. Light pouring down from the skylights seemed noticeably muted, making the weird, quiet atmosphere thicker than yesterday. Hot. Almost suffocating.

Keith's knees shook in spite of his efforts to control them. The best defense was a good offense. He stepped over to the Lookout and knocked. Perhaps Thomas had them in there. No answer. He waited a moment, turning his gaze toward each distant corner. The wooden Indians stood in their places, staring fiercely, like warriors who expected an attack to come at any moment. He took another breath and turned the knob — the door opened.

Thomas's office was dark, lit only slightly by the skylights' glow filtering through the side windows. He leaned over to peer out of one. The side of the balcony dining room on the second floor was visible from here, tables empty. Hurricane-style streetlamps muted. Beyond the railing, the main dining room on the first floor lay in shadows. Back in the old days, the boss of the water works could have seen a lot from up here.

A greenish glow came from the face of the clock radio on the credenza behind Thomas's desk — the only modern convenience in evidence. The desktop was swept bare, tidy, like everything about the man, except for his graying shock of hair. On the credenza, the ball-in-jack lay, along with what appeared to be a hand-crank music box, and a wooden Parcheesi set, all placed just so. No marionettes.

A sound. Keith turned, suddenly out of breath. Thomas? On the stairs? He rushed out and closed the door behind him. Nothing. For an instant, he could only stand, breathing hard. Then a movement caught his eye. Across the landing, over the narrow catwalk in the tiny storage room, a waitress was moving boxes, partly visible behind half-drawn curtains.

He swallowed, wondering if she had seen him, thinking it might be best to disappear, but something about her movements held him in place. The garter around the sleeve of her puffy waitress shirt, the way her full skirt moved—her hair—my God, it was she!

Heart pounding, he made it to the near end of the catwalk. "Hi," he called out.

She stopped moving boxes in the cramped space, but did not look around.

"Hello? Remember me? We met the other day?"

A beat. Finally, she turned to face him, her long hair draped around her shoulders. Her gaze settled to his, and those piecing eyes erased the last doubts. Heart beating. Another deep breath. She glanced downward, perhaps embarrassed. "Be careful on the bridge," she said, as if she knew that nothing would stop him from crossing over it.

Instantly, he put his hands on the shaky railing and looked down. Three stories of darkness and shadows cascaded below. Perhaps he would hit the slanted roof over the ground floor restrooms if he fell. Either that or the hard concrete of the electrical room between the lower dining room and the kitchen.

He laughed nervously. "Hope it holds me. I weigh a lot more than you."

She did not answer, but leaned against the boxes, her hand brushing her hair back in the most exquisite motion.

The first steps were excruciating, then he scrambled forward, using a tall tortilla chip box to cushion his sudden stop.

"Hi," he said, unsure of whether to offer his hand. "I'm Keith, remember?" She looked up at him. No smile, just pure sensuality and honeysuckle perfume.

"I knew you would come," she said. "Let me show you."

Stepping back, she pulled a drawstring, and a single hanging light bulb exploded the tiny room in stark shadows. Cardboard boxes were stacked up the two side walls. The back wall was brick, the side of the restaurant, he figured, and she backed toward it, motioning for him to follow. It took only two short steps for him to crowd in next to her. Her perfume was suffocating. Intoxicating.

She pointed. A horizontal board had been mounted on the wall. Like a single bookshelf. On top of it were some toys: a small version of an old flatbed wagon, complete with a little wooden man as a driver, and a wooden horse pulling it. She reached forward and adjusted one of the horse's legs, making it stand more securely.

"God, there are toys all over this place aren't there? Are these Thomas's, too?" He moved closer, so that his arm pressed against hers.

"Not toys," she replied flatly.

In the bed of the wagon, a tiny marionette lay. Its features were smooth, as yet uncarved, but strings had already been run through small holes in its hands and feet.

"Yes, they are. Wow – another puppet, but this one's a lot smaller. And they didn't finish it." He pointed, and took the liberty of gripping her elbow at the same time. She didn't jerk it away. "Do you know who took the big marionettes away?"

She turned, so close that her breasts brushed against him. A long look up, black hair, strong face. To hell with the puppets. This woman seemed to know who she was and what she wanted. Had he ever really known one like that? Was there a chance she could want him?

A tension sizzled between them. She kept staring. Eyes searching for something in him. He resisted, but not for long.

Suddenly, he was grippng both of her arms. "Please tell me your real name."

Still gazing. But now a slight smile. Softly, deftly, her hands rose to his neck and pulled him down. "I knew you would come." A whisper. A glorious, deep whisper from lips just brushing his.

Then those lips pressed full on, lingering, tongues touching. The world spun. Perhaps the two of them together were too heavy, because the storeroom felt to be tumbling down into the blackness. Didn't matter. He held on. Wished this moment could last forever.

When he finally pulled back, gasping for air, she answered his very thoughts.

"It will last forever."

She gave him a sudden, desperate hug, and his mouth opened, but words would not come out. He blinked, and she let go, pushed past him, then moved swiftly, out through the half-parted curtains and jumped across the catwalk, like some sort of gazelle.

He tried to follow, but the skylights glared brightly now. Spots floated before his eyes, and his chest heaved as he balanced across the wobbling walkway – not daring to leap, as she had –but she was gone. He strained to hear her footsteps — on the stairs? — the Lookout? No sound, except for lonely clangs and voices rising from the kitchen. They would be gearing up for the dinner hour.

Should he tell Ben the quarry had been located? Not important. He had come here to find her, and now he had. It didn't even matter that she kept up the strange, elusive act. Coming from her, it did not feel like game-playing. A deep, inner calm told him not to worry.

She had already kissed him. Twice. So, she must know, somehow, too.

She was the one.

CHAPTER 5
A DANCE

Chavo and the others were drinking beer tonight, spending hard-earned money instead of sending it home. "Robbing their fathers," it was called. When a party was planned, they whispered among themselves, but never invited him. *Brujo*, they called him. Warlock. *Pendejo*. Bastard.

The broom's swishing soothed his frayed nerves. Twice tonight he had performed the chant with no success. Last night, the same.

He had heard things said about women. She was making him wait—was that some sacred woman's game, mandatory even after a female soul was free of the body? Uncle's chants were commands, in the nether world, so how did she resist them?

With each crack and pop of the old building in the darkness of midnight, he halted the wide brush. Silence.

He swept by feel. Already, these floors seemed as familiar as Uncle's porch. Like a muted paintbrush, the wide broom head glided into the red glow of the exit lights, then plunged back into shadows under the table.

The only woman he ever really knew was *Madre*. He remembered her standing over his bed in the middle of the night, eyes glistening like an owl's. What a jumble of emotions a female could be. Relief, happiness, shame—all poured out of her at once.

Her real wish stung him, though, like a lash from Uncle's switch. She wanted both Lionel and his brother to die, so that she would be free.

Little Raffy did die of a fever. Lionel was young then, but he knew that *Madre* had caused it, somehow. They were her property, weren't they, to do with as she wished? The evenings in the yard, when she gave him pomegranates — those were the best times.

Thinking of *Madre* brought a bright tune to mind. The broom handle swayed, and he moved around it, dancing as if it were the partner he longed for. The dance grew spastic, funny, as he hummed.

A twirl, and the broom head swooped the air. His high-stepping feet made the floor talk. He bumped into the salad bar, and froze. Was that a noise out in the dining room?

Silence. Long moments. Only the rushing air conditioners and his own breathing.

"Carlotta?" He said it, and the echo of his voice sounded eerie.

Slowly, the broom began to sway again, the tune came back. Something touched his elbow, and Lionel jumped.

"*Que?*"

Slender fingers retreated from the reddish glow. He grabbed them.

"My love, why didn't you come before?" he said, barely able to hold back tears of joy.

Her face remained in the shadows, but her hand rose to caress his cheek. "I am frightened," she answered. "My master watches so closely. It takes all of my power to hide your pull on me. It reminds me of desire. I have not tasted desire in a long time. This is so dangerous."

"I am the one full of desire," he said. He embraced her as if she were already alive, and felt a tear fall from his cheek into her black hair. "Enough to light the candle of life for you." Was this love? He hoped so. "Let me bring you back to this world."

He felt a wave travel through her when he said it. With a halting motion, her fingers traveled up and down his spine.

"Are you so powerful?" she finally asked. "You would not only have to defeat my master, but his hellhound, too." She seemed to weigh the possibilities. "No, dear one. When I send my mind along the course of the river, I see our paths crossing, but for you, your whole life awaits. I am patient now. I can be content with just the memory of these few moments."

"Listen to me, *querida*. There is a way." He grasped her shoulders, straining to see her eyes in the dark. "My uncle taught me how to reach across the lines of the worlds. I want you to live again, taste a life that is happy. A life for us both, together. Let me talk to this master of yours. I will convince him you deserve another chance."

She sighed and pulled away. "Talk to me of courage forever – but courage cannot save me. Already he has betrothed me to another. It is always this way. Do not call me again, dear one. Find love among the living and be safe." Her voice became a whisper, and before he could touch her again, she was gliding away.

He gave chase, broom thrashing behind him like an unwieldy tail, knocking over chairs, but swift – too swiftly she moved, a graceful shadow fluttering through the alcove, flashing red eclipses darting between tables, then up, onto the balcony railing, where she danced, like clothes flapping on a clothesline, until she merged with the darkness.

"Come back." He thumped against the railing and leaned out into thin air, calling. "There is a way we can be together."

CHAPTER 6
ALBERTO

Mexican music blared from a huge cream-yellow Cadillac in the middle of the Water Company's back parking lot. The driver's feet stuck out the open door onto the gravel. Keith parked on the far side, under a tree. Hopefully, she would also be on the brunch shift. Perhaps he could even find a corner in which he could kiss her again.

The door to the kitchen was locked, so Keith shuffled aimlessly, kicking gravel into puddles of rainwater, until he finally walked toward the Cadillac. The driver remained seated, squinting against the sun.

"Hi. I'm Keith. I'm new here--in the kitchen."

"Alberto," came the grudging reply. The accordion and bass from the car's tape deck blared a mariachi-polka beat.

"Nice music," Keith said after an awkward pause. Alberto offered him the tape case. *Miguel Garcia!* the flashy cover slip announced. A handsome, well-dressed man clutching a guitar stood beneath the name, posed on a sandy beach in front of resort hotels. Beautiful women in bikinis surrounded him.

"He very rich," Alberto said.

"I bet."

"You waiter?"

"No-no." Keith smiled. "Training for the kitchen. I'm a cook."

"Cook? You chef?" Alberto's scowl deepened.

"No, not a chef." Keith found himself echoing Alberto's Pidgin English. "Just a beginner. Apprentice."

"Ahh. You're a cop? Here for the Mexicans?"

Keith scowled. "Of course not. Why did you ask that? Do I look like a policeman?"

A shrug. Shy smile. "*Si.*" Of course. Larry had said the place was staffed with wetbacks.

"Well, I'm not. I'm as desperate for a job as you are. What do you do here?" Keith asked.

"I cook, *tambien*. My brother is Cisco."

Keith had met Cisco yesterday. The only Mexican in the kitchen with a green card, according to Ben. Alberto made nervous adjustments to the tape deck, but Miguel Garcia's voice remained undaunted.

"Nice car," Keith said, wishing like hell more people would show up.

It must have been the right comment to make, for a huge smile erupted on the young man's face. "*Gracias.* I have it six months." He climbed out, clutching a rag and began to polish the vehicle's perfect finish. Shorter than Cisco, Keith noted. Their facial structures were varied enough to make him wonder whether they had different fathers.

"I got a chip." Alberto pushed the car door to, muffling Garcia and combat between an accordion and guitar.

"A chip?"

"*Aqui*—here," He squatted down and pointed to a tiny blemish in the paint, rubbing carefully around it.

"God, you can't even see it," Keith exclaimed. "If you think that's bad, don't even look at my rattletrap."

Still squatting, the young man glanced over, then smiled. Thomas's aging pick-up truck appeared, and Keith breathed a sigh of relief. "Ola, amigos!" the boss called, waving a cowboy hat. He leaped from the truck and unlocked the back door, then led Keith over to the linen stacks where aprons and paper chef's hats were kept. He turned and pointed a finger.

"Big brunch, Alberto. Mucho eggs this week, no? Extra, maybe."

Alberto's gazed drifted toward the floor. "*Si.* We won't run out this time."

"*Bien. Gracias.*" Thomas excused himself upstairs.

Keith stared after him, his fingers struggling with the apron strings. "I wonder how he stands to be up there all alone in that spooky place?" He chuckled, trying to make it a sort of joke, but Alberto only scowled. "What do we do first?"

Puzzlement turned to bother. "We open up. You don't know how to open up?"

"This is my first day."

"Light the stove." Alberto said, and produced matches from a drawer. No other narration followed, and Keith was reduced to ask questions about each little motion the young man made. Answers — when they did come — were single syllables or grunts.

The pattern persisted. Minutes felt like hours, and Keith concluded that he had tasted enough of this blue-collar hell. He would tell Ben as much, and get out of here as soon as possible.

He watched as Alberto mixed ingredients in a large bowl. "Biscuits?" Keith asked. "Do you have the recipe written down, somewhere?"

"Mmm. John show you when he gets here."

Keith took a breath. It would be so easy just to walk out the back door. But then, what chance would he have with Carlotta? He reached across the table and gripped the edge of the bowl. "Alberto, aren't I supposed to learn this stuff?"

Unfazed, the young man glanced up. "Towels," he said.

"What?"

"*Yo necessito* towels. Dish towels. Towels." He pointed. "Upstairs. Storage room next to the manager's office. This much." He gestured with his hands.

Keith trudged up to the room of stacked shelves — boxes of durables on one side, condiments on the other. He gathered an armful of the linens, moved past Ben's darkened office, then stopped. A movement down the hall set his heart pounding.

"Thomas?"

The figure moved quickly, through the alcove, and into the dark doorway.

"Hey — hey, Thomas?" Keith heard himself call out. He edged forward, but stopped with one foot on the stairs to the attic. Up above, the black ceiling was just visible, far away, streaked faintly by light.

"Anybody up there?"

No answer.

Hugging the towels, Keith fairly leaped down the stairs. When he landed on the brick floor, he was startled to see that Alberto had left his batter, and was poised beside the prep table, eyes wide, looking ready to make a quick getaway.

"Why did you yell? You say something to me?" he demanded. Fingertips clawed the table's edge.

Keith felt certain that if he gave the wrong answer, Alberto would fly out the back door. "No," he lied, too uncertain to say anything else. "I was yelling for Thomas. What's the matter?"

The young man's eyes narrowed into slits and he pulled closer. "Upstairs." He pointed with his chin. "You see the devil, no?"

"What?"

A sly smile. "*Si*, you see him, I think. They tell you about *El Diablito*? He lives up there."

"*Diablito*. That's little devil, right? Come on, Alberto, don't freak me out just because I'm the new guy."

Alberto looked incredulous, examining Keith's eyes, perhaps for the lie. He gave up and returned to his bowl. "Ehh. You fulla shit." The mixing whisk moved in quiet thumps. It was as if the inscrutable Mexican countenance had been open, reachable for a moment. Now Keith felt him closing up again, like one of the heavily tinted windows of his Cadillac.

"I did see something. A shadow, maybe."

Alberto's head jerked upwards, the skin in front of his ears drawn taught, like a scared animal. He wiped his hands, the batter again unimportant.

"Alberto, what the hell are we talking about?"

Eyes squinting. A slow nod. "Chavo, Emilio, they all see him. I never did, because I don't go up there, unless there are lots of people. You know? He doesn't like people. Brenda went up there alone, and he pushed her down the stairs. She quit."

All morning, he had begged to have the guy start talking. Now, Keith realized the young man was off his nut. "This Brenda resigned just because of some — some superstition?" Perhaps they were all like this.

Alberto returned to his whisk. "In Mexico, we believe in God. *Norte Americanos* don't believe. A *diablo* like this can reach out and get you. Cause heart attack. Cause a wreck. You know — car wreck. These things happen." The short speech had purged him of something, leaving his face peaceful, like that of an evangelist giving witness. "Cisco says Thomas will move to a new building. Bullshit. I only work here long enough to find another job. Chavo, too."

Keith leaned against the table. "That's my situation, too. I'm looking for a new job. Sorry, I wasn't trying to argue. This is an old building. Full of noises and shadows, nothing to be afraid of — "

But Alberto wasn't listening. "In my dreams — " he waved the metal biscuit cutter, " — I see his face."

The cutter clanked onto the table, and Alberto strode across the floor, his scowl suggesting that no one should follow. He disappeared into the smoke of a huge freezer, emerged quickly, his arms laden with small boxes, came back and dumped them onto the broad prep table. Green beans, succotash, corn. Frozen.

With quick motions, he dumped the contents of four green bean boxes into a deep pan. His hands grabbed boxes of salt, pepper, seasoned salt, onion powder and others. With careless flicking waves, he flavored the beans, then lowered the canister into the water of the warming steam table. Keith finally decided he had no intention of finishing his sentence.

"So? You said you see his face. What does he look like?"

Alberto glanced up, pale. A loud scraping sounded outside, and the back door flew open with an earth-shaking slam. Cisco himself barged in from the bright sunshine.

"*Ola.* John is sick today. I gotta work," he said, and tied his own apron. He leaned over the steam table. "Mr. Keith, welcome to the kitchen. You start these?"

Alberto immediately returned to the dough, and started rolling.

"No. Your brother--"

"Ahh, the brother--" A flicker of a smile. "You show Mr. Keith how to season these?"

Alberto wielded his circular cutter with a vengeance. "I put it in, but I don't know if he watched."

Spanish streamed from the larger man, and Alberto's lips pulled tight. Almost apologetic, Cisco began showing Keith locations of supplies, explaining things in detail as he did them.

Charles, a waiter Keith had met yesterday, yelled as he burst in the back door, "Hey, Cadillac Boy!" He wrestled with his tie.

"Shaddup," Alberto replied.

Undaunted, Charles flexed his eyebrows. "Whatever you're cooking today stinks." Alberto picked up a spatula and a chase ensued. Cisco broke them up. It was the first time Keith felt like laughing that morning.

Alberto remained tight-lipped in his brother's presence. Keith was dying to ask him more about the devil's helper, but whenever he brought it up, Alberto brushed him off, using his eyebrows to point to first one, then another waitress. Keith played along, and they teased each other about which ones they would prefer to sleep with. In spite of his knowledge of the waitresses, Alberto played dumb when Keith tried to describe Carlotta.

"She sounds good, but that one is better." He nodded toward an attractive girl with frizzy brown hair who was filling buckets with ice from the ice makers. "Fuck Cheryl. Go ask her."

Keith ignored the mischievous look, but couldn't help watching Cheryl as she exited to the dining room, groaning beneath the weight of the buckets, her lithe, strong legs evident beneath her short black skirt. My God, if he could only get Carlotta alone.

Keith mimicked Cisco's methods, turning frying sausages and bubbling eggs. He learned several new dishes, but could do nothing right the first time. Thomas appeared only once during brunch, clad in his chef's coat, and settled against the cutting table with a hand-held video game while a customer in a tailored suit jabbered in his ear.

Time zipped by much more rapidly than it ever had at the agency. The amazing pace of orders from the wait-staff finally slowed. There was no clock on the wall, but somebody said it was almost two. Finally, Cisco slapped his towel on the steam table, and led Keith through clean-up procedures. Ben arrived for the late shift, and the big man gave the new apprentice a favorable grade.

Ben studied Keith for a moment. "You still with us?"

"Maybe." Both Cisco and the manager laughed.

"We get paid, Boss?" Alberto interrupted.

"Huh? Oh, yeah." The Ben's brow furrowed. "The checks are up in Thomas's office," he said. "You want to go get them for me?"

Alberto shook his head vigorously, eyes downcast, and took his apron off.

"No." Cisco laughed, "Alberto won't go up there."

Ben's eyes rolled. "Well, do you want to go get them?"

The big man smiled sheepishly. "Not so much."

"Hey, I won't have a check yet, but I'll go with you," Keith volunteered.

Alberto brightened. "Send Mr. Keith."

"What's the matter?" Charlie said from the dining room entrance. "Is the Cadillac Man too lazy to walk up those stairs?"

"Ehhh." Alberto headed for the back door.

Ben nodded, and Keith trotted through the wait-people loitering about, likely waiting for their checks, too. But pulling off their arm garters and flirting seemed just as important. Up the main stairs, through the alcove, he moved briskly, halfway up the spiral staircase before his resolve took a dive. He found himself panting. Alberto's remarks about making sure there were always people around came back. Nonsense. Mexicans had a more superstitious culture, didn't they?

The air conditioners fell silent when he reached the top step. No one in the little storage room. Neither had the marionettes returned. He ducked hurriedly into Thomas's office, and was relieved to find a stack of envelopes — obviously containing checks, the top one addressed to a *Sam Spalding* — on the otherwise bare desk. He grabbed them, leaped back down to the landing, and froze.

She stood there. Holding onto the railing at the top of the spiral stairs. As if waiting for him.

He swallowed, heart pounding, chest tight. Why wasn't it a surprise that she was here? "Hey. Good to see you. I just finished my first shift. You working this afternoon?"

She smiled, for the first time, and came toward him, skirt swaying easily around her shapely legs. For an instant, she studied him, and his heart pounded as her arms wrapped around his torso.

Alarm bells. What kind of woman was this?

"You joined us today." A hug. "I am glad."

And now the suspicions vanished. So fresh and real, that smile. So powerfull and searching, those eyes.

It was automatic. He bent to kiss her, but she slipped his grasp and slinked off toward the wooden Indians.

"What is your name? Come on, just tell me your name, Sweet Thing. It's driving me nuts."

She paused beside the statue Ben called Cochise. Her fingers went out, tracing the lines on the Indian's arm, and she turned. "Do you have someone to love? Someone whose love can hold you here?"

Keith felt his jaw drop. "Hold me where?"

She waved her arms, both directions. Smiled. "Here. You came to this place, joined us, because of me." She left the Indian and wandered across the landing like a coquette taking her time before granting the next dance to a suitor. "I vowed not to do this with you, but he took my will, long ago." She stopped again, and looked at him with eyes suddenly sad.

"What's the matter?" Keith asked. A step forward. Careful, for he knew how fast she could move. She resisted, but he took her hand, held it tightly, and kissed her perfect fingers. "If you're upset about something, I can make it better. And don't—" He shushed her with one hand over her mouth. "—don't worry about – you know, doing something with me. We'll take it slow and easy. As slow as you wish. I just want to know you. We could just start by going out to dinner, maybe the movies."

He stopped, breathless. She was stroking his neck, fingernails caressing, waking every nerve in his body.

"Parties. Get to know each other's friends. You know, uh--" Another deep breath. "The whole nine yards. Slow and easy."

"You don't want to know my friends."

She tried to pull away, but he took her chin in his fingers, made her look into his eyes. "Something's happening between us. I'll call you Carlotta, if I have to. But it would be better if you told me your name, and agreed to go out with me this Friday."

Now she did work free, seeming about to weep. With folded arms, she stalked toward the catwalk.

"What's the matter?" He followed, tracing his fingers along the back of her blouse. "You're not married, are you?"

With no warning, she whipped around. The shine in her eyes stopped him, sucking all the oxygen out of the air. He didn't feel the checks slip from his fingers, but he heard them slapping the wood floor.

Slowly, she let her body come near again. On tiptoes, she gripped his shirt and pulled him down, until they were kissing, over and over again.

For an instant, she broke the luxurious contact. "You see?" Her eyes were placid, sated. "That is all I can do. Until you are taken."

"Oh, I'm taken—" He barely got the words out before their mouths pressed together again, tongues mingling.

Finally, she pulled back, out of breath, looking as drunk as Keith felt.

Her hand came out to keep him at bay, and she breathed hard, using the other one to grip the catwalk railing. Would she take him into the little room again?

"You're incredible," he managed to say between gasps. "Tell me—"

The hand came higher, cutting him off. She nodded toward the storage room. "Never cross this bridge. Leave this place. Promise me you will find someone to love. Hurry, or this will happen, again and again, until it is too late."

He reached for her shoulders, but she escaped and swept left, toward the staircase.

"Wait," he yelled. "I want it to happen again." His feet slipped, sliding apart on the scattered checks. He sank to his knees, and could only watch as she drifted down into the darkness below. "What about Friday?" She didn't stop, pounding the steps until they were silent, replaced by the wailing Mexican music that started playing once the last diners had gone.

He called out even louder, not caring who heard. "I'll keep calling you Carlotta, if I have to." How could she move down those dark stairs so quickly without falling?

"Goddam it." He gathered the paychecks, brushing away swipes of his black shoeprints. He would search the dining rooms for her. Stay through the whole evening shift, if that was what it took to talk to her again.

Somehow, though, talking no longer seemed that important. His lips, his head, every part of him tingled. There had simply never been another female like her. In the kitchen, he could only smile at Ben as he gave up the checks.

"Let me guess. You couldn't find them. Hey – who messed 'em up?"

Keith looked him straight in the eye. "What the hell's going on up there?" he asked.

The checks were handed out to eager, smiling employees, and Keith stood, studying each one of them, feeling like a deflated ballon. He didn't realize how exhausted he was. Knees aching, a tiny burn blister on his hand throbbing. He gave up the idea of going back up, scouring the dining rooms. She already made her escape – somehow he knew that, and tossed his apron into the linen bag.

A girl like her – part goddess, part head case – might not like being swept off her feet in front of the whole staff. He would play it better than he had with Linda – she would see that he could be strong, patient. He smiled again, wallowing in the glow she had left inside him. He had a future with that woman, and he would stay in this crazy place until he landed her.

CHAPTER 7
THE TWO-WAY STREET

"Light is a two-way street," Uncle said, rocking in his chair that made the porch creak and creak, sometimes all through the night.

Only eight years old at the time, Lionel listened intently. Anything less would cause Uncle to pull a switch from the pear tree.

"The light of the moon gives. Do you understand?"

Lionel nodded, though he didn't.

"It also takes. The light that washes over us, pulls us at the same time." His grizzled finger pointed at the white ball in the sky. "It can catch a strong man at a weak moment and draw his spirit away — to be lost among the demons out there."

Even now, Lionel sometimes thought he saw the old man's eyes, sharp and focused, like a hawk's, hovering in the darkness.

"It is the same way when you are dealing with the spirits," he said.

"It is?"

"If the spirits decide to talk to you, always remember. They give to those who are brave enough to ask, but they also take. Show them you are unselfish, but strong. Demand things from them. If you want to stay alive, you must make the spirits dance to your tune."

"But if I do that, must I give them something in return?"

The big smile. The one that said that Uncle was pleased.

"Very good, my little conniver," the old man said. "I think you know what you will give them. Your good looks. Your hot temper. Your excited energy. They rarely see the likes of you where they come from."

Lionel remembered the old man's face pulling very close, the stale breath, the white stubble, and being terrified. Yet those crazed, wolf-like eyes full of white moonlight suddenly softened.

"Remember your Uncle's place, the warm fire, the hot soup. This is your home now. If you are ever taken by the spirits in the night, demand that they return you here."

Lionel promised, though he had not the faintest idea what the old man was talking about, and hoped he would never find out.

So far, Carlotta had called the tune. She was like the moon, beautiful but ever pulling.

He swept a pile of dirt into the dustpan, silently rehearsing what he must do and say the next time. He would tell her when and where he would chant the spell of exchanging. She must obey, he would insist. Once she grew into her new body, once she became his lover, she could take all she wanted.

CHAPTER 8
THE WOP

On Monday afternoon, Ben led Keith downstairs to finally meet the chef who would be his trainer. In the lounge, an old popcorn machine percolated against one wall, spreading a pleasing, nostalgic smell. The front of the room was dominated by a small stage for folk singers and the occasional rock or country western bands. Keith had drunk beer here, back in the days before his credit cards were maxed out.

A husky man with a bushy black moustache glared at them from the serving window of a small cubicle against the back wall. As they drew closer, Keith remembered that the cubbyhole held a compact kitchen. The burly man stepped out, wiping his hands on his apron.

"Paisan," Ben yelled.

"Will you shut up? When you talk Italian with a Texas accent, it makes me want to puke." He laughed, his thick hand squeezing Keith's. "How are ya?" His own intonation sounded more like Brooklyn, not Italy.

"Keith, this is our chief caterer and one of the best cooks around, John Belotti."

"One of the best *chefs* around," John said. "There's a difference." He looked Keith up and down. "Goddam, Ben. I thought you were going to hire some beautiful dame with big tits for me to train." He exploded in laughter and gave Keith a playful shove.

"Sorry. He's the prettiest thing we could find on short notice."

He grabbed Keith by the shoulder. "Hey, you know how to cut up *jalapeños*?" A motion to shoo Ben away. "C'mere."

In the cubicle-kitchen, a cutting board and bowl were piled high with the hot peppers. Ben shrugged and rolled his eyes. "Good luck."

"Wash your hands first." John demonstrated a slicing technique while Keith obeyed. "Your fingers go straight up and down. They act as a guide while you're slicing." With quick jerks, he positioned Keith's hands the way he wanted. "These are good ones for you to start on. They're not that hot, you know. Thomas orders 'em special." He held one up to study it. "More flavorful and nowhere near as spicy. Get a whiff of that."

"Smells hot to me."

"Nah, g'head. Eat one, for chrissakes. How are you gonna learn to cook without knowing what the food tastes like? Mmm--" John popped one into his own mouth and began munching, eyebrows raised.

Keith sniffed the pepper again, then bit it in half.

"Ahhh--" He choked, his throat suddenly afire. To his horror, John pulled his own pepper back out, unmolested, and burst into laughter.

Keith scrambled to the cubicle's sink and drank directly from the tap.

"Come on, Bastard-o, I thought you Texans ate these things for breakfast." John laughed uproariously, leaning back against the cutting board. "You should have seen your face."

"You're not going to catch me with a sophomoric stunt like that again," Keith said when he could stand. "Persuasive asshole. I hope you're not one of those practical jokers."

John chuckled, slicing peppers more rapidly than Keith could ever imagine being able to. "You're a sport." The position, he explained, combined two jobs: fixing hors d'oeuvres out here for bar patrons until happy hour ended, then back in the big kitchen, working on the Line for the remainder of the night.

"Here. Have a meatball." He opened a warming oven below the cutting board and skewered two tiny meatballs on toothpicks. "No tricks this time." Even with his tongue ruined,

Keith found it delicious. As they both chewed, John emitted a low moan.

"What's the matter?"

He nodded. "Julie."

Through the serving window, a blond cocktail waitress served drinks to a table. "God, I can't stand it. You met all the girls yet?" A grunt.

"Only Andrea. Ever date any of them?"

"Every chance I get," came the booming reply. John shook his head. "Goddam, there are women here. Whoo. But if you don't like practical jokes, stay out of the attic. You been up there yet?"

"A couple of times." Keith was suddenly excited. If anyone knew who Carlotta was, surely this clown would. "What do you mean, practical jokes? Alberto told me there was some sort of evil spirit running around up there."

"Evil spirit?" John interrupted himself by bending over and hauling a large burlap bag out from under the prep board. He reached deep into the bag and extracted an oyster, held it under the running tap, and opened it with a small knife. "Do me a favor. Don't listen to the Mexicans. They spook easy. Whoever tried to rape Brenda was flesh and blood. The fucker. She was a nice lady." He dug at the mussel inside with a knife, then dipped it into a small dish of red sauce and swallowed down in one easy motion. "Want one?"

"No thanks. Wait a minute. There was a rape here?"

"*Attempted* rape." He was busy chewing, stretched for another oyster. Finally, he swallowed. "He grabbed her, didn't he? Hell, we don't know his real intentions. Thank God she got loose, but no one's gotten a good look at him, and he apparently climbs around in those rafters like a monkey. We'll find him. Thomas'll hold him while I punch his lights out."

Keith leaned against the bricks, digesting this new information. "Shit, Ben never mentioned this. Did someone call the police?"

John sipped from a glass of ice water. "Way ahead of ya. A couple of times. They took fingerprints. The police are just a bunch of wimps. One officer was totally freaked out by the marionettes. It would be funny, if it weren't so pitiful."

Keith laughed, squelching a sudden nervousness. "Heck, they spook me, too. Who keeps hiding them? I haven't even seen them since the first day."

John shook his head. "I don't care if they are antiques—" He washed his hands, his gaze directed out the window at the people who were starting to fill up the lounge. Happy Hour was almost here. "I say Thomas ought to take those goddam toys home. Stuff like that doesn't belong in a restaurant. The same goes for all this rusty farm tool shit on the walls. It's a fad--crap."

"Is there a waitress named Carlotta?" Keith blurted. "I mean, one with long, black hair? Sort of looks like a Spanish noble-woman?"

John scowled and reached for another mollusk. "You know how to shuck these? I'll have to show you." Keith let him think for a moment. A shrug. "Beats me. We got eighty employees. Is she pretty hot?"

"I see that look. I saw her first."

"You haven't seen shit. You're confused—Carlotta is the name of one of those fucking puppets."

"That's the point—" Keith bent over, his gaze following John's out the serving window. Julie was brushing something from the upper leg of her fishnet stockings. "These two waiters—it's a long story. Anything else I should watch out for besides pranksters and puppets?"

John shrugged. "It's a nice place to work. Just be here on time, and if one of the ladies back in the kitchen, or Cisco, or *me* tells you to do something, do it. Look at that—" He nodded a tall girl, likely a Sironia State coed, sat down at one of the tables. A new, melodic groan.

"Oh, yeah, another thing." He slapped Keith's arm. "Every six months or so, the phone rings in the kitchen for one of the dishwashers. Whoever's calling tells them the feds are coming. Every Mexican—except Cisco, of course—hightails it. It's their own early warning system, but when it happens, this place turns into a circus."

"Do they all get fired?"

"Hell, no. The rest of us have to bust our hump until closing. Last June, we were only one hour into the shift. It was hell. Sometimes the immigration guy shows, sometimes he doesn't. Next day, the Mexicans are back, and everything returns to normal. It's a fucking game." John laughed heartily. Keith joined him, though he was not sure why.

"Don't worry." John dropped several tortillas into the deep fat fryer. "If your lady fair is a waitress here, she'll wander by sooner or later, or you'll see her back on the Line." A lecherous look. "Is she really that pretty?"

"She's perfect. Either that, or being a hermit for so long made me nuts."

"You here for the job, or pussy? Christ, boy, this place is full of it."

Keith nodded. "So I've noticed."

"Goddam straight." Finger pointing. "But don't waste my time. If I teach you something, you learn it, *capiche*? Cooking is an art, and nobody fucks it up around me. Hear?"

"Yes, sir."

He nodded out the serving window. "You wanna see how a pro does it?" With his chin, he indicated a young girl wearing Water Company overalls and the shirt and garter. "There's another one I haven't met yet. Damn, Ben keeps 'em coming. I'm taking her out. Pay attention."

"That's a bus girl." Keith laughed. "Why not try one of the cocktail waitresses?"

"Huh?" John washed his hands in the sink. "Hell, no. They're wise to me." He rushed out the side door, and as Keith watched, he backed the young lady up near a corner table. She smiled sheepishly. Very young. Blondish-light brown hair. Sort of odd, rough features. Definitely the ugly duckling type, but Keith fancied he could spot some real potential once she matured a little more.

Now the girl laughed, but a customer interrupted, and while John answered the man, the young lady picked up her bus bin and skedaddled through the swinging doors to the kitchen. John returned in a huff.

"Well?"

"Too young." Back to the oyster sack.

"Damn, John, don't eat all of them."

"Shut up. Her name is Branwyn. Or some goddam foreign name like that. She's like you — just hired. She ain't even eighteen. Says her mother doesn't let her date yet. What the hell is he doing hiring minors?"

Keith stifled a chuckle, but in moments, they both collapsed, laughing. John rubbed his own temples, and sobered up.

"So, if you strike out with your mystery gal, does that mean you quit?" It was just what Keith was thinking.

"Dunno. I don't think I'll get promoted to waiter quickly enough to make enough money here."

John looked incredulous. "You don't want to be a pansy-assed waiter, do you? Cooking--that's the heart of a restaurant." One-by-one, he extracted the crisp tortillas with a pair of tongs. "Wherever you work, you want to be near the source of things. Cooking is the source here, bucko. Waiters come and go. Cooks remain."

Keith was not listening, but mentally replaying last night's last kiss. "She wears this incredible perfume. Honeysuckle."

A tortilla dropped to the floor, and the tongs followed. "What did you say?" The ruddy face had turned pale.

"Her perfume. Never came across it before. Smells just like honeysuckle."

John's mouth twitched, then he picked up the mess and washed his hands again. "Long hair? Sort of a big nose? Eyes almost slanted?"

A nod.

"There used to be a chick…" his voice trailed off.

"What? What are you saying?"

At that instant, another cocktail waitress leaned into the window. "That table over there — nachos, please. No sausage." She smiled at Keith. Reached her hand through. "I'm Emily." Nice.

"Keith--" He got it out before he choked on the tortilla chip John had given him. Coughing, there was no way he could say something smart.

"What, your customer ain't macho enough for sausage?" John popped his dish towel. "John's famous nachos, coming up." She winked and left, and he scratched his head. "Don't worry. Couldn't be the same broad. She worked here when I first arrived, three years ago. Don't know what happened to her. But that was her perfume."

Keith slid off the stool. "God, this is driving me crazy. The way you described her is right on the money. That could be it—maybe Ben hired her back."

John was lost in his memory. "What a bitch. We went out once. A disaster. Drove her from here across the bridge to the park. She wouldn't go any farther. Told her we could get pizza at Ira's, go to a movie, but she acted like a wet cat. Wanted to just sit in that cul de sac over there, and watch the river." He lay three crisp tortillas out, then carefully pasted them with refried beans, shredded cheese and jalapeno slices. He slid the plate into the small glass oven that dominated the counter.

"I mean, that's fast, even for me." He raised his knife to the heavens. "Damn it. Honeysuckle. Goddam that Ben if he hired her back." Sharp look. "And if she's *your* little filly, watch out. I'll find something else to do with this blade."

"So what did you do? I mean, back then. Just park and neck?"

"Are you kidding?" A tortilla was broken, and John began munching. "I suggested we go skinny-dipping." He gestured, illustrating the tale, then a finger shot forward. "And if you tell this story to anybody, I'll kill you. We strip down, I jump into the river, but she won't get in the water, no way. Then the bitch turns and walks off. Said something like I had failed the 'moonlight test.' It was the only time a woman has totally humiliated me." By now, his face and neck were bright red. "Sure, I'm not Mr. Perfect Physique, but I'm a demon in the sack—and that part you can pass on." He laughed loudly.

Keith smiled, but a profound shiver kept him from being too jovial. "Don't think I ever saw her at work after that."

"Do you remember her name?"

John grabbed a towel and pulled the order out of the oven. "Huh? Carla or something."

Keith's stomach cramped. "Carlotta?"

John paled, almost dropping the hot plate. "I said Carla, goddam it."

CHAPTER 9
THE DREAM

Keith tossed around in darkness, waking every few minutes, it seemed, from montages of hot plates of nachos, chicken wings, men in suits sipping highballs, drab-faced women gazing into space, coeds giggling over their beer. There was Cisco, smiling as he squeezed between the tables, bringing a sample of his guacamole dip out to the little bar kitchen. And John, belching loudly at the back door, warning him that he would have nightmares about food.

He sat up in bed, wiping his face. My God. Would it be this way every time he worked the late shift?

He rolled over at dawn, and finally felt himself sinking into a deep rest. A light feeling, floating, flying above something — an old western-style wagon.

I'm dreaming, he thought, though he had no control over his movements. Just as if he were on one of those zooming Hollywood cameras, he started dropping, closer, until the view of the wagon came clear. A single old horse pulled it – big brown globes for eyes – and the spoked wheels wobbled in a rutted path in the middle of a grass-covered prairie.

The floating sensation made him laugh and half-expect to see John or Ben driving the wagon, but when he drew closer, he saw only a shabby elderly man, with dark eyes that sank far back into his head. Beside the wagon, a lithe young woman in a long cotton dress, the type pioneer women used to wear, walked, one hand resting on the wagon bed. Behind them, a short, forlorn-looking man completed the procession on foot. He was not dressed roughly, but wore evening clothes, as if he had stayed up all night at some elegant plantation party. A bizarre trio, those three, Keith found himself thinking. What had brought such weird types together?

He blinked, having a hard time holding the concentration, bobbing up and down through the air in uncontrollable swoops. Though he could not always see clearly, it was the woman's face that kept stealing his attention: sharp features and dark, flashing eyes. Where had he seen her before?

The old man spoke. "Your new lover's home is almost finished. When he comes to you, Princess — " He stopped talking, turned in the seat, and gave her a long hard stare. " — you'll know what to do. Look at him."

As if his words had sent a shockwave through them, both the woman and the man behind the wagon focused their attention on a tarp that lay in the back of the wagon bed. Their interest spurred Keith to want a better view, too, and that thought brought him lower, directly above the creaking vehicle.

He turned his head in time to see the woman's face as she stretched to lift one edge of the heavy covering. For a moment, the look in her eyes softened, until they resembled those of a child opening a gift she wanted. She pulled. A human hand flopped out, dangling at the end of an arm, and hung over the edge of the wagon. Keith felt her shock in his own stomach and recoiled. A dead body. He knew it instantly, and barely stopped himself from crying out. That was the wrong thing to do.

Frantic, he waved his arms like a drowning swimmer, as if one could swim in the sky. Get away from these people he did not know, gain altitude. Then a cloud moved, and sunlight hit the curled fingers. They glistened, and his own thrashing slowed. The appendage was not human, but carved out of wood.

The woman's gaze was riveted on that hand – but now her head turned upward. She was looking at Keith. It felt as if gripping fingers seized his insides at the very moment she made eye contact. He had thought himself invisible, but felt the air move around him as some force pressed him closer, until he was almost brushing the top of the tarp. Its smell enveloped him, stale wet cotton. Somehow, his movement stemmed from the woman's eyes — she had the power to hold him there, floating.

Wake up. The clear thought crashed down from somewhere, but thoughts of rebelling against the pressure evaporated each time he glanced at her perfect face. Soft, ruddy cheeks. Sharp eyebrows. My God. A gasp for breath — this woman was Carlotta — but so much more real here than in the hazy dimness of the attic. She had changed dresses - this one, calico and bright checked - but it fell around her hips the same way. Except this Carlotta seemed much younger. Like a girl still in school.

Her red lips moved — was she speaking? A invisible film surrounded him, and when her words did break through, like heavy drops of water falling through cloth, they were cloaked, infinitely soft, full of love, it seemed, but harsh at the same time.

"Leave this place. Hurry, before he sees you. It's not me — find someone else to love."

Keith blinked, disbelieving. His heart started to pound. Who would see him? Some instinct told him it was not the man in the suit, but the wagon driver.

Another jolt. She seemed so much in control. She could visit his dreams? Like in a horror movie? Well, why couldn't he just make it somehow to the ground, grab Carlotta's hand and run away with her across the prairie? He strained, but the muscles in his arms and legs obeyed none of his commands.

At that instant, the rough tarp brushed his cheek, and whatever force held him began pressing harder. Down, down, against the dingy cloth, until his cheekbone smacked against the hard wooden form beneath the tarp. More — he could not stop the movement, and looked up frantically, trying to catch Carlotta's eye again. She only walked, her gaze straight ahead, as if she thought he had already followed her advice and disappeared.

No — the force would not stop pushing — he was actually going through the cover. He held his arm out, but it fell limp, inches above the wooden one, brushing the surface — so much smoother and polished than the tarp — then the bright sunshine blinked out…

Keith catapulted out of bed, breathing heavily, wiping his face, rubbing chilly sweat all the way down his torso. Thank God. The eerie, disturbing sight of that hand — why such a nightmare?

He paced. Dawn seeping in, threatening to remind him he had to go to work today.

This was wrong. Sick. Was he drinking wine last night? Why would he have a dream like that about the woman who was so free with her kisses?

Was he depressed? No – he was employed now. The depression was over. Besides, every moment he had spent with Carlotta in the restaurant had been glorious, not a downer.

He scraped his belly with a shirt, then his sides, legs, trying to brush off the invisible itchy particles, identical to the tiny shards of fiberglass that used to cover his body during the summer he worked construction. It was the scratchy feel of that tarpaulin in the dream. He sniffed his hands — the same musky wet fabric odor lingered on them. Impossible — did his sheets smell like that?

He climbed into the shower to get rid of the prickles, and the weird thing he was trying to remember came back: *Leave this place*. She said that the other day. Would that make him construct such a nasty dream?

He dried himself, then tore the sheets off and lay down on the bare mattress. He tasted too many different dishes last night. Rich food always gave him weird dreams. He closed his eyes and dozed, focusing on the memory of her kisses. So sweet, but they kept twisting, changing back into her cryptic warning, layered over by that foul odor and the creaking of the wagon wheels.

He finally gave up, dressed, and drove to the Water Company, determined to stick around all day. He would catch her on whatever shift she worked, drag her to see Ben, and put an end to all these guessing games. Unfortunately, when he pulled up and saw Alberto's car, and a few others, he remembered that the wait-people would not show up for another couple of hours.

Instead of going inside, he ambled around to the front. Across River Drive, an old black man sat on the grassy bank, fishing with a cane pole.

"Catch any?" Keith asked automatically.

"You bet." The answer came with a laugh. "River's been good to me today."

Keith made small talk for a moment more, then trudged back to his car. Simple old man. Talking about flowing water as if it were a living thing. He pictured John trying to seduce a woman with skinny dipping, and started to laugh.

CHAPTER 10
IN THE LOUNGE

"Ben, this is it." Keith blocked the manager's exit. The hall behind was filling with wait-people tidying up their shirts and garters.

"This is what?"

"You come over here." Keith led him to the time clock in the hall, and proceeded to pull out each timecard with a female name on it. "OK. Describe her. Now her."

Ben set his jaw, but acquiesced, giving rough descriptions of each person named, until they had made it through a half-dozen cards. "Keith, I told you, I don't remember any one of them with long black hair."

"OK. That's an idea." Keith stuffed the cards back in their places. "You look. Just pick out the ones with black hair. Go on."

Ben's gazed went up and down the rack. "Just black hair?"

"Really black."

"Hmm." He pulled one. "Sandra. She's all I can pick out. But her hair is short, and she's on a leave of absence until the end of the summer. She goes to State."

Keith felt himself getting flustered. "That's all? What about any other brunettes? Or ones that are Spanish, or Mexican? But hell, her skin seems pretty white--"

Ben's finger dodged from one card to another. "Jenny — but you've met her. Audra — waitress — she's black…" He named a few more. "Goddam it, Keith, I'm busy. You look through them. You probably know most of the girls by now."

He was right, of course. Keith had been riffling through them since he arrived. Ben led back into his office.

"Let's do it this way. You just be ready. When I see my lady, I'm bringing her down to you. Your job will be to tell me her name, rank, and social security number."

"Oh, of course." Ben's smile turned to a frown when Keith blocked the doorway again. "Hey, I'm in a hurry, Dude. And so are you — aren't you supposed to be prepping in the bar kitchen?"

"Ben."

"Yeah?"

"This is bullshit. You're hiding that girl. Or someone is. Now I'm having nightmares about her. Worse — " He dropped his arm and moved out of the doorway.

Ben rolled his eyes. "What's worse? You're starting to go mental? No one's hiding — unless she is. I dated a girl once, for a few weeks. She said she loved me every day. Later, I found out she hated my guts from the first. Maybe you've stumbled into a deal like that."

"Which of your many conquests are you talking about?"

"Nobody you know. It was after high school. Shut up and go to work." Ben stepped into the hall.

Keith was suddenly talking to the empty doorway, his voice growing louder, not really knowing what he was saying until it came out. "What if there's really no such person? What if she doesn't really exist? Are you sure Thomas's wife doesn't have long black hair?"

He looked around the doorsill. Already several yards down the hall, Ben turned, wearing a silly grin. "Janine is a blond, and Thomas'll skin you if you even look at her. Hey - if your lover doesn't exist, who have you been making out with in the attic? Cochise and Geronimo?"

They laughed, then Keith thought of the marionettes, and swallowed. "Just putting two and two together. The Mexicans think the upstairs is haunted. No one seems to know her, and — "

Ben held his hands out, as if asking, why me? "Come on. This is an old building. Lots of different people work here. I would never have lasted six years if I freaked out every time something odd happened."

" — she told me to leave."

Ben turned and started down the stairs, wagging a finger behind him as he did. "Then leave. But you gotta give me two weeks notice, or I'll hold your check, asshole."

Bar traffic was starting out slow. Keith prepped, cruised through each dining room, looking for her, then made a salad and sat munching and gazing out of the serving window. No Carlotta.

"You're looking glum, you bastard." John barged through the doorway, carrying a plastic bucket. "Here's your goddam turkey nuts." Keith stuck the bucket into the cooler under the sink. He liked almost everything on the bar menu, but battering and frying turkey testicles — turkey fries — almost made him sick.

"Do you believe in fate, John?"

The Wop wiped his hands on his apron, studying a table in the middle of the room that was surrounded by coeds. "Huh? You mean that predestination shit? Naw, man, the dice are rolling. Look at those women. You could score with any one of them. Don't give me all that college pre-destination bullshit. Like there's just one girl meant for you. There's lots of girls – *unh, unh*." He gyrated obscenely, thrust his elbow into Keith's arm."

"OK, OK. Maybe so. It's a plausible theory." Keith leaned back on the stool until he felt the cool bricks through his shirt. "But I mean — well, I could be going crazy, but I was just wondering what I'm doing here."

"The blond." John nodded and took a breath, never moving his gaze from the coeds. "I'll take the blond in the middle. With the big hair. You can have the rest." Then the spell broke and he slapped Keith's arm. "What do you mean, what are you doing here? You're learning to cook. You made a choice, and you changed careers without even knowing it.

You're better off, Bucko." He waved his hands, encompassing everything. "None of that stuffy office crap. You want to be here. It's even more creative than writing or whatever kind of shit you were doing."

"Copywriting. And you're wrong, John. I didn't make a choice. Not really. I followed a girl here, and now she's disappeared."

John scowled, forcing his eyebrows together. "Are you gonna start that again? Look out the window." He pointed. "The best pussy in town passes through here. Wake up and take your pick."

"But that doesn't answer my question. Why would I hallucinate someone? I even kissed her. It's like some big staged event, and I'm the only one they're not letting in on the joke. I think I'm going crazy."

John sawed an imaginary fiddle in the air. "Spare me. You're just horny, and that bitch, whoever she is, is just a prick-tease. Might not even work here. We're like a family at the Water Company, Bucko. Everyone has slept with everyone else."

"That's not a family. That's a rabbit warren."

John laughed. "Have it your way. Of course, there are exceptions. Some of the women are Confederate snobs. Won't give a poor Yankee boy the time of day. What I'm saying is, if I don't know her, she don't work here."

He held his hand up. "Moral of the story? If fate brought you here to find the love of your life, start circulating, instead of moping around after that mystery bitch."

He started out through the door. Susie, the slinky, ever-present girlfriend of Manny the bartender, had risen from her place at the bar and was walking toward the serving window. John nodded. "Uh-oh. There's another exception. Don't get mixed up with her. I've seen Manny kick the butts of customers who hit on her. She's creepy, and god knows why she's looking at you that way. She ain't the type to fuck every new guy who comes on board."

Before Keith could protest, the Wop stalked across the room and through the swinging doors to the kitchen. By then,

Susie was perched on a stool just to the side of the serving window.

"Why did John leave?" She asked. "I don't think he likes me. She set her daiquiri on the shelf, and extended her hand. Keith shook it.

"Goof to see you again, Keith."

"Uh, thanks. You, too. John just has chores in the back."

A smell of patchouli drifted through the window. Up to this moment, she had never acted like Keith even existed.

"Can I get you something?"

"Oh, no. Just tired of listening to Manny kiss ass with the dull business me. They're always trying to get him to go deer hunting. Imagine, killing defenseless, beautiful animals with big guns." She fluttered her eyelashes. Had doe eyes, herself. But what caught Keith's attention was the heat from Manny's choppy glances.

"Hunting's the oldest sport—" No, that was taking the conversation the wrong direction. "I mean, surely they're not all dull."

Susie grimaced. "They are tonight. Rich and dull. The regulars." A sigh. "But yeah, on the weekends, there's a few new faces. I do like to sit here and watch those. Especially the ones with interesting colors. I can see people's auras, you know."

Keith nodded.

She traced patterns on the counter with a toothpick, dodging the plate of nachos Keith handed out to Joanie. "This place has power." She said it quietly.

"Did you say power?"

"Supernatural. Psychic power. You know what I'm talking about?"

"Maybe." Oh, brother. "I heard the place is haunted.'

"Of course it is.' She flashed a seductive look and took a drink.

Keith's heartbeat quickened. What did she know? "How can a restaurant have power? It's a place, not a person."

"No, dummy. Power can reside in anything." She exhaled, as if his education were lacking. "Weird things happen here. Like in the Bermuda Triangle. This place is a portal that strange things pass through. A passageway. Parapsychologists say there are thousands of little Bermuda Triangles scattered all over the Earth. The Water Company is one of those places."

"Oh?" An older man caem up, smiled at her, ordered wings. Manny's irritation — even from this distance — was beginning to be tangible, but Keith hoped she wouldn't leave yet.

The man went back to his beer, and she twisted on her stool, seeming to peruse the clientele, stopping midway to give the big bartender an animated wave. "Watch the people who come in here. Even some of the employees."

Automatically, Keith scanned several faces.

"Can't you just feel it?" Her eyes sparkled, and for a moment, Keith imagined her wearing a cheerleader dress instead of a long printed caftan. Not possible.

"I'm looking for a waitress that keeps disappearing. Is she hiding in one of your Bermuda Triangle things?"

She looked surprised, and giggled. "Could be."

"No. I'm serious. I've seen her, but no one else seems to know what I'm talking about."

She pulled the plastic straw from her drink and sucked on it. Perhaps she was reading his aura, perhaps only trying to get him beaten up. "If no one else has seen her, how do you know she's not an apparition? Some spirit just passing through the vortex?" She straightened up on her stool, excited now. "Manny doesn't like to talk about stuff like that. Do you?"

From the corner of his eye, Keith could see Manny stop drying a snifter.

"Uh — sorry, I need more utensils from the back." He dodged out the back, stalked across the lounge and through the swinging doors.

When he returned, Susie had been replaced by Jeremy, Manny's assistant. He accosted Keith.

"Listen, get the code straight. I missed that beauty you had sitting at that corner table until they got up to go into the dining room."

"Huh? Sorry, I got busy. What was the signal again?"

"You know. Two shooters. You call out, *two shooters*, like a drink order. That bitch in the beige dress — she ordered nachos. God, if only she would eat my nacho."

Keith nodded in Susie's direction. She had taken up residence at a table with some familiar patrons. "What about her? Is she nuts?"

He grinned, then whispered. "Yes, she's nuts, and Manny's insane. The perfect couple. Don't tell me you've got the hots for her. Danger, Will Robinson."

"No. But you know the waitress I'm looking for? Susie says she must live in a vortex — or something. Is this place really that weird? You still haven't seen her, have you?"

The assistant bartender was already walking away, pausing only to sneer over his shoulder. "If I see her first, you'll have to settle for sloppy seconds."

"Could you put this up?" It was Emily, another of the three cocktail waitresses on this shift. She held out a small stack of empty plates, balancing her tray with the other hand.

"Sure."

She smiled, and turned back to her work. Brown hair. Green eyes. But she had a boyfriend. He had heard her say it unequivocally one night, fending off the advances of an older guy with too many drinks under his belt. For a moment, he fantasized, then remembered Carlotta's desperate kisses, and felt guilty.

He sat back down, wiped a streak of cheese off of the outside of the oven, and resumed picking at the remains of his salad. If only he could sit Carlotta down and really talk to her. A slow, cold shiver passed through his body. What if he dreamed about her again tonight? Why couldn't he have a good dream about her?

A shadow fell across the cutting table, and he jumped.

"What are you thinking about so intently?" Emily stood in the doorway, arms folded, leaning against the sill. Such a soft smile. In the close space, her perfume mixed unbearably with a hint of female sweat.

"Huh? Oh, nothing. Had a nightmare last night. Just can't shake it. Probably the shock of getting a new job." She laughed with him. "How's Paul?"

"Who?" A scowl. He kept his gaze riveted on her smooth face. In spite of the cocktail outfit. In spite of the cleavage.

"Your boyfriend. I heard you tell that drunk the other night your boyfriend's name is Paul."

"Oh. That Paul. I guess he's OK." She blushed, moved a step closer, and leaned against the bricks. "Ooh. These are nice and cool." A shock of hair fell out of place, across her cheek. She blew from one corner of her mouth and tossed her head at the same time, sending it back into place.

"Well? How is he?"

She ignored the question. "You like working back here all by yourself?"

"I guess so. The music's nice. Usually, the people are nice."

"Yeah. The clientele at a high-end restaurant is better. Makes the night tolerable. I used to work at the Catfish Hut. The drunks there were a different breed." She laughed. A customer raised his glass, and she was off.

When the bar patrons thinned out, it was Keith's duty to clean up the bar kitchen, then report back to the big kitchen, to help with clean-up. While he stooped to turn off the deep fat fryer Emily returned. Green eyes, with a cast of easy indifference. He found himself comparing each feature to Carlotta: nose--softer, rounder, but maybe immature; cheeks—definitely softer skin; lips—fuller, maybe, pink instead of firehouse red.

"So, tell me about yourself. Going to be a waitress all of your life? Making some extra money until Paul gets out of school?"

"No, silly. To both questions." She smiled and bent over to brush the knees of her black fishnet stockings. Keith studied the smooth skin of her neck, the way her breasts wobbled softly in the molded top of her cocktail suit. She straightened up and met his eyes. "I'm working on my education credential at Sironia State. I finish at the end of summer. Gonna teach high school science. Psychology."

"A scientific female. That's scary. Are you and Paul engaged?"

She held up her hand. "Don't see a ring, do you?"

"No. I don't. I'd still like to meet him. Maybe one of these lovely ladies--" He nodded toward Andrea and Julia, chatting at the bar, "--will go out with me sometime. We could double date."

A slight smile formed. "Oh? Who have you got your eyes on?"

"I'm not that particular just now." His cheeks felt suddenly hot. He was blowing this, wasn't he? "You're all so attractive."

"Why, thank you, sir." She laughed and gave a small curtsey.

There was a long pause. Eyes met again. Both looked away. Again. It didn't hurt. He was the first one to regain his voice. "Did you say psychology? Can you analyze dreams? Nightmares?"

She blushed again. "Any you would care to share?"

He was speechless again, and she hit his shoulder playfully. "You're bad, you know. Gotta check my tables."

He watched the smooth, zippered back of her tight suit, and her hips as she walked away. She stopped, looked over her shoulder, and smiled, as if she knew he would be watching. If she had not had a boyfriend, he could swear it was a come-hither look.

Forks and spatulas fairly bounced into the busbin. Then the whole mess spilled onto the floor. Keith didn't care, but moved to the band's rhythm as he cleaned them up.

"'Bout time you got back here," Katy scolded from the stoves. "Bring me one pack of squash, young man."

"How'd it go out there?" the Wop yelled from the prep room.

"Fantastic," Keith said.

Ben leaned against the dessert Line, re-tying his tie. "Haven't seen you. I thought you were bringing the mysterious maiden by. Still no luck?"

"Well, no. And maybe yes." Keith hustled into the walk-in freezer, grabbed the squash pack. Wondered why he felt so suddenly free. Emily was already taken. And the puzzle of Carlotta loomed bigger than ever. Still, he was giddy, and every time he returned to his little plan of searching through the rafters before the night ended, his mind was invaded by the image of Emily's perfect torso, her stockinged legs.

Later, the employees came out in small bunches, revved their cars in the parking lot. Laughing, making plans to meet at the Catfish Hut, calling insults back and forth. Emily stood there at the foot of the steps, hugging herself against the nighttime chill. She wore a white sweater above her enchanting cocktail outfit, but her legs were bare, except for those maddening stockings.

"Need a ride?" Keith asked it with no hopes. Obvously, Paul was on his way.

"No, thanks. My cousin's coming. She's throwing a birthday party for my aunt tomorrow, so she wants my help."

"This late? Planning a party in the middle of the night?"

"Yeah, I know. She just wants someone to drink wine with. Doesn't have any friends." A little chuckle.

"Darn." Keith stepped close to her. "Need any help drinking that wine? Or would Paul object if a male crashed the party?"

A sly look. "I don't know. But it's not a party, Nosy."

"Sorry. Just trying to help."

"I bet." She reached over and pinched his elbow. "Maybe some other time."

"You just say when." What was he doing? If he ever did get something going with Emily, the Water Company gossip would take it straight to Carlotta. Or would it?

More workers came out. They stood together, telling some goodbye, trading verbal jabs with this one, that one. Cars kicked up dust in the gravel, and Keith had an urge to brush it off of the cocktail dress. Then held his breath, and one of those awkward silent spells descended.

"So, Paul's a nice guy?" he finally asked, acknowledging the 600 pound gorilla between them.

"Why do you keep bringing Paul up?"

"Oh, you know." He smiled. Shuffled. "Just not – not trying to get too fresh with another guy's girl."

"Why don't you speak for yourself, John?"

The earth shook. He knew Longfellow's story about Miles Standish and John Alden, but did she really mean –

A breeze picked that instant to come off the river, and Keith shivered. Another long pause, and he might have screamed, if he could figure out what the thoughts in his head were trying to tell him – but it was all a jumble, and she smelled like a mixture of perfume and sweat, and the parking lot was almost empty, and he silently vowed not to leave until she did. The thought of Emily alone in the darkneww in this part of town –

"The stars are beautiful tonight," she said.

"Yeah." Above, a few white ghosts of clouds reflected the downtown lights, but not enough to dim the swirls of stars, which were maybe more stunning than any he had witnessed before.

Flash of headlights. Waving hand. Again, Emily reached over, pinched his elbow.

"Night. Thanks for offering me a ride."

"Sure. Some other time, huh?"

Her only answer was a wink. Then she was gone.

"What's with the goofy smile?" Ben asked, coming down the back steps. "You look like your brother does after he smokes a joint."

"Nothing." Pretty Anna, the pastry chef, came down behind him, clutching her purse and a bag of leftovers for Arkie. Keith blew her a kiss, took a deep breath, looked the manager in the eyes.

"The river was just good to me tonight."

CHAPTER 11
BLUE JEANS

Keith was confused – trying to go to sleep, he thought – but when he opened his eyes, it was daylight. A few blinks, and his body went as rigid as a corpse.

He was back – floating above the old wagon. You can't repeat a dream – but that thought flew away when he saw Carlotta's dark hair. He tried to call out her name, make her look up, for he was still fifteen, twenty feet above the creaky old vehicle. But his voice was only a whisper. The fishy, grassy, dirt smell of the river filled his head.

"Look at your lover." It was the voice of that disgusting old driver. He looked back over his shoulder, straight at Carlotta, who walked in fluid, easy strides. A jolt surged through Keith's body. He didn't like it here, especially when he knew he would wake up screaming.

A gnarled finger gestured toward the wagon bed.

Carlotta lifted the dingy tarp, and the hand fell out, as before. She kept pulling. Farther, farther up the canvas climbed. The smooth wooden arm, then perfectly formed feet. More – the the legs and lower torso were clothed in a modern-looking pair of *Levis*, unlike the period clothes that she and the little man behind the wagon wore. Keith found himself mesmerized by the faultless workmanship that could make wood look exactly like human skin. Those feet – perfect toes, a high instep, the wood almost looking as if it had pores – like skin.

Something broke his gaze. It was Carlotta's own hand, waving insistently above the slowly emerging life-sized figure. It was wearing an old cotton shirt.

Yes – she wasn't just looking up now, but glaring at Keith, no mistake. An angry gaze. He could read the fear in her mind. Next, she would whisper, warn him to leave, but before she could, the dream broke apart.

He woke in darkness. No screams. But his hand rose to his face. Tears. He was crying, and couldn't remember exactly why.

CHAPTER 12
CARLOTTA

Lionel tried to will the voices and music rising from below into silence. The restaurant was still awake, but he felt time pressing in, and wished the old building would just disgorge all its aimless souls and go to sleep. He moved the broom along the landing, pausing after each thrust to look at Carlotta, who hung between the Indians again, swaying slightly in the draft from the air conditioners.

Why not just grab her and run away? Steal her from whatever forces held her here? No, it did not work that way. The Old Ones imprisoned their enemies in wood and rocks, his Uncle told him, since long before the *conquistadors*. Simple physical separation would not protect her — this was an affair of the spirit.

He looked down, held his hands out, shaking. Mustn't underestimate the task at hand. He remembered how spells took it all from Uncle. That one, with the coyote *brujo* left him so spent, he had to stay in bed for three days, eating only the poor chicken gruel that was Lionel's only dish at the time.

The spell to free her would take every bit of energy he possessed – of that he was certain. And the receptacle, the receiving host body — finding that would be the hardest part of all. The Old Ones just took whomever they wanted. The *Norte Americancs* had a different way. If he tried to take someone without care, without finesse, without her willing permission, he would be signing his own death warrant. The people in this land were asleep, mostly. But not stupid.

Above all, she must be beautiful. It was only proper, for a spirit like Carlotta to have the proper home. But how? Here, pretty people had something to live for. With no knowledge of the spirit, what desirable woman could possibly be glad to be rid of her shell and take his lover's place in the marionette? *Dios mio.* The gravity of the thing made him feel like he was suffocating, even with air blowing straight onto his face.

Slowly now, the broom traversed the catwalk. Specks of dirt tumbled off, flickered for an instant, then disappeared into the blackness below

Suddenly, a chilling breeze parted the curtains to the storage room. As if the airconditioner had learned to blow another direction. My God, it was happening. Even without calling her, it was happening.

He stepped across, thrusting his fingers into the shadows, reaching for the light's pull-string. They found, instead, shafts of iciness that interlaced with them. His breathing accelerated.

"You wish to know why I am captive." Her wonderful voice came from the shadows.

Take control, he reminded himself. "No, my love. I am only thinking of your new body." He moved closer, remembering his speech — she must know every detail of the plan. She did not stay in one place, however, but tugged, pulling him farther into the little room.

Pitch black surrounded them, then they were suddenly outside, in the empty grass by the river.

"Wait," he said, staggering back. "I can't go with you – I'm not ready." In a single instant, his hopes and dreams came crashing down – he must appear a frightened schoolboy to her, not a man.

Instead of listening, she kept pulling him toward a strange man and a woman who stood talking on the knoll where the Water Company should be. Their crude garments identified them as natives of a period long past.

The man was tall, muscular, hair crudely cropped, his face scarred in two places, but handsome. The woman's hair fell long and black past her shoulders. She turned, and a new shiver passed through Lionel – it was Carlotta, only younger, more girl than woman.

The handsome man paced, waving his arms, professing his love, his dreams for their future. He seemed to be facing an impossible task of some sort. His words, though, could not come through clearly enough for Lionel to understand. Nevertheless, the man's hope and boundless determination shined through the stressful feelings that surrounded them both. Lionel liked him.

Young Carlotta, however, turned away, brooding, then suddenly screamed at her suitor.

"You are a simpleton," she said. "Do you honestly think you can become as rich as they are? With skins on your feet?' Though her friend withstood the upbraiding proudly, Lionel could see the effect of her words, could see the man's resolve wither, like a flower dying in the sun.

She tossed her head and folded her arms. "I will marry one of them, because they are not stupid."

In this dimension, Lionel was accustomed to becoming one with the feelings of another — the man's inner pain was excruciating.

"Warn her," a voice whispered.

He turned to his Carlotta - not the young maiden - and felt the sorrow in her eyes stab at his heart. Frantically, he raced up the knoll to beg the ghost Carlotta, the young phantom, to shut up, to see the true heart of this man she was refusing. Before he could top the hill, though, a whirlwind came out of the blue and pushed him back down, toward the river.

A crowd of people were marching toward Lionel, through the grass. A procession. The middle braves carried a lifeless body - the young man!

Now the girlish Carlotta stood alone. The parade came to her, and broke the news: there had been an accident on the farm where the boy worked. The girl's eyes flashed darkly, but only for an instant. Then she straightened up, proud, defiant. As if she had never cared at all.

Now it was Lionel's turn to be alone on the knoll. Cold wind blew, and the low thunder of the river blotted out all sound. In a shivering, fast motion, the sun went down, and darkness fell.

He gripped something – the catwalk railing! Hnads shaking, sweaty, drops falling from his fingers, glistening like tiny falling stars into the shadows.

Almost afraid to find her, he glanced around – only the old, quivering attic. The curtains to the store room had been drawn, and her voice came from there, carried on chilly air:

"Be careful, my love. He is watching. It angers him for me to tell my story, because it is his story, too, and I have defied him. He has called the Children. They come in threes."

"*Que?*" Dark blotches hovered before his eyes. He held on.

"You are a beckoner of souls--" It was a rebuke. Here, he boasted of wielding such power, but stood on a flimsy board high in the air, shivering like a scared toddler.

"So, be brave or die," she continued. "You must help your friend. He is tired of life..."

"My friend?"

"I refused to be part of the taking this time, but my master catches me when I am weak. He can use whom he wishes, when he wishes."

"I will do away with him," Lionel called out, not caring if anyone were still in the kitchen below. "Show me this monster. I'll kill him."

Behind the curtain, she let out a small laugh. "You aren't that powerful, my love. But he knows you have some talent. He might decide to take you, instead, to punish me. Please leave this place. Do not be here when the Children of Rage come."

It was gibberish, but terrifying. His eyelids felt heavy. He didn't have the breath to question her, was too afraid to open the curtains, because he knew she wouldn't be there. Who were these "children of rage?" Would he have to fight every demon in the cosmos to secure her freedom?

He clinched a fist and waved it in the air. "I won't leave until you are free." But his voice was only a whisper.

For a long time, only the hiss of the fans. Finally, she spoke, as if from far away. "There is no freedom. Go away. Go back into the world, where from you came. You will know the moment."

The curtains quivered, and Lionel shifted around on the catwalk, from one railing to the other. His gaze drifted to the puppets. Carlotta's wooden body hung there still, swinging softly with the others.

Being with her was nothing like love-making. More like talking to Uncle when the old man was drunk and vomiting riddles. For the first time, too, she had urgency in her voice – didn't she understand it would take time to find a beautiful woman who would give up her body?

He staggered to the landing, closed his eyes, slowly sank to his knees. Enough thinking — it only led to mistakes of the ego. Let the Great Spirit tell him the answer…

He knew he had to return to his cleaning. There was the entire second floor to vacuum, but first he had to silence the fears and doubts that bubbled up, base, defeatist thoughts that he had to whip back into their holes, like disobedient dogs. Eyes closed tightly. Darkness. *Please, Grandfathers, let the spirit speak to me –*

Tired, panting like a man who ran a marathon – was he asleep again?

He saw something in the distance – a ray of light. Slowly, materializing from empty space, a face appeared. Yes! He knew who she was — she worked in the restaurant — one of the bus girls! Pretty in her own way, he had watched her many nights from the shadows.

She seemed quiet, as Carlotta was quiet. Observant. A bit like himself, actually. Always watching. An excellent candidate, but was she — to use Carlotta's phrase — tired of life?

He asked for the answer to that question. Yes or no? Silence. He knew the Cosmos wouldn't answer. It never did.

But then the impossible happened. A voice, unknown to him:

"The lady is trying to decide whether to stay on Earth, or give up her dreams. Because none of them have come true…"

It was earth-shaking, the energy that possessed him now. He bounded to his feet and took his broom down the stairs, silently reciting Uncle's spell of transformation. Yes— the girl was beautiful, but her shell was filled with sadness. It might be possible to convince her. Why didn't he see it before? She was the perfect choice.

Voices in the kitchen – he wasn't too late. Before Ben came up and demanded they lock up, he would rev the vacuum cleaner, make it look as if he'd been working the whole time.

The machine roared. He swept quickly, thinking back to Uncle's explanation of how such exchanges proceeded: When Carlotta first took over, the young lady would still seem like her old self. Slowly, though, her face would change, re-form, re-shape while its new soul became accustomed to life and gained strength. In a few months, maybe a year, the identity of the sad one would be erased and his beloved could take full control.

It was a night to remember – his soul, finally open to the Universe, receiving its commands – not the least of which were his Uncle's thoughts. The foolish old man, trying to speak to him even now –

"My son, think. You can't do this. Don't throw your life away tilting at windmills--"

Then,

"The spell of giving life is like a rose – its body, full of thorns--"

Foolish old man. So accomplished in the ways of Knowledge. But never smitten with a woman's love. Lionel laughed. Raised his fist again, and spoke over the vacuum cleaner's whine:

"Grandfathers," he whispered, praying, "ignore your ancient prejudices. Look kindly upon the enterprise of your humble servant, for earthly love will be the result."

He clicked the machine off. Stuck it back in its closet, strode to the alcove, and down the steps, heart pounding happily.

Cisco looked up from his steam table, and pointed a finger. The prep room would need mopping.

CHAPTER 13
THE MOONLIGHT TEST

"Is Emily scheduled tonight?"

"No," Andrea answered, her eyes narrowing. "Why?"

"No reason." It was the truth. She was taken. Keith's stomach churned. He had never actually seen Paul pick her up after work, and neither had Julie or Andrea, when he asked them.

His body jumped involuntarily every time he glanced out the serving window and saw a waitress of Carlotta's stature, or even female customers with long, dark hair. If Ben were telling the truth, if there were really no conspiracy to make a fool of him, if Alberto was miraculously correct, and there really was something unholy upstairs —

He ate his salad, remembering last night's dream bit-by-bit. The wagon. The horse. The empty prairie. Were her little horse-and-buggy toys still upstairs somewhere? He had never given a damn about stories of the Old West.

Women came and went. Dressed up. Perfumed, smiling. Clumps of them, or escorted by sullen men who, Keith knew, might never be able to give them the happy time they were looking for. Most had barely gotten their drink before Charles came in to tell them their table was ready in the dining room. As they shuffled in and out, he studied them, always seeking to discover that one might be Carlotta in disguise.

Ben was right, though — her kisses were real. And her telling him to leave. He pictured the Carlotta marionette, hanging up there in the darkness on her strings. Yes, they were back, and whenever he asked who it was that sometimes took them away, blank stares were the answer.

If only Emily were on the schedule. My God, was he crazy? Wanting to go after two women at once?

At the end of the night, Keith trudged down the concrete steps to the parking lot. "Go home and get some rest," Ben called from his aging pickup truck. "You've been acting squirrelly all evening. Again."

For a moment, he thought about joining one of the clumps of wait- and bus-people that loitered in the gravel. The normal contingent were headed to the Catfish Hut to drink beer. "Where's John?"

Ben shrugged. "Saw him talking to Melissa earlier. Maybe he finally got through her defenses. Wait—" He fumbled with something.

The Wop had been chasing Melissa for several days, and Ben had already declined a beer. Keith looked around for Charlie. He was in the mood to talk.ig

"Here." Ben tossed a substantial ring of keys. "As long as you're standing there, go back in and make sure the ovens are turned off."

Keith held up his hands, letting the keys dangle. "You forget some pretty important things for a restaurant manager." He waved Ben away. "Not my job, *Señor*. I'm sure Chavo did it."

The keys clinked. "No. John made me a pizza at the end of the evening, remember? Don't make me get out of this truck. Please? Chop-chop."

Keith stopped halfway up the steps. "Wait a minute. I don't know how to disarm the burglar alarm."

"We don't have a burglar alarm. It's just a box with lights." None of the chattering waiters flinched at this. Everyone must know, except Keith. He stared, and Ben rolled his eyes. "We have a guy who comes around. "Old Larcinter will be by in a while."

"Larcinter?"

"The night watchman. Works cheap, so of course Thomas hired him."

Keith looked through the small window as he fumbled with the key. The lock clicked open. "Hey," he yelled over his shoulder, "the lights on your little box by the wait station are flashing."

"They don't flash."

"Wait—" It was all he got out before the door swung open. "Someone's in here." Then, to the moving form, "You. Hold up, there." Could it be the night watchman? With long strides, he made it to the short hall that led to the lounge. At the far end, the doors were swinging. "Ben—in here," he yelled over his shoulder. Heart pounded — they had a security guard? Security guards didn't run like sprinters.

He froze in his tracks.

"My God," he yelled, hoping the others would hear. "It's the prankster. Ben!"

This might be their chance to corner the criminal.

Keith jogged, stumbled through the lounge doors, and bumped into tables and chairs in the weak red light from the exit signs. At the front, next to the stage, he stopped, scanning the shadows. Nothing moved, but he did feel a draft—where was it coming from?

No music or ventilators, no murmuring barflies. He might hear voices entering the kitchen, yet there was something else. The drone of the river?

He turned, feeling what was about to happen before it did. The side door to the lounge - the one leading outside, always locked, pasted with signs that warned the fire alarm would ring - stood wide open, letting in the night.

She stood in the doorway. Her name whispered automatically from his lips. "Carlotta."

She smiled. "You're alone, finally." She shook her head, sending long hair flying, ink-black, tinged with red from the exit sign above her, and silver from outside—or somewhere. "The moon is shining," she said, reading his thoughts. Her hand came out to take his.

Shaking, he let her lead him. Out the door, into the night cool.

"Where have you been? Why do you do this?" Tried to pull back. "Why do you run from me?"

Another shake of that long hair, and she came to him. Her forehead sank against his breast. She started to meet his eyes, then turned her head to face the river.

"You have so much, it hurts to be near you." Only then did Keith notice an old wagon lodged up against the side fence. Even in moonlight shadow, he could see how weatherworn and crumbling it was. A neglected antique he had never noticed before, but no one ever came over to this side. Now she was staring at him. "It is too rich, being here. I want to tell you to run away, but I can't. You know that."

"I don't want to run away—" His head was a jumble of the stinky river breeze, the crickets, the locusts. Large clouds blotted out most of the stars, and the moon played hide-and-seek between them. "Are you real, or just a dream?"

No answer, but her hands gripped his arms like vices. Real enough. Another pull, and he was dragged across the cement entry walk, until her back was against the wagon. Her lips were on his, until, in one swift move, she pulled away and hopped up onto the wagon bed. He started to protest, but she pulled again, with surprising strength.

Dizzy, he landed on top of her.

"Will this old piece of junk hold us?"

But she smothered him again, her tongue darting in and out, first fire, then ice. They rolled, and between kisses, he glimpsed the delicate white lines the moon painted on the river, out in the middle where the current ran. Only the moon, and the single streetlight far across in River Park, and shadows—

The wagon creaked, sending shivers through him. He'd heard that sound before – in his nightmares. He sat up. A dark shape glided across the river, a skiff, or boat of some sort. There were people in the back of it, or something hunkered down. In the bow, a single man.

"A boat—" he said, as her fingers traced his back.

"I told you," she answered breathlessly, perhaps drunk, or part of the way to ecstasy, "that this would keep happening. See? Now he is coming."

"Who?" His body jolted, but her lips were on his again. He strained to keep his eyes open, just making out the man's outline. That shadow felt somehow malevolent and the craft moved with purpose. They were going to land.

Cricket songs screamed to a crescendo, the moon hid, her lips kept pressing, her tongue taking away his thoughts — He wanted to let his hands roam, but how could he be romantic when that boat was coming? Where were Ben and the others? Didn't they hear him? My God, the boat was almost here.

"Touch me," she insisted, almost whimpering. "Let me have as much energy as I can — before he takes it all." A deep kiss. She fell back to the wagon bed, her chest heaving. "Quickly — touch me before he touches the river bank." The moon had come out again, more silver on the water, flashes of mercury behind the skimming craft.

"Carlotta, who is that guy? Who are they, in the boat — we should go inside -- "

But she pulled him back down to the wagon bed. His hands moved by memory, automatically, urged on coaxed by her soft fingers, her wet lips. Down, to her calf, then up to her knee, still sliding up, beneath the full petticoats of her Water Company costume. Higher. The crickets crowded in, the lapping of the waves against the shore, even the slick whisper of the boat's hull in the water. He was drunk on the fishy river odor, mixed with her potent honeysuckle perfume — then he froze.

Disbelieving, his hand grasped her thigh. Then the other. They were smooth, warm. No, cold. Too smooth. He squeezed, but the skin did not respond. He ran his fingers up and down, not believing. Again. Her legs were made of wood. The air gushed out of his lungs as if he had been hit in the stomach. He jerked away, breaking her embrace. The wagon creaked and he was on his feet.

"What the hell —" he started to say, but the boat thumped against ground, and the man in the bow leaned forward with a rope. He could cross the grass and the street within moments.

Carlotta sat up, her eyes glowing in the moonlight. She was panting, like a woman sated. Her fingers spread, waving him away.

"He took my will," she gasped. "Find someone to love, or he will take yours."

Every hair on Keith's body stood up. The man was on the grass, coming up the bank. Back to Carlotta. She nodded. "And he will never stop coming."

Keith leaped down, stumbling on the broken concret walk below. Groped for the doorway. Gulping for breath. From the corner of his eye, saw the man's shadow moving quickly – then he was inside — carpet under his shoes, red light filling the air – he didn't dare look back to the wagon -- He slammed the door and latched it.

A sound — he turned quickly. Ben and a waitress named Jackie banged through the swinging doors from the kitchen.

"What's wrong?" the manager asked.

Keith shook his head, panting, stalked past them, rubbing his fingers together, trying to understand the feel of what he had just touched. He fought to maintain, to not cry out. He grabbed onto a chair, a table, anything to keep the room from spinning.

"Someone left the goddam side door open," he finally said. If this was a dream, he couldn't tell if it was over yet. If not a dream, then he must hurry to catch some of the waiters before they all left for the Catfish Hut. He was suddenly in the mood to get drunk.

CHAPTER 14
THE TRUTH ABOUT MADAME X

As he lay writhing between the sheets, Keith remembered the
story his grandmother used to scare them with — the one about
the kid that swallowed a watermelon seed, only to have an
entire vine grow out of his mouth a few days later.

It felt like a seed had been planted in Keith's
stomach — nourished by too many beers, growing, pulsing,
sending a belching vine up his esophagus, making him taste
her kisses again, sending him gliding across the moonlight
river with that heavy shadow behind him, plopping him
down on the stool in the bar kitchen, to wait and wait for an
Emily who never returned to work.

He had never moved his shotgun to his apartment, but
found himself plotting how to sneak in and out of his parents'
house, get the gun, buy shells at an all night convenience store,
wait in the attic after work some night, and use the weapon to
blow the puppets to bits. Then he would go downstairs and
chop that old wagon to smithereens, if it really existed.

Wooden legs. How could they be? She was flesh and
blood, with a tongue, and moist lips. But if he went shooting,
he would like to include those two smart asses at the
Laundromat. My God, was he going insane? Is this how
homicidal maniacs were born?

He wished Emily were lying in this bed with him,
listening to all that had happened. Maybe she had read
psychology books about things like this. Of course, after he
spilled his guts, she would console him, climb out of bed, and
never speak to him again.

Perhaps he fell asleep, for the ringing phone almost blew him out of bed.

"So, how's your love life?" Larry's too-cheery voice blasted over the phone. Bright sunshine poured in through the cracks in the blinds. "I want to know the results of the hunt for Madame X."

"No results." Keith yawned. "Except that your brother is in need of a shrink. Better yet, an exorcist. That restaurant is all fucked up."

"Then get a real job." Mr. Positive was apparently short on patience this morning. "I'll hang up. Just wanted to know if you landed a date with Ms. Weirdo yet. Ever find out her name, at least?"

"Look, Baby Bro," Keith sighed, "it's a mistake to start with you, but there's no one else to talk to. I'm not sure she's real, anymore."

"Then grab yourself a cocktail waitress. You gotta score a few times before you quit that dump and get back with an ad agency."

His brother's omniscience was always his most disgusting attribute. Keith sat back. Was that what he was doing? Would his little fantasies about Emily turn into a one night stand, distracting him from the real prey?

"I told you, the agencies aren't hiring. Not in this economy – Oh, crap, what's the use of going into this again--"

"Shut up, Keith. Don't be beat before you start."

"Hey, Larry, I'm way past starting. And I'm beat, anyway. She's not real. She's made of wood."

"OK, OK, I'm getting tired of --"

"Listen when I'm trying to tell you something important. Somehow, I'm having hallucinations about a marionette. A life-size fucking puppet. She's never there when other people are around, and then she's made of wood, and keeps telling me to leave. I'm about to die, I'm so tired, but I don't dare go to sleep. Go read your ghost books and tell me what all this means so I can get on with my life."

Now silence.

Finally, Larry's studious voice — quiet. Not such an asshole. "You sound too pissed for this to be a joke you cooked up with Ben."

"I told Ben a thousand times. You and he are the jokers, remember? Hell, I'm the one who kept you both out of jail when you pulled that prank on the lady at the discount store."

Larry talked fast. Never wanted to admit how stupid that had been. "What do you mean, made of wood? Is she just stiff?"

"No. Idiot. I felt her legs."

"Come on, Keith, maybe she has a wooden leg or something. Some people can walk just fine — "

"I'm not going to yell at you, Larry." Keith stuck his head under a pillow, blocking out the light. "It's not a wooden leg. She is wooden. She comes into my dreams. She tells me to take a lover or get married or — something."

"Sounds like Mom."

"Goodbye, Larry."

He slammed the receiver down, trying to be mad, but wound up chuckling at the smart-ass remark. It felt good to laugh. What else was there to do? Either Carlotta existed and he was having some sort of cerebral episode, or there was no such creature, and he was now schizo. Either option was a hopeless case.

He had forgotten to check the schedule. Oh, please let Emily be on tonight. And maybe there was a God, and she would break up with her boyfriend.

He pulled the pillow over his head. What did it matter? If he hit on her, she would dismiss him like a drunk in the lounge.

Light stabbed in, but he tried to doze. Always starting awake with the same image in his head. The smooth wood of those legs.

Even if Emily agreed to go out with him, would he ever want to touch a woman again?

CHAPTER 15
ONE CHANCE

Keith drove to work through a fresh rainstorm, straining to see through the streaks of the defunct wipers. As he turned off River Drive, he heard a thump, and a glance in the rear-view mirror confirmed he had run over a large snake. That was an omen, his grandfather had always claimed, of an impending flood. A flood was impossible, of course, since they built the new dam. Nevertheless, Keith stepped carefully between the puddles in the back lot. Where there was one snake…

"Well, goddam. Working in the big kitchen all night, huh?" John bellowed inside the back door.

"Oh, shit." He had forgotten he was scheduled to work behind the Line all night, so there would be precious little chance to corner Emily. Could nothing go right in this place? "Want to trade?"

"Hell, no. It's my turn to sit on my ass out there and stare at all the beautiful women. Here, help me." Keith took an armload of pans and followed him into the cool lounge. A nervous glance at the side door. A couple of characters he had seen in the bar before picked that moment to enter. No one else. Julie was setting tables in the corner, but no Emily.

John worked his teeth with a toothpick and fiddled with the deep fat fryer's temperature control while Keith primed the popcorn popper. Another look at the side entry. Was the old wagon still out there? He'd forgotten to walk around the side and look when he arrived. Going through the alarmed door was out of the question.

The popper took only seconds to start belching out a rich smell of butter flavoring, and he could hear the little rake inside start mixing up the kernels. Stay focused, he told himself. Don't be obsessive and go looking for the wagon, or the marionettes, or any other meaningless thing, and hopefully the insanity would not return.

"Have you ever met Emily's boyfriend?"

The Wop was wiping the counter. "You want to ask her out, huh?"

"Is it that obvious?"

"Only to a pro." John sneered. "Does this mean you've quit searching for that dream girl?"

Keith ignored him. "He's probably some jealous maniac. Just wondering." He turned to leave.

"Listen, shithead." John spat out the toothpick. "You guys would be perfect together. If you don't have the balls, I'll ask her for you."

"Relax. I'll do it. Just don't rush me."

John's eyes widened. "Well, now's your chance." Keith turned to see Emily coming around the front of the bar, greeting Julie and Manny.

"So, Keith?" John stuck his head out of the serving window, talking loudly. "You gonna ask her?"

Panicked, he felt his face get hot. "Shut up."

"I said," — even louder, his sneer resembling the devil himself — "are you going to ask her?"

His mouth worked. Curse words almost poured out.

Emily drew alongside, holding her small tray aloft. Impish, irresistible smile.

"Who is he asking what?"

John didn't miss a beat. "Don Juan, here, is trying to get up the nerve to ask his new girlfriend out on a date."

Keith's heart felt like it would burst. Tongue thick, too heavy to move. Inexplicably, his feet moved and he barged past her, through the back swinging doors, and down the hall.

"Chicken shit," John's voice followed him. Two giggling waitresses looked up, spread apart to let him pass. In the kitchen, heads were up, looking for the cause of the commotion. So he turned at the register, and proceeded up the stairs.

Goddam it. He would kill the bastard next time he had him alone. In a few huge strides, he reached the back dining room on the second floor, panting. Now he paced, cursing himself for running away like a child. Deep breaths — he drank in the cool silence, glancing from the burgundy-colored velvet curtains to the gay nineties wallpaper. The salad bar stood fully stocked, the only sign that the room was part of this century. Finally, his heartbeat slowed.

"Don't be so upset." The voice was low, like a melody. A new jolt rocked his heart back into high gear. Carlotta sat on one of the antique-style chairs. Relaxed. Her legs stretched out – legs that looked absolutely flesh and blood. How long had she been there?

"Stay away," he sputtered, struck all over again by her amazing beauty, regretting the words the instant they came out. "I'm sorry, Carlotta. I didn't think I would see you. I get confused when I'm with you. Last night — I thought — "

His voice withered, and he could only watch while she leaned forward, elbows buried in her fluffy period dress, and casually adjusted the buckles on her old fashioned shoes. She was ravishing — perfect features, carefree air, as if last night had never happened. Her legs — he couldn't keep his gaze from them. My God, they were real — the thought occurred to him that he shouldgrab her arm and not let go, drag her down to Ben's office, and demand that his friend tell him what was true. Or take her now. On the floor. He ached. In every part of his body.

Carlotta rose. If she could read his thoughts, she wasn't threatened. Invulnerable to him. To anything. Just like any other waitress, she brushed her hands across the front of her period dress, as if eager to start on her tables. But then she smiled, and moved toward him at a seductive pace, her dark gaze riveting him in place.

"Don't lose your temper," she whispered, bringing her hands up his arms, then around him, while he stood, shivering. Her breasts pressed against his chest. Not wooden at all. If he touched them – but she was speaking. "You have been given a gift from the Great Spirit. It's what I wished for you. Don't ignore it."

"A gift? Tell me who you are. How the hell do you appear right when I don't expect it?"

Her hands touched, then intertwined with his. Cold. She stretched up and kissed him, her tongue so chilly that it sent a freezing wave through his mouth, down his neck. He tried to push back, but his muscles were asleep, and the kiss went on forever, until he felt like he was spinning around, his heartbeat shifting gears yet again, throbbing slower--slower--

Just at the point where he thought he might pass out, their lips parted.

"You are mine. He gave you to me. But I know what he does to those he gives to me," she said, caressing his hair. "Now you have a chance—the only one you will ever have."

Soft eyes. Long lashes. Honeysuckle fulling air that could exist in any Time, from the Beginning until now.

"The swarthy one is right." A little smile, as if she were his best friend in all the world. "Tell her how you feel. Do it now, before he closes the trap. You cannot fight the battles alone."

She released him so suddenly that he went flying backwards, stumbling across the carpet until he landed on his butt. In that same instant—he saw it only from the corner of his eye—Carlotta traversed the distance from the salad bar to the stairs beyond the alcove. He tried to get to his feet, but fell back down like a drunk.

On the bottom step, she turned. "The Children of Rage will come," she said. "And they think you are mine. You must know what that means. Tell her how you feel tonight. A chance comes only once. " A step backward, and she merged with the darkness.

"Wait," Keith tried to yell, his tongue a wad of dead meat in his frozen mouth. Emily? Did she read his mind? Overhear his thoughts about the waitress? "I didn't mean them," he tried to say. Couldn't. Blood surging. Heart pounding. His mind a mish-mash of feelings for the mysterious woman. And for...?

Gradually, his ears stopped ringing, and the dining room righted itself. Rational explanations rushed in, but didn't hold up. No one—not Ben, not a single waitress or busboy—had happened by during the encounter. It lasted an hour, or maybe only seconds, as if staged for his benefit, similar to so many ghosts sightings he remembered from Larry's books, where a specter was visible to only one subject. Hell, if every waitress in the place had been standing up here, would anyone else have seen her?

But what did that mean? That ghosts were real, and that she – Carlotta was a ghost?

He worked his way to his feet. My God, he should have listened to Mom, gotten a job, any job, right after he got laid off. Lying around on the couch all day ate at your brain. But was he insane beyond repair?

And why – with Carlotta – was it always warnings? The man in the boat last night—dreams, nightmares. Garbage. He was just horny, it had been so long since he was with a woman. And his last chance—was she talking about Emily? Was that man going to do something to Emily?

Two thoughts resounded in his head, maybe logical conclusions, or perhaps realizations she had planted, left to thaw out with his frozen tongue. She didn't want him. She said that plainly enough. But who were these Children of Rage? Was that the title of a video game? A movie?

Each time he repeated the phrase silently, the image of those two boys in the Laundromat came to mind. For a few brief moments, her words and actions possessed a sort of logic. Perhaps he had been hallucinating last night.

No – she wasn't a phantom. Why would a phantom give a damn about what happened to him? He could always walk out of here. Ben would forgive him. But then he would never get to know Emily.

Noises from the kitchen filtered slowly up the stairs, until he could hear everything again. Katy would be getting antsy, and he needed to stay on her good side, if he wanted

time later to duck into the lounge, at least to apologize for
storming out earlier.

He grabbed one side of the ornate alcove to keep his
balance. Emily. Another fool's errand. She was taken. Was he
just picking on her in order to follow Carlotta's warped
warnings?

He tossed that thought around for a while, picturing
Emily's face, her hair, the line of her legs. Such a happy –
impudence – in her eyes. Her laugh. Emily was not an omen
or a plaything or part of any conspiracy — she was something
else. She was real. Was he really ready to choose her over
Carlotta?

Now his tongue could move, and breathing seemed
almost normal. He rubbed his eyes. Wouldn't hurt to try. Ask
her out or something. Emily would decline, and then where
would he be? Looking for a job. This infernal place muddled
his mind.

He took a few steps, wound up holding onto a table,
then moved, pausing again by the alcove. If he followed
Carlotta upstairs, what would he find?

No. Prep time was half over, and he had fallen way
behind.

CHAPTER 16
EARLY WARNING SYSTEM

Katy stood there, hands on her hips, eyebrows raised, as Keith trudged across the brick floor. "Did you forget where you were working?" She offered a plate on which a fresh bacon, lettuce, and tomato sandwich sat. "We were about to split yours between us." She laughed. Keith began eating with a vengeance, thankful his mouth could work again.

"Why bacon? It's not on the menu."

Katy waved at the steam table stocked with pots of vegetables. "I'm tired of all that crap."

Chavo stuffed the remainder of his own sandwich in his mouth. His family ran a small leather shop in Mexico City – purchased, supposedly, with money the little guy sent home. He wore a fancy monogrammed belt, and even Thomas had reportedly bought one like it from him.

Keith ate in spurts as they prepped, Katy's delicious sandwich radiating warmth into the hollowness he felt from the encounter upstairs. He was the only one who could see her, wasn't he? Carlotta. If she came down now and dropped an order, he was certain he would faint. What the fuck was happening?

Katy was black, rotund, and cheerful. Daughter of a Pullman cook who derived her name from the nickname for the Missouri, Kansas, & Texas railroad. Her cooking talents, she claimed, had come from him. Especially her ability to tell how well a steak was cooked just by looking at it.

Orders began, and the traffic picked up quickly, multiplying Keith's jitters. Ben paused by the cutting table, and Keith flagged him down, not really sure what he was going to say. "You ever meet Paul, Emily's boyfriend?"

"Calm down, Mr. Available." Ben straightened his tie cockily. "Your mystery princess might get jealous."

"More spaghetti, Chavo," Katy demanded. "Keith, you start some shrimp."

Minutes passed, an hour, and the heavy supper rush forced him to concentrate on the frying, dipping, mixing wiping spills off the edges of the dishes passing through his hands. He was the new guy. The weak link on this Line, but thanfully Chavo seemed always as far behind as he. Only Katy seemed unperturbed, as she stacked the tickets chronologically, laid steaks on the grill, doled out the proper vegetables for each order and ordered them both back to the coolers when a hotel pan got low.

"I'll bet we're a sight, running around back here like three dogs fightin' over the same dish." She chuckled. "Keith, you looks like the jolly green giant, Chavo's not much more than a midget, and me a big old hippo." The laughter was a release, and as Keith dumped spices into the shrimp, and it was a while before he remembered he had something important to do.

But what was he going to say to Emily? And how could he get away, with orders coming in this fast? And what if this was one of those nights when they let her off work early?

"Don't burn the chicken fried steaks, hon." Katy nudged him. "Who are you looking for? Someone to come give you a coffee break?" She laughed.

"No. Sorry." He tried to be cool, but when the slightest of lulls came, he had reached the breaking point.

"Uh, can I have five minutes? Go out and check on John?"

She looked at him. "John can take care of hisself." Now her eyes were slits. "Tell you what – I'll give you two. First, get me a packet o' peas. That pan's gettin' low."

He trotted through the prep room and into the big freezer. "Hello, Mr. Thieu." The small Vietnamese man breaded fish at his prep table. A banker at one time, John contended, who escaped from Viet Nam with his family

during the "boat people" exodus. The only time he appeared
was to dart behind the Line to replenish steaks, fish, shrimp,
chicken and breaded chicken fried steaks, sliding trays of them
into the ice boxes below the stoves.

"Too busy?" A toothy grin below coke-bottle glasses.

"Too busy, Mr. Thieu."

"No good."

Emerging with the cold packs, Keith collided with the
Wop.

"We're gettin' hammered, man," John yelled. "I've gone
through two buckets of turkey fries." He disappeared into the
walk-in cooler on the far side. Keith's stomach churned. Katy
would see him back here, so there'd be no reason to go out
and check on him. Worse – Emily would be too busy to talk.

Praying that the big woman wasn't looking this way,
Keith strode quickly past the pastry Line, and was right next
to the wall phone when it rang. He almost jumped out of his
skin.

Lionel, the quiet janitor, had appeared with his broom
from nowhere, blocked his path. A nod, as if directing Keith to
answer. Keith picked it up. Pea packet freezing his hand.

"Hello?"

The man on the other end rattled frantic Spanish. Keith
tried to pick out familiar words, but heard only something that
sounded like "Chavo."

"Chavo! I think it might be for you." Keith held the
receiver aloft.

"*Para mi*?" Chavo stood as one thunderstruck. The
janitor reached over, intercepting the phone before Keith could
pull it away.

"*Bueno*," he said forcefully into the receiver. A long
pause, then emphatic whispers. Keith trotted behind the Line,
handed the box to Katy.

"Good Lord," she said, looking past him.

He turned in time to see Lionel make a twirling motion
with his hand. As if choreographed, Chavo, the two
dishwashers, and Jose – a holdover from the early shift –

untied their aprons, dropped them into the laundry bag, and exited, single file, through the back door.

The janitor remained. Glanced at Keith with a slight, helpless-looking smile, laid his broom against the wall, and followed the others into the night.

John emerged from the prep room and took it all in. "What the fuck. Say it isn't so!"

"It's so." Katy sighed.

"Amen," said Anna from the Pastry Line.

"Where are they going?"

"You dumb shit," the Wop answered. "Immigration's on the way." He raised his arms. "And in the middle of the night, goddamit." He barged past a couple of dazed waiters and stormed toward the passageway to the lounge.

"You mean they're gone for the night?"

"That's about the size of it, Hot Shot," Anna said, holding her icing spatula in the air.

"John?" Katy's voice was heavy.

"I know, I know." He waved her off. "I'll take Chavo's place when it dies down out there. Right now, Thomas is busy kissing the mayor's butt." He disappeared down the short hall.

Katy rotated her gaze to the Pastry Line.

"Don't look at me, girl," Anna said with a shake of her head. "I'm up to my eyeballs. There ain't enough pies cut up to hold us ten minutes, and somebody's got to clean up this cheescake I dropped."

A hush descended. A waiter named Rodney barreled through the front doors, elbowing past the scattered bus- and wait-people, and slammed a ticket down between the warming shelves. "Order up," he yelled.

Jeers rained down on him from all sides.

CHAPTER 17
DIVERSION

Lionel was caught up in the moment, found himself joking
with the others as the station wagon turned onto River Bridge.
They weren't such bad guys, really. The beer tasted tart and
made him cough. A smell he remembered from childhood.

"I thought Jose was going to wet his pants," Patricio
said. The others howled.

"Are you afraid to go back home?" Manuel punched
Jose on the arm. "You think the police will be waiting?"

"It's an all-expense paid trip, *pendejo*," Patricio added.
"Hey Lionel, you ever been taken by the INS?"

Lionel shook his head.

"I have," Chavo said sheepishly.

This brought a new uproar.

"We know your story. Did you sleep with the officer,
you little pussy?" Manuel asked in a syrupy whine. "Is that
how they let you come back?"

For an instant, it seemed that Chavo would leap over
the seat, but he stayed put. "I was home three months. They
don't know I came back," he said through clenched teeth.

Lionel could not help but laugh out loud, and finally
the little man cackled with them.

"OK, one of you *cabrones*, we need an I.D.," Patricio
demanded. They would buy more beer before they left town.
As fake documents were compared, Lionel thought he heard a
voice.

"Stay away, the Children are coming." It came from
above the car, crystal clear. From nowhere. The others kept
jabbering. If any one of them heard it, he didn't flinch.

Dios mio. The Children. Carlotta's words. Of course-- there would be no Immigration man. Somehow, she had tricked him into leaving the restaurant.

"Stop the car." He slapped Patricio's shoulder.

"Ehh?"

"Shut up." Jose shoved Lionel down. "We have the night off. In the morning, we call Cisco and find out what happened. Your precious dirt will still be on the floor tomorrow."

They all laughed.

"Tonight, we drink."

Sneers from the others made him sit back. He waited, making note of the streets they took, until there was finally a pause in one of Patricio's speeches. He leaned forward and asked, as innocently as he could, "Where do you take us, amigo?"

"To my cousin's. He lives on a farm on the west side."

"*Estupido,*" Manuel added, "did you think we would drop you at your room? The INS officers could be there, waiting."

"They know where we live," Jose warned. "Don't they, Chavo? They only toy with us, like a cat with mice."

"Don't be a bashful *pendejo,*" Patricio said over his shoulder. "You'll be a very funny drunk."

Manuel perked up. "Hey, if Lionel gets drunk enough, he can teach us how to fly." The remark brought a new riot of laughter. Lionel made himself chuckle. Through the back windshield, the bridge receded until it was out of sight. He would never make it back in time.

"The powers that be make the world turn 'round," Uncle was fond of reciting, "while fools sing their songs..."

"A store." Lionel pointed.

Manuel was elected, and collected money. To allay their suspicions, Lionel donated three dollars. The moment they pulled in, however, he twisted over Chavo and opened the back door.

"No, *Amigo,*" Chavo cried.

Lionel's tattered tennis shoes hit the pavement, and he ran.

"*Alto.*" "*Pendejo.*" "You goddamed *chupacabra*," their voices called after him.

He guessed it was at least three miles back to the bridge, then two more to the restaurant. He had walked that last leg many times in the dead of night.

Thankfully, they did not pursue him with the car. He felt bad, for this would tear it with them. There would be no end to their taunts. And what if he were wrong? The INS men would take him and he might never make it back to Carlotta.

Before he even reached the bridge, he had to slow to a walk, lungs bursting. Was he being a fool? After all, Carlotta's time was different. Her warning, which felt so urgent, might not mean tonight. Maybe it would be years in the future. Or the past.

A cluster of vehicles sped past his outstretched thumb. The *Estado Unidos* was a place of wonders, but no one would pick up a tired-looking Mexican going down to the river in the middle of the night.

The Children of Rage, she had called them. What were they mad at? And who was this *friend* he supposedly had? His only friends were in the car, or else, they would be friends no more.

Once he crossed the bridge, he stopped again, stomach aching, calves cramping.

"Don't go down a path that starts with pain," Uncle said more than once. Then he would laugh and state the obvious--every path to the other world begins with pain.

What if it were not Carlotta who tricked him out of the place, but her master? If he was so powerful, why would he call children to do his mischief? What sort of monsters could they be? His mind went back to the vision she took him into, and the shadowy figures that set the fire when she lulled the little gentleman to his death.

A police car turned onto River Drive. Lionel moved off the road and down into the brush that lined the water. By now, the others would be halfway to the cousin's farm, drinking beer, cursing, telling their dirty jokes.

He forbade himself to envy them. Crouching, he let the nervous lights pass on the road above, while his legs shook in the cold reeds.

First, they took his parents, then Uncle. Now, his own beloved was risking herself by sending him astray. It was his job to protect her, not the other way around. Why was his path was always the hard one? He had asked the spirits that very question so many times. They had yet to answer.

CHAPTER 18
COWBOYS

"Where is that Ben?" Katy cursed under her breath while she laid order tickets next to two outgoing plates. Wait-people loitered in front of the ice machines. Shaking heads. Clenched fists. Keith was aware of Ben's history at the restaurant, but in this moment, it really came home. He had started as a dishwasher, advanced to cook, then waiter, maitre 'd. He knew the business inside and out, just as Thomas was purported to. Of course Katy would ask for him. She probably had him back behind this Line three or four years ago.

"Out there," Charlie answered. "He knows about the Mexicans. Doing his PR thing. Everyone's getting pissed-off over the delays."

The big woman flipped through the tickets again. "Start two more Shrimp Orleenz, Keith hon."

"No more pans." Keith handed her a plate of fish, fresh out of the fryer.

She added French fries, then peered through the shelves toward the vacant dishwashing cubicle. "Well, start 'em when you can. We're gonna run out of clean dishes in 'bout five minutes."

At last Ben appeared, shedding sport coat and tie, and donned an apron. "What do you want me to cook?"

Katy grimaced, pointing at the towering stacks on the dishwashing conveyors.

"Oh, yeah," he said, and reached for the spray gun.

For a short while, Keith thought they might be holding their own. Then a new wave of tickets appeared on the smooth stainless steel shelf. Even so, he was careful to wipe spills off of every plate he sent out. Katy was a stickler for perfect presentation.

"You're catchin' on." She laughed. "My daddy always said that if you mind how the food looks, the good sperrits'll take care of the taste."

"Spirits? Do you believe in ghosts, Katy? Is this old building haunted?"

She chuckled again. "Just talk, I reckon."

"Well, what scared Brenda?"

"I wasn't there." This time, a little edge in her voice. "Poor thing. Got a job at a diner up on the Dallas Highway. She don't call me much anymore."

"But she was scared, right? There's a prankster or something fooling around up there?"

Her brow furrowed as she turned the steaks. "I'm not sure I believe that one. Don't know of anybody crazy enough to go up there by theyselves to play a prank. This old place is just too spooky." Her eyes twinkled.

Hands gripping order tickets pulled her from her rest, and in minutes, Mr. Thieu's last tray of meticulously lined-up shrimp was reduced to cold crumbs. Keith trotted back to the freezer, to look for trays the old Vietnamese might have forgotten.

Why didn't anyone want to discuss what was going on upstairs? Finally, another pause came. The waiters peered through the shelves with calmer faces, somehow. Katy leaned back against the steam table and sipped her ever-present glass of water. "Maybe it's 'cause we're so close to the river," she said quietly. "Daddy said sperrits collect in the river bottoms. It's the water that draws 'em."

Keith felt his jaw drop. After a night like this, he didn't know whether to ask more questions or scream. Here he was, about to go crazy, and everyone else seemed to be aware of a vast, hidden set of crazy rules that governed this place – and took it for granted. Had they all gone daffy, working here?

Like a blast of fresh air, Thomas entered from the main dining room. "Sorry, Katy. I was stuck out there with the *big money*."

"You heard about Chavo and Patricio--" Keith began.

"They were due some vacation." Thomas smiled, snatching a ticket in one hand and dropping spaghetti into the steamer with the other.

The restaurateur seemed to take twice as long with orders as was necessary. In spite of that, he quickly surpassed Keith in volume. Working on a pan of Shrimp Orleans, Thomas sautéed the crustaceans before adding spices.

"Just put it all in at once," Keith heard himself advise. "It's quicker."

The chef nodded.

Katy scowled. "You gonna tell the boss how to cook ever' dish?"

After another eternity—order after order, a hundred glances up, afraid Emily might leave early—traffic finally dwindled. Thomas bowed to Katy, then disappeared back into the lower dining room. The Wop ambled in, chef's coat half unbuttoned, sipping from a glass of beer.

"Sorry, folks." He jiggled the cashbox in his hand. "New record for the bar kitchen." A meaningful look passed between him and big lady, then he motioned to Keith. "I beat your shit, Big Boy. Don't sweat it. Luck of the draw." He winked. "I'll bet you're in the mood to clean up out there for me."

"You got it." Keith glanced at Katy, who only shrugged. His heart pounded as he rushed through the hall. Should he start off with a speech of apology, or just ask her outright? If she said 'no,' there would be nothing more to hold him here. He could quit this asylum. Hell, maybe forget the whole thing.

"You're like a wanna-be Chinese general," Linda had told him when they read *The Art of War* together. "You won't act until you are sure of winning. You have to take risks to be successful in love." Linda talked too much.

The lounge looked like a tornado had come through. Quiet now, with its sour, night-is-over smell. Only a few patrons lingered, and Emily was writing on her pad, taking orders, and grabbed an empty beer glass from another when she turned toward the bar.

Andrea groaned as she helped stack dishes into the bus-bin Keith had carried in with him. "The night from hell," she said.

The long-haired, sweaty country rock band was packing instruments. Keith scraped the counter, started draining the deep fat fryer, all the while watching Emily's every move from the corner of his eye. The overhead music framed her, seemed written especially for her graceful motions.

Finally, she looked his way. "See me before you leave," he said in a stage whisper. She looked puzzled, but gave a slight nod.

He turned back to the dirty dishes, and remembered that Andrea was one of the few staff members he had not yet asked about Carlotta. There was no point to it, really, but the question came out, without him being able to control it. "Hey, Andrea, do you know all of the waitresses here?"

She held up a finger and left to wait on three cowboys who entered just as Manny bellowed "last call." The cowboys were dressed for a night on the town--new jeans, snap shirts, and beaver-skin Stetsons that were weathered with sun. Only one — the oldest — was polite enough to remove his hat. He set it down meticulously in the table's only empty chair.

"Little darlin'," he told Andrea loudly, "just git us started on a pitcher. That's enough, ain't it, boys? Unless you come along with it." All three laughed, as if he'd come up with the best joke ever.

After filling their order, Andrea returned. Keith was scraping something stubborn off one of the pocked tables. "What did you say about a waitress?" she asked. Seductive smile. "Got the hots for somebody?"

"No." Bad move. He didn't want her to dwell on this with Emily. Still, he described the dark-haired woman, leaving out mention of Carlotta. "Ever see anyone like that?"

A grimace. "Waitress? Doesn't ring a bell. You work in the back. When she brought orders, did she come from upstairs or down?"

"She didn't place any orders."

A scowl. "On a night like this? Impossible. Maybe she's a hostess. When was the last time you saw her?"

"Want us to go look for her?" the youngest cowboy interjected, sipping his beer.

Keith's hackles rose. These guys had obviously had a few before they came here.

"Why, here she comes now." The middle cowboy motioned with his beer toward Emily.

The young one cackled. "Good one, Hank."

"What are you guys so serious about?" Emily poised her free hand on her hip.

"It's nothing." Keith stifled a nervous laugh. "I just asked Andrea if she had seen someone. No big deal."

"Hell, I've used that line before, Missy," the oldest cowboy said. "This boy's two-timing you sure as hell." The two younger ones slammed their beers down, laughing.

Without reply, Andrea snatched up the bus bin, as if she were the lucky one who was smart enough to get out of here. Keith nodded toward the little kitchen, and Emily followed.

"Are those creeps bugging you?" he asked. She stood close, her perfume tired, but intoxicating. Keith leaned against the cutting table, his back to the serving window.

"What a night," she sighed. "Swamped in the back, too, huh? I heard they had to cut the dining line off. Stretcehd out to the parking lot." She took a shoe off to examine the condition of her stocking. "Oh, my aching feet…"

"Sorry I ran out so fast earlier. John was getting on my nerves," he began, then halted midstream. He watched her light brown hair, the way it brushed the top of her collar. Perhaps, for once, his body knew it was not the time to talk. His hand thrust out to touch her chin. Her eyes lit up.

Slowly, unstoppably, he leaned forward and kissed her. The turmoil of this night, even the loneliness of the last few months, maybe, unraveled in the gentle click of their lips as they parted and joined again.

"Hot damn!"

The cry made them both jump. The young blond cowboy filled the cubicle's order window.

"Hell, I came up here to see if I could get somethin' to eat. I didn't know it was a kissin' booth," his voice boomed through the bar.

Keith gritted his teeth. "Sorry, we're closed." He took Emily's hand and started out of the little kitchen's back door.

"Well, the kissin' booth ain't closed," the cowboy said, voice ringing the pans that hung over the glass stand-up oven. With lightning speed, he stretched through the window and grabbed Emily's arm. A bin tumbled, raining dirty dishes down onto her feet.

"No--let me go." Her face — so pale — Keith had never seen it like this.

It was automatic. Keith's right fist shot forward, landed landing squarely on the punk's forehead. The cowboy flew backward, releasing his grip. Emily collapsed against the bricks.

"Stay here." Keith leaped from the cubicle, determined to throw the jerk out. His partners, though, scrambled from their seats and moved to protect the young punk's flank. Crap. They wanted to fight.

"Jeremy," Keith yelled. "Get Manny." No one would mess with Manny.

"Manny's off tonight." The bartender looked ready to duck away, then seemed to collect himself, stepped out from behind the bar. The middle cowboy was prepared, put a fist into his stomach. Andrea screamed.

The blonde punk regained his balance and rushed. A fist. Keith saw stars, unsure whether he was hit once or twice. Why didn't it hurt? Hands on his chest. He resisted, but fell back against the bricks, bracing, but he heard a loud pop, anyway – his head on brick. The room swam. He watched his own left fist fly out, land a glancing blow on the cowboy's jaw, but it had no juice. The young man shook it off, sneering.

"I told you the kissin' booth was still open," he hissed. Another fist plowed into Keith's middle. No breath.

"Leave her alone." But it was only a pitiful wheeze.

Emily emerged from the doorway, and the young cowboy moved toward her. Keith struggled to his feet, intending to intercept him, but the entire lounge swam before his eyes. The lights went out.

CHAPTER 19
TUXEDO MAN

In the shimmering splotches that reflected lights from the park across the river, Lionel could see pock-marks--light rain impacting the water's smooth ripples. The moon's face vacillated in the wavelets, then disappeared behind dark clouds. A bad omen.

In the harsh streetlights, Lionel scanned the license plates in the lot – no government cars. Tense, he climbed the steps and opened the door. Against the far wall, the manager, himself, was spraying dishes, getting more water on himself that on the plates. Bodies rushed in every direction, but Lionel felt the Grandfathers watching out for him, because all eyes were strangely averted while he hustled across the floor and up the stairs.

The climb took forever, but finally he collapsed on the upper landing, swallowing gulps of air that made his whole body shudder as he crawled on all fours toward the marionettes.

The glow from the light bulb hit them strangely, then he realized: where was Carlotta? He had not moved her. The elf, too, was absent. *Dios mio.* Had the Children done this? Had they already come and gone?

He glanced through the storage room, laying out a strategy. They could not hide the puppets forever. Even magicians and dead souls left tracks of some kind.

He needed a moment. One more moment to rest, to analyze, but tears began on their own, streaming down his cheeks. A terrible pressure gripped his stomach — Carlotta could be gone forever. Of course. Her master was jealous and sent these Children to take her back — to wherever he existed.

A sob. For the first time since he found her, he felt truly alone. Fool. He had always been alone, and thought himself suddenly rich, destined never feel that again. Fool, Uncle would say.

Time sifted by, and with it, he felt his chances being pulled farther and farther away. How could he track down entities when he had no idea what they were? He lay motionless, sprawled out on the cold boards, weeping for long minutes, looking this way and that through blurry eyes, as if that would bring Uncle from the dark rafters with the answer. Thomas's office windows were also dark, but Lionel no longer cared if he were discovered here.

Spontaneously, he began to quietly sing a lullaby from childhood. That turned into a prayer, and then he found himself speaking aloud, begging shamelessly to the silent tuxedo man and the dragon.

"*Por favor, amigos.* Tell me where they took her. I will return her and polish all of you twice a day. Please, help me rescue her from the Children."

He drew closer, pleading. The round dots on the tuxedo puppet's cheeks glistened. The dragon eyes stared cockily, as if skeptical of anything a mortal might promise. Lionel's muttering prayer devolved into one of Uncle's incantations, though he did not remember its purpose.

At last he gave up and lay again on the cool floor. Where in the Universe could he go to find her? His heart slowed. Sleep. Please, God, grant a moment to rest. Perhaps in his dreams, he would be shown the next step.

A noise jolted him upright. The little tuxedo man's face had turned—yes, there was no mistake—it stared straight ahead. How?

"Who's there? *Patron?* I can't see you."

Eerily, the tuxedo man began to swing. Softly at first, then his arc increased in amplitude. Lionel shivered, squinting in vain to see who was touching the strings.

"Am I dreaming?"

Sickeningly, the little man's head swiveled again, until he looked straight at Lionel. The large wooden eyes blinked.

Lionel felt his heart stop. *"El Diablo."* His arms flew up, as if they could block anything such a monster could do.

The puppet began to move — an arm. A leg. Stretching, like a human child just waking up, perhaps.

"No."

But his cries could not stop the demon. The wooden feet reached out, scraped the floor, stopped the little man's swaying. Then the monster flipped forward, until it stood upright. It shook its body, causing its strings to fall away like water off of a dog.

"No. What do you want?" Lionel choked, backing up slowly, until he bumped against a wooden Indian. The puppet cocked its head and stepped high, marching smartly in place. Yet, the demon did not advance on Lionel, but swung its cane and pranced across the landing, swaggering like a rich man in Guadalajara.

Lionel pushed back harder against the wooden statue. Uncle never told him something like this could happen. It had to be the devil. *"Señor,"* he said, teeth chattering, "are you going to find Carlotta?" He hid behind his fingers as the little man started to turn. The evil eye!

But the wooden eyelids only blinked, as if the *Diablo* could be a thoughtful man, calculating, almost seductive. But now it stopped, standing very still, moving only its arm, raising its small black cane into the air. Suddenly, the walking stick came down with a resounding *crack* against the floorboards.

Caca. A magic wand. Lionel jumped up into a squatting position. He could not remember Uncle's chants of defense! Instead of attacking, though, the *Diablo* turned and disappeared down the stairs, so rapidly that it kicked up a cloud of unswept dust.

Lionel collapsed, drenched in sweat, gasping and pushing down, trying to quell his convulsing stomach. *Dios mio.* He cursed himself for a novice. All this time, he had ignored the obvious fact: the other marionettes were possessed by lost souls, too.

The hairs rose on his neck. He stared at the dragon and backed away, scraping across the landing on his butt.

CHAPTER 20
COME HITHER

Light pierced Keith's eyes, colored smudges that coalesced into the young predator grabbing Emily by the shoulders, ready to try another kiss. From somewhere, a second wind burst inside Keith. He leaped to his feet in one smooth motion, grabbed the punk's arm, and twisted him around with scant effort. The boy's hat flew as he stumbled toward the middle of the room. At that instant, though a loud bang echoed off the walls.

My God. Keith froze. They've got a gun. But the young one's hands were empty, and he came again. Keith blocked the kick of a boot with his shoulder, just managing to stay in front of Emily.

The world had shifted to slow motion, and in Keith's peripheral vision, he saw the swinging doors to the hall blow outward, releasing a short, darkly clad figure into the room. The young cowboy regained his balance yet again, but Keith could not take his focus off of this intense, swiftly moving newcomer.

"Enough," the short man yelled, in a voice larger than his lungs should have been capable of. All three tough guys turned at the noise. Keith blinked. The man was dressed in a tuxedo.

The tuxedo man kept moving, raised a black cane in the air, brought it down swiftly, smashing the oldest cowboy on the side of the head, sending him flat out on the carpet.

The young one flinched. Keith groped for Emily's arm, pushing her back toward the cubicle. The tuxedo man came, the cane *whooshed* again, and the young cowboy punk yelped and collapsed, writhing, onto the floor.

"Shit," Keith yelled.

The kid was sobbing.

"OK, OK, King's-X," the oldest called, rising to all fours. Bystanders surged from around the bar. Even Anna and Katy budged through the swinging doors, followed by Ben, then Thomas.

Jeremy was helped to a chair, but Keith's gaze remained on the tuxedo man, who everyone else seemed to have forgotten. The man paused to brush off his own elegant lapels, then sauntered toward the side entrance. He gripped the doorknob, as if he had no care of the fire alarms he might set off. He turned for an instant to stare at Keith with deep black eyes. Keith gasped, unable to catch anyone's attention.

The stranger slipped out the door.No alarms sounded.

"What's going on here, Cliff?" Thomas stood resolute over the cowboys' ringleader.

"Chet—name's Chet." He stood with a groan and brushed off his pants legs, perhaps mentally in some old-west saloon instead of a carpeted restaurant. "Shit, I'm sorry, Thomas." The scoundrel made an attempt at sounding sincere. "I guess the boys are a little high-strung tonight."

"You all right, Keith?" The head chef's look was stern.

Emily supported Keith, her hands holding him from behind. "You OK?" Her voice—so soft.

"I think so."

A pause. "Well, I won't call the police this time." Thomas folded his arms. "But you're banned. All of you."

"C'mon, boys." Chet's temple bore a purple welt. They shuffled toward the side door. The young one—still sucking injured fingers—picked up his hat with his good hand and pointed it at Keith in a silent threat.

Play-by-plays erupted from the witnesses.

"Did you see that little guy?" Keith asked Emily breathlessly. "Who was he? Have you seen him before?"

She shook her head, and helped him walk to the kitchen.

A meeting convened in Ben's office. A doctor friend of the chef had been dining downstairs, and studied Keith's eyes. "No concussion as far as I can see."

Later, they all crowded around the back door.

"The gallant knight, driving home his damsel in distress," John held the door and gave a mock bow.

"Asshole," Keith replied. "Wish you had been there, John."

The Wop gulped the last bit of a glass of beer. "Damn me. I was upstairs counting the cash. We would have taken them in a fair fight."

Katy gave Keith a hug and pointed to his swollen eye. "Put some ice on that, Darlin.'"

"It was a crazy night, Katy."

"Yours was crazier than mine." She winked at Emily.

Several members of the staff tarried in the parking lot, rehashing the drama. No one else, it seemed, had paid attention to where the tuxedo man went. No one knew him. A socialite, probably. Or government muckity-muck, too drunk to stick around.

Keith's stomach roiled. This was no dream, for everyone's accounts matched his own memory. Two certainties could not be reconciled, but he did not dare propose them to anyone else. The fight-stopper was a dead ringer for Poindexter, the marionette. Worse. His face was also that of the man in his dreams, the one who walked behind Carlotta's wagon.

He intertwined his fingers with Emily's. Her hand was so warm. What the hell was happening?

Ben's pickup ground to a halt behind them. "Hey, Champ."

Keith noted the ring of keys twirling on the manager's fingers. "Sorry, Ben. I won't go check your alarm this time."

"Don't worry. Already done. Take Emily home. She's had a rough night, too."

"Yes, she has." Keith hugged her.

"Please," Ben's face became serious, but he started to chuckle in spite of himself, "don't sue the restaurant."

Emily laughed. "That depends on whether I get a raise at my annual review," she said.

Keith kicked the front tire. "We're meeting our lawyer tomorrow —" But Emily's fingers were digging into his arm. "What?"

She pointed. "My God. Are those cowboys coming back?"

Across the parking lot, behind the dark corner of the building, a flashlight beam flitted back and forth. Thick ivy covering the fence on the property line was illuminated, then fell dark. Now a couple of discarded tires, and a rusted-out wheelbarrow lit up, then returned to shadow.

Ben craned his neck, leaning out of his window.

"Please tell me it's the night watchman," Keith said. "Those bastards wouldn't dare cause more trouble, would they?"

A shake of the head. "It's too early for Larcinter. I think. Come on, get everyone in their cars, just in case." Ben waved at the others. "Hey."

"Larcinter? Weird name. Stay here a minute." Keith planted Emily next to the truck and set off in long strides. "Ben, I want you to come running, if I yell."

"Keith —"

He felt the faces of the others turn to watch, and for some reason, he knew the light would retreat as he approached. It did, but when he rounded building's back corner, placing his feet carefully through the unkempt area's thick grass, he almost jumped out of his skin. There, just ahead, a stocky shadow stood, and the flashlight beam turned to blast Keith in the eye.

"Who are you?" Keith demanded, shielding with his arm. "Mr. Larcinter? You're early."

For a moment, the form was silent, rock-still behind the blinding beam. Then it spoke — a man's voice. Deep and grating. A superior air, as if Keith had no business asking questions.

"Are you lonely?" he said.

"What?"

"Come with me." It was a suggestion, but also a command. The man turned and stalked along the side of the building, using the light's beam to point the way, but keeping his face in darkness. Only a glimpse. White-gray hair. Stooped stature. Slight limp.

Keith followed, stepping carefully around the scattered rusty cans and sticks the flashlight hit.

"Why? Did Thomas send you? You're the night watchman, right? Where the hell are we going?"

"Look up here."

When they neared the old mausoleum's front corner, Keith's body registered another shock. Ahead, against the fence, the old wagon was indeed there. On the right, a wash of reddish light poured from the wide-open side entry to the lounge.

"Oh, shit. Did you open the door?" He looked in. Tables and chairs stood in their places, eerie and quiet. Keith's heart was pounding. Were the cowboys in there? "You didn't answer. Who opened the door? I saw Ben lock it."

"Keep walking."

The watchman waved his light along the concrete walk that led to the top of the side stairs, then down to the parking lot. River Drive lay quiet, lit faintly by the parking lot lamps. Across the water, in wooded River Park, a pair of street lights burned steadily, but the whitish cast to the river's surface was from the full moon.

A delicate scene, almost, except for a black mass attached to the near bank, just beyond the street. Keith blinked. It was the unmistakable shadowy form of the boat Carlotta had shown him.

The flashlight blinded him again, and the same gravel-filled voice.

"Are you lonely?"

"What kind of question — is that your boat?" Keith's chest heaved. Did Ben follow him? But he could not turn to look, for the light was drawing closer.

"What have you done with your life?"

"Nothing. Nothing special…" The answer came as easily as the sweat on his temples.

"They don't love you. You know that, don't you?"

Keith answered between chattering teeth. Why was he even responding to this stranger? But the words came out on their own. "Someone probably loves—"

"No, they don't. You know this. Have told yourself so, many times. Be honest."

He thought of Emily.

"That will fail, too," the voice behind the light said, as if the watchman knew his every thought. "In time, her feelings will be nothing. It is time for you to come home."

"Home?"

The light flexed, down to the ground, to the stairs, drawing a straight line—too straight—across the front lot, the road, all the way to the boat.

As he watched, the voice droned, a soft whisper barely above the level of the crickets. "You have no one, just your secret thoughts…" The light flashed on the sleek wooden side of the craft. "—your sorrow, the pain of your failure—life is not what you thought it would be--"

The boat was old, but smooth, worn, like an old ship. Keith's body shook in heavy, grounded shivers. The light paused at a long oar that extended from the rear. "—your pain, your empty nights waiting – are over—"

The light stopped. Sticking up from the bow was a carved figure, like in pictures of Viking boats. Keith shook his head to focus. It was an animal—a dragon. No, the scrapes and marks were the same—the bow of this boat was identical to the dragon marionette upstairs.

"Come home. Now."

"No." Only a whisper. For an instant, it seemed that Keith was choking for air – then, in a sudden rush, he found enough air to scream: "Who are you?"

The light flicked off, the stocky shadow turned to face him. Keith backed up, hit the balustrade that bordered one side of the walk.

"Come home."

Keith groped, feet sluggish, turned, frantic to reach the reddish doorway. Fuck. Was this what Larry meant by a boundary? He stopped, unable to draw a full breath. Carlotta stood there, only inches away, blocking the doorway. Face in shadow, but it was her, staring at him with eyes that glowed red – mirrors of the glow of the exit lights.

She gestured toward the bar behind her. "He wants me to take you to the wagon. So your body may be finished." A hand came up. Long fingers spread. "I refused. Leave this place. Hurry. I may not be able to resist you very long."

Over his shoulder, Keith heard a sound. Larcinter was coming up behind. Keith twirled, fists out, as if that would stop a demon.

"No. Turn it on," he cried. "Turn the light back on."

In a blinding flash, the sky lit up. Not sky, but the lights that ran along the kitchen ceiling. He was sprawled out on the cold bricks.

"Are you all right?" Emily's voice — soft, but it made him jump, all the same. She looked down, cradled his head in her lap, her eyes searching his. "The side door was open. We found you in here. You must have slipped on the bricks. Did you hit your head?"

Waiters, bus people crowded the back doorway. Ben next to the icemakers, twisting closed a plastic bag. Keith knew it was for him. Emily rubbed Keith's temples lightly.

"Can you hear me? Are you OK, Keith?"

He grabbed warm fingers.

"I am now."

CHAPTER 21
PHANTOM FOOLS OF FORTUNE

A peal of thunder jarred Keith's eyes open, and rattled the windows.

"Damn. That was close." Larry's voice, though it didn't seem connected to the silhouette standing against the gray-lit window that was speckled with rain drops. "So, you decided to join the living after all."

"What the hell ar you doing here?" Keith rubbed his eyes. "Ouch." One was swollen, almost shut.

"Visiting. That's what brothers do when a psycho winds up in the hospital.

With a grunt, Keith made it to one elbow. "Hospital? What happened? I'm not dead?"

"No such luck." Larry pulled the room's only chair closer to the bed. "They gave you a sedative hours ago. You don't remember?" Another peal of thunder.

"Good God, what a nightmare."

"Barroom brawls will do that to you." Larry wagged his finger. "I'll have to teach you my method of ducking out the back door."

"Emily — where is she? Is she OK?"

"You just missed your lady fair. She was here all night, watching over her hero. You've been holding out on me. I thought you were hot for some gypsy broad."

Keith glanced around the room.

"Ass. Ben took her home."

"What time is it?"

"Dawn."

"Ben was here, too?"

"He's a wimp," Larry answered. "He apologized to mom and dad for the last two hours about how this was all his fault for giving you the job, blah, blah, blah--"

"Mom and Dad?"

"Yep. So that girl has already met your parents. This could get serious before you know it." Larry laughed.

"Will you shut up? I've just come through hell. I think."

"OK, so what? Like I've never been in a fight? Nobody gave a shit when I had a concussion." A smile. "Forget it. The doctor said you need to rest today." He stood, a silhouette again. Stretched. "They'll probably let you go in a few hours. Man, were you out of it. Talking in your sleep like a drunk."

Sinking back into the pillow, Keith closed his good eye and heard himself start talking, even though it was against his better judgment. Everything came out—Carlotta, her elusiveness, her wooden legs, even the final straw—the night watchman and his bizarre boat.

Larry listened silently in the dim, mediciny air. Didn't argue or smart off. In fact, Keith thought he detected his brother's mouth opening wider and wider. When the tale was finished, a long pause ensued.

"Well?" Keith prompted. "Embarrassed that your big brother's finally gone loony?"

"Who's the guy in the boat?"

"What?" Larry never failed to pick the detail that was most inane. "A relic of a tortured mind, I guess. I shouldn't have told you. It might all go away soon."

"But you never saw his face?"

"No. These are hallucinations, Larry. Waking dreams. How else can I explain them and stay sane? Thanks a lot for telling me to get a job there."

"Keith—"

"Sorry. I can't blame you. Been reading your psychic books, your ghost books for ten years. Well, my subconscious finally constructed a fantasy from all that shit..." His voice ran out of steam.

"They were your books, Dummy. Remember? And it ain't a fantasy. That place must really be haunted. I can't believe it. It's – I goddam can't believe it--"

He trailed off, too, and Keith's headache took the silence as a chance to roar back to life.

"Just shut up, OK?"

"Bullshit." The shadow shook a finger. "Concentrate on the man in the boat. He's the one." The shadow rose from the chair, became Larry in the tiny light over the room's sink, then started pacing. "It's amazing. I thought all the ghost stories came from New York, Virginia, you know, places old enough to have some history. Now we've got some raging spook in an old building on the Brazos River?"

"Oh, my God, Larry. This isn't about you. Shut up, so I can get well. Then you can go do your paranormal investigations 'til you're blue in the face."

"Damn right I will. Hell, you're in this, too. For some reason, they've picked my big brother to be a player – what's it called? Help me--"

"No, you help me by getting the nurse and get the hell out."

"A focus – that's it. They usually pick one person's energy to focus on. You know, they're drawn to super good energy – or bad – which one are you?"

Enough. Keith pulled the pillow over his eyes. The growing light outside was playing havoc with his headache.

"That stupid Ben. I'm going to kill him for not telling me the restaurant was haunted."

"He did tell you. Are you crazy? You're the one that told me. That's what I'm talking about. Everybody planted the seeds of it, so my subconscious dremed up a stupid psychotic episode."

Larry leaned against the wall, parted the sheer curtains, peered out. "Don't start with that Freudian stuff. Oh, sure, everyone talks about it being haunted, just like the Cox mansion, or the Terrace. But that's normal old wives tale horseshit. But this – this joint is really *haunted*. Oh, crap!"

"Please go away."

"Did you hear what I just said? The Terrace – it's right across the street--"

Keith fingered the crusted skin above his eye. "Come on, Larry. We're too old to believe in fairy tales. Hell, it's not Ben's fault. He's never even seen Carlotta. No one has."

"Exactly." Larry pounded on the bed. "You see a woman, recurring times, no one else does. You're a focus – no, a receiver. That's what they call it. On our sleepovers, you were the one who saw the white blobs first. Whenever we did the ouija board, it was you the channeling came through."

"We were kids, for god's sake." Keith brought the pillow up again.

"Keith, remember the hauntings we used to read about? That theater in upstate New York. The toy store in San Francisco. The ghosts appeared only to one or two receivers. The rest of the people just witnessed their effects. Put two and two together, for chrissakes."

"I'd rather look for a psychological explanation. Even if it mean's I"ve gone crazy." Wait – Emily was studying psychology. Somehow, that thought made him warm.

"To hell with that. Psychologist can't explain ghosts or UFOs. And they'll go broke if they admit there's something they can't explain. You're the one that explained it all to me.

"So, hush – that dame you keep seeing? How do you know her name? Carlotta. Did she tell you?"

"No. Those two asshole waiters in the Laundromat."

"Great. Just ask them about her. Have you seen those bozos on one of your shifts? They're waiters, or what?"

Something shook. He'd looked around several times, but had never seen either of them in the restaurant. He didn't even describe them to Ben. "Damn. I never even looked for them – well, maybe once that first day. Crap, what the hell's going on, Larry?"

"Wow. They must be ghosts, too."

"Oh, come on. Now you're going overboard."

"Am not. Quit playing dumb." Larry leaned forward, his eyes almost dancing with excitement. "Remember that book by Heider. Hell, you used to quote it to me. I remember the passage: *Visitations or apparitions are often heralded by nondescript third parties – possibly apparitions themselves – who introduce the entity –*' or something like that. Then poof, those heralds are gone. He called them 'phantom fools of fortune.' Wake up and smell the coffee, you bum. That old joint is a ghost-hunter's goldmine."

Keith groaned. "OK – so what? Let's talk about it later for God's sake. Where's the button I push for the nurse?"

"OK. I'm going – they're letting you out this afternoon. I'll pick you up. Damn, your car is still at the restaurant. I'll call Ben –"

"Fine."

"But when you're out, we'll look for a conventional explanation first. That's the responsible first step. Gotta be scientific about this."

He stopped at the door. "Wait. Nobody has it in for you at the restaurant, do they? Could anyone be pulling practical jokes on you?"

"John thinks it's a prankster. The Mexicans think it's a hobgoblin."

"A clue. What is this Carlotta like? Is she cool? Or dysfunctional?"

"She talks like a space cadet. Get the hell out and let me sleep."

Larry shook his head, oblivious. Off on one of his tangents, big time. "Doesn't jibe. Ghosts aren't hippies."

Against his will, Keith felt tears welling. He couldn't look pitiful in front of his baby brother. "Things have been fucked up ever since Elmer fired me."

Silence.

"OK, OK. You're tired." Edging out the door. Stuck his head back in. "Just promise me we can check that place out. Ben will cooperate. I'll make him, by God."

Gone again, but damn if he didn't push the door open again.

"Hey. I'm sorry. Got carried away. It's just so exciting." Larry took a deep breath. "Guess I'm being selfish. I forgot – maybe you're not going back to work there anyway?"

"Hadn't thought about it. Can't think of anything, you're jabbering so much."

He was clear now, the light in the room enough to see everything. The poor punk looked like a little boy whose toys had been taken away.

"Guess I have to stay there, until I find another job. Dad's not paying my rent anymore."

A pause. "Bullshit. IF you stay, it's not because of my investigation. It's because of that Emily girl. Am I right?"

"We haven't even gone out. Yet."

Larry leaned forward, and counted intensely on his fingers as he spoke. "Just remember. There are only two dangers an apparition can pose. I know you recall those. One, heart attack from fright. Two, an apparition can lure the victim across a boundary. You know, a line you cross to get into the other world. That's what you have to watch out for. You'd better quit while you're behind, goddamit."

"I'll remember that. Can I sleep now?"

Larry looked at his watch and stood. A hand rose thoughtfully to his chin. "That might be a bad idea. I mean, with a concussion and all -- What if you have another one of those dreams? Christ, you're the one who taught me this stuff. They can lure you across a boundary in a dream, Keith. That's obviously what they're trying to do. That guy in the boat – Maybe I'd better ask the nurse."

"They wouldn't have given me a sedative if it weren't safe. But I need a stronger one if you're here."

His brother smirked. Waved a hand. Door open again, swinging back and forth. "Did Ben ever say why they have puppets in a restaurant?"

"They're just there."

"He never told me. I'll kill him."

"Go."

"This time the ghosts have an address, Keith."

"Goddam it."

"OK. Don't cross any boundaries." Finally, the door shut behind him, and didn't re-open.

Keith lay, listening to the sounds of the hospital coming awake, kicking himself for not prodding Larry about the most important thing:

What, if anything, did Emily say about him? Did she even care?

CHAPTER 22
SHE WOULD MAKE A FINE NEW HOME

Lionel sorted the dust into small lines with the broomhead, lines he would collect in their proper order. Perhaps shifting dirt was his true calling. It certainly wasn't sorcery.

What in the name of the Virgin had happened? While he shivered like a scared girl in the attic, the Children had come. Anna said that several people were knocked out. The tall gringo was taken to the hospital. Perhaps he was dead, by now. Had the Children settled for him when they could not find Lionel? Who was their real target? Somehow, he had never really thought rich *norte americanos* would have to fear such things.

Now the poor fools around the restaurant were talking about the mysterious man who broke up the fight. Only Lionel knew the rescuer's real identity. And his countrymen – only sullen glances, when they deigned to look at him at all. He remembered those few precious moments in the car, when he felt like one of them. Would he really have been foolish enough to get drunk with them?

Dismiss such thoughts, Uncle would say, were he here now. *To envy the sinners is to invite the Devil to your own funeral.*

The broom lagged under the puppets. They were all back, too, safe in their places. Even his beloved. He doubted that Ben had brought them. Maybe Thomas, for there were things that man knew that no one else did – but, no. These creatures moved on their own, propelled by the spirit.

He reached out to caress Carlotta's frozen face, but his hand paused in mid-air. Her eyes were closed, like an embarrassed lover pretending to sleep. Was she unwilling to

discuss her infidelities? Why did she send him away? Surely
he might have helped, but she still doubted his power.

And helped whom? The gringo? The Children came for
someone The stupid white cook was nice enough, but strange.
He just got in the way. Was that it? In his head, Lionel put the
reasons together every which way, like a puzzle whose pieces
changed shape each time you touched them. No configuration
that made sense.

He turned his gaze to the leprechaun. *Dios mio*, the
thing fairly oozed evil. Why had he never detected it before?

His hand stopped short of Carlotta's smooth cheeks,
and he used it, instead, to wipe sweat from his chin. Hot
tonight. Three puppets, besides his lover. In which one did the
monster reside?

Not the little man with the cane – the memory of him
walking on his own, racing down the stairs – it was a vision
that would haunt him forever – but he couldn't be the evil one.
Wasn't he the one who stopped the Children? The kitchen was
buzzing with talk about the man in the tuxedo —

That left the infernal dwarf or the angry dragon. What
if he grabbed both of them and threw them into the ovens
downstairs?

Now his hand was shaking, but he put it out again,
until he caressed Carlotta's wooden forehead. "I forgive you,
mi amor," he said. Why be afraid? After all, things had not
really changed. He would stick to his plan, find her a body.
Uncle would call it bad medicine to destroy the others. Yes, it
would seal their fate, but also his own – true demons could
reach out from the beyond and do god-knows-what.
Nevertheless – he set his jaw – if any of them got in his way —

Plodding downstairs, back into the hustle and bustle,
he spotted the bus girl. The pretty one he often caught looking
his way. An enchanting creature!

Now it was time to bag up the dirty linens, because the
truck might be here any minute. An apron hit him, dropped to
the floor. From behind the Line, Chavo was sneering.

But the disdain from the others wasn't what ate at him – it was -- it was -

Of course! He looked over in time to see the bus girl taking a tray, heading out the door to the main dining room.

She was the one. What a fine new home for Carlotta *she* would make. But a girl like her, one that beautiful, vibrant would never agree to such a thing. What *yanqui* girl could ever agree to give up her rich life?

The whole plan, so sudden in its glory, came crashing down just as quickly.

But wait. He closed his eyes, peered intently at the air she had just passed through.

Maybe – Yes, this one seemed different. Lonely. Or lost. Like a baby chick born before it was time. Either way, seeing her at that instant, at one of those exact moments when he could feel fortune's wheel turning, was a good omen.

Perhaps.

He tightened the bag, started to hoist it over his shoulder, and she appeared again! Back through the same door – hauling her bin of dishes toward the washing cubicle.

But she passed him.

And when she did, she smiled.

The second omen. Unmistakable.

Lionel wished the spell had already been cast. Could he hope for a miracle? He would never know until he worked up the courage to talk to her. Ask her about her life. Jesus, if such a beautiful being were to agree to leave her physical home, bequeath it to Carlotta, he would never let her pass him again withough taking her arm, kissing her, proclaiming to the others that she was his!

If Carlotta only knew the reach of his designs – he, Lionel, would be the master of his beloved's destiny. Not the wooden dwarf. Nor even the dragon.

And to hell with everyone else.

CHAPTER 23
WARM FLESH, COLD FIRE

"How about a movie Friday?" The question came easy. Keith leaned against a post in the entryway, slightly dizzy from his first foray back out into daylight after two days of resting on his couch, eating mom's ketchup-y meatloaf, suffering Larry's unending speculations about what they would find when at last Ben permitted an "exorcism" in the restaurant, after work some night. Thank God, Keith assumed, the manager would never put up with that.

Emily's face was a welcome sight, and, miraculously, he was not the slightest bit nervous. As if surviving a single fistfight made him tough. Even if he was the loser.

"What are you doing here?" He waved his paycheck. "Oh," she said, and slipped her arm around his and walked him to the front door. A laugh. "Do heroes not have to come through the back door anymore?"

"Are you kidding?" The afternoon lull was half over. A light drizzle fell on the few vehicles in the paved front lot. "Have you seen the mudholes out back? I was afraid my car would sink. No big loss, of course."

"A movie, huh?" Her smile was sly, but her bright eyes made him think he was home free. "Don't know when I'm off next."

"I already checked the schedule. You have Friday evening open. So do I."

"Yeah? Who's working the bar kitchen?"

"John. Ben's working me back into the schedule slow. John thinks I'm a baby for putting up with it, but that's what the doctor advised."

With an abandon he had always lacked with Linda, he hugged her arm to his side. There was still the issue of Paul, but he did not care.

"You seem pretty sure of yourself." She did not resist the hug. "Are you sure you don't still have a concussion?" They laughed.

"No, I'm not sure. Ever since I got clobbered the other night, things seem more — well, hopeful." He kept his gaze locked with hers.

"I guess I would be pretty rude not to accept an invitation from my rescuer. A movie sounds good."

The next night, he reported for work. Back on his stool, shaky, he prayed for a quiet night. Just prepping had almost worn him out, but there were tiny flashes of feeling – good.

"You OK?" Ben asked through the order window."

"I could use a nap."

Emily entered the little kitchen's back door several times. Usually to park dishes for the bussers, but her smile seemed wider each time. She didn't speak of Paul and he didn't ask. When traffic finally dwindled, he started packing up to move to the back. She leaned through the empty order window.

"Uh, about Friday?"

Keith's stomach fell away. "Oh-oh. Change your mind?"

She blushed. "Not that. I was just thinking that Friday is a long time from now."

If his head weren't still full of cotton, he might have whooped for joy. Heart pounding, he could clearly feel blood rushing into capillaries that must have shut down since the fight. How asinine he would look if he fainted right here. Gripping the counter for support, he took a deep, deep breath. "How about my apartment before work tomorrow?" he heard himself say.

"No. Since I moved back here to go to school, my mother has been tracking me down like a hawk. I'll get the third degree if she can't get me by phone. I spend a lot of time at Mary's. I could get her to take my shift tomorrow afternoon. You're off, right?"

Bar music played. The room threatened to start spinning. "Yeah. Every other night. Full time next week."

"Then we could meet at Mary's?"

He nodded. "Afternoon. *Early* afternoon."

A maddening smile. "Slow down, there, sailor."

He lifted the bus bin of utensils. "Gotta go slow. Doctor's orders."

Driving over, Keith did not know what to hope for. Rain again, and huge lakes of it slowed traffic at every intersection. By the time she met him at the front door, he was breathless. They had never really been alone before.

She took him on a brief tour. Mary's bedroom was a disaster, like Keith's. The small living room contained a portable TV and a stereo system. Large pillows and beanbag chairs were strewn about. He paged through her CD collection. Vinyl, too. And a turntable.

"Looks like she's into the seventies," he said. "Or is this eighties?" A window unit hummed, taking the edge off of the steamy air.

"Let's see what she left us." Emily inspected the fridge. "There's some wine."

"Being with you is intoxicating enough." *Oh, God, how lame.* He descended to a large striped pillow against the wall.

She entered with the bottle and glasses. "You really know what to say, don't you?"

"Actually, I never do." In spite of himself, Carlotta's admonition echoed in his head: *Tell her how you feel.*

How *did* he feel? Life was out of control and he wanted to grab onto something, but what was this with Emily? Infatuation? Or just desperation, giben that Carlotta was – well, whatever she was?

He watched while she poured the wine, slipped off her tennis shoes, and stretched her legs. Her faded jeans and plaid shirt fit perfectly in the out-of-date decor.

She said something about predictions that the river would crest above flood stage. He heard only his own breathing. The afternoon light played in her hair. He moved forward and lifted the glass from her hand. She seemed surprised, but maybe not so much. He pulled her close and kissed her.

She responded. Within moments, they were gasping from exertion. He pushed her back into the beanbag chair, and his fingers found her buttons.

The plaid came off and soon she lay, vibrating as he moved his lips across her breasts. The hum of the window unit merged with the buzzing in Keith's ears. He pulled her jeans away, then his own. Slowly, they joined on the creaking wood floor, cushioned only by the vinyl beanbag chair. The cooler's thermostat clicked urgently. Locust songs segmented in her groans.

A breathless eternity later, the thermostat downshifted, idling the cooler. They lay in each other's arms. Her eyes were dreamy, half-open, and she wore a soft smile. Keith rolled off the bed, borrowed the bedspread from Mary's room and lay back down, covering Emily while he kissed her. She fell asleep first.

When Keith opened his eyes, he found himself in a strange city full of very short inhabitants, like elves or dwarves. They wore odd, antiquated costumes. *Medieval*, a quiet voice said. But it was impossible to just sit there and observe them, because some sort of crisis was going down. The little people ran around frantically, eyes wide with fear, like they were all looking for a place to hide.

Keith found himself scrambling with them, wondering if one of the small, stout thatched-roof houses could hold him. He towered over even the tallest of them, and, ridiculously, none of them seemed to have noticed him yet.

"There he is," a miniature voice cried. Too late – they noticed him now. A throng of the little abominations surged forward, surrounded him, and pushed him out ahead of the crowd. He looked down, and saw that a handful of the short males had been chosen as victims with him. But victims for what?

Keith's heart pounded. Tangible tension in the air — a pressure in his head that threatened to become unbearable. The instant he had that thought, the nervous little mob perked up in unison.

"The dragon's coming," one of the elves whispered, and winked.

They pushed Keith farther forward, out into a clearing near an intersection of two paths. The clump of little men came with him.

"A dragon?" he asked them, trying to follow their frantic gestures. Only tiny huts, and a larger barn, also roofed with straw, littered the landscape.

He grabbed the scrawny arms of the elf nearest him. "I'm a visitor here. You don't understand," he said.

The man looked at him blankly. Finally, a whimper came from his little throat and he pointed at the rising water that already covered Keith's ankles, almost up to the knees of his own brethren.

"It's flooding. I can't stop a flood, for God's sake," Keith told him, for it was obvious they thought he could save them, somehow. "Move to high ground," he cried out. "Are you all helpless?" He pushed, and the little man fell splashing down into the water, then scrambled, splashing away on all fours.

Keith turned in time to see a shadow fall across the waters ahead of them. He looked up. Finally, he felt the little peoples' raw panic.

A dark creature towered above the stunted trees and houses. Not a bigger person, or a giant – but some sort of beast, at least twenty feet tall, with red-glowing eyes and huge leathery wings that darkened the sky when it flapped them. The glare of those monstrous eyes bathed the crowd like lasers.

Keith turned to his "honor guard."

"Weapons. We need guns," he yelled. "Do you have guns? Spears, at least?" The tiny, dysfunctional bastards just stood there, quaking with fear.

An unearthly noise – a mixture of a moan, a growl, a pained breath – and the monster opened its gaping maw. Keith knew that in the next instant he would be roasted alive by the dragon's breath. Elfin cries for mercy filled the air.

The swaying head pitched forward and a massive wind--not fire, but an icy hurricane, washed over them. Keith could feel the waters beneath them solidifying, and still the frozen air poured out. In moments, they would all be lifeless popsicles.

He woke with a jerk, shivering from the chilly air belching out of the window unit above them. Emily stirred.

"Damned crazy dreams," he muttered.

"What?" she asked sleepily.

"Just a nightmare." He nestled closer, kissing her repeatedly, then pulled her up and led her into the bedroom.

They made love again, this time on Mary's bed, to the sound of more insistent thunder outside. The locusts went silent when the rain erupted, and they lay back, still joined. The heat from her skin made him shiver. If only he'd had that when he faced that dragon.

"I like this," she whispered with closed eyes.

They showered together and dressed. She poured more wine and they huddled on the covered balcony, watching huge drops shudder the large puddles in the parking lot.

"I think we should live here," he said. "This apartment. Decorated just like it is now. It will always be raining and we'll be hipsters, and only come out when we want to watch it. Inside, we'll do nothing but make love and drink wine."

"No food?" she said, laughing. "I thought you were a cook."

"Maybe. But mostly, it'll just be wine and love."

"Mmm. How about mostly love?" She gave his arms, which were draped around her, a squeeze.

"Even better."

The drops came harder, along with new rolls of thunder through the clouds.

"Wow. What was that?" Emily nuzzled closer.

"A dragon."

They listened while the "dragon" rumbled slowly away, invisible behind the gray thunderheads. A vibration started somewhere inside, a disturbing shiver that he braced against, intent that Emily would not feel him shaking. The dragon in the dream had a large gash — one that started above one green lip, and continued down to scar one or two of its massive teeth. Keith glimpsed the mark just before it belched out the icy wind. A scar identical to the one that marred the face of the dragon puppet up in the attic.

"They're not real," he said, and exhaled.

Emily snuggled against him. A single drop of rain hit his forehead. "Who?"

"The waitress. I was looking for this waitress at the restaurant. When I first got the job. Thought we might get something going. I just realized — she's not really a person."

"That's sweet of you to say." A giggle. "Guess I'd better confess, too. There is no Paul. I use that name when drunks try to paw me. Every cocktail waitress has a Paul. They're big and mean, if anyone asks." She stretched up and kissed his lips lightly. "So we're even."

"Yeah. I guess we are."

Find someone to love, Carlotta had said. An hallucination, giving him direction. Had his subconscious actually conjured a phantom to lead him — to a new job? To Emily? Did that mean he really was crazy? And if so, was it crazy bad?

"No," he said. "Crazy good."

Puzzled look. He brushed the hair from her face. "Never mind." He kissed her.

CHAPTER 24
BRANWYN

Branwyn! The name rolled off his tongue, dancing through his head until he released it in little snatches of singing to the broom's happy beat. A strange name. Not English, maybe. What did it mean in its own mysterious language? Cisco helped him say it at the back door.

"Bran-wyn."

He tried it.

"No. Do not roll the 'r.' You sound like a priest at mass." Cisco laughed and eyed him suspiciously. "Why do you ask, *amigo*?" He waved a finger. "You finally starting to notice the waitresses? Maybe you feel an itch? Do you watch her butt when she cleans the tables?"

Let Cisco think what he would, his heart was too light to protest. Even the haughty waiters laughed as he clowned past them with the broom.

Branwyn. She was the one. Perhaps he knew it that first time he laid eyes on her, as she stood forlornly by the upper salad bar. Today, at last, the spirit had moved him to speak to her.

He watched her get out of her mother's car. A ritual that could be seen every day. Sad, really, the way the girl's eyes turned earthward under the harpy's tongue.

"Now you make sure those drunks keep their hands off of you." Her mother's intense eyes flashed harshly.

"Yes, mother. Please, not so loud."

The lady — always dressed up, wearing gaudy necklaces and earrings — ignored Lionel's presence completely, as did most people. Branwyn, though, saw him standing on

the gravel. Her eyes told him she knew she should be
embarrassed, but really didn't care.

"And if you don't get a ride, you'd better call me by
nine." The voice grated more with each word.

"Yes, mother."

"If those older girls want to go out drinking, tell them
you have to go home." The speech was nearly identical every
day.

Head down, she walked to the steps. But perhaps she
heard his thoughts, for she obeyed his silent command and
turned to look into his eyes again. He had waited for this
chance.

"*Buenos tardes*. How are you?" he asked politely.

"Not so good." She shrugged in the direction of the
departing car.

"I am Lionel."

Not a grimace, but a smile. "I know. I'm Branwyn."
She must have read his face, for she pronounced it again.

"Your mother is a strong lady."

"Life sucks. She's the worst part."

"I am sorry." He did not know what else to say, but still
she stood, quietly, rather than hurry inside to the time clock.

"Can it really be so bad for a beautiful young lady like
you?" He did not believe such daring words could come out of
his mouth.

She smiled again, her cheeks growing red with blood.
"Oh, it's bad. And it doesn't end, you know? I'll never have a
normal life with her around, and I realized the other night —
she won't ever change." A look — was she asking for help?
Such lovely features. Freckles.

"What is a normal life?" he asked.

She ignored his question completely, and came up with
her own. "Do you believe in reincarnation?" He had no idea
what the term meant, and only shrugged.

"It's when you die and you are reborn into a new life, a
totally different one."

He could not believe what he was hearing.

"You live in a whole new world, you know? At least in a different time. New friends. New parents." The afternoon sun caught the gold in her hair. Again, her freckles caught his attention. Abundant and perfect, scattered below her eyes, across her cheeks in accordance with an undiscoverable formula. She sighed. "The next time around, that's the only way I'll ever get to really live. 'Cause this ain't living. Don't you agree? I mean, don't you want to do something besides push a broom?" She was rambling, shaking her head, still smiling. "I mean, young people like us deserve better, don't you think?"

Thank you, Grandfathers! He wanted to dance for joy. This was the finest omen he had ever seen. A powerful rush — uncontrollable, a feeling he had never really experienced before — coursed through his chest and down his arm, until his hand reached out and grasped one of hers. She looked up, startled.

"I am not sure what you mean with your words, but I can help you find what you are looking for." He coated his words with gentle syrup, the way Uncle spoke on tequila nights. Her gaze locked with his. She understood.

Yet he was too bold. She pulled her hand away and mounted the steps. "OK." Was she breathing hard? Worry on her face, but also another enchanting, perfect smile.

What happened next? Maybe he finished taking out the trash, maybe he slapped the broom against the concrete steps. The heavens were spinning and he felt he could fly.

"Branwyn!" A magical name. Almost as lyrical as the name Carlotta. His beloved would be pleased with the choice. No, not his choice, he would tell her, but a choice made by the Great Spirit itself.

"For a true magician," Uncle said, "things fall into place effortlessly." *Dios mio*, Lionel had never really believed that until now.

A little later, though, as he watched the mop's watery tracks under the prep table, the itch started in his belly. Grew, until it rose to his head, like a storm cloud – something wrong. But what was there to worry about?

Being a magician is – above all – a never-ending struggle, the old man often said. *When your path seems too easy, beware. The fearful beasts of the unknown can hit you without warning…*

"Shut up, old man," Lionel said aloud, to the ancient mnolded ceiling. He had struggled. Now victory was in sight. Carlotta would have a home in the world of the living. A beautiful home: Branwyn!

CHAPTER 25
A FLOOD

Emily's hand burned in his as they ambled down the steps. The rain had stopped, but the dark clouds seemed certain to burst at any moment. A car splashed through a gutter river and pulled into a parking space. Mary's face beamed from behind the steering wheel.

"Yikes. We almost got busted," Keith said.

"What are you doing off so early?" Emily yelled.

"Thomas closed up. The water's almost up to River Drive. The cops barricaded the bridges for the next twenty-four hours." She beckoned. "Come on, you've got to see something." They climbed into the back seat.

"It'll just take fifteen minutes." A glance in the rear-view mirror. "I had to go the long way around or I would have been home earlier." She looked over her shoulder, blushing. "Almost caught ya, huh?" A laugh. "Darn."

They crawled through a town transformed. Cars glided atop a sea of red-brown undulation. Streets and yards had become one, separated only by lines of autos along the submerged curbs. Kids splashed through knee-deep brine while old people stared from porches, women wringing their hands.

Keith kept his arm tightly around Emily. The looks on the faces, the motions of the scattered citizens seemed disturbingly like those of the elves in his dream. But he determined to ignore that. It was just a bizarre fairy-tale. They joked about the flood, until they came upon a stalled yellow taxi. Mary's bravado suddenly evaporated.

"Want to go back?"

"What the hell. This sort of flood is once-in-a-lifetime," Emily said. She squeezed Keith's knee and laughed.

Inside the grounds of River Park, the road slanted upward, out of the water and toward the cliffs. Mary found a spot between cars, and they climbed out.

A carnival atmosphere dominated the entrance to the bridge, complete with a hick-looking family perched on the back of their pickup truck, selling T-shirts that bore the logo, I Survived The Great Sironia Flood. A man in sun glasses hawked bags of popcorn from a card table, and Keith bought one for them to share. An old high school buddy whose name he did not remember hailed him, holding a beer aloft.

"Man, this is nuts." Keith waved back.

They worked their way through the throng for a turn at the bridge rail. Below, the river boomed past, angry and yellow-brown, a torrent four or five times its normal width. The force of the water made the bridge hum, more a vibration than a sound.

The churning water smashed against the walls of "Lover's Leap," the legendary cliff on the west side where two Indian lovers supposedly jumped to their deaths. Keith was in college before he learned that every other town in the West had a Lover's Leap. The bottoms of stately cottonwoods along the base of the cliff were swallowed up, and the road to River Park had disappeared.

"Look, Mom! A cow." A small boy pointed frantically. A red Angus carcass bobbed carelessly in the waves.

"Crazy," Emily said, "how people will make a sideshow out of awful things like floods and fires."

"It's sick," Mary agreed.

A pause.

"But it sure can be fun," Keith said quietly. They laughed.

"Well, well, who do we have here?" a voice came out of the crowd. A large black lady approached.

"Nosma," Mary exclaimed and gave her a hug.

"You know Nosma, don't you, Keith? She works the lunch shift." He remembered seeing her, but had not been introduced.

"I'm pro'ly gone before you come on," Nosma's deep voice boomed as she took his hand. "They don' catch me sittin' idle when my shift is over."

A retinue of children crowded behind her. If Katy was substantial, Nosma was exponential; taller, a giant girth and a smooth, pretty face dominated by steady eyes. She wore her hair in a bun. Keith explained he was scheduled for the lunch shift during part of the next week.

Her vise grip still held. "Well, if there's still a restaurant for us to cook in, we'll have a good time." Her smile melted into a scowl. "But ain't you the one who's always droppin' things on the floor?"

When their laughter subsided, she turned on the girls. "What you doing, hangin' 'round with kitchen help? You're supposed to be out findin' rich husbands."

"Not doing too well, are we?" Emily winked.

The youngsters remained anonymous, but Nosma leaned over to explain things to them every few minutes. Mary asked her how much damage she thought the water might do to the restaurant.

"No tellin'. This one looks bad. The Lord must have some purpose to it." Nosma sighed.

Oohs and *ahhs* came from the crowd as an old Plymouth emerged from under the bridge, bouncing through the water in leaps, like a rudderless boat.

"Hope nobody's still in there," someone said. Keith lifted Nosma's charges up one-at-a-time, high enough to see the old sedan as it tumbled through the white crests.

The throng shifted and Keith found himself pressed against the railing. Nosma's musical voice rose above the chattering, but his thoughts kept drifting back to the dream. There was nothing weird about a flood dream in these circumstances. And the dragon—it meant nothing. If he was going to dream about a dragon, of course it would look like the puppet. That made sense.

The sound of Emily's voice above the crowd's din, answered by Nosma's deeper tones, blended with the surreal river. Yes, the dream was powerless now. Not one of Larry's "boundaries." What counted was that this afternoon had found Emily.

He watched the angry clouds wheeling overhead and caught Emily's attention. "We'd better leave soon."

Holding the thick rail tightly, he leaned over for one last look. Silt, trees, fence posts, and trash of all sorts danced atop the waves at high speed.

Then he saw it--a hand!

"Hey, a little help here." Keith anchored himself and leaned farther.

"What is it?" a strapping high school kid next to him asked. From under the bridge, a hand flexed its fingers frantically, feeling for a place to grab.

"Here," Keith instructed the kid, "grab my belt with one hand, and get my leg with the other. I can almost reach him."

"Who?" The kid seemed ready to retreat, then followed directions.

"Someone's stuck down here." Keith leaned — farther, farther — and felt dizzy, hanging above the pitching current below.

"Watch out there, guy," the kid yelled.

"Shit. Hold on." Keith swung lower — the boy was losing his grip.

He stretched, almost touching the outstretched hand. "You. Under the bridge. Reach, for God's sake."

Yells, other voices crying, "Help him--"

But a faster motion took over; the river smashing angrily below, strange hands grappling his feet, the waving arm, extending from beneath the bridge's concrete understructure, a hand flexing its fingers lamely. At that same instant, a deafening peal of thunder sent a shockwave through everything. For a sick millisecond, he felt weightless, then realized it was true — the kid and the others had lost their hold.

Then he was falling, clawing upwards for the rail, the concrete ledge, then only air. The raging water rushed upwards, and he braced.

Something smashed him in the stomach. He grabbed leaves, a limb – but it broke with a sickening *crack* – tumbling, until he hit something hard. His shoulder – my God, was it dislocated? – black splotches swam before his eyes, then turned green. How could death be so green? He shook his head, and the cosmos righted itself –

His feet stuck out, making furrows in the brown-yellow river rushing beneath him. He was a-straddle a large branch – from a huge cottonwood tree. The damned thing had broken off the trunk -- no, it was still attached, but the base of the tree was underwater.

Holding onto wet bark, he forced his left arm to work in spite of its throbbing. Rain started again, and, too winded to yell out, he grappled downward on a slant toward the bank, he hoped. Slid down until his crotch came to rest painfully in the crook where the branch met the trunk.

"Emily--help--" Below, through the leaves, people moved at the top of the steep bank. Commotion.

There was commotion "Up here." He wheezed, and coughed until he thought he would vomit.

Finally, a deep breath. Then he remembered the hapless climber trapped under the bridge, and looked up at the structure's underside. Nothing but old dirt-dobber nests and hanging strings of moss. Where was the stranded guy?

The tree vibrated in a sickening rhythm, one that seemed to rise in pulses from the crashing water. He squinted – a shadow moved, behind the curtain of green.

"Who's there?" he called out. "Did you fall, too?"

"We are in hiding," a whining voice answered.

Just above, and to the side, branches rustled. A hand stuck through, and moved the dense leaves. At last, a face emerged, and Keith felt a jolt.

"You – Christ, you're the guy from the bar – you're – " He scrambled to retreat, but his shoes couldn't take hold.

Gulping air, he looked up again, barely able to voice the words. "You're Poindexter…"

The deep black eyes kept Keith from looking away. His face looked human enough, but moisture from the rain made the little man's cheeks shiny, like well-varnished wood. A buzzing in Keith's ears blocked out the roar of the river, the frantic voices above.

"Who the fuck are you? Who are you people?" He heard himself screaming, far away. "What are you doing? Am I insane now? What do you want?"

Yes, it was the man who had come to rescue him in the bar – maybe Keith knew it was Poindexter all along. But it couldn't be. Had to be – the man's eyes shifted right and left, like a puppet's. His mouth clacked open and shut. The words came, calmly, deliberately. "He is looking for you." Quietly, almost like a kid telling a big secret. "We disobeyed, so he will punish all of us." The plaintive eyes blink.

"Who are you?" Keith could not catch his breath. "You were in the bar. It was you. Is Carlotta—she keeps saying strange things. You—" Another gulp of air. "Is this all a trick, or am I too far gone already? My dreams…Are you ghosts? Who the fuck are you?"

Thunder rolled, and the eyes kept blinking slowly, as if Poindexter's thoughts came in their own time. As if anything Keith said did not really matter.

"You are still here. She speaks in her old language, so you did not understand. You must leave the river." He pointed down, at the raging water. "See? He made it angry because he can't find us." Now his hand swept back through the green leaves, upwards until it touched his chin, thoughtfully. "We will never escape. We can only hide for a while. He will hurt us, and everything will be as before. But you, with your energy—" More blinking. "I know she told you about your energy."

Below, two firemen emerged, carefully working down the slope of the riverbank, carrying a ladder between them. "Told me what? What am I supposed to escape from?"

Poindexter cocked his head. "When your new body is polished, not even you will be able to flee. But she thinks things can change. If you get away, if the spell is broken this time, then perhaps—" The big round eyes shifted again. "They are coming."

With no warning, his head pulled back, leaving only a dark shadow behind the blur of green leaves.

Was he afraid of the firemen? "Up here," Keith cried automatically. The ladder clanged against the tree trunk, propped from the hillside, but the men were not looking up. If he could keep Poindexter talking, would they see him?

"You still haven't told me what I'm escaping from."

"You're a fool." The voice was singsong, muffled by the foliage. "Listen." A new crash of thunder. "They are almost here."

"It's just firemen. They're here to help us out of the tree."

"Behold." A hand—now looking more wooden than human—emerged from the leaves, its pointing finger aimed at the high ground of the park. The land sloped up steeply, covered with scattered grass and bushes, until it reached the stone wall that ran along the lip of Lover's Leap. On the grass patches, gawkers stood, smoking and chatting.

Up higher, on the cliff side of the wall, cedar trees wavered like victims of an earthquake. The wind could not be blowing that hard, Keith thought. As he strained to see, an old man stepped out from behind a large bush. My God. Keith blinked. It was the old man from his dreams—the one who drove the wagon. That exact face, grizzled and ugly, missing only his regular sneer, for the man seemed desperate right now, glancing this way and that.

"Hide," Keith said automatically, though Poindexter was already more invisible than he. Keith ducked his own head behind a limb that was too thin to conceal anything. Large raindrops plopped from the leaves above, mixing with the sweat on his temples.

"Be very still, or he'll see your energy," the small voice whispered. "You must run away and break the spell. Rage is flying. When Larcinter and he get together, they are unbeatable." The slick hand retreated back into the leaves.

"Larcinter? Is he that same guy? What about you? I've go to know if all this shit is real."

A pause. He might have heard a sigh cross those little vocal chords.

"Who is Rage? Who are these people?" Keith tried to keep his voice to a whisper, but it came out as a scream. On top of the cliff, the old man now shaded his eyes with one hand, peering toward the crowd on the bridge. "Goddam it, tell me what's happening here." Then, to the firemen who kept slipping on the bottom step of the ladder, "Up here. Hurry, for God's sake."

Limbs thrashed, and Keith could see the shadow moving higher. "Leave the river," the small voice repeated. "I will make him look away."

"Where are you going? Come down here so they can rescue us, for God's sake." Keith shook with cold, and tears came. What was happening?

A *crash* – the shadow fell right through the leaves above, tangled with branches, broke through – it was Poindexter, dropping through the air, holding his coat above him like a parasail.

"No," Keith yelled. His own stomach fell away with the little man's plunge. The smallish form did a half-turn against the breeze, then knifed into the brown water and did not reappear.

On the high cliff, the old man waved a hand, like a sergeant directing invisible troops, and disappeared into the bushes.

"Hey, mister, slide down to the top of that ladder," a voice commanded. "We'll catch you."

Keith gestured toward Poindexter's point of impact. "Did you see that?"

"Come on," the fireman urged.

Emily broke from the crowd when he reached the top of the hill. Rain resumed in earnest.

"Keith, what happened? Are you crazy?" Her hair hung wet and stringy down both sides of her face. She threw her arms around his neck and kissed him.

"No. Just a moron. Thought I could save somebody," Keith began.

"Now I know why you're always droppin' things," Nosma said. She held a makeshift newspaper hat over her head, and laughed, laying her broad hand on his arm. Her grip tightened and those big brown eyes turned serious. "What'd you see under that bridge, hon?"

"A guy--" He pointed toward the river, but his voice faded. The moment was now. Either the little man was real, and had actually been in the tree with him, or else he had been caught for a moment in one of those—what did Larry's books used to call it, an *astral middleground*?—where there was no difference between reality and dreams. This was it. Either a flesh-and-blood person had plunged to his death or Keith was raving mad.

"I went over because I thought I saw someone fall into the river." Looks of concern covered the faces of the large-coated men, plus a policeman behind them. Emily gasped.

"But I can't be sure," he hastened to add. "I know I sound goofy, but I can't be sure if anything fell in or not." It was the truth, mostly.

One fireman scowled, then looked over his shoulder at the cop.

"Well, we can't do any looking here. If someone bit it, he'll show up downriver." A shrug.

"We've got a medic over here," the other one said. "Want to take a ride to the emergency room, just in case?"

"No thanks, sir," Keith said. "I just left there the other morning." Emily laughed, perhaps from nervousness. "Just some cuts and bruises." He displayed his scraped arms, and Emily hugged his waist.

Nosma frowned and poked Emily with a finger. "You take care of him, girl. He got the *dropsey*." She excused herself to collect the children, who were knee-deep in a puddle of mud.

Hours later, Keith's apartment was too quiet. What more could he tell her? Did he have to feel so ridiculously guilty? That look in her eyes — when he stumbled up the hill — was it love, or was she calculating, trying to figure out if his quirks were worth it or not? At the instant his hand reached for the phone, it rang, nearly sending him out of his skin.

"Hey, Numbskull." Larry. "What were you doing in that tree? Check out the news."

Keith flicked on the TV. The crowd, the firemen, an excited newswoman, and a pale version of himself paraded across the screen, his adventure recorded for posterity.

"Oh shit," he moaned. "Mom will have a cow."

CHAPTER 26
A CONFESSION

"Hi, you okay?" the voice on the phone asked. At last. Emily.

Keith rubbed his eyes. "Yeah. Guess I fell asleep. Can you come over?"

"That's what I was calling about. Bad news. I'm going to Brownwood."

"Brownwood? Why?"

"Mother's all freaked out about the flood. We owe my Aunt Orby a visit. She's ninety-four."

"Will you be gone overnight?"

"She doesn't want to come back until Friday. Her work's closed down, anyway. I begged off last time, so I can't get out of it. Sorry. Make it up this weekend?"

"Sure you can't come over tonight?"

"They're predicting another storm. Mom has us packed to leave in fifteen minutes." Was she telling the truth?

"Forgive me?"

"Of course. Hey, Brownwood is only sixty miles away. Maybe I can come visit."

"You would hate it. If they don't have me tied up shopping and quilting, I'll call you. OK?"

Her mother yelled in the background, and Keith panicked. He could not go the rest of the weekend without telling her—but what? "Uh, sorry I was so clumsy at the bridge. This afternoon was—was incredible."

"Quit apologizing—"

"Emily, I saw a hand sticking out from under the bridge. That's why I went over."

"A hand? In the water?"

"Under the bridge. The guy was in the tree that caught me."

"Really? The rescued him, too? The news didn't say anything about it. "

He exhaled. "But that's the tricky part. He may have been sort of a--a *vision*. A phantasm, I guess you'd call it. Hell, I don't know if it was real or not."

"I've heard of that. Wow. It's called having your whole life didn't flash before your eyes."

"That happened, too. This is different — "

"You need to rest. We'll talk every night, but I have to spend some time with Aunt Orby. Oh, God, she'll want to take me shopping."

"You've suffered a trauma," she continued. "I had a whole class on trauma. Practically. Your mind protects you in this type of situation. It may try to forget. What you should do is to rest and think all the way through it, no matter how horrible it was. I wish I could stay and help."

"Emily, I'm trying to tell you something. You know all that bullshit about the restaurant being haunted? Well, the guy in the tree with me was one of the marionettes. You know, from upstairs?"

A pause. Was she laughing?

"Keith, you're so crazy. Probably the funniest guy I know. I'm bummed out about having to leave. Sitting at Orby's is so *boring*."

"Emily, I see those puppets in dreams." The words kept coming. "The guy who stopped the fight in the bar? Remember? I know you saw him. In the tux? He's the one who was in the tree with me, too."

Silence.

"I know it sounds crazy. Emily?"

Another pause, then finally, she sighed. "I'm sorry to be such a wet blanket. I ll be in a mood to play when I get back. Promise. You and John are just so full of it."

"Emily--"

"Oh yeah, call me if the restaurant opens before the weekend and if I'm on the schedule." She gave him the number. "Mom's signaling me. Gotta go. Miss you."

He had done it. He sat, elbows resting on his knees, a sour taste in his mouth. She thought he was joking. Why couldn't he just work with her a few more days, solidify the relationship, then quit the infernal job and get on with his life? Get away from the river, Poindexter said. That was easy enough to explain. It was just Keith's own subconscious, repeating his innermost wish.

As he settled back into the couch cushions, the phone rang again, jerking him upright.

Ben's voice, not Emily's. "Hey, *paisan*, we're shut down. It's unprecedented."

"I heard," Keith said.

"You bastard. Thomas is scheduling clean-up later this week. We'll get paid. Can I put you on the list?"

"Yeah, go ahead." Shit. He forgot that he would lose money as long as the restaurant remained closed. "You're in a good mood for a manager whose job may be washing down the river."

"I'm stoked. If we can't work, we party. You coming?"

"What, in this weather?"

Ben laughed. "Not tonight, butt-brain. Tomorrow night at Charlie's apartment. The whole staff is invited. Even you."

"I don't have a boat." A night surrounded by Ben and his favorite smoking material did not sound that exciting.

"Your car will float, ass. High water is supposed to be tonight. Tomorrow is just a day off, finished up by a great drunk with your favorite pals. Bring Emily."

"Can't."

"Uh-oh. Lover's tiff?"

"She's going out of town."

"Too bad. All the more reason to get drunk. Charlie said to make sure you showed. Everyone will be there."

Keith copied down directions in a daze. Ben chattered a while longer, then his voice became a dial tone. What could Emily think of him after all that insanity?

The scrapes on his arms were starting to scab. He sat back and closed his eyes. Trauma. That made sense. Looking back, it felt like he'd been in a state of shock for months. If trauma could suddenly let him see things that would give Larry an orgasm, those hallucinations could go away, too, just as suddenly. It was all in the mind. The only real magic was what he had with Emily today.

He kicked off his shoes. Larry's books said it, themselves. The unknown was better left alone, and keeping your mind clear, sticking to the real world, was just a matter of focus. *She* would be his only focus from now on. By this weekend, today's nonsense would be forgotten, and together, they could recapture the magic.

CHAPTER 27
BRANWYN'S DESTINY

Lionel worked late into the night, helping his landlord and neighbors with sandbags. Their beer, their music, the festive air in the face of such danger, both impressed and grated on him at the same time. Did they think the river was playing?

"It won't go much higher. Maybe a foot more – just up to the bags," a gringo policeman said from the window of his police car.

"*Muchas gracias, Leo*," his landlord said and pushed another beer into his hand. "You take a rest, *si*?"

"But the man said--"

The landlord shook his bronzed, gray-haired head. He had come from Zacatecas twenty years ago. Built a shack into a roomy house with a courtyard. No permits. When he first landed in Sironia, he built things for a man who was now a city councilman. No one bothered him.

"The man may be right," he said, a helpless smile. "But maybe the river is smarter than the police."

When the others started quieting down, and the women went to bed, Lionel climbed over the bags, and splashed across the street. Cold water in his shoes, but he couldn't sleep. He walked aimlessly for some time before he realized his path led relentlessly toward the higher ground, through neighborhoods surreal with drawn faces, filling windows lit by candles. The great lights and power of the *Norte Americanos*--all of it was rendered useless by the water. He might as well be in the countryside outside of Monterey.

He climbed up a hill into River Park, wandering aimlessly until he sat to rest on a short stone wall. The stunning power of the river churned at the bottom of the cliff that yawned below his dripping feet. Like a low, thoughtful thunder, the growl tumbled upwards from a dark void. Clouds, no moon, and for the first time, no street lights to glisten in the water's surface. The river was like a long, monstrous snake who claimed the land in both directions.

The flood was totally unexpected, an upsetting of all routines. Sudden cataclysms that made all puny humans scramble for the safety of their God, Uncle claimed, were the grandfathers' method urging one to rest, be quiet, gather power. *Get out of the way when the Spirits are busy at their chess games.* Lionel always resented him when he said that. It just meant the old man was weak, didn't know what to do.

He looked down at his hands. What a child he'd been, back in Mexico. In this frightening moment, the fulcrum on which the whole future was perched, he had no idea what to do, either.

He rubbed sleepy eyes, rehearsing his strategy with Branwyn in whispers. It must be perfect, if he were ever to convince her to give up her mortal shell. Such a surrender was set on its path by a simple choice, but the actual exchange would require a considerable act of will.

"No one is ever really ready to give up," Uncle had cautioned. "No matter how brave he might seem."

Poor Branwyn, so sad. Other employees talked and laughed with her, but only as a pretense. He saw their looks after she walked away. She was every bit the outcast that he was.

With closed eyes, the roar of the angry river far below became the Universe. He practiced the chants, and meditated until he could clearly see the red and yellow stars. He mouthed English words he might use to direct Branwyn's spirit toward those two great lights that served as a gateway for seers journeying into the other realm.

What if he misjudged her? If she would not take the ultimate flight willingly, then what?

"A true magician," Uncle's voice returned, a soft whisper above the teeming flood, "is simply a person who ushers others into their destiny, when otherwise they would stray."

Lionel opened his eyes and peered into the roaring darkness below. How could a novice like himself know Branwyn's destiny?

Then again, what was so bizarre about what he proposed to do for her? The trading of one spirit for another happened all the time, all over the world, with or without the help of magicians. It was not his fault that ignorant people could not see it.

CHAPTER 28
CISCO'S PROJECT

Keith found Charlie's apartment, one of three flats that made up a once-stately house, in a dingy neighborhood not far from the university. The water had receded, but muddy children still pretend-fished in the flowing gutters. A dark brown line remained where the water had climbed the raised foundation.

Charlie met him on the porch. "You should have been here last night, man. Ben and I shot bottle rockets into the water from the window up there."

Rock-and-roll music blared. Keith accepted a can of beer and greeted those he recognized.

"Where's Emily?" a waitress asked.

"Out of town."

Cisco perched on the arm of an overstuffed chair. A quiet- looking Mexican lady occupied the seat.

"This is my wife, Barbara."

"Pleased to meet you."

The big man smiled sheepishly. In the kitchen, the stern master of everything, but out in the Lounge, or near the bar kitchen, his public set of manners took over, and he became the retiring, shy observer.

"Her real name is `Rolinda,' but in the United States, she has decided to change it."

"I like that my new name," Barbara explained in halting English, smiling with a soft, child-like beauty.

"Is Alberto coming?" Keith asked.

Cisco took a long drink of beer and rolled his eyes with a very American shrug.

"I don't think the brother is coming." He chuckled. "I think maybe Alberto is not very comfortable at parties unless it's just *his* friends, you know? When he drinks, he makes a *tonto* of himself. You know? He acts like an ass."

"Cisco!"

Keith laughed.

The big Mexican's eyes lit up as though he had just realized something. "Oh, Gringo, I have a favor to ask you."

"Sure. What is it?"

"You pretty good driver, huh?" Cisco nudged his wife. "This is the Gringo I told you about--a very good driver."

Barbara looked appalled. "Cisco, don't call him that name."

"No, no, it's okay. He's just the Gringo." They laughed as she sputtered.

Barbara blushed and issued a rapid rebuke in Spanish.

Cisco looked at Keith. "Did you understand that?"

"No. Too fast. *Mas dispasio, por favor*," he recited, asking Barbara to slow down.

"'s OK," Cisco chuckled.

"Anyway, you good on the highway? My wife's cousin--he just came over the border at Laredo," Cisco said, keeping his voice low and glancing around as he spoke. "He and some friends need transportation."

Keith's stomach sank. The man wanted him to cart wetbacks from the border to Sironia.

It made sense, really. A month before the big chef had asked him for a ride home, and made him stop at the Catfish Hut, upriver from the restaurant. While Keith nursed a drink, Cisco spoke at length in hushed tones with the Shack's owner and evaded Keith's questions afterward. It was like a scene from a movie.

"You want me to what?"

Cisco glared. "Shhh! Gringo, you want to maybe be very quiet. Please, do not go if you don't want. But we have no work this week. My wife's cousin and some friends already have jobs promised."

Keith tried to think of a polite way to refuse. Emily – of course – he would tell Cisco he had to go to Brownwood to pick up Emily.

"Is Thomas going to hire them?"

"Oh, no, I don't think so. Other jobs."

He promised to pay for gas and food. They would be back Friday, just after noon. The chef cajoled like a veteran salesman. Keith liked the big Mexican, and the idea of getting out of town, especially with Emily gone, made such a trip more palatable. Getting arrested for smuggling, though, would be serious. He saw an out.

"I guess it might be fun, except," he felt his cheeks redden, "my car would never make it. No way could we fit more than one person in the back seat, even if it did. Sorry. *Lo siento.*"

"Would you like to go if you had a better car?"

"Well, yes, but my car--"

" 's okay. The Brother has said that we could use *his* car."

Damn. Cisco had him. He put his arm around Keith's shoulder in congratulations. "Alberto would go himself, but it would look too--you know--suspicious to have so many Mexicans in the car." He laughed uproariously. Barbara blushed and hid her face.

"Drive Alberto's car to Laredo? Me? That car is his baby. If I got one scratch on it, he would kill me."

"Don't worry," said Cisco. "I'll take care of the brother."

Keith grasped for one more straw. "Uh, Cisco, is there any danger they might be carrying drugs?"

"Oh, no, Gringo." Cisco seemed offended. "My wife's cousin is a very hard-working young man. From a good family, all of them." He topped off these assurances by revealing that Ben had driven on just such a trip.

"Well, I dunno--" Keith felt himself nodding, in spite of the knot in his stomach. Was this really illegal? There was a debate on TV only last week where on pundit claimed the government wasn't enforcing immigration laws. No one had been arrested for a year for transporting illegals. It was the drug lords they were after. Keith couldn't check the luggage of strangers. What if Cisco was wrong? What if every one of them was just a drug mule?

"Day after tomorrow," Cisco said. "We meet in the parking lot. The trip will go so fast." A big smile

Keith excused himself and went to the kitchen for another beer. A trip might not be so bad, after all. Might get his mind off of his train wreck love life. If Emily forgot his confession entirely, if he never had to talk about his hallucinations again, if he could only count on that somehow, it might even be fun.

"Hey Keith, watch this," John bellowed from the doorway. He and Jeremy stood toe-to-toe, engrossed in a beer-chugging contest.

"You're idiots," he replied, and leaned against the counter. Oh, this was stupid. Smuggling wetbacks.

He hadn't even checked to see if Ben had actually made such a run. But Cisco wasn't a liar. Or else he was a very good one. This was insane. Who was he trying to get back at? Emily, for leaving him? This was a crazy time of dreams and floods and marionettes who came to life, and every second that passed made him more certain he would wind up in jail , this time.

Did he like the Mexican cook that much? Was he trying to prove something?

Or, just maybe, he saw helping the poor Mexicans as a way of buying a ticket out of the Water Company. A way to escape all the predictions of doom he kept dreaming about.

He stepped into the kitchen, and poured himself a scotch and Dr. Pepper, a drink Manny had christened "the Sironia." With the first sip, he felt a smile form on his lips. Falling into a ridiculous situation like this would never have happened at Elmer's ad agency.

CHAPTER 29
THE FLOOD PARTY

Keith switched and made small talk with Julie on the couch.
As his head swam in the mixture of her perfume and his
frustration with the Ciscc thing, he tried to work up the nerve
to ask what, if anything, Emily might have said about him.
Finally, she rose to drift to another part of the room.

Emily might call soon, so he gulped at his drink, now
cursed with the duty of telling her he was going on such a
stupid jaunt. With his luck, she would invite him to
Brownwood, and he could cancel the whole thing.

"Hey — you're not leaving." Ben grabbed his arm.
"You're crazy brother is back there claiming you found some
new evidence that the Water Company is haunted. Come fill
us in."

"No thanks. No dope smoking for me."

"I promise--they put the stuff away. There's a bottle of
scotch back there with your name on it."

Keith looked at his watch. "I can't stay. I'm pissed
anyway."

"Pissed about what?" Ben looked absolutely hurt.

"OK. Fifteen minutes." The music was getting too loud
out here, anyway. They weaved through milling bodies, and
Keith paused to freshen his drink.

In the back bedroom, Keith settled into a stuffed
rocking chair that had seen better days. Charlie smile,
obviously high, with his feet propped up on the bed. Larry
gazed into his beer, yawning.

"So tell us your bullshit," Ben urged.

"I ought to kick your ass, Ben. Cisco just roped me into transporting wetbacks. Said you'd done it before, too. I thought you said you guys didn't hire them anymore."

"Goddam, lower your voice." Ben waved his hands. "We're not hiring any. We're just not firing the ones we've got. Thomas can't sponsor another green card until next year."

"What does he get? One per decade? Doesn't matter. They're going to work somewhere else." Keith rubbed his eyes. "Wasn't there some sort of amnesty last year?"

Again the shushing hands. Ben leaned over to whisper. "Don't make a big stink. Just go out there and tell him you can't do it."

"He already left."

"Ben-ny." Larry wagged a finger. "Still trafficking in slaves?"

"You're drunk. Shut up." Ben sucked down the rest of his own beer. "Now, did Keith see something weird or not?"

Keith rocked back. It was no use. He was going to miss Emily's call. Maybe he wanted to. By now, she had probably gone over their last conversation a dozen times. She would just tell him she wanted out.

Staring at the eager, intoxicated faces, he took a deep breath and chose his words carefully.

"I think Emily said it best. I've been suffering from trauma. Or maybe depression. Hell, I don't know. I already told you about the waitress." He pointed a finger. "For the last time, Ben, are you sure you don't know the one who looks like the spitting image of Carlotta?" Keith tried to conceal a shiver. Talking made it all seem real again.

"No such person." Ben put his beer down. "You're blowing me off, dude. Tell me something new."

"Sorry." Keith closed his eyes. "I'm bored with it now. Got other problems to deal with."

"Don't we all. Larry claims you believe that girl — or something you've seen — is really a ghost."

"That's right, he--" Larry began.

"Shut up, ass-hole. I know *you* believe it," Ben yelled. Charlie frowned.

"I never said that." Keith made a face at Larry, then looked at Ben. "You're the expert on the attic. I don't go up there anymore."

Larry would not be suppressed. "There's an explanation for all this, and we--" he waved a hand, "we--"

"--have got to find out the answer, I know. Bullshit." Ben finished for him.

"I know the attic is spooky. But what's this about the door down at the bar? Come on, quit being coy." Before anyone else could speak, he took another gulp of beer and shook his head. "Damn. Thomas has been talking about relocating the restaurant, anyway. I wish he would hurry so we could be rid of all this nonsense."

Charlie grimaced. "Won't work. If it's not in that old building, it's not really the Water Company, is it?"

"I swear to God," Ben's head was still shaking, "I never would have hired you, Keith, if I had remembered that you guys used to read all those flaky Tarot and UFO books."

"Shut up, big shot." Larry did a sarcastic pantomime. "Just 'cause you're the big-ass manager doesn't mean you know anything. Every time you interrupt me I'm going to get another one of these." He held his beer up, downed it, and stomped toward the kitchen.

Charlie leaned forward. "Hey, Ben, keep it up. Let's make him puke."

"It won't take that many more," Keith observed.

"Spooky as shit." Ben said.

"What?" Keith sat back, closed his eyes, imagined his phone ringing. "I haven't said anything."

"Yeah, but I hear crap all the time. Especially from the Mexicans."

"Yeah? What do they say?" Keith leaned forward. "No one's filled me in on anything, especially not you, Mr. Immigration-law-breaker."

Ben blushed. "I told you, we're not hiring. So, what— you've seen a woman who looks like a puppet. What about the side door, goddamit?"

"I've seen them all, I think. Except the dragon. Oh, yeah—"

Charlie sat forward, eyes wide. "You've seen the dragon?"

"Nah—in a dream, if that counts."

"In a dream?" Ben sneered.

"It might count," Charlie said, then hiccupped loudly.

"What did I miss?" Larry returned, fresh beer in hand.

"Hey, where's mine?" Ben sneered. "You were supposed to get me a beer." He winked at Keith and Charlie.

"Idiot. You were discussing neat stuff while I was out of the room. No fair."

In a level tone, Ben said, "We have a theory--but you can't know about it until you get my beer."

"Crap." Larry shuffled back toward the kitchen. "Nobody say nothing until I get back!"

They jeered, but when Larry left, Ben seemed defeated. "It's always the puppets. The Mexicans are always worried about them, for some reason."

"Who? Who's worried?" Keith demanded. "Which ones?"

"I don't know." Ben grimaced and rubbed his forehead. "They talk to Thomas, really, before they talk to me. I think Chavo was one. Maybe Patricio."

"The dishwasher?"

"Yeah. Maybe Lionel."

Charlie brightened. "The Intellectual? I saw him tucked away in the corner in the other room. We could bring him in here and ask him."

"I think he was one of them. Shit, I don't know. Can't we just shake all this off? I'll get on Thomas's back. Those spooky marionettes came with the building. Maybe he'll leave them there when we move."

"Hey, I told you to shut up while I was gone." Larry stalked in and threw the unopened can at Ben.

Charlie took pity. "You didn't miss anything. Ben just said that some of the Mexicans had told Chef Thomas about spooks or something."

"Not spooks, necessarily." Ben tapped the top of his beer, trying to wait until its pressure died. "More like--"

"What?"

"Lionel told him the marionettes were alive, and Chavo was afraid of them."

A chill crawled up Keith's spine.

"He said that?" Larry. Sloppy. Waving his finger. "He told you that to your face, and you're just now spilling the beans?"

"Shut up," Keith said, but the the others stared with open mouths. For whatever reason, he started talking, heard himself narrating the details of the incident in the tree during the flood, something he had not even shared with Larry. When he finished, the wide eyes were filled with fear, not booze.

Clearing of throats. Getting late. No one moved, though.

"So who was it in the tree, really?" Charlie inquired.

"I guess I'm nuts. I think it was Poindexter."

"Bullshit. It's all bullshit." Larry pointed his finger at each of them in turn. "This sort of thing is not supernatural. It doesn't sound right. Don't you agree, Keith?"

"What? You're the one who convinced me it *was* supernatural. Are you drunk?"

"I've reversed my field. Now, I think there's a scientific explanation for it." With the word `scientific,' a fine spray of beer rained over Ben.

"Goddam, quit spitting on me." Ben shook his unopened beer, popped the top, and sent a shower of foam over Larry's face.

"Screw you." Larry stood up. "Now I'm going to smell like beer." He shook his own can and a duel ensued. Keith and Charlie retreated, laughing. Larry took aim at Keith.

"Don't shoot! I've got a mixed drink."

"Good God." Ben wiped at his soaking shirt. "You got any towels, Charlie?"

"Thanks guys." Charlie stomped his feet. "I vacuumed today." He produced towels from the bathroom.

"What I would like to know," Keith said, once they were re-settled, "is what Cisco thinks about those damn puppets. His judgment I can trust."

Ben shrugged.

"Why doesn't Thomas just throw them out?" Charlie kept licking a finger, dabbing it on his clothes, sticking it in his mouth.

"My God, are you eating shreds of dope?" Keith asked.

"So what? They work, even if you don't smoke them. I say burn the old relics. Have done with all this shit, if they're the problem."

"Wait," Larry bellowed. "You didn't let me finish. I said that there has to be an explanation. They aren't haunted. It's something else." He spoke his words slowly, succinctly.

"Sounds the fuck like they are to me."

"Do you know anything?" Keith studied Charlie. Acting weird, and it didn't seem all marijuana.

"Yeah, Charlie," joined Ben, "You've been squirrelly. You're usually the loudest bastard around, so what's the big secret? "

The waiter, rocked back, shrugged. "No big deal. I went into the bar one night. Patricio and Manuel wanted some drinks."

"Hell, I want some drinks," Larry mocked him.

Mutual flipping off.

"Anyway, Manny and Jeremy were – somewhere – nobody behind the bar." Charlie took a careful drink. "We need to smoke another joint."

Ben gave a sour look. "Later. When Keith's gone."

"Oh, we gotta cater to Mr. High and Mighty, the bar cook--"

"Shut up, ass." Keith stood, brandished his drink. "Don't you know I'm looking for an advertising job? If I have to take a drug test--"

"Oh, sure. I wouldn't work for a crrep who made me take a drug test." Charlie stuck his tongue out. "So, shut up and let me finish. I got the drink gun, and out of the corner of my eye -- I saw there was this guy in the wine closet-

-" Thumb thrown over his shoulder. "I almost came out of my skin. He's not an employee, but he don't care. Just stands in there like he owns the joint."

"So? Doing what?" Ben's voice fairly shook, and Keith could see they all shared the same nerves. "Stealing a bottle?"

Shrug. Arm raised again, painting the picture. "Maybe. He's just looking up and down the racks. I'm not *this far* from him." Hands poised a couple feet apart.

"And?" Keith prompted.

"He wore a tux. Like that clown who stopped the fight in the bar. I just remember his eyes." A visible shiver. "I was going to tell him to get out of there, but he – he finally looked up at me – those eyes..."

"That's it." Keith pounded on the arm of the chair. "That's him. You've seen Poindexter!" He could not have been happier if Emily had walked in. "Ben, listen to him. I'm not crazy, after all."

"What about his fucking eyes?" Ben demanded.

Larry seemed suddenly converted by Charlie's testimony. "You wouldn't understand," he said condescendingly.

"Shut your ass." Ben sneered.

"It was the same guy--"

"Eyes, damn it!"

"OK. Well, they were – they weren't human."

Silence fell over the room, and the waiter went back to harvesting dope shards, with no luck.

"You saw him." Keith stood again, raised his glass in salute.

Ben dismissed him. "So? Go on, go on – what happened? Did he leave?"

"Beats me," Charlie said. "I couldn't speak. Meant to yell out for the others to look, but everything went black. Next thing I know, Manny's asking me what the hell I'm doing. I was standing there with the drink gun in my hand, pouring *seven-up* all over the floor."

"Man, I don't need this shit." Ben shook his head. "You guys are asking me to believe that there is a whole other world of some sort of creepy beings going on behind this one. And they've all congregated at the Water Company."

"Who made those goddam puppets, anyway?" Larry slurred.

"Larcinter," Keith said absently.

"Larcinter? The night guy? He's old, but not that old."

Keith looked at his watch. They weren't getting anywhere. It wcertain he'd missed Emily's call, and nobody was being honest until you pulled their teeth out.

"OK, that's enough," he said. "You know this Larcinter bum. Who is he?" Pointing a finger. "Ben, you tell me the truth. Haven't you even noticed that he looks just like that leprechaun puppet?"

Ben paled, but wasn't having any of it. Even if it was obvious. "He's just an old drunk that Thomas gave a job to, Keith. He ain't stopping any robberies, but if he shows up some nights, it keeps burglars away."

"Slow down. The puppet told me that name. In my dreams — I think he's the one who carves — or carved the puppets –"

"So that's where you got the name from, Larry howled. "Psychology one-oh-one."

"For once I agree with the town drunk." Now Ben raised his glass.

"I can't believe this shit," Keith muttered.

They were silent for a while, each of them staring into space.

Larry emitted a great belch, then seized the floor. "What I've been trying to tell you bastards is that we all ought to get Thomas's permission to spend the night there. If there are burglars or cowboys or whatever the explanation is--" he burped again, "— especially if they really are spooks, which, in light of this testimony, they might damn well be, it's the only way to find out."

"And what?" Keith rolled his eyes. "They won't show with all of us waiting for them, and what would we do, anyway? Take their picture? Throw water on them and hope they melt like the wicked witch?"

Larry's smile had only grown goofier. "Remember what the books say. You may not see a ghost's reflection in the mirror, but you will in the water. Water is life."

"I give up," Keith said. "I'll do it—once, if it will shut you guys up. I gotta get another job. No offense, Ben."

"I'm game." Charlie was enthused. "It makes sense. If all this is just a series of creepy pranks, whoever the joker is won't be able to resist sticking around to mess with our minds. Thomas is a player. He'll let us, won't he, Ben?"

"Crap, I don't know." Ben was obviously sorry he had praised Larry for anything.

Keith's focus, though, remained on his brother, who had become a pale shade of green.

"Come on," Charlie urged. "He'll let us if you explain it to him."

"I don't guess he'd be against it, as long as we don't drink his booze and get busted after hours. We have to agree, though. No one else is invited."

This was a blithering mistake, but how else would Keith get home tonight? He held out his hand. "Just we four. And if we find anything, then yours truly won't wind up in the nut house."

Larry and Charlie stacked their hands atop his. Finally, Ben put his in, grudgingly.

"The four musketeers," said Charlie. "Spook-catchers. Ghost-busters."

"M-musketrs--" Larry said. His hand jerked away and he bolted out the back door.

"Oh-oh."

They shuffled out to a grim scene. Larry lay prostrate, his long torso stretched across the wooden back porch, head hung over the side, rudely depositing the night's alcohol intake into the flowerbed.

"Look at that," Keith cried. "A goddam beached whale." The others laughed.

A few minutes later, Keith started for the door, but, catching Ben's frown, decided it was better to bed down on the couch. He had to make it up to Emily, somehow.

Fantasies about that day in Mary's apartment kept him tossing and turning. He would cancel on Cicsco. Drive to Brownwood -- Did she call? Laced through his fantasies, Larry's ghostbuster scheme intruded. Folly. As stupid as his trip to Laredo would be. Plus, it would probably never happen.

Yet, Charlie had seen something. That fact brought a measure of solace. Maybe the damned place really was haunted.

Even that thought, though, was losing its power to relieve. With his face in the foul-smelling couch pillow, Keith had to admit that his problems had started before he came to the restaurant. Perhaps Emily would know the right psychological terms, but it made more sense to explain the visions as splintered pieces out of his subconscious. Get out, something was trying to tell him. Carlotta — whatever she symbolized in the inner recesses of his brain — had led him to the restaurant, and now she wanted him to leave. Why?

Nothing would make him happier. But first, Emily. Once he made things good with her, he would bail, job or no job.

CHAPTER 30
LAREDO

The back lot lay strewn with an amazing assortment of trash and tree branches. Water stood in the deep potholes, steaming under the hot morning sun.

Neither Nosma nor Katy were in evidence, but most of the rest of the staff--clad in grubbies--filed in and out through the back door, emptying buckets of pure sludge.

Cisco arrived in dress-shirt and pants, looking more fit for a wedding rehearsal than a smuggling mission.

Keith waited by Alberto's pride and joy. In two days, only one short phone call, and Emily sounded more detached than he had ever heard. He was careful not to quiz her about the issue at all, but her attitude had changed. When he tried to call her back — twice — answering machine.

When Cisco and his brother emerged from the back door, Keith laughed in spite of his funk. Alberto looked ashen, his car keys clenched in a fist. Like a man in pain, he opened the car door, took out his chamois, and gave the finish a final, tender caress.

"Don't worry, amigo, you'll look great in Keith's jalopy," Ben goaded from the steps. Cisco waved him away. Alberto had never driven a standard transmission before.

"No problem. Alberto, come over here. I'll show you," Keith volunteered.

Reluctantly, the young student climbed behind the steering wheel. Cisco piled into the tiny back seat and Keith sat shotgun.

"Let out on the clutch slowly," Keith instructed.

"What?" Alberto hollered.

The car lurched across the lot, bucking violently into and out of potholes, rocking Keith's head against the roof.

Alberto tried again, cursed in Spanish, opened the door to leave, and stayed only under Cisco's threats.

"*Pendejo*," Alberto said bitterly after the car died for the umpteenth time. In spite of that, he had successfully reached second gear more than once. He scowled viciously and climbed out of the car to the applause and laughter of the staff.

"Way to go, *puta*," Charlie yelled.

Alberto took a bow, returning all curses in kind. He held up Keith's car keys to more cheers.

"Don't worry, Mr. Keith," Cisco said quietly. "He will take good care of your car."

"Sure. He can get home and back in second gear."

The crowd applauded wildly when Keith and Cisco took their places in the Cadillac and moved it slowly onto the side street.

"Don't get too drunk," Ben called from the door.

They opened their windows to the warming air. The smell of the railroad tracks was replaced by the fishy tinge of river water. In turn, pungent smoke from diesel rigs on the highway intruded, then the bacon and sausage fragrance from Jeff's Pancake Plaza across from the university. Keith pushed the "aircraft carrier"--Larry's name for cars this big--up to speed, and piquant odors of buttercups, bluebonnets, and Indian paintbrushes took over from the sides of the highway.

They chatted about the beautiful day and how the roads were so much better here than in Mexico. In spite of that, Cisco contended, the flowered landscape of his homeland put the brightly hued Texas prairie to shame, especially down near Mexico City.

They made good time, stopping for lunch at a Mexican restaurant Cisco knew in San Antonio. Afterward, the chef dozed and Keith thought of Emily and grew both horny and confident that he could put things right. How, he could not quite figure.

Cisco awoke. Eventually, the talk turned to Alberto. Cisco sighed. "My brother's a good *muchacho*. He just needs to grow up, you know?" He had his arm propped up in the window, looking out of place, an Aztec god in a modern car.

"Alberto looks different," Keith said gingerly. "Did you have different fathers?"

"Different mothers, gringo." A cryptic smirk. "No, you don't want to know the circumstances." He laughed softly.

The hours had flown by, and they were nearing Laredo before Keith got up the nerve to ask what he knew about the marionettes.

"Ah, yes. The puppets between the wooden Indians." He seemed amused.

"Are they haunted? Do you believe in that sort of thing?"

A pause.

"Gringo, you have the habit of the *Norte Americanos*. You want to put into words something that should remain silent."

"What does that mean? They are haunted? Or not?"

Cisco laughed freely. "No, *Señor*. I don't mean that. Has the Gringo been listening to stories from Lionel? He is a young man with a huge imagination."

"Lionel?" Keith protested. "I doubt he would even talk to me." That made two people who talked as if the janitor knew something. "Sorry. The reason I bring it up is that I've been having some weird dreams — visions, even — about them. And I can't seem to get them to stop."

They entered the city limits of Laredo, and Cisco gave directions.

"Dreams that won't go away? You sound like the young ones — Lionel and Chavo." His face took on a serious scowl. "Gringo, I'm a Catholic," he said. "As a Christian, I was taught to avoid witches and magicians. I had a friend in school, before I had to quit and get a job.

"My buddy met a witch and started taking some kind of medicine, or dope, or whatever they use. He died. Only nineteen years old." Tears welled in the big man's eyes.

"Lionel thinks like my friend did. I'm afraid he will meet the same end. Believe me, Gringo, we Mexicans are maybe more spiritual than Texans, but that does not mean there are really ghosts who come from the beyond to try to capture people."

"I didn't say anything about ghosts capturing people."

Cisco smiled sheepishly.

"That's what I'm talking about, *Patron*," Keith said, exasperated, "everyone seems to know a whole different set of rules than I do. Don't say it's just Mexicans. Katy talks that way. And Brenda. She wasn't Mexican. What happened to her?"

"I think, like you, Brenda maybe talked too much with Lionel or the dishwashers. Patricio kisses his medallion once an hour to keep evil spirits away.

"She asked me questions like yours. She claimed she had to quit to be safe. I would rather go to my priest than lose a good job. Turn here." He pointed abruptly. They entered a gravel road and pulled up in front of a well-kept house.

Two older Latino men were smoking cigarettes on the front lawn. They waved and called toward the house. Immediately, a throng of men and women of all ages issued from the door of a screened-in porch.

"Do not worry, Gringo," Cisco's face was happy, devoid of any ridicule, "you will like Mama Luz. She knows about witches. Maybe there will be time to talk to her." They got out and a crowd of welcomers engulfed Cisco.

Señora Luz was introduced among a flurry of other names he knew he would never keep straight.

"Call me Mamá," she said, and put her arm around him.

"Call him Gringo," Cisco bellowed. Everyone laughed.

"You have a dirty mouth, Cisco." Mama Luz shook a finger.

She introduced the four young men they would transport to Sironia: Eduardo, Rafael, Renaldo, and Humberto.

The modest house had an immaculately kept living room. The den looked more lived-in; cushions, chairs and a television. The air smelled of tamales.

The four wards were quiet. Each had a small vocabulary of English, except Eduardo, Barbara's cousin, who handled the language remarkably well. They studied Keith continuously. They answered promptly when Cisco addressed them, and laughed at his jokes.

An old man they called Fernando--a neighbor, perhaps-- entered with bottles of Mexican beer for everyone. The young men looked automatically at Cisco, who nodded permission.

A few women camped at the kitchen table, drinking coffee from china cups that were elegant, though chipped with age. Several men loitered on the back porch, smoking cigarettes and looking through the windows occasionally.

After more small talk, everyone adjourned to picnic tables in the back yard as tamales and more beer were passed around. Luckily, everyone spoke English as much as possible.

"We have many guests of honor tonight," *Señora* Luz announced. "Each guest must tell us his life story. It is a tradition. We'll start with my new nephew." Her gaze roamed the table and stopped on Keith.

"Me?"

"*Si*, nephew. How did you get a job working with Cisco?"

Keith stumbled through an account of the ad agency, omitting the black hole of this last winter. Several of the listeners nodded in polite approval.

"And now our four other children," Luz insisted, motioning for the illegals to stand. She required of them where they came from, and the jobs to which they were traveling. No mention was ever made of the consequences of being caught as illegals.

"To the young *patron*," the last wetback said and raised a glass to Keith.

"Young *patron*," others echoed.

"To my four new *amigos*," Keith responded, as drunk on the goodwill as he was on the beer.

Cisco was charming, as much a maestro here as he was in the kitchen. A radio blared music Keith was now quite accustomed to. *I'm actually having a good time*, he thought. If only Emily were here to share it.

As darkness grew, a single light bulb on a wire switched on. The air grew thick with mosquitoes and the fragrance of Mama Luz's roses. Cisco seemed to know everyone, asked about their families, and made Keith laugh with stories he told about many of them, teasing them right to their faces. Finally, the neighbors excused themselves.

Señora Luz offered Keith a blanket and a fresh pillow in the den where the young men would sleep. After they settled down, though, Cisco appeared in the hall and asked Keith to come with him.

He followed the chef down a hallway, into a dark room where Mama Luz sat, smiling, seated before a dozen candles surrounding a picture of Jesus on a table.

"*Ola*, Nephew," she said quietly. Cisco handed Keith a full cup of clear liquid.

"It's rum." Keith tried to decline politely. Liquor on top of beer had never worked for him.

"It's good for you. Drink, drink," she motioned with her hand. Cisco held a mug, as well. Keith submitted.

"Your friend Cisco tells me you have been seeing some strange things. No?"

Keith barely heard. He was looking at the large, hanging crucifix above the bureau. His home had not been a catholic one, and the flickering candles added to the sudden eeriness. Things began to connect. The candles, the black lacquer tables, small decanters and incense burners--he had read about such settings. These were the tools used by witches in South America.

"Is Cisco correct, nephew?" she prodded. "Tell Mama what is wrong with your dreams. *Por favor.*"

Keith came to and looked at Cisco for direction.

"'s OK, Gringo. Mama Luz knows about these things."

"But is she a witch?" Keith blurted without thinking.

The big lady laughed aloud.

"Gringo, I told you. I'm a Christian. So is she." Cisco smiled and took another drink of his own rum.

"Nephew, there are all kinds of witches." Mama Luz spoke consolingly, "but the Savior--" she crossed herself, "-- does not begrudge us the weapons to fight the bad witches."

"OK. I hope you don't think I am too crazy." Keith recited the chronology of his life, beginning with the Big Day, the afternoon he first met Carlotta. She listened intently. The tart rum mellowed. Cisco seemed bored for a while, then actually dozed off.

Mama Luz motioned toward the nodding chef and whispered, "Now we can pray in privacy."

She rose and lit more candles, all the while asking Keith to clarify certain details.

"Pray with me," she said abruptly, indicating he should kneel in front of the picture.

"I'm not Catholic."

She pointed. He knelt.

Luz murmured a long, intense litany in Spanish. Afterward, she motioned him back to his seat and ordered him to hold out his hands. Into them, she dumped what appeared to be old dried chicken bones from a leather bag she had tied to her waist.

"Yuck."

"Throw them," she said soulfully.

"What? Where?" He was dulled. In younger years, he might have been excited to take part in such a ritual. Now, he simply felt wiped-out. He shook the bones in his hands, like large dice, and tossed them awkwardly.

Mama Luz pressed his rum cup back into his hands, then knelt close to the bones, softly humming a tune. Keith fought his own immense drowsiness. For a moment, he thought he saw Emily coming through the door.

Keith's eyes fluttered open. Mama Luz was knitting, rocking herself slightly, back and forth, though the chair she sat in was rigid. Cisco was nowhere to be seen. Neither was Emily. The candles stung his eyes.

"Where's Cisco?" He felt embarrassed.

"You have a very pretty girlfriend." Mama Luz put her knitting down and took a sip from a glass.

"How do you know what she looks like?" Of course, Cisco had told her. "Sorry. I must have gone to sleep."

"*Si.*"

"Well, what did the bones tell you?"

"You are being stalked by a river spirit," Mama Luz said simply.

"Is that bad?"

"So many people come to me when they don't really have an ailment. They just want someone to talk to." She spoke matter-of-factly. "But you, Nephew, have a real problem." Her eyes rested on him and would not move.

"I do?"

"Yes. A river spirit will kill you if you do not find a way to escape."

He laughed nervously. Was this how they entertained stupid gringos when they came down here? Yet, her eyes were clear and friendly.

"Of course, we never really die. But you will be taken to a place you do not want to be. Believe me. It happens every day."

"What do you mean? I have to move away from the river? Like Brenda did? I can't even get on a boat in the future, or go fishing?"

She laughed and it irritated him.

"Are you serious, or just playing with me because Cisco told you I'm an idiot? This can't really be happening."

"But I just told you, Nephew. It happens all the time." Mama Luz leaned forward. "People are taken by the demons of the Great Beyond constantly. Just because we explain it in a way that makes us less afraid doesn't mean it's not happening."

"OK, OK." Keith didn't want to sound rude, but now his head hurt. The way it usually did when he mixed his drinks. "So I should quit my job. Is that what you're saying?"

"No, nephew. It's an old fable that you can escape such a creature by staying away from it. It is not bound by the space and time like we are." She put her cup down and moved her knitting onto the table.

"Then what can I do?" Keith was genuinely alarmed.

"You seem to be sensitive, nephew. Do you know what that means?" Her eyebrows went up.

"Maybe."

"You are. The bones say so. Your face says so. If you are sensitive, then can you tell me why this monster is hunting you?"

"If this isn't all just a bunch of crap--pardon me--then I guess it's because I screwed up. I used to have a nice job. I worked twelve hours a day. We – I mean, my girlfriend and I – hung out with the same group, had long dinners, talked current events, philosophy – I kind of got lost in the lifestyle. And when that was taken away, I guess I forgot who I really was. Damn, it sounds so trite when I say it that way."

He looked up, feeling his cheeks burning. "Is that it?"

"Are you still lost? This is important, Nephew."

"I don't know. It's all bullshit. I can't trust women. My job turned out to be no security at all. So what can I do? Land another executive position somewhere and find out that means no security, too?"

"Is that where you get your security? From your job?"

"No. You're right. But relationships blow up, too. It makes me wonder what the purpose of living is, anyway."

Mama Luz nodded her head vigorously. A hand shot forward. The finger shaking at his face was both gnarled from arthritis, but graceful, too. "That's it precisely. You don't have a reason to live. You just said so."

"So? Isn't everyone like me? Why aren't they being hunted?"

"No. They are not like you. Everyone has certain gifts. The Great Spirit doesn't really care what happens to you if you do not use them. And it is when the Great Spirit does not care that demons such as your predator have the leeway to make their move."

A long pause. The warm lady's nonsense rang true.

"Maybe. But you still haven't told me how I can keep from dying and being turned into a marionette." He grabbed his aching head. "Listen to me. I'm talking like an imbecile."

She shushed him.

"Do not worry, nephew. You are a smart boy with a big heart. If Cisco and I like you, you must have something going for yourself. Just listen to the Great Spirit. He speaks to you from inside--" She tapped her own chest. "--Learn to use your talents. Do not be afraid to love. But do these things intensely. Only if you are sincere will you capture the Great Spirit's attention."

"And the next time I see that old man? Or the leprechaun? Or the next time Carlotta comes out of the shadows?"

"Laugh at them. Tell him you have much to live for. Make sure you are not lying, though. There are no untruths in the spirit world. Shake off the self-pity. If you don't, neither I nor anyone else can help you."

Mama Luz stood and crossed the room. She opened a desk drawer, found what she was looking for, and closed it in her fist. She returned, passing her free hand over the burning candles.

"How insane it is not to live life deeply." She exuded energy. "Use every breath. We do not have time in this realm to spend years enjoying being depressed. The spirits will snare us!" She whipped her fingers together in a snatching motion, and swept her closed fist only inches away from his face.

"To help you." The hand opened, revealing a small locket *sans* chain. She flipped the tiny latch, and pointed at the miniature picture of a young Mexican man inside.

"This was Ernesto," she said. "He was fourteen years old."

Keith studied the photo, then saw the tears in her eyes.

"Was he your--"

"Nephew," she smiled. "Like you. He was lost *tambien*. The spirits took him too early. He never realized how loved he was. Just thought his life was over. Thinking that made it so."

She closed the locket slowly and pressed it into his hands. "So you will remember," she said.

CHAPTER 31
THE VIEWING

The stench of wet carpet scraps escaped, no matter how tightly
Lionel twisted the plastic bags. He had done the heavy stuff
since daybreak. Now, he chewed on a roll, watching Branwyn
laughing and talking with the others on lunch break. Even
grubby clothes could not hide her beauty – they fell around
her perfect torso like royal robes – but she had not met his
furtive glances all morning. Not once.

Carlotta, too, had refused to come for many nights.
Since the evening the gringo was attacked, she had only hung
on her strings silently, eyes downcast, as if pouting.

For the thousandth time, he noted the mark made by
the water, halfway up the stairs to the second floor alcove.
Chairs had been moved upstairs for safekeeping, and as he
shifted a stack of them, a noise made him turn around.

He saw a vision of unexpected grace. There, by the
salad bar, stood Branwyn, one leg poised in mid air, like a
ballet dancer doing exercises, floating rhythmically through
space, humming a tune. Her figure--so lithe--lit from behind
by the huge stained glass window on the building's side.

Dumbstruck for a moment, Uncle's words jarred him:
He who hesitates is lost.

In a flash, he set the chair down and was at her side.
He grasped her hand and bowed, pretending to dance with
her like a gentleman. The shock on her face gave way to
laughter. They did an impromptu, silly *minuet*, and he bowed
again.

"You're crazy," she cried. "I almost jumped out of my
skin."

"Nice to see you." Even he noticed the unexpected manliness in his voice. "What are you doing up here, all alone?"

"Ben wants me to polish the chrome," she pointed at the rail around the salad bar, "then vacuum. Dancing was my own idea." They laughed together.

So fresh. So full of life. Her mouth--a treasure of expression. How could her fellow beings fail to appreciate her?

Move, Lionel reminded himself. *Strike, before she remembers how lowly you are…*

"Would you like to meet my friends?"

Branwyn retreated. Shyness clouded her eyes. "What friends?"

"Upstairs. Have you never seen them?"

She thought. "You mean the puppets? Of course."

"But have you really?" He felt the wave of charm touch her, and held out his hand. She did not hesitate.

"For a minute, if Ben won't miss me."

He led her up the dark steps, drunk with feelings he did not recognize. She chatted cheerfully, too quickly for him to get all the English meanings. He grunted and laughed when he thought he should.

On the landing, he knelt, and recited the same history Thomas had told him about the wooden Indians. As unobtrusively as possible, he made sure the eyes of the monster dwarf faced away from Carlotta's hiding place. That done, he took Branwyn's hand again, reveling in its warmth.

They crossed the catwalk and he pulled the light cord. Boxes lined the walls, stacked up almost to the short ceiling. On two lower stacks, Carlotta and the tuxedo man sat.

"Why aren't these two out with the others?" Branwyn asked. She did not resist when he placed the gypsy puppet's hand in hers, as one joining two lovers.

"To be safe."

"Safe from what?" Branwyn pulled away and leaned against the bricks. "Are they scared up here in the dark?" She giggled impudently.

"Does the dark scare you?" he asked. Perhaps she saw his feelings, for she quit laughing. Still, she did not harden. If anything, she softened.

"No."

"You are not afraid of a long journey? Even into infinity?"

"No." A deep breath. She searched his eyes for something. He must not let her have it, not yet. He fingered Carlotta's dress, then held it up.

"Here. Feel it." She did.

"Beautiful, no? *Bonita*. Without an equal--"

"Yes, she is."

Careful.

"Can you think of what it would be like to be so beautiful? Would you like for this to be your new home?" Slow down. Don't rush.

"My home?"

"Yes. A home away from your mother. Away from the pain of life. A house whose front gate opens to the worlds— out there--" He gestured and could have said it better, but did not have the English.

Her eyes left him and focused on the puppet for another moment. She caressed the fingers, stroked the hair so much blacker than hers.

Lionel's heart leaped--she was accepting it all.

Her eyes returned to his. "I would live wherever you wish," she said simply.

The words hit like rain on a drum, like blasts of longed-for truth. He saw something like devotion in those exquisite eyes, but now his tongue failed him.

"They all said you were a clown of sorts." Branwyn patted Carlotta's head and smiled softly. "They were right. And I like it." Swiftly, she stepped closer and kissed him.

But it did not end. Kisses were quick, short bursts of electricity. Not this overflowing of a river! The world closed in, twirling, surging. Her tongue cam into his mouth, and he almost screamed -- His heart boomed, trying to burst from his chest, a feeling he had experienced only with Carlotta.

His eyes remained closed until the young bus girl pulled away. A little smile that ripped him in half. Colored circles darted this way and that before his eyes.

"See you downstairs," she said. Her footfalls echoed until they faded into the joking and music far below.

He leaned against the cool bricks, colors still dancing through his field of view.

A motion on the box made him jump, and blasted his heart into high gear. Slowly, the figure of Carlotta shifted. The puppet hand raised, jerkily, wooden, through the air, as if someone controlled her strings — but those were hung limply, down the side of cardboard. The head turned — but this was not his Carlotta, was it? He stood, shivering, consumed by the shine of the wooden face, the slow motion of the mechanical eyes.

"*Que bueno*," she said, her mouth moving in perfect synchronization with the words. "You have found a reason to live. Now he cannot touch you." The wooden eyes blinked, and as he felt the air exhale from his own chest, her form slid back down on the jumbo carton of tortilla chips, lifeless again.

"*Dios mio*." He fell to his knees, ignoring waves of fright. "Carlotta? My love, what are you saying?"

The mouth remained shut, but her voice echoed quietly from the air conditioning duct. "You cannot save me."

"No," he protested. "I was born to save you. You and I will be lovers." He picked up the body, immutable wood and floppy leather joints, and shook her.

"Carlotta, my love, open your eyes. Please, God." He pulled each string in turn, with no effect. "*Por favor, mi querida.*"

CHAPTER 32
THE BASEMENT

On River Drive, colorful banners on the fence surrounding the
Terrace advertised the annual River Festival in two weeks.
Late this year, because of the flood. When they turned onto the
side street, Keith got a better look at the old mansion — a new
water line had been added to its century-and-a-half collection
of such marks.

Two of their four refugees knew the dishwasher,
Patricio, and a happy reunion ensued in the parking lot.

"So, how'd it go?" Ben entered the kitchen from the first
floor dining room. He wore a ridiculous combination of work
shirt, khaki shorts, and rubber waders. "No immigration
problems?"

"Did my car survive? Are you going fishing?"

Ben produced keys. "Alberto left these. He bailed out a
while ago. Couldn't take the smell."

Keith followed him into the dining room. Mud had
been scraped away and the wood floor looked almost normal
again, but the rancid odor had worsened.

"Cisco's great. I really like him. But when you brought
a load up, did you feel guilty?"

"Guilty?" Ben grimaced. "Can't feel that way. You're
one of the only *legal* people in Sironia dumb enough to stay
back in the kitchen at little more than minimum wage."

Ben led him toward an opening in the floor where a
table had been moved away.

"What the hell is that?" Keith exclaimed.

"A goddam trap door. What does it look like?"

"There's a basement here?" Keith bent over, craning his neck to see. Concrete stairs led down into what was obviously a walled room. Someone sloshed through water that lapped up onto the steps, just visible in dim light beneath. A thick hose snaked down those steps. Its other end led out the restaurant's front door.

"You've never been down there?" Ben chuckled and stepped onto the top step. "I was sure you knew about it."

"Bullshit."

"What the hell do you think is stinking so bad? The floor's dry."

Keith squatted into the opening as Ben moved down. Two men worked the hose against the far wall, dirty water halfway up their calves. Keith breathed through his mouth to keep from puking, and took a seat on the lowest dry step.

"This is so big," Keith marveled. "Why doesn't Thomas use it for a dining room?"

"There's another the same size down that passageway. A lot of little cubby-holes between the two." The dark opening in the back corner gave Keith the creeps. Out here in the light, an archway dominated the side wall, but any opening had obviously been bricked up.

Ben followed his gaze. "Supposedly, a tunnel went from here to the Terrace, believe it or not, back in the old days. They closed it up."

"The more I know about this place, the weirder it gets."

Ben chuckled. "Thomas does let people have banquets down here sometimes. We're having a group in a couple of weeks. One of the biggest banquets we do all year, so we gotta get it cleaned up." He took a mop and began pushing invisible things beneath the brine. "There's another drain here, somewhere."

Keith exhaled, wasn't sure if he could suck air back in. "You're crazy. If it were dry tomorrow, it would take longer than two weeks to get rid of this stench. What group?"

"It'll be ready, by God." Ben held a finger to his lips, and shook his head. Keith watched in silence until the two workmen climbed the stairs to get more equipment. At that moment, the manager wiggled his eyebrows and said in a stage whisper, "The Scalded Toms."

"The Scalded Toms? You're shittin' me." The *Toms* were a super-secret organization, founded after an infamous episode of Texas history. "They have a banquet here? Nobody knows where they have their meetings – are you sure?"

Ben ignored him, catalogued the other tasks the clean-up crew had accomplished in two days, laid out the plan for doing the rest, but Keith didn't listen.

His mind drifted back to the first time he heard the Toms' story. In those days, it was a sort of right-of-passage for young boys. He could still picture Miss Prudence Ellam, his fifth grade teacher, reciting it.

The portly spinster paced in front of the class, wielding her punitive fly swatter, while sniggering boys and blushing girls listened to the tale of Texas' most notorious gang of peeping Toms.

Their founder was Bill Talley, son of a well-to-do merchant in the east Texas town of Paris, in the nineteen-twenties. He was never known as a troublemaker until late one night when he was walking home and stumbled upon the visage of Miss Melinda Johnson.

Melinda was the prettiest of the town's sixteen-year-olds, and she disrobed that night in front of her window with no thought that there might be passers-by. "A good lesson for any young girl to learn," Miss Ellam declared, waving the swatter for emphasis.

Bill Talley was so enthralled by what he witnessed that night, that he founded a club, *The Peeping Toms*. The "scoundrels," as they came to be known, ranged throughout Paris with impunity.

"Conspiracies are doomed to discovery," Miss Elam continued smugly. One night, Melinda Johnson's father lay in wait and caught Bill Talley, himself. Up came Melinda's blinds and out came a pan of boiling water.

Young Talley ran screaming into the night, horribly disfigured for life. Some idiots, though, never learn from their mistakes, Miss Elam complained. With a supreme stubbornness, he created a new club, *The Royal Order of the Scalded Toms*, a super-secret and illegal society which spread throughout the state and which was eventually co-opted by adult males.

"Dirty old men," Miss Ellam concluded to the rapt class.

The tradition grew, formed sub-chapters, was handed down from one generation to the next. It was said that each local chapter of the Toms convened once a year in a secret place, their members adorned in outrageous Halloween-style masks, a holdover from their founder's need to conceal his maimed face.

"Oh, pshaw," Keith's grandmother once summed it up at the dinner table. "I wish every masked society was as harmless as that crowd. They're just a bunch of lecherous fools who never grew up. Like they never saw a *nekkid* girl before. Hooey."

Ben's wagging finger brought him back to now. "As for the banquet, don't tell anybody. Especially Larry, for God's sake. If word gets out, they'll switch to a new place."

"Mum's the word. I swear. Are the phones working yet?"

"You coming to the picnic?" Ben asked suddenly. "Oh, yeah. You've been gone. We're having a picnic at State Park tomorrow. Everyone meets at my parents' house and we bicycle from there. Lots of beer and good food. Thomas is footing everything. You know, to celebrate surviving. Why don't you bring Emily?"

"I will, if she's not still out of town." Keith started to climb out.

"You didn't ask."

Careful not to bump his head on the ancient wooden beams, Keith turned around. "Ask what?"

"We had a flood, numbskull. It destroyed almost everything in the place. Thomas has to buy new tables, carpet, even one of the cash registers was left too low on the stairs.

Don't you want to know what happened to your precious puppets?"

"Yeah, I guess. Never really thought about it. The flood didn't get up to the third floor, did it?"

"No, actually." Ben's eyebrows went up. "We found them all on top of the roof."

"How the hell did they get there?"

Ben looked sanguine, and went back to his thrashing with the mop. "None of us could figure that out. Just thought it would tickle your fancy. Make your phone call."

The phone at the wait-station emitted a dial tone, but the eternal answering machine was the only response on Emily's end. When he got home, he tried several more times, then made the mistake of lying down on the couch. He slept until the morning sun came through the blinds.

CHAPTER 33
THE PICNIC

Emily's mother answered with a flat, bored air. "It's Keith? Oh, she's already left with some of her girlfriends for the picnic."

It was a hollow drive to the rendezvous at Ben's parents' house. His bike would not fit into his car and he was in no mood anyway. He had already lost Emily. Only the formalities remained.

Several wait-people and busgirls were mounting their bikes and waving as he pulled up.

Ben seemed puzzled. "I thought you weren't going to make it. Emily took off with the first group."

"No problem." Keith stood around aimlessly for a few moments, then returned to his car.

"Hey, man." Charlie stuck his head into the window. "Come on. We can dig up another bike."

Keith managed a smile. "No, thanks. I might blow the whole thing off."

The Wop pulled up in the large white catering van. "Keith, my boy, get over here." Keith took a breath and climbed out.

John barreled out of the driver's seat and tossed Keith the keys. "Get in there, goddam it. We gotta cruise behind all these shitheads and pick up the laggards. You drive. I want to start drinking."

Grudgingly, Keith set off at a snail's pace, allowing the last cyclers to work ahead while John settled in the back among the beer coolers.

"Goddam stupid bastards." John was full of energy. "Who in hell would want to ride a bike on a day this hot?"

"You're hittin' it early today," Keith observed.

"Damn right." A defiant smile. "Hey, keep it slow enough for me to chug it all before we get there. Want one?" He laughed.

"Thanks, I'll wait." Even the Wop's annoying exhuberance could not calm his churning stomach. This was worse than losing Linda.

"Well, now what the fuck's the matter with you?" John bellowed. A belch ensued.

"Nothing. Women."

"They're all bitches."

There were stragglers to pick up. By the time the van reached the large pavilion Thomas had reserved in Texas Park, a forested oasis out in the middle of a dry prairie, the riders were laughing and drinking as the Wop regaled them with vulgar jokes.

Chef Thomas presided over the feast. Salads, vegetable dishes, and dips had been supplied by the ladies of the kitchen. Katy and Chavo stood watch over hamburgers and hot dogs on the grill. Nosma reasted against a stone table, working a cheap Japanese fan, while Anna and Arkie fretted with the plastic place settings. The Thieus' children frolicked on the lawn near the pavilion.

The rest of the staff concentrated on flying Frisbees on the well-kept grass and impromptu bike races on the chalk-gravel roads that ran through the small park.

Keith approached Emily cautiously.

"How was Brownwood?" he asked.

"Oh, fine. We got home late."

"I know. I talked with your mother."

She blushed, close in the protection of her girlfriends. "Sorry I didn't call. Mary's having boy trouble. We're trying to console her. You know how it is." Mary called her away at that instant in an obviously scripted move.

Keith let her go and fetched himself a beer.

Alberto arrived with a boom box, and a battle began between those who wanted it tuned to rock songs, versus country-western, or mariachi, or rap.

Keith wandered, trying to keep from exploding. He played volleyball, then touch football. Emily and company seemed always to choose a game he was not involved in.

Ben egged him into a bike race. The road began near the pavilion and coursed down a slight decline, through a thick tunnel of trees and underbrush, curving at last into a semi-circle on the well-worn forest floor.

A creek fed a small pool surrounded by felled trees that had been carved into benches. A group of cyclers sat there already, passing a joint around.

"Sorry," Ben said with a sheepish shrug. "I never pass up good weed." He climbed off his bike and joined them.

Keith started back, wishing he had brought his car. Thick cedars and oaks created an opaque green roof above the road. Absently, he felt Ernesto's locket through his jeans pocket. Did the boy ever feel this way?

Rounding the large bend near the bottom of the road, he slammed on the brakes. Branwyn and Lionel were walking together, unmistakably holding hands, but they jumped back, separating, when he almost ran between them.

"Ola, Lionel. Hi, Branwyn." They made a strange couple—but cute, in a way.

Her eyes were wide, as if she were looking for a place to run, but Lionel feigned coolness. "Ola, Gringo. This lady wanted to see the trees."

"I needed an escort," she added.

"*Muy bien*," was all Keith managed to say.

When Branwyn blushed, she became irresistible. Lionel looked--well, happy.

Emily and Mary disappeared at one point, and did not return until later when Keith played hide-and-seek with the Thieu kids. When enough burgers and sausages were ready, employees lined up to fill their plates. Once, Keith caught Emily staring. She looked away and made a point of sitting down to eat with her friends.

Games resumed, and weary employees stretched out in the long shadows under the trees as locusts beckoned the

night with their buzzing. Nosma and Katy laughed over
Arkie's stories of the old days. There were arguments about
whose salad tasted best. Bikes stood in rows just off the gravel
road, like horses tethered for the night.

"This is a good group," Chef Thomas said, holding his
beer aloft.

"Bullshit—we just have a good boss," Ben replied.

"To the *Patron!*" Cisco toasted.

"The *Patron!*"

Thomas bowed. "*De nada,*" he said. "But now we're
going to have to work hard to pay for all this."

Moans echoed through the camp.

"So what's with you and Emily?" Ben sat down, beer in
hand and toothpick in teeth.

"You tell me."

"Did you piss her off?"

Keith could only shrug and watch. She seemed to be
working hard to have a good time. A campfire leaped to life
and the party entered a new stage. The Thieus took their leave,
followed by the ladies behind the lines.

Nosma ambled past, squeezing Keith's shoulder as she
did. "I'm gonna get out of here before they start tellin' ghost
stories."

"If they do that, I'll go with you," Keith said.

"Bull." She turned around. "You pro'ly be the one tellin'
'em." She climbed into her car with a saucy laugh.

The night sky slowly sparked to life, brilliant over the
park clearing.

"Look, a shooting star," Julie called out.

"There's another."

"Idiots," Charlie yelled. "Those are lightning bugs."

Patricio produced a guitar and the young Mexicans
danced whirling jigs around the campfire. The waiters joined
in.

"C'mon," Charlie shoved Keith from behind. "Let's take
a ride."

Ben and others took off on bikes, fading out like
specters as they moved down the unlit gravel road, away from

the pavilion lights. Keith stayed put, sipping yet another brew, and laughing in spite of his mood when he heard the sick sound of bikes sliding on the gravel, followed by the scraping of metal against metal.

"Goddam!" The Wop's voice boomed out of the darkness.

He watched Emily, her face all the more striking in the campfire light, and his fingers traveled into his pocket. The locket was still there. No, Ernesto could never have made it to this point, could he? Too young to feel the cruelty of women. Too young to be the fool that Keith, himself had become. Still, maybe the boy's memory had something to say. Life was too short. This could go on no longer.

With sure steps, he advanced on her clique of giggling friends. She tried to duck his gaze, then faced the inevitable. All eyes seemed to be turning toward them, and maybe some voices grew quiet. He spoke over a wailing accordion on the boom box.

"Hi." His voice held a definite edge.

"Hi," she answered shakily.

"Take a bike ride with me."

Their gazes locked.

"OK."

She followed him to the line of bikes and found her own. He picked one at random.

"Where are we going?" she asked.

"This way," he nodded toward the woods. Thankfully, she followed.

Keith led, glancing back to see Emily bathed in the pavilion lights, until the dark shadows of the trees swallowed her. He squinted, barely able to see the white roadbed ahead. The gravel crunched, spewing puffs of chalk dust from their tires. Then the pavilion disappeared behind the trees entirely, and they were free agents.

"You there?" He called back.

"Yeah. Hard to see the road," Emily said, sounding exasperated. "How can we keep from winding up in a ditch?"

The downward slope took over and it was no longer necessary to pedal. They glided slowly, weightlessly, and, as if the forest had heard her complaint, tiny flashes started exploding in the branches above them.

"Wow," Emily said. The lights multiplied, like a cold fire spreading on a wind of cricketsong. Within moments, they were coasting through a high-ceilinged tunnel lit by a million blinking lightning bugs. The explosion of tiny lanterns did not really illuminate the road, but the contrast improved the going.

"Christ, did they all wake up at the same time?" Keith wondered aloud.

He guessed they were almost halfway down, and no other bikers could be heard on this part of the road. It had to be now. He stopped, and Emily scraped to a halt just in time to avoid smashing into him. Here, the lightning tunnel stretched in both directions, like a magic corridor in some sweet dream. Her face remained in shadow, but he could feel her warmth.

Carefully, he gripped her bike, walking them both until he could toss them onto the top of a low cedar bush. She made no protest. He had composed a long speech, one that would cover all of her possible anxieties, but the words failed and all became feel. Her lips were scalding, and they stumbled, out of breath, backwards into the brush.

Poison oak, scorpions, even snakes might be waiting on the forest floor, but that did not seem important. Prickly leaves crunched under them as he pulled her clothes away and felt her burning skin against his own. They joined, and everywhere he touched her became a hot refuge from the chill night.

The lightning bug nebula reflected in her eyes, and her soft moans, along with the deafening roar in his ears, drowned out the thumping of the distant boombox. She kissed him hard, squeezing him tightly, seeming every bit as hungry for this as he. Finally, it was over and they lay still in the forest peat.

He traced her thigh, stomach, breasts, with a finger.

"It tickles." She laughed and pulled him over her for warmth. Bikes barreled down the road, only yards away, spitting gravel that landed near their feet.

"They either have eyes like owls or they're totally bombed," Keith whispered.

"Sorry I acted like such a creep," Emily said.

"Forget it."

"I--I saw him. I thought you were playing a trick."

"Saw who?"

"That man." She kissed his neck. "The one in the tuxedo who broke up the fight."

"What? You saw him?" Keith almost yelled. He sat up, only to have her pull him down again.

"Quiet." Voices passed at a slower pace. Walkers.

He whispered. "You actually saw him? Where?"

"In Brownwood."

"What the hell was he doing in Brownwood? Is it some real guy? Does he--"

"If you'll shut up, I'll tell you." She laced her fingers behind his neck. "I thought you sent him to check up on me. You know, like he was some friend of yours and this was all a gag." She thrust a hand over his mouth. "Wait."

She suffered a kiss, then resumed. "I knew it wasn't a joke when I looked into his eyes. He scared me to death. Still, I guess I decided to take it out on you. I didn't want to think I was having hallucinations, too.

"When I saw you today, somehow I knew all that stuff you told me about, the tree, the puppets — all of it might be part of a shared psychosis or something. Or, it might really have happened. That made me even madder."

"Are you sure it was him?"

"Keith, those eyes--I thought I was dying. He was this close." Her grip tightened.

"What were you doing when you saw him?"

"We were sitting in the car and he appeared in the headlights, staring for a moment, as if he had to make sure it was me. Then he came at us very quickly. We screamed bloody murder. Kristen barely got the car started, and when she turned around to leave, he shoved his hand inside the window on my side. I almost called the police. You know what this is?"

She gazed downward, her voice shaking.

"Why didn't you call the cops? What do you mean?"

"It's the power of suggestion. A really strong, transferred hallucination. It's the only possible explanation. I'm thinking about talking it over with Professor Durban. At least ask him if he's heard of something this vivid before." She shook her head. "It was real, Keith. He was real. I don't want to be crazy. I don't want you to be crazy."

"Forget telling your professors. Can you come over tomorrow?" He kissed her.

"Maybe. But we've got to confront this, Keith. Don't you see? I've caught some touch of whatever you've got. Psychological diseases can't be transmitted –"

Maybe she felt him jerk. She looked down.

"I don't believe it, Emily. You really think I'm crazy."

Flustered. "No, no. I swear, Keith. That's not what I'm saying. Or – if you're crazy, I am, too. I don't – look, I can't explain everything. I don't have a graduate degree."

He wrapped his arms back around her. "It's OK. I might have doubted myself before Laredo. But there's a big world of other things out there, Sweetheart. Things your precious science can't explain. I guess I knew that in high school, but maybe I forgot--"

"Of course it can't be explained. But I'm going to try. There has to be some sentinel event that causes this sort of thing."

"Explain it tomorrow. In bed." He kissed her, and they both rose, groping for their clothes. Emily's bra remained elusive for some time, much to Keith's enjoyment.

"Here it is." He found it in a small tree.

"Give it to me. Hurry, I hear voices."

"No," he teased. "First, one more kiss."

"You're a monster. And you're trying to dodge the subject."

"No, I'm not." They retrieved their bikes and started

walking them through the tunnel of fairy lights. "Start from the top. Where were you when it happened, and are you sure your friend Kristen saw him?"

"Yes, she saw him. That's the thing that blows a hole in my theory. We went out to see *Jane*."

"Another friend?"

She laughed. "You never heard of Jane before? I'm sorry, I've been there so many times, I take it for granted."

"Jane's an *it*?"

"Not a person. Well, she *was* a person, back in the forties and fifties. Her husband had money--some banker or rancher or--"

Screams and scraping tires interrupted, then faded.

"Anyway, Jane died. Her husband was so distraught, he moved to town and never came out of his house, except at night. Right next to the town cemetery. For like a year, neighbors heard him building something in the dark--"

"A memorial to her?"

"Good boy," she teased. "He built these short walls in a big circle, with a curving driveway running inside, just big enough for a car. In the middle, he constructed huge concrete letters--almost as tall as a man, J-A-N-E."

"Concrete letters? That's all?"

"Not just cement. He mixed in little stones and chips of quartz and big pieces of broken beer bottles, all sticking out of the top and sides so that it all glistens if you shine your headlights on it. But if you touch the letters, you'll get cut. It's a hang-out for young people in Brownwood."

"So Poindexter was standing around those letters?"

"Staring."

"At JANE?"

"At first, then he was staring at me. I recognized him — I thought — and almost had a heart attack. I had been thinking about what you told me all week."

"Did he mean to hurt you? Did he talk? Say anything?"

"Don't know. I was too scared. I think he said something, but I was panicked. He was moving — weirdly, like he didn't have complete control over his muscles."

"That's Poindexter."

She drew closer. "I was going to call you this morning, but I had a bizarre dream last night. He was there – somewhere – and he told me to take you away. That's all he said. 'Take him away.' And I knew he meant you. By the time I woke up, I was really upset — at you, I guess." Her face sank into his shoulder. "Sorry."

A loud crash came from up the slope. "Damn," a voice yelled. Other expletives followed.

Hair stood up on Keith's neck. No mistake – he knew that voice. He gripped Emily – almost too hard – a whisper, "Did you hear him? I know who that is."

"Stop, Keith. You're scaring me."

"It's that fucking cowboy. Shit."

"Who?"

Whispering. His heart beat like a hammer on an anvil. "The one from the bar, for God's sake."

"Over there. If he's down in the circle, you have to forget it--" Clear, too. *The second cowboy.*

"My God. They came in a pack," Keith said.

"Forget, hell--"

In the hazy glow of dust kicked up by the bicycles, shadows moved. They weren't coming this way. Yet.

"Shh. Quiet." He guided Emily toward a tall cedar bush – something scraped, close in – he looked over his shoulder –

Grunts. A bike clanged to the gravel. Short breaths -- unmistakable sounds of a struggle. The bodies — whoever they were, came tumbling closer on the ground, just off the road.

"Keith--" She let him push her back against a tree trunk.

"Shh. I can't see how many there are." Keith hunkered down. Did all three of the bastards come out to wreck the picnic?

"Hey!" The voice again. A dull thud — more blows falling.

"Son of a--" Keith's arms came up automatically for protection – but the shadow didn't fall toward him. Twisted away, instead huffing, jumping.

A cry of pain, and the cedars shook, the oaks rattled, sending lightning bugs swarming, twirling into a circular cloud, like a mini-tornado. Through the sparks, the shadow retreated — stumbling across the road, bent over like a cripple. The hat - that white cowboy hat - was the final proof.

"It's him," Keith whispered. A sudden wind blasted the trees high up, crashing branches together, scattering even larger clouds of fireflies. A push back to cover Emily — "Look—" he started to say, then froze.

Up the middle of the road, kicking gravel, then smashing into the brush - the form stopped, just long enough for Keith to catch the shape of her face. In the hoar-fire of the bugs, his gaze locked with hers for an instant—Carlotta, her eyes reflecting a million lights.

It was as if his muscles had gone on strike. Movement was impossible - until she looked away.

With a lightning-fast turn, she vanished into the woods on the far side, perhaps chasing that cowboy.

"It's—" He coughed, unable to finish. Had Emily seen?

Another volley of scraping, and heavy footsteps pounding across the gravel. Swirls of dust melded with the blazing bugs. Keith bent over, coughed violently, kept his head low. The noise of the thrashing bodies faded into the woods on the far side.

"It was the cowboy," he said, almost choking.

This was a nightmare. How could such a perfect moment twist into Hell itself? The cowboy was here, with blood in his mind, and how on Earth could Keith beat him - especially if the other two were covering his flanks?

He shook, asked her to repeat her words --

"I saw."

"Someone must be chasing him. Maybe John saw him."

"It wasn't John," she answered with assurance.

"Then who? Did you see? Did you see everything?"

Emily's hand dug into his arm so firmly, he thought it might stop his circulation. "Don't talk about it, Keith. Take me back. Now."

The forest up and down the gravel road had become a scary chorus of shouts — bikers warning to stay clear of the race that dozens - it seemed - had joined.

"This might be our chance," Keith said, shivering. He pulled their two bikes off the flat bush, and motioned for her to hug the road's edge.

Still whispering, though no one would have heard them over the hilarious screams –

"I don't know what the hell is going on, but don't let it spoil what happened, OK?"

"Shh." She pulled up behind him, took his face in her hands and kissed him. "Just take me home, and don't talk about it right now."

They emerged from the forest cover, out onto the wide lawns, and he looked back down through the remarkable tunnel of lights. She squeezed his hand.

Alberto's face lit up as they neared the campfire. "Ohhh, Gringo-o," he taunted.

They joined the clean-up, which was in full swing. Keith found Thomas and Ben chatting, putting out the grill fires.

"Did you see them?" he said, still out of breath.

"Who?" Ben wielded a bucket of water.

"We heard a fight. I swear those cowboys were down in the woods. Somebody kicked their asses. I thought it might be you and John."

Thomas scowled.

"Hell, no, but I will kick them if those jokers are anywhere near here. Want me to look around?" Ben volunteered. Together, their gazes drifted over to John, who seemed thoroughly sloshed on a picnic bench, putting the make on Lydia. Thomas's eyes rolled.

"I'll take some of the waiters," Ben said. "That goombah couldn't beat a fly right now." He and his posse set off on bicycles.

A Spanish guitar began from the boom box. Thomas leaned back, returning his attention to the pocket puzzle he was working.

"How do you see that in this light?" Emily asked.

"Can't really," Thomas answered without looking up. "I do this mostly one by feel, I guess."

"Have you always liked those little games?" Keith asked.

"Mmmm." A smile. "I guess I didn't really have many toys when I was little."

"That's sad," Emily said.

"Not really," the chef spoke slowly, focusing. "'Cause now I still like playing. I haven't used it all up." A nod demanded silence. "There."

He held the small disc for them to see: a tiny silver ball sat in each eye of a cartoon gorilla, another one in the palm of the beast's hand, and one on each foot. The ape sat on a unicycle, arms and legs splayed in a balancing act.

They applauded.

"Come on, assholes," John called, wavering even as he held Lydia's delicate hand in his huge fist. He let her go with a kiss and began supervising the loading of bikes into the van. Those remaining would have to fit into several cars.

Keith took Emily's hand. "Can you spend the night?"

"Can I leave my bike in the van tonight?" she asked John.

"Babe," the Wop answered. "A beautiful dame like you can leave it there permanently."

From inside the van, Keith gazed back at the pavilion through clouds of chalk dust kicked up by the tires. Now Thomas was sitting atop a table, flanked by waitresses.

He touched Emily, and pointed. "Look." Branwyn stood there in the dust, a lone figure by the campfire, arms closed around herself, against the chill. Lionel was nowhere to be seen.

CHAPTER 34
A SPELL, A SEDUCTION, A FIRESTORM

Lionel opened his eyes in the dark – yet he could see everything clearly. A soft, milky light. He was still dreaming. Held his breath as he scanned the room, waiting for – whatever had awakened his spirit body – she sat in a chair, simply watching him sleep, as a lover would. At least, he had heard stories of that…

Still not daring to inhale – squelching the jolt that rumbled up his body. In Mexico, he had never been able to keep the spell. When he woke in dreams, the elation of it always jarred him awake for real. But here, in Sironia, by the river, he had somehow learned to hold on –

He opened his mouth to speak. The beautiful princess blinked. Her gaze sucked him in. She wasn't here as a lover. Reflected in her eyes, he saw again the scenes of her suffering when she was alive. He was beginning to learn – but didn't we all suffer? Was her own life horrible enough to trap her in wood?

Then came the fire – he reached out to take her hand, console her – finally, the spell popped.

He shook his real head, chilled by the night air. "Patience, my love. Not long now," he whispered the words to the ceiling, then rose and got dressed.

When Alberto honked, he went out. Swifts twisted and turned, diving in a unified dance in a cloudless sky. An outstanding omen. Today was the day. Would Carlotta be ready? Was that why she came? To remind him?

Chavo and Patricio cut up, as usual, on the trip to the park. Would they act like such children if they knew of the ordeal that lay before him?

What if Branwyn didn't come to the picnic? She must. The air, the hopeful smell of the morning flowers, everything his senses touched oozed with the promise — the Grandfathers would let it happen.

Succeeding in this, the most precarious funneling of the forces of the Universe, would mean he had graduated above his teacher. He would become like the ones who came before, long ago. At least in ability.

No pride in that. No ego. He would be happy to put down his spells and live simply from now on. Maybe return to Mexico to a small farm. With Carlotta at his side, he would care only for this world, no other.

Remember. You may be a spirit, but you are also a farmer. You must plow this world, and eat of the fruits it gives you, Uncle told him.

As always, though, his happy thoughts scattered like quail when the heaviness of the task at hand returned. A deep breath. He must still procure Branwyn's vow to surrender. She must say the words — clearly, to the cosmos at large, let her voice echo through every realm. Once that was done, magic would take care of the rest.

"The words of humans," Uncle used to say, "carry more weight than one might imagine."

He thought of Branwyn, that time in the storage room, when she was so sweet. Her kiss muddled his memory, but he was certain she understood. Her inner wish to fly from her mortal shell shone from her eyes.

Once the decision was made, things would go easily for her. Uncle had demonstrated to him time and again how normal aspects of life always move out of the way when confronted with endeavors as novel as the transfer of souls. That same moment, however, would herald excruciating suffering for Carlotta. For Lionel, too. All of their resources would be taxed immeasurably, for entering this life was always painful, no matter how it was done. Until she gained her bearings, his job would be that of midwife to her soul. A daunting challenge, but she was worth it.

But why had she refused to answer his call these many days? *Peace,* the voices whispered. She was only hiding from her master.

At the picnic, Lionel got caught up in the festive mood, the music, the smells. It reminded him of market day in the village near Uncle's.

Chavo cajoled him into different games. In short glances while he played, he watched Branwyn. Thanks to God, she had come, and had never looked more radiant. When he went to get a soft drink, she approached him.

"Hey, Lionel, I don't think volleyball is your game."

He laughed with her. By now, he had practiced the correct phrasing of the question a thousand times. But how to get her alone?

"Come on, they're having a three-legged race," she said excitedly. He let himself be pulled across the smooth lawn, feeling every pulse of her blood. How could the hand of another feel so alive?

Branwyn deftly tied her right leg to his left. Other couples laughed and fell down. He tried to hop, nearly fell, but she grabbed and held him up. White teeth and freckles. A smile that vied with the sun for a claim to the day. Then she gave him the lightest of hugs. The kiss in the storage room came to mind. *No. Don't. You must follow your destiny*, he told himself with closed eyes.

"Hey, Lionel," Thomas yelled from the sidelines, "try to keep your mind on the race." Laughter.

"Don't go too fast, *tu cabrones,*" Manuel called.

"Come on, catch them," Branwyn screamed. The other couples bounded ahead, and he hopped, mesmerized by the sheer electricity pouring into his leg from hers.

He stepped too wide and Branwyn tripped. Down she went, taking him along. Colors swirled as they rolled--green, blue, the yellow of her shirt. Against his will, his body came to rest on top of hers. For an instant, he could not move, his hips pressing down. From beneath her shirt, two mounds pushed up against his chest, her heart pounding inside. He jumped up quickly, gasping for air.

"Whoa, Lionel. Why don't you lie down and rest?" Thomas called. More laughter.

"That was fun," she said as he helped her up. She loosened the rope that joined them.

"There is something we must talk about," he heard himself say automatically.

"OK." She gripped his hand and led him across the grass toward the trees.

It was happening. The spirits were paving the way.

What would the others think, seeing them going together into the bushes? Once Carlotta came over to the living, the opinions of others would not bother him.

They picked their way through the trees, then down the road. His mind was a swirl of feelings, waves of yearnings and dizzy glimpses that would not let up. She was speaking, her voice lilting up and down in such a lively manner. About her job, her hopes and dreams. As he suffered her small talk, he rehearsed his own speech, focusing vigorously through the fog in his head and the convulsing of his stomach.

She smelled like something—strange flowers and limes. Huge chalk rocks lined parts of the roadway, and when she occasionally stepped up, balancing on them like a dancer, her hand squeezed around his all the more tightly. Too much—there was too much data for his mind to take in.

What was happening? A true magician would be wary—stop the whole process the instant he felt things going off-track. But to stop meant to lose Carlotta, didn't it? There would never be a better chance. But Branwyn—what would happen to her after the transfer? For the first time, he admitted to himself that he could not be sure.

Worse—out of the morass of swirling colors inside his head, Uncle's raspy voice kept echoing. Too far away to make out the words, but he knew the old man was squawking, parroting his eternal and dire warnings about the beyond: "At the moment of crossing celestial boundaries, one is attacked by *toll-takers*, natural forces from many realms who will join to

stop the transfer of souls. Only the strongest magicians can
endure such a battle and still achieve their goals."

His blood pumped to the boiling point under his skin.
My God, would he be strong enough to execute a maneuver
that required total control over two worlds at once? Why
hadn't he spent more time preparing?

Bikers on the gravel yelled to them, and Branwyn
colored in embarrassment.

"My mother is weird about these things," she said. "She
would go crazy if she thought I was interested in anyone
who's not rich. That, and--well..." He knew. In spite of that,
after more walking, they left their fingers together when
others passed.

"One day, I'll have a big house. With a big yard. Maybe
an orange tree," Branwyn said, swinging her other arm. "Is
that what you want, too?"

It sounded nice. "I like dogs," he said.

"Oh, I do, too. Do you have one?"

"Not now. When I was small. A very small one--named
Chacho. You know, from *muchacho*?"

"Oh, he sounds cute. Did he die?"

That horrible childhood afternoon swam back, through
the colors, from so many years ago. Mean Mr. Vargas raised
his stick and brought it down again and again. The poor pooch
screamed, and Lionel saw his body go limp. His father was too
drunk to wake up. When he did, he only scolded Lionel, and
said that no one gave Mr. Vargas problems. He was too
powerful in the town. The day was hot, and the night hotter.
Lionel lay on the cool kitchen floor, watching the setting sun
in the whiskey bottle as his father slowly emptied it. That
night, without Chacho to snuggle up to, he had bad dreams. In
the morning, the house filled with people who said that Mr.
Vargas was dead. Then they took his father away, and he
never came back.

They left the road and found a soft place in the loam. They talked for a long time as the light faded from the sky patches in the trees.

"We're not rich," Branwyn said. "But my mother always wanted me to be in high society."

"Is that why you are tired of life?"

"Hmm? Yeah, I'm sick and tired. All she thinks of is being in the bridge club, going to society functions. Showing off clothes she can't afford. She thinks she's a failure because we're not wealthy. She makes me and my sister miserable."

"You would be happy in another life?" He had to press on, move toward the goal, though her bubbly movements and wan smiles made it so much harder to ask her this.

She smiled. "Tell me about this new life you keep talking about. Would I like it? I don't need to be rich. I just need a house. The house can be simple. Big, in case I have a lot of kids. You know? But plain, sturdy. Mom always whines because she doesn't live in a brick house. I would be happy with wood."

Lionel whooped in victory, though he meant to stay silent.

She giggled. "What I mean is, it's better to be poor and have someone whom you really love--"

Then she was very close, and she took other hand, as well. Smells of woodsmoke drifted through the trees. The wind had changed and dusk arrived. His breath came in short gasps. She was so very ready. What could he say next?

Closer. Her lips found his and the colors inside became a fireworks show. No—this was not in the script. Who was making this happen? Were these the fingers of the toll takers?

They rolled in the brush, kissing so hard they were forced to stop for breath.

"It's okay, this time," she said, a frightened look in her eyes. She placed his hand on one of her bulging breasts.

"Do you--" he panted, still trying to recite what was prescribed by ritual, "--want me to take you to the other world?"

"Yes." He heard her answer, but the tide crashed over him again, breaking down the careful walls to his heart, unleashing every forbidden desire. She tugged. He rolled onto her. The dark landscape tumbled, and he fumbled his way into a place where—obviously—neither he nor Branwyn had ever been before.

They were separate, and moist, and on fire. Then came a sound of fluttering, and crickets, bugs, and birds, and suddenly they were one, flexing, and hotter than the sun. They moved together, instinctively riding wave after wave, smothering each other until the faraway laughter and music became a single, deafening hum.

He was sunk—immersed in a deep ecstasy no one had ever predicted. Even hinted at. The hum became silence. Pulses of silence, like air bubbles rising from deep water, each bursting as it hit the surface, releasing her moans of perfection. Still, in the instants of deafness, a recondite voice nagged to be heard: *Stop--Do not let the building blocks of a lifetime crumble to satisfy one moment of hunger.*

Drunkenly, from sheer rote, Lionel began to sing.

Branwyn's body lurched when the first words came, but she relaxed under his caresses. He cast the spell from memory, chanting it perfectly, mesmerized by the feel of her sweating skin.

Visions flashed through his being, memories of Branwyn working diligently at her tables, laughing at him when he clowned. Her perfume tangled with the smell of cedar. His hands played on her, inside her, leading her spirit out. Chanting. Chanting. Her body squeezed him and made his head swim.

With bleary eyes, he glanced skyward, and was shocked: the trees appeared to burn with thousands of blinking candles. Something moved, on one side of their tiny bed of leaves. The little lanterns exploded in a bush that was previously dark.

No! It could not be. From behind the coldly blazing bushes, a beast extended its huge head. The whitish scars that stretched along one side of its neck made the monster

unmistakable: the dragon marionette had been brought to life
and grown ten-fold. Had Lionel used the wrong chant?

The wind rose, stars flashing on and off behind a great
flapping of wings. In torrents, the tiny blinking lights gushed
out of dragon's gaping naw. *The dragon's fire.*

"What is it, darling?" Branwyn's voice drifted up softly.

He could only watch as the beast mounted the air on a
whirlwind. It moved into the trees, broke out into a patch of
sky. The size and power of the beast turned Lionel's body
cold. Higher, toward the clouds the winged lizard climbed,
and now he could see the terrible leprechaun perched on its
neck, driving it, up, up.

Dios mio, Lionel cursed himself. These were the toll-
takers. The leprechaun craned his neck, gazing earthward –
looking – for what?

From the other side, shadows darted through the
burning bushes. He recognized the shape of one--Carlotta.

"No," he screamed.

"Kiss me," said a voice below him. Branwyn's spirit still
hovered in that beautiful body, not Carlotta's.

In the sky, the dragon belched another universe of
stars, and began to descend. Of course – the leprechaun was
here to recapture Carlotta!

"Carlotta," he screamed. In one motion, he disengaged
and ran through a myriad of little lanterns – chasing the
shadow into which his lover had flitted.

"Wait. Don't go." Branwyn's voice came from the earth,
but he ran, crashing through trees and bushes that tried to
snatch him, slow him down.

"Come back, Carlotta. Your new body is here." Almost
to the perimeter of the road, he fell headlong. A vine had laced
itself around his ankle and would not let go.

Whop--whop--the great wings stirred the air above him.
With a roar, the dragon lit the entire road with fireflies. Lionel
tugged but could not free himself.

A black form emerged from the brush, came crashing
down atop him, knocking out all his breath. Shadows

scampered this way and that. More toll-takers? He felt the leg of a man across his back.

The heavy body jumped off, and Lionel rolled, instinctively. When he looked up, a jolt passed through his body. Carlotta stood in the middle of the road, arms raised. The little gentleman came from around her side, rushing toward their shadowy attacker.

"*Mi amor*," Lionel screamed. The damned vine not only held him – it was trying to pull him back into the trees!

Blows fell. Carlotta's voice rattled something in a language strange – and haunting. The little gentleman raised his cane—once, twice, the loud *cracks* sounding like thunder. Fireflies scattered, and a body crashed down into the gravel.

Lionel scrambled to his feet, but another shadow appeared. Before he could dodge, it slugged him in the stomach. Down again, choking on clouds of dust.

Then the two shadows were together, swinging huge fists. The little gentleman parried with his cane. Carlotta waved her hands, weaving the dust around their heads—the shadowy monsters couldn't see – A voice cursed angrily, and the cane smashed into them again.

Then silence. Lionel panted. He could hear the boom box, singing from another world. Then a moan, and the sound of something being dragged on the gravel. Carlotta and her friend started to give chase.

"*Mi amor*," Lionel called out.

She stopped halfway across the road, and turned, her ravishing shape illuminated by the bugs.

"Up there," he warned.

More burning bugs rained down. Again, the wind came, a gale sending them every which way, like shooting stars. She looked up at the very instant the dragon's gigantic form dove, directly above her.

Carlotta and the little gentleman broke across the gravel into the trees. The flying lizard's great mouth snapped, but missed. The vine let go and Lionel ran after their shadows.

"Carlotta!"

But the dragon was in the trees, huge eyes blazing like streetlights, casting an eerie darkness over the trees and bushes, a green glow that fought with the yellow of the bug lights. The Serpent belched, sending a thick curtain of the tiny lanterns across Lionel's path. In the firestorm, Carlotta's form shivered, then disappeared. The air rang with diabolical laughter, cloaked in wind. He knew who it was.

"No," Lionel scraped through the sharp limbs and leaves. "Please, Jesus," he prayed, "bring her back."

He dove onto his belly in the clearing and grabbed, but a swirl of dark shadows hovered above him. He crawled, through the shining bugs, under a bush — she was there. Out on the grass, Carlotta's unmistakable form huddled with the little gentleman's. Lionel advanced, on hands and knees.

"*Mi amor*," he cried.

He reached, but a great wind blasted, throwing him into the dirt. A million tiny lights, swirling, swirling. He screamed, but it was too late. The tornadic wind ceased, the swarm of fireflies receded, and only dust and dark leaves remained in the air, floating specks against the stars.

He rose again to his knees, clawing forward with his fingers. A single glistening in the grass caught his eye. He picked it up, holding it this way and that, straining to see in the darkness. Then a ray of light hit it — the moon was just peeping over the horizon. No. How many times he had fingered this relic while sweeping the attic — it was a button from Carlotta's ancient blouse. She was gone.

Far away, the wailing boombox came back to life. He looked up, trying to spot the demon lizard against the stars, but he could only see the bugs, streaks of fire made blurry by his tears.

"You were right, Uncle," he cried, falling to his knees, sobbing. "The toll-takers are very powerful."

CHAPTER 35
THE MONKEY HOUSE

For many mornings after the picnic, Emily came over, woke Keith up, and they made love. Keith didn't really like working evenings, but this was a luxury he could never have afforded at the Agency.

Afterward, they lay luxuriously in his bed, debating what to fix for lunch, and chatting about the future. Her plans to teach. His lack of any real plan. It had been several days, and he decided to risk bringing it up: "Tell me again about that night. You know, when you saw Poindexter."

Her mood shifted abruptly. "That's not me, Keith. I don't dwell on things in the past that can't have any possible effect on my future. It was the power of suggestion, or—I don't know what. I thought about it for a while, but I made myself stop."

She snuggled into his arms. "This is too good. All that other stuff is over. You haven't had any more of those dreams, have you?"

He glanced over. Ernesto's locket lay next to his watch on the end table. "No." It might be a lie.

"I still think you had a touch of trauma, from losing your job and everything," she said. "People get the mistaken impression that they are their jobs. That's not healthy."

The dreams had continued, he realized, but with less urgency than before. Some nights, it even worried him when the dream didn't come.

He remembered floating above the wagon each time, and the malevolent glare of the old driver, Larcinter. They seemed only smudges in the night now. His hand traveled across space and he fingered the locket. It was true — Emily was saving him from Ernesto's fate.

As he drove to work that afternoon, he wondered if he could ask her to move in with him. But a teacher — even a starting salary — dwarfed what he was making at the restaurant.

Nosma's great grin accosted him when he arrived. The shifts had become confused since the reopening, and she was now staying well past lunch each day, until Katy relieved her just before the dinner rush.

"I'm not late am I?"

"You're early if you come to eat. You're only late if you come to work."

Alberto laughed too loudly, his normal response when someone else got an upbraiding.

Nosma moved so ponderously, Keith wondered how she got more work finished than he did. It was as if she somehow squeezed time together. Her *piece de resistance* was her cream gravy and new potatoes. They included ample portions of butter, salt and pepper, garlic salt and monosodium glutamate (MSG).

"I don' like this stuff," she explained, holding up the MSG shaker. "Neither does Thomas, but he says sometimes people need to have their taste-buds woke-up."

Keith tasted the finished product and declared, "I'm going to get some of that for tonight."

Nosma leaned over. "I didn't hear, hon. You gonna *get you some* tonight?" Her deep brown eyes twinkled and she laughed her deep laugh.

Mr. Thieu pushed between them, loaded down with two trays for refrigerator under the stove. These held battered fish, breaded shrimp, and chicken fried steak – all ready for the deep fat fat fryer.

"There ain't enough o' him to feed my cat," Nosma whispered.

Mr. Thieu wore the thick eyeglasses associated with caricatures of World War Two Japanese. He and his wife miraculously managed to bring their six children out of Viet Nam with them, though rumor held that not all the kids were really theirs.

Keith followed the wiry man back into the prep room, where John launched into his regular taunting.

"Mr. Thieu! How are you?"

"Fine. Fine." He smirked at Keith and rolled his eyes.

"You go Viet Nam?" It was a question John asked every day while he chopped up beans for refrying.

Mr. Thieu grinned. "I go Viet Nam--they kill me."

Thomas laughed, standing at a dry processor, mixing his famed Shrimp Orleans spices. He winked. "Mr. Thieu! You have very pretty wife."

"My wife very pretty." The aged man giggled.

"Very young, Mr. Thieu. Maybe she need younger man."

"No. She no need."

"Oh, yes. Young man," Thomas insisted. "Maybe she needs a young man like Keith."

"No, no," Mr. Thieu grinned broadly and waved a butcher knife at Keith. "You no like."

Keith choked on a laugh, and changed the subject. "Mr. Thieu, you lived in Mexico?"

"Live Mexico one year."

Alberto passed on his way to the walk-in freezer. Keith pointed as he disappeared into the smoking cold. "Alberto lives there," he said.

"He monkey." Mr. Thieu pointed, just as Alberto emerged again. He giggled uncontrollably.

"Ehh," Alberto replied, "You monkey."

"I no monkey. You monkey."

"No, you monkey." Alberto stopped in the doorway.

"You monkey — " Mr. Thieu pantomimed a monkey scratching under his arms, and pointed toward the freezer, " — and that monkey house."

"Ehh." Alberto wielded his vegetable packs, as if he would throw them, then headed back to the line.

Arkie, the old and frail neighbor of Nosma, stopped Keith at the doorway. "Can you get me one of those big buckets of butter?" She asked Keith.

"Sure, ma'am." Keith retrieved one from the walk-in cooler, and carried it to the pastry line.

"How you doin', girl?" Anna asked, when they rounded the corner.

"Just fine," Arkie said in her quiet singsong. "Got me a helper."

After she scooped out the amounts needed for the three different pans of cake icing, Keith lugged the bucket back to the cooler, marveling at how the people here worked as a team. Politics, petty squabbles were unknown. He remembered his days back at the agency. Long. Mind-numbing. If a copywriter was mad at an artist, projects might languish for days. The arrogance of wealth, Larry called it. Hell, Keith never felt wealthy at Elmer's. Though he made five times what he was making here.

But how much time would have to pass—if he took John's advice and stayed in the restaurant business—before he could make a salary that would rival Emily's?

The phone rang in the dark living room, just as Keith entered after work.

"Hey, big bro," Larry's voice boomed. "We need to talk about this ghost hunt. I've been brushing up on the fundamentals."

"Oh, shit. Are we still going to do that?"

"Re-reading some stuff. Here's one part we'd better not forget—listen—"

"Larry, can this wait? I'm going to call Emily."

"Don't be a spoil sport. We're going to have fun and you know it. Has anything else happened you're not telling me?"

"Not a thing. The whole thing's blown over. I think I had an overactive imagination."

"Stop it. Don't torture me. Listen to this--it's by Heider --you know, the *clairvoyant of Vermont*? If we ever chase a ghost, ever actually see one and follow it, we have to be very careful. Supposedly, Heider documents cases where people chased apparitions, and were lured across a special line, a boundary."

"I know. The boundary to the hereafter. We used to say that was the curb, and if we stepped out into the street, we would be dead. Blah, blah, blah. Look, Larry, I had those dreams. I came back. I'm no longer mentally disturbed, I'm thinking about asking a girl to move in with me?"

"What? Emily? No shit?"

"It'll never happen unless you get off the fucking phone."

"Keith--Keith, wait. This is serious. Think of how many people cross one of those boundaries every day — maybe they're chasing a ghost, or maybe being lured across, without knowing it — and never come back to tell the tale? Maybe that's what happens to everybody when they die."

"Which boundary? A ghost's, or asking someone to move in?" Keith stretched out on the couch. "We had this same conversation when I was fourteen. Didn't your clairvoyant-genius who wrote the book wind up in jail for drunk driving?"

"This stuff rings true, Keith. I'm just trying to warn us — you, especially. If we see anything, we have to make sure not to go past a certain point. It could be an optical illusion, we could walk off the staircase the wrong way — anything could happen."

"Listen, Larry, I think we should call it off. I'm getting bored with the whole thing."

"Well, we sure won't witness anything with you being so negative."

Keith sighed and gave up. "Ben's got an idea about when we should do it." If he thought of it like a sleepover back in high school, maybe he could stand it. They could have a few drinks and bullshit all night.

"Great! When?"

"Three or four weeks. I forget. The incidents have stopped, so we can just look through the joint on the run. How about thirty minutes, then go home? I'm not going to screw around all night."

"Oh God. You were more fun when you got all grown up in junior high, sourpuss. This may be the calm before the storm. You've forgotten everything you ever read about parapsychology, haven't you? That restaurant is a classic haunt, and supernatural entities can outlast humans. They never let up."

"Right." Keith put the phone down. The want ads lay on the table, and he hovered over them for a moment. Then he picked up a legal pad and tried to re-start the poem Emily had requested. It must be sensual, he decided. By the time he called her later, the first stanzas had been crossed out a dozen times, and his only success was in making himself horny.

CHAPTER 36
RIVER FESTIVAL

The flood delay had allowed summer to set in, making it the
hottest opening day for the River Festival that Keith could
remember. He parked in the Water Company lot, then took
Emily's hand to cross the car-choked side street to the ancient
gates of the Terrace estate.

The sound of an old-fashioned crank organ mixed with
smells of outdoor-cooked foods to cast a spell as they waded
into the crowds that spilled out of the striped tents on either
side of the makeshift midway.

Inside one of the craft booths, homemade wind chimes
clanked in an electric fan's artificial breeze. The proprietor, a
gray-haired hippie, excused the marketing gimmick. "It's too
damned hot for the wind to blow," he said with an
embarrassed smile. The hippie wife, clad in a homemade
peasant dress, twitched long crochet needles in a rocking
chair. It occurred to Keith that she might be right at home
among the mansion's original owners.

Pecan trees protected the midway from the sun. Taller
oaks and cottonwoods shielded the Terrace mansion, itself.
Milling fairgoers were a cross-section of Sironia — middle-aged
couples who looked to be right off the farm, yuppies in golf
shirts, scruffily dressed teenagers, and screaming kids,
swarming around the game booths set up just for them.

"This is great," Emily said, fingering the top of a
lacquered music box. "They don't have anything this quaint in
Dallas, where I grew up."

Keith shrugged. "It's mostly the same stuff for sale
every year." He put his arm around her as they strolled. "The
old mansion was just used for hoity-toity bridge clubs, until

the city ran out of money for its upkeep. So they started these money-raising festivals." He leaned closer, to whisper in her ear. "We've seen enough. Why don't we go to my apartment?"

"Hold on, tiger." She slapped his chest. "We haven't seen a third of the booths, and you said we would eat lunch here."

Great black pots hung from tripods in the manse's "back yard," bubbling out enticing aromas of the annual chili cook-off.

They bought enchiladas and sat down under the big cottonwoods near the art tent. Keith tried to mimic the art auctioneer's cadence, until Emily giggled.

"Shut up," she said, "I can't eat while you're making a fool of yourself."

A figure plopped down beside them.

"Branwyn," Emily exclaimed. "Did you come alone? You should have called. We would have given you a ride."

"A couple of the others were hanging around earlier," the busgirl said sheepishly.

"*Donde esta Lionel?*" Keith asked.

Emily threw a scolding look and Branwyn blushed.

"Don't know. I think he's mad at me. He's been weird lately."

"Weird bad or weird nice?"

"Keith, hush," Emily broke in. "Don't mind him, Branwyn."

"It's OK," Branwyn said. She fiddled with a snap on her overalls. "He's nice, but I guess being with him was doomed from the start, anyway.'

"Your mother?" Emily asked.

"Of course. He's a Mexican. Worse than that--he's a boy."

Keith laughed. "God forbid."

"Keith, can't you see she's upset?" She turned to Branwyn."Who knows? Things might change for the better."

"I doubt it," she said. "Besides, he's kind of strange." Keith watched her eyes, dancing and girlish, but always that undertone of sadness.

"Kind of?" he asked.

"But that's just what is so--*uhhnn*--about him." She said it. Then blushed.

"Uhhnn?" Keith looked to Emily for help. She laughed.

"Some things are just not meant to be, I guess." Branwyn sighed.

Emily's eyebrows raised. "And some things are."

Branwyn sat back, scanning the passing people. Between bites of enchilada, Keith watched her and drank in the atmosphere. Contrary to the old hippie's prediction, a warm breeze had started out of nowhere. The wind played in the hair of both women, the sounds of a fiddle and dulcimer lilted from the bandstand, and the dry cottonwood leaves scraped high abover them. Life was good.

At one point, Branwyn leaned forward and spoke confidentially, "He says the restaurant is alive." Another blush, but she was not too embarrassed to talk about it, obviously. "He says he wants me to stay late some night and listen to it *sing*. What do you think that means? Some come-on, huh?"

The hairs on Keith's neck rose. "That's the most bizarre come-on I've ever heard."

She shrugged. "I think I see one of my friends. Gotta go." She squeezed Keith's shoulder as she left, and he watched her progress down the midway. She met no one. It didn't matter. Today was too perfect to be spoiled by whatever superstitions guys like Lionel wanted to cling to. So far, ignoring all that shit seemed to be working.

"Can we leave now?" he asked when they stood up.

She pecked his cheek. "Let's go on the mansion tour," Emily insisted. "I've never been in there."

Keith moaned. "I'd rather give you a tour of my apartment."

"I've seen it." in reply. She slapped his leg and handed him her dirty paper plate.

While they stood in a long line, the dulcimer's pinging, mixing with the rustling of the tall cottonwoods, softened his irritation. Keith squeezed her close, and whispered in her ear.

"Do you know what I'm going to do to you if we ever do make it to my apartment?"

"Calm down, Keith, for God's sake." Another slap. "The tour won't take long."

At last, they stepped through the large front door, joining a group of twenty people or so.

"Hi, I'm Kelly Gilles, your guide for our tour of the Terrace Mansion today," a beaming young *debutante* said, brushing her hands across her full hoop skirt.

The cool air inside reeked of old closets. The opulence of the place seemed dimmer than Keith remembered from grade school, the rooms not a spacious, yet it all must have been gaudy a century-and-a-half ago when one of the five Sironian founding families built it in the middle of nowhere.

Neatly lettered signs denoted the few pieces of furniture that had survived from the original house. Antique carpeting had been removed after the flood.

"Some of it will be a total loss," Kelly Gilles explained through a pasted-on smile. "But don't worry. These old oak floors have survived worse, and we have dried them from above and below with hot lamps and fans."

That means there's a basement to this place, too, Keith thought. Instantly, he was tantalized by the idea of investigating this end of the tunnel that supposedly reached all the way to the Water Company basement.

Ms. Gilles recited the list of floods the structure had survived, but Keith's attention became riveted on an old brass hand-held telescope that lay on a mahogany desk, behind a thick velvet rope to keep trespassers out. Without warning, an urge made him step over the rope, grip the seeing device, and raise it to his eyes.

He pointed it through the aged window glass. Though the cheerful music and carnival noises continued outside, he could see none of the brightly colored tents out there. Only a few figures in a tranquil yard. He turned the scope's barrel, focusing.

The blood in his veins turned to ice. There, close-up and clear, he saw Larcinter, the man from near the bridge. The wagon driver.

He scanned the scope, following Larcinter's pacing, then opened the aperture for a wider view. The old man's jerky path traced an ellipse between two oaks. Carlotta and Poindexter were each lashed to one of the tree trunks, struggling against bindings that appeared to be their own marionette strings.

Instinctively, Keith stepped back, twisting the instrument again. Where was he looking? Who would stage such a scene? Zeroing in again on the face of Larcinter made the evil man look up. Those deep eyes leered, pulling somehow, tugging, as if their darkness hid invisible strings that went directly into Keith's churning stomach. He couldn't pull the glass away, felt himself starting to scream, but thoughts boomed into his head, projected by those wild, motionless eyes in that old man's head.

"Come home," they commanded.

"Please, sir!" Kelly Gilles's bodice blocked his view and she snatched the telescope away with no ceremony. "That's exactly why we have things roped off."

"Oh, sorry."

"You're lucky nothing broke," she said. "This belonged to the young master of the house himself and is irreplaceable."

"Why did you do that?" Emily whispered incredulously, after he stumbled back over the velvet rope.

"I'm sorry. It just sort of happened." He tried to smile. Now was not the time to tell her.

As the crowd shuffled toward the next room, he glanced back through the window. The edge of the bandstand, and several bright craft tents stood, clearly visible in the mottled sun and shade. No empty yard. No one bound to any trees.

"What's the matter?" Emily demanded in a whisper, as they followed the group up the stairs to the second floor. He licked his dry lips.

"Uh, something I ate, maybe." *No, that's not it--she won't come over if she thinks you're sick*. He took a deep breath, raised one of her hands and kissed it.

"Emily?"

"Yes?"

"It's not over. I saw the marionettes through that telescope. I didn't mean to — it just happened."

She took his hand, and practically dragged him behind the crowd, into the next room.

"Why do we get to talk about the spooky stuff only when you want to?"

When they stomped down the big entry stairway, and reached the ground, she walked so fast he could hardly keep up. Keith finally grabbed her arm and turned her around.

"Look, I'm sorry," he said. "I couldn't help--let's forget it. We don't have to say any more about anything."

"Oh, please, let's not." Emily shut her watery eyes and clung to him. "We've been doing fine, haven't we? We just have to hold on a little longer."

"A little longer? What a cryptic thing to say."

"All that nonsense is behind us. It has to be. I've been thinking. If those cowboys were really stalking us at the picnic, we should both just quit anyway. There's nothing supernatural about jerks. But they can be dangerous."

For a long moment, they stood there, inseparable. Long enough to make festival-goers stop milling, and look over at them. My God, was she shaking? "Emily, what you're saying is right. We can control it. Just ignore it and live our lives. We'll both be in new jobs before long, anyway. I hope. Now quit worrying and let's go home."

She looked up through tears, and tried to smile. Near the gate, they ran into Jack Conrad, head of Sironia's largest advertising firm. Keith knew him from the annual ad awards banquets.

"Keith Clayton, I'll be damned. Great to see you." He shook hands with more gusto than required. That's Jack, Keith thought, always eager for bystanders to think he had a big deal going. Emily and Mrs. Conrad were introduced.

"Hey, Keith, we were talking about you the other day. What are you doing now?" Jack's asthmatic wheeze had increased in volume since the last banquet.

"I'm cooking--over there." He pointed across the street.

"Well, that's fine." Not a flinch. "You always were a go-getter."

"Is your agency keeping busy?"

"Can't complain." Jack laughed. "Without your old boss Elmer as competition, it just keeps coming in the door."

"How's Bruce Hardy?" Bruce had served as Keith's mentor when he started at Elmer's firm.

"Bruce? Creative son of a bitch. He retired here last month. We're going to miss him."

"Too bad." Another handshake and the Conrads were off into the crowd.

"What a nerd," Keith said quietly. "Who else would wear a goddam suit to a River Festival?"

"Sounds like they might have an opening for a writer." Emily's eyebrows went up.

"Emily, he's the biggest creep in Sironia. Of all the agencies, his has the biggest turnover. I need a job, but not that badly." He did not mean it as harshly as it came out. "Right now, I'm happy just where I am." He hugged her.

"I didn't mean--"

"It's okay." They navigated through the crawling cars on the side street.

"Been writing lately? Where's my poem?" she asked.

"Working on it." He could hear her wheels turning.

"I've been scanning the teaching positions." Emily began, obviously trying a different tack.

Keith interrupted. "Do me a favor. Please? Let us have this afternoon just for us, OK?"

She seemed about to protest, but permitted a kiss.

He held her chin. "You don't get it, do you? I want you. When I'm in your arms, it's the one place the marionettes can't touch me."

"Shh." She put her finger to his lips. "I do get it. And I'll do almost anything, if you just promise not to talk about the puppets anymore."

He squeezed her hand and winked. "I can do that."

CHAPTER 37
CARLOTTA'S ADVICE

Lionel cursed in whispers and stomped on the hollow landing floor. It was clear the marionettes had again been tampered with. Who else would come up here in the darkness? He glanced toward Thomas's empty office. The *patron*?

He approached the beam between the Indians. Whoever it was had tangled the strings of Carlotta and the little man so badly that the knots might take hours to unravel.

"My love, why don't you come to me?" he asked as he tugged at the strings.

He passed the night in the basement cell, and chanted two candles' worth. Nothing. Though the leaded glass windows showed no brightness yet, his body told him that dawn was quickly approaching.

"I know you can hear me. Be patient and I will free you." He returned to the knots, glaring intermittently at the leprechaun. "One sign from you and I will take your wretched carcass down to the ovens." Peace, Uncle would say. There can be no flight of magic without a sober head.

His breathing quickened until his fingers faltered in the strings. *Santa Maria*. Tears came freely. Again, he could not achieve the concentration he needed to sort things out. That night in the woods — it would not leave his memory! He could still see Branwyn's face, looking up from the leaves on the forest floor, streaked with ecstasy. A true magician would never make such a mistake.

No good. The knots simply would not be undone. There were plenty of knives downstairs.

"A metal blade is good for nothing natural," Uncle's words resounded. "Use one made of stone."

"Enough, old man," Lionel said to the dark attic. Time was running out. He rose and stalked to the top of the circular stairway, then froze. Carlotta's vaporous form stood there, watching him from the shadows several steps below, just out of the glare of the light above Thomas' office.

"I am happy for you," she said. "You dodged the master well. You ignored my warnings, yet survived and fell in love. An amazing proof of your power, my grandmother would say."

He choked words out, "If I am in love, it is with you."

She seemed not to hear. Her gaze wandered, focusing this way and that into the dimness. "The master grows weaker every day you thwart him. He curses and conjures new magic, but can't defeat you. His flame grows thin."

"You are his prisoner again, my love." Lionel fell to his knees. "It's my fault. I was trying to cast the spell, but that woman – I know the Children of Rage came for me at the picnic. You and the little tuxedo man saved me – like you saved the Gringo."

Down one step. Another. Slow. She didn't retreat. He reached out a hand. "Let me take the monster to the ovens, my love. I know you will say it can't help, but I know it will weaken him"--

She looked up, bottomless eyes that might be showing fear for the first time. "No, *mi amor*. He is too strong, and his flying monster is still mighty. They could still win the day, unless you and the other one could combine forces."

"*El Otro*?"

"Leave me, sweet one. Take your new love, and move away from the river. If my master follows you, he will run out of energy in the desert."

"You are my love." He raised his voice, "Can't you see that? I only want the new one --" he stammered, tongue-tied. "--her body – I want it only for you. When I cast the spell, you must be ready to come to me. For -- forever. "

Carlotta's hand rose, holding him in his place. "You will save me only if you save yourself."

Lionel squinted intently, could not prevent the dark shadows from swallowing her. Long moments passed, heavy and empty. A silent voice warned that someone was watching him from the landing. Quaking from tears that threatened to come again, he did not turn around.

CHAPTER 38
GOVERNOR HOGG

Keith and Emily paused to chat with Patricio, who guarded the entrance to the back lot, when a sudden explosion ripped the afternoon air. Cautiously, they moved toward a gathering of people on the hilly lawn at the restaurant's front.

"Was that a gun?" Emily asked.

The crowd applauded. *CRACK!* The noise repeated, inspiring more cheers.

"Hey, guys, come see this." Ben waved from the inside of the group.

Mary stood in a clearing in the center, posed unnaturally, one arm lifted into the air. An aged gent, well-dressed and sporting white moustache and Stetson, strutted in the open space around her. He wore a string tie over a starchy checked shirt.

"Come on in, folks," the wiry old man said with a mischievous smile. A long black bullwhip writhed at his side. Mary waved meekly with one hand, holding a lit cigarette with the other.

"Just in time to see us curin' this young lady of a bad habit--" the old man spouted in the tone of a carnival barker.

"Mary doesn't smoke," Emily whispered to Keith.

The old showman raised his voice. "Ladies and gentlemen, this is the very same thing we done with Richard Widmark, the movie star when we wuz a shootin' *The Alamo.* Now hold it up, there, darlin'." He directed Mary's clenched fingers away from her body.

"Mr. Widmark played Jim Bowie, you'll remember. True, he had longer arms than this little lady, but I hope that don't make any difference."

The whip flexed, climbing up itself. A titter passed through the crowd.

"Now, now...right there, very easy, little lady..."

The wrinkled face narrowed in fierce concentration. The whip grew agitated, now a live snake. In a lightning move, the arm raised, the wrist flicked — another explosion rent the air.

Only the butt of the cigarette remained in Mary's hand. She exhaled, her face a chalky white.

The crowd cheered. The old man bowed, then patted Mary on the shoulder.

"Who is this guy?" Keith asked in a whisper.

"Governor Hogg," Ben confided.

"That's not Beauregard Hogg."

"No, this is Pryce Hogg."

"Young man," the Governor interrupted, and drew closer, looking at him with clear blue eyes. "You're confusing me with my older brother, Beau. He was Governor of Texas way back in the fifties. That ain't me." Laughter. He had the crowd in the palm of his hand.

"Y'see, my brother was in so good with them Democrats, he got President Lyndon Johnson to appoint me Governor of the Marshall Islands.

"Served six years. But I missed the plains, don't you see. My ropin' skills were suffering, so I gave it up after one term."

He turned to the crowd, continuing the impromptu show.

"This is the very bullwhip I used when I was hob-nobbin' with John Wayne. Hope you've all seen that picture. You know that scene where the Texans rode into the Mexican camp to destroy that big cannon? Remember, Thomas?"

"Very well, Governor." Laughter.

"Me and my ranch crew were those Texans. They were chased out of camp by a passel of Mexicans. Well, we rode hard back to the Alamo, got off, changed into Mexican soldier uniforms, got back on the horses and chased ourselves to beat the band." Pause for effect. More laughs.

"I am, therefore, one of the few veterans of both sides of the Texas Revolutionary War." He doffed his Stetson to cheers.

"Anyway, we visit Thomas when we're in Sironia, and eat some of his good food." He winked in the chef's direction. "We've got time for one more demonstration." He worked the whip again. "I'll need another brave volunteer."

Murmurs rolled through the crowd. A syrupy smile spread over Ben's face. "Keith," he yelled.

The restaurant workers and Thomas laughed and chanted, "Keith! Keith! Keith!" They pushed him ahead.

"Mighty good. Come on out here, Mr. Keith. Has somebody got a cigarette?"

Before Keith knew it, he had awkwardly lit a cigarette and held it out in the same fashion Mary had.

"Well, now that's just fine, Mr. Keith. It don't appear that you smoke as a regular thing. I'll demonstrate to you just what a dangerous habit it can be. Allow me."

In a sweeping motion, the Governor took the cigarette from Keith's fingers and wedged it into his mouth. Emily gasped. Ben could hardly contain himself.

"Now, young fella, you hold real still." The old cowboy backed off. From the corner of his eye, Keith saw the whip writhe. "Mr. Gary Cooper himself was always impressed by this one. Now don't be a draggin' on that weed. You don't want it any shorter." Laughter.

Keith's lips quivered, while dripping sweat tickled his left temple.

"Did this with a Lebanese once." The sudden pause sent another titter through the crowd, "Fine-looking feller, but had a large nose. I don't mind telling you that it was touch and go there for a spell."

Everyone tensed except the smoothly twisting snake. "*CRACK!*"

A firecracker exploded inches before Keith's eyes, sparks and all. He tasted tobacco on his lips. Only a tiny butt remained. The crowd burst into applause. Ben guffawed, re-enacting Keith's expression for some of the waitresses.

"Mighty fine." The governor stopped coiling his whip long enough to shake Keith's hand. "You're even braver than Mr. Clint Eastwood, young man."

"You really know Clint Eastwood?" he asked shakily.

"Why, shore. I'll have to tell you all about him sometime."

Slowly, the crowd dispersed, some heading for the River Festival, some for the restaurant. Emily excused herself to go to the ladies room with Mary. Thomas seated the governor and his friends at the VIP booth near the register. The old statesman ordered Shrimp Orleans.

"You know," it was Thomas speaking, "Keith has something in common with you, Governor. He's very interested in the puppets upstairs."

"Why, the Indians! How could I forget?" Governor Hogg climbed out of the booth. "I haven't even said howdy to them. Come on, young man." He grabbed Keith's arm and hustled him toward the stairs. "Thomas, you just keep those shrimp warm when they come."

Though he had to be at least seventy, the old man mounted the steps with ease. It was all Keith could do to keep up with him.

"How long have the marionettes been here?" Keith asked.

"Most of the century, I guess. Old Jasper — he was a peddler. Woodcarver from Europe somewhere. He made 'em." He gripped Keith's elbow as they started up the last flight to the high landing.

"You knew their creator?"

"'Course Jasper wasn't his real name. My granddaddy knew what it was. Yannis or Johann or somethin'. Shoot, my folks wuz from Arkansas, so they just called him Jasper. He wuz a gypsy, you see."

"You actually talked to him?"

"Why, shore. I was just a little tyke, and he must have been a hundred years old, so he never paid me much mind."

The upper reaches of the ceiling loomed above, blind from the white sabers of quietness icing down from the skylights. The Governor babbled about what a nice job Thomas had done with the restaurant, but when they climbed into view of the puppets, the old voice fell silent. They crossed the landing.

Governor Hogg's eyes sank into his wrinkles, and his face grew wistful. Barely tall enough to do it, he reached up to caress the face of the taller of the wooden Indians.

"Well, there you are, you old warrior," he said in a tone of ultimate friendship. His hand coursed down along the Indian's muscular arm, and he patted it.

"Ol' Thunder Horse." He addressed the statue. "You durn near made it as long as I have, didn't you? Longer, I bet..." He grinned. "Old Jasper carved the Injuns, too. On consignment, you see. Early in his life."

"Thunder Horse? Is that his real name?"

"Hmm?" The Governor paused, then seemed to come back from wherever he was. "Well, I 'spect so. That's what we called him when I wuz a little boy." He pointed across to the other Indian.

"That one, we just called `Red Man.' These two wuz parked on opposite sides of the street downtown.

"We would get toy pistols and play on these Indians when Mother brought us in on her shoppin' trips. Boy we would have a hell of a gunfight." He chuckled and took off his hat.

"I guess downtown was a lot different then."

"Yep, I knowed Sironia from way back. Way back. Our ranch lay south of town. Jasper the gypsy went back and forth between here and Austin with his rickety ol' wagon. Full of pots and pans and rope and every piece of junk you could find on the prairie. He used to stop by, and mother would feed him. Hell, she fed every bum that came on the place."

A cock of the head. "But ol' Jasper weren't no bum. No ways. He was old school, you understand."

Maybe Keith's expression told the old man he had no idea what that meant.

A smile. "Old school means he could live off the land. You set that old demon loose out in the old West, he would'a survived just fine. Sure he took my mom's vittles, but he always paid with a carving. Or else he would polish the pans and the silver before he left."

A wrinkled hand stretched out to the marionettes, brushing across the strings as one would play a harp, setting them into an awkward chorus of motion. Only the leprechaun faced away from them. The Governor's fingers curled around the dragon's strings, and jerked the heavy puppet up and down.

"This here's the oldest one o' the bunch. 'Least that's what he claimed. Named it *Rage*. Said he carved it right after his wife died, when he wuz a young man. Married a Karankawa, if I recall."

He pulled his fingers back, and his hand danced this way and that as he talked.

"Weren't many Karankawa left, you understand. Cannibals. But they was some other natives livin' 'round here then, I guess, when he was a young buck. The rumor was that she didn't die of illness, but that he killed her. Somebody said she had a thing for some Comanche boy. Or Apache. I don't know. Back then, ever' thing was rumor, mostly. Facts were pretty hard to come by."

For another instant, the old man's attention drifted. Keith seized the chance. "Governor Hogg, have you ever heard stories about these marionettes being haunted?"

Hogg's eyebrows rose, and he chuckled with delight. "Why, son, of course they're haunted. Didn't nobody ever tell you? Why, that old gypsy wuz crazy as a bedbug. And spooky--" He nudged Keith's arm with the hat brim.

"You ain't gonna believe it, but he always claimed that a marionette wuz just a piece of wood unless he put somebody's soul into it. He said that very thing, sittin' there on the porch, in front of my brother and me.

"That's why the Dragon's name is Rage--he said he put his own anger from his wife a-dyin' into it." A knowing smile. I know it's crazy talk, but my granddaddy would just sit there in his rocker, drink his cider, and listen to the old coot.

Usually, my brother and I would be scared and hide under the porch."

"You're pulling my leg, Governor."

"Well, that's one old man's memory of another old man. And both of us crazy, I guess." His gaze went far away, and he licked wrinkled, chapped lips.

Voice quiet, weary. "Said he didn't know how, but if you picked the right wood and carved the puppet just so, a lost soul would come along and claim it. Then he would chant an old gypsy curse to lock him in there!" The governor's hands snatched the air. "What a character."

"What did the old gypsy look like?" Keith asked.

"What'd he look like? Why, I 'spect someone would have told you that by now, as interested as you seem to be. He looked just like this--"

The governor's hand shot forward and he seized the leprechaun, turned it around, and held the face close to Keith's.

Keith gasped and groped for the nearby railing.

Those staring wooden eyes glistened, as if washed by real tears. They might blink at any moment. He had never noticed — the chiseled jaw was identical to that of Larcinter. If the wood melted and warped at that instant, and the grizzled old face emerged, it would be no surprise.

The Governor laughed outright. "Well, it startled me, too, young man, but that's his spittin' image. Finished it just before he died, or so the story goes."

He let the puppet fall back and saluted the wooden denizens once more with a wave of his hat. He held onto Keith's arm more firmly on the way down, as if the visit had sapped his strength.

"Yes, sir," a visit to this ol' place ain't complete without seein' ol' Thunder Horse and Red Man. And ain't it curious, those marionettes windin' up there next to those wooden Injuns? It's a world of coincidences." He sighed. "Time goes by, young man. And now it looks like my native friends will outlast me. Make your move when you can, my Daddy used to say. If you tarry, your chance is gone."

"Yes, sir."

"Perfect timing, Governor." Thomas placed the hot metal plate of barbecued shrimp on the table.

Keith thanked him again and set out to find Emily, but the governor's voice turned him around. "Now just you remember how bad it is to smoke, young man." Everyone laughed.

CHAPTER 39
THE PEARL

As Keith saw it, Emily was very circumspect about avoiding the subject of advertising. Yet, that look in her eyes remained, an atmosphere that had been ever-present with Linda. The afternoons she spent with him in bed erased all doubts for a while, and pushed him closer and closer to asking her to move in. But what if she said no?

Before happy hour one evening, Keith fixed a salad and returned to his stool to eat it. Only a handful of quiet drinkers sat in the lounge. The ventilator hummed, and he tried to contain a growing excitement. He had booked a motel room in Dallas for the next night. She told her mom she was going shopping with Mary. They would spend the entire night together for the first time. Then he would ask her.

"Take a break," the Wop said, crowding in through the side door. He thrust his hands into the small sink and washed them.

"What?"

"G'head, get the fuck outta here." The oyster bag came out and he deftly popped one open. A finger pointed down to the refrigerator. "Get me some red sauce, for God's sake." Keith complied.

As he stepped out into the lounge, John issued a prodigious belch. Keith flinched, then leaned back in. "I won't be gone long. Anything the matter?"

A brusque shrug, as he reached for another oyster. "Don't take offense. I'm leaving."

"Oh." Keith moved back onto the stool.

"No, shithead, I'm not leaving this instant. Right now, I'm staying so you can take a break. That's the kind of nice guy I am. In two weeks, though, I'm gone. I gave my notice."

"I don't believe it."

"Oh, Christ," John said and pointed the oyster knife. "Your break is almost over, already."

Keith moved his half-eaten salad. "Where will you go? The Catfish Hut?"

A sneer. "That dive? Come on. Dunno yet. I called St. Louis today. They're gonna get back to me."

"You're moving to St. Louis?"

John's movements calmed. With this new oyster, he pried slowly, until the low-pitched 'pop' sounded. "St. Louis is where my agent is." He dipped, then chewed thoughtfully. "They got me this job. They'll be back to me in a week with some offers for the new one. Get good at this stuff, Bucko, and you can work anywhere."

Two ragged-looking young men with long hair entered through the large swinging doors by the bar and climbed onto the stage, each carrying a guitar case.

John shook his head. "Why the fuck can't Thomas get a real band in here?"

Keith left it to the burly Italian when a man came up to place an order. He chatted with Emily and Andrea, then walked aimlessly through the still sparsely populated dining rooms, until he stood before the alcove on the second floor. Perhaps this was good. He could not imagine the Water Company without John. It would make it all the easier to quit, himself.

He didn't know which was more daunting — the dark stairway that beckoned before him, or tomorrow night with Emily. Could things remain the same if she turned him down? Or would the world come crashing down again, and the wagon dreams reacquire their sharpness?

"Stupid," he said under his breath. Was Emily only a shield to him? Something to keep the boogey-man away? Or was she a luxurious creature that he should spend the rest of his life with?

"What did you say?"

He turned. The speaker was Branwyn. She looked up with a faint smile.

"Oh. Nothing. How are you doing?"

She shrugged. It seemed she grew more beautiful each time he saw her. "Same old chores, different day."

"Still seeing—uh, how is Lionel?"

She leaned against the wall, her eyes wistful. "Strange. Friendly some days. But sometimes he avoids me. Are all guys the same?"

"I don't think any guys are just like him." He laughed, but instead of sharing the joke, her gaze only grew more intense.

"No. No one is like him."

He excused himself and jogged back down to the bar kitchen.

"Goddam, 'bout time." John shook the fry basket full of chicken wings.

"Busy?"

"Nah. Oysters and wings."

Before Keith could reclaim the stool, John held up a single mollusk, its top shell gone. "Look, Paisan." His thick finger pushed the mussel aside. A black chunk lay in the shell.

"What's that? A slug of oil?"

"It's a pearl! First one I ever found here."

"My God." Keith picked out the black, irregular form. "You asshole. I'm out here for months popping thousands of oysters, then I take a short break and you find a pearl."

"Some got it, some don't." He put the prize back in its bed.

"I can't believe you're going." Keith sat down.

John leaned back against the bricks. "I'll miss the place. But if I'm ever going to own a restaurant, I've gotta make all the right moves. It won't happen in this town." Their eyes met, and he punched Keith's shoulder, full-force. "Gotta follow your dream, man."

Watching the stout figure carefully carrying his treasure toward the swinging doors, Keith had to chuckle. He tried to remember what it was like to have a dream.

It was that realization that bedeviled him in Dallas the next night. They had a fabulous dinner, went to the motel and made love. When it came time to ask her to move in with him, he chickened out.

CHAPTER 40
THE INTELLECTUAL

"Ridiculous," Keith told Ben inside the walk-in cooler. He put down the container of salad dressing he had come for, and paced in the tight open space. "We can't have the fucking ghost hunt after the Scalded Toms Banquet."

"Its official name is the *Toms' Tea*, and it's the only night it can possibly work."

"We'll be wiped out. You told me yourself that it took you all night last year to clean up after the bastards. Do me a favor and tell Larry it's off."

"He'd be heart-broken. Come on, we'll have a few beers and unwind. The bastard will poop out by three or four a.m., and we can pack it in."

Larry called, too early, on the morning of the Tea, to confirm when he should report.

"The banquet — " Keith chose his words carefully, knowing that even this late in the game, Larry inability to keep a secret could find a way to prove disastrous, "--doesn't start until ten. God knows when it will end. Be here at midnight, and remember, no dope. Thomas could lose his liquor license."

"Don't be such a grouch."

"I mean it, Larry."

He took Emily to lunch at the mall. "I got a job," she announced with a proud smile.

"Where? You're not even through school yet."

"Teacher's aide. I can do that even though I'm not credentialed. September first. The best thing is, the principal said she could almost guarantee me a teaching position in January."

"We celebrate. Lunch is on me," Keith said resisting the instant pressure her news had created.

"This time, I'll let you, Mr. Gotrocks."

Emily was waiting in the bar that night, but her evening would be abbreviated. On Thomas's orders, all female employees were to be out of the building by nine-thirty. Ben called a meeting in the cellar before they opened for dinner.

"We need to get as much equipment down here as possible. After the customers are out — remember, no one is to be seated after, say eight forty-five — we'll have twenty or thirty minutes to bring food to the buffet table down here. John and Alberto will make sure all the cooking is done by nine-forty-five. Except the steaks."

"Paisan, you gonna work-a you ass off," John whispered to Keith.

"That's another thing," Ben said, scowling. "This is going to be a training session. You're stepping into John's shoes, Keith. From now on, you'll be running the catering detail. This is the same as catering, it's just that you go downstairs instead of across town."

"Thanks for the going away, party, Ben," the Wop yelled.

Ben reddened. "If you weren't such a damned Yankee, I'd hold your check for a month--"

"What?" Keith panicked. "When is he going?"

A helpless look. "This is his last night."

The Wop draped his arm around Keith and launched a punch into his stomach. "Got my marching orders yesterday, Bucko. A brand new restaurant in Cincinnati. You're looking at the head chef of the Top Hat Steak & Seafood Emporium."

"So," Ben continued, "the ghost hunt will be the only goodbye he's gonna get. OK, guys? Quick, so we can open up for dinner."

John got in another punch — this one on the arm — as they climbed back up to the dining room. "Let's move it, you scumbag."

"I can't believe this." Keith's stomach felt like it had a hole in it.

Negotiating the concrete steps wasn't easy, and he could imagine the overgrown adolescents taking a tumble – but, then they'd been there before. A huge table and chairs, plus a portable bar had been set up, a few cheap signs. Otherwise, this whole level resembled a cement dungeon, and the thought of getting trapped down here made his skin crawl.

When the place was full of water, it was had been impossible to see anything, but the most obvious feature was the two – well, pillars, that had been cemented right into the wall. Above them a brick archway, also surrounded by the masonry. Obviously, the passage to the Terrace.

He stood gaping for a moment. "What the hell was this, part of the underground railroad for the slaves?"

Ben shrugged. "Beats me."

"That wasn't just a tunnel entrance, it was ornate, before somebody ruined it."

"Doesn't matter. The tunnel caved in decades ago."

Keith aimed a spatula at him. "You S.O.B. You've been in it, haven't you?"

"Hell, no. It caved in, I told you. Put those utensils in that basket on the corner table. Hustle, Cool-Jerk."

On his second trip down, Keith heard a noise from the dim passage that led down to the large room. The hairs rose up on his neck, but it was only the Intellectual, sweeping the small room John had designated for stashing supplies.

"*Ola*, Lionel." Keith heaved an oyster sack against the wall.

"*Ola*." The broom kept moving for a few seconds, then the janitor straightened up, a strange light in his eyes. "You talk to the marionettes?"

Keith's heart immediately shifted into high gear. Lionel had never permitted more than a couple of seconds of conversation. Now, to come out with something like this—the very thing Keith had wanted to ask him—

"*Si*. I mean, no. I'm sorry, Lionel, I feel weird talking about it. I had some dreams. Who told you?" He was not sure he wanted to know the answer to that. "Maybe we'd better keep setting up."

"Chavo told me your story."

Keith tarried, speechless, wondering which gossip chain had let Chavo in on it.

"You have great--" Lionel groped for a word, "--vision? Seeing?" He smiled. "Greater than me," he continued while the broom resumed. "I have called them out. But that is very hard. Meeting them in dreams, like you, is more natural. Better."

"Called them out?"

"*Si*."

He nodded. Against his better judgment, Keith followed him warily through the dank hall, squinting to see in the light from the weak bulbs.

Lionel stepped into the farthest room on the right. Grimy, mismatched couch cushions had been strewn across the floor. A thin paisley bedspread lay crumpled in a pile near the center of the room next to a small black lacquered table. A plume of smoke rose from an incense stick that burned in an ashtray beside a candle. *Mama Luz's parlor*, Keith thought. How many Mexicans had some connection to witchcraft?

"What's all this?"

"'s okay." Amazingly, Lionel actually looked a bit embarrassed. "Thomas knows about this room. In here, we call the spirits." He sat down easily by the table, draping the bedspread over his knees in the process.

"Who's we?" Keith asked.

"Some of us."

Keith sat across from him. "The spirits of the puppets?"

"Yes." He thought. Then, "No. We only have spoken to ancient spirits--power spirits." His finger went to his chest. "Only I have talked to a marionette."

Like Mama Luz, the young man had an authentic air. Larry would pummel him with questions. For some reason,

Keith could not think of anything meaningful, and spouted out the first thing, "Ancient spirits? What do they tell you?"

"Not for you." The Mexican shook his head solemnly.

"Oh, well, excuse me." How ridiculous. Still, Lionel did not flinch. "So, you have talked to Carlotta, too?"

At last, the sphinx-like face seemed lost. He sat back, gazing around to the stained concrete walls, for a moment, then looked up with actual tears in his eyes. When he did speak, Keith's attention had shifted to the room's artifacts, the pillows, especially.

What if Lionel, and maybe even his "others" spent the night here sometimes. That explained a lot. Illegals sleeping here or just hanging out during their off hours. My God, perhaps there really was a prankster. Who could prove that one of his buddies didn't just hide in the attic, working puppet strings? How many of his own visions had been just bullshit?

"I'm sorry, Lionel. I didn't hear."

"You are in great danger."

Keith felt a jolt, and looked into those deep brown eyes, all the darker in the harsh shadows. The young man who seemed so vacant, always puttering in the corners with his broom—if someone's imagination ran wild, he could even look evil down here.

"Oh?" Keith tried to hide a sneer. "Which spirit told you that?"

"Carlotta."

"Did she say I was supposed to leave the river?" It came out suddenly, more snidely than intended. "I mean – uh, isn't something like that just a vision? Why would you listen to Carlotta, even if she did say that?"

A cool look. "I think you know that it is real. But *mi*, I am in love with her."

Loud scraping came from the direction of the cellar banquet room, followed by the Wop's deep-throated cursing. They both rose automatically.

Lionel touched his sleeve. "You must listen to her. This place--it is not so good for you."

"Why does everyone seem to want me to leave? Lionel, *amigo*, I'm just trying to make a living." He was verging on taking out his frustrations on this poor weirdo, who had never been anything but polite.

Thankfully, his outburst seemed to have little effect. "If you stay, maybe we--" Lionel grasped for words, "could talk to the spirits together."

His eyes possessed a strange light. But was it really malevolent? A plan began to hatch, though Keith's brain was too befuddled to grasp the details, yet. If he played along, perhaps he would find out just what Lionel's friends did down here. The conspiracy theorist in him was blooming. Christ, what if all the weird stuff here was just a cover for some hidden plot? Drugs? Wouldn't Thomas find out if there were a drug ring running from this basement? But what if Thomas, himself, were the kingpin?

Deep breath. Impossible. It wasn't in the chef's nature. Nor Ben's, even if he liked a toke once in a while.

"I don't know how you talk to spirits, but let me know the next time you try it. My brother loves this shit."

He stepped carefully down the hall, then turned. Lionel was behind, uncomfortably close, seeming nervous, maybe even sad. "Are you in love with her?" The words came quietly, as if he would find a place, somewhere in his mysterious world, to tuck any answer Keith came out with.

"With Emily?"

The janitor's head shook slowly. "Carlotta."

"No." Once upon a time, maybe, back when things still made sense. This guy was too hard to read, and should be kept at arm's length. "Speaking of love, *amigo*, what are you doing to Branwyn? I hate to see an innocent girl like that be taken advantage of. You've got her confused. Either be with her or don't, but don't hurt her."

Lionel drew back. "She is not happy in this world."

"Son of a bitch," John's voice echoed down the hall.

"We'd better go help," Keith said.

"Where the hell have you two been?" John demanded. "The banquet's in here." He sucked on a finger. "Help me. Quick."

"Some farewell party, eh, John?"

"I've had worse."

With great heaving, they maneuvered the portable bar into the corner, and the Wop's eternal, intimidating scowl melted into a huge smile, and his arm went around Keith's shoulders. "Let's go up to the prep room and get drunk."

"Down boy," Keith led up the stairs. "It's going to be a long night."

CHAPTER 41
THE BANQUET

After they set the heavy table back into place over the trap door, Keith wandered to the lounge, where he found Emily discussing with Andrea and Jeremy how different teaching would be, compared to this job.

"Hope you have fun tonight," she told him with a roll of her eyes.

"Sorry you girls can't stick around."

"Are you crazy?" Andrea broke in, "Sandra was almost raped at the one last year."

"Yeah. Thomas says it's not a good idea." Emily loaded a tray with drinks. "He hates those creeps as much as we do."

"They're that bad?"

"You'll have to see them to believe them," Jeremy added.

"What will you be doing?" Keith called after Emily.

She turned, her short skirt twisting against those perfect thighs. God, how he would rather go home with her.

"Mary and some of the girls thought we would drink a few beers."

"No fair," Keith said, and pinched her. "You'll go out and get picked up by some millionaire, and I'll be history."

She winked. "Then you'd better behave."

An hour before the start of the banquet, Larry sauntered through the back door, and stationed himself beside the cutting table.

"Gosh. Gets busy here, huh?"

"You're early," Keith said coolly. He could feel the night going down the toilet. "Go up and wait in Ben's office."

John appeared at the door of the prep room with two glasses of beer. He motioned Keith in.

"Join me. By God, we'll have our own party."

Keith shoved his glass behind a mixer. "John, we're on duty. We're going to drink later, anyway."

"Bullshit." John raised his glass in an imperative toast. "What're they gonna do, fire me? C'mon, drink-a with-a your old Wop." He drained the glass in two huge gulps.

"They can sure as hell still fire me." Keith sipped.

"You worry too much, Paisan."

Shortly after nine-thirty, Ben interrupted them in the prep room. "Have at it. The last two tables are leaving."

"*Muy bien*," the Wop said, too loudly, and belched.

They moved the center table and hustled down to set up the buffet. Fried shrimp, fried zucchini, lettuce, four-bean salad, sliced bread, meatballs, a large bowl of guacamole which Cisco prepared earlier, chips, chicken wings, and a dozen other delicacies were positioned quickly under warming lights on a the long table.

"Where's Larry?" Keith asked.

The last members of the staff not working the party were filing out. Thomas had departed an hour before, leaving orders for all of them to keep the restaurant from being destroyed by "those scoundrels."

Ben shrugged. "He was in the office for a while. I thought he came back down here."

"Christ, Ben, did he go snooping around upstairs? He'll break his neck." Keith slapped the prep table with a dish towel. "This whole ghost hunt thing is stupid. Are ghosts going to come around with a loud party going on?"

"Hmm." Ben's eyes were impish, amused. "Sounds like you think ghosts are like fish, scattering when you hit the aquarium."

"Look, go up there and find Larry, OK? I'm busy learning the catering business."

John pronounced everything ready. He hauled Keith into the side cubicle to take inventory: ice, plates, and extra utensils. A second burlap bag of oysters lay against a chair, upon which sat two more glasses of beer. He shoved one toward Keith.

"Here's to the best damn chef's apprentice I ever had."

"Well, I guess I have to drink to that."

"They're here," Ben yelled from the first floor.

"Manny and I will hold the fort," John directed. "You go up and watch the scarecrows come in."

Cars rumbled into the front lot. Lights across in River Park wavered on the flowing water. A passing raft sporting cane fishing poles caught Keith's eye, and he breathed the cool night air. Honeysuckle. A shiver. Crickets talked. A whippoorwill called in the distance.

"How will we know if someone's just here for a late dinner — you know, not part of the group?"

"We'll know. Look."

At the foot of the wide concrete stairs stood the first of the Scalded Toms to arrive. He was slim, dressed in black pants and dinner jacket, brilliant white shirt, sporting a carnation on his lapel, with a cape hanging from his shoulders. The man's face, however, hid behind a Halloween mask, the likeness of a popular cartoon woodpecker.

"Ahoy, Citizens of the Water Company!" The woodpecker saluted, and mounted the steps. Other elegantly dressed figures moved quickly out of their cars, patting each other on the back, and crowded behind him. More masks of cartoon characters: a penguin, a bunny, a donkey, and a bear. Like woodpecker, they did not simply walk, but moved forward in a stately and affected strut.

"Greetings, Infidel," a few muttered to Ben as they passed through the front door. Keith was ignored entirely.

Two elephants came through, followed by a giraffe, a pair of raggedy Andy's, a cartoon mascot for a popular seltzer, a Frankenstein, two draculas, a sea serpent, an improbable mask of a deli-sandwich with eye holes. They chuckled and chatted among themselves as they disappeared into the trap door in the floor.

"I'll stay up here for the stragglers," Ben said, after a lull. "They'll be getting busy down there." Keith descended, well after the last of the odd men.

"Welcome, Brother," Woodpecker exclaimed from the lectern at the far end of the room. He toasted Keith, the did a double-take.

"Alas, 'tis not a brother, but another infidel!" Glasses were lowered 'to boos and hisses. At the buffet table, John laughed.

"Repent, Infidel. Forswear your infamous ways, that ye might escape perdition," the Woodpecker preached, his finger pointed at Keith.

"Repent! Repent!" came the call from several more.

"What's all that about?" He edged in behind the table, next to John.

"They're fulla shit. Get used to it or it'll be a long night for you."

Buffalo-mask rose for a toast.

"Bar-keep!"

All eyes now turned to Manny, who was pumping the beer keg.

"'Tis a fresh, clean ale you have brewed. You lend honor to a sordid profession. *Hip hoo-rah* for a veritable son of a Scalded Tom."

Applause rippled weakly through those not engrossed in their own conversations.

"My dear scalded and deformed brethren," Woodpecker tapped the lectern with a fork. Chairs scraped on the concrete, plates clacked. Calls for more beer.

Woodpecker:

"Against all odds: death, taxes, the police and protective mothers, we meet again--in heat!" *Hoorahs.*

A walrus rose. "Avast, Bally Woodpecker! Demur and leave us to our grog!" Laughter. Cheers.

"Thank you and none of it, sir." Woodpecker's chest swelled. "To our grog, it shall be. But not until the election of officers, the annual report, and official notice of *Windows in Which One May Peep.*"

"Hear! Hear!"

"Can we have our grog while we're doing all that?" said a meek voice wearing a coyote mask.

"Capital," bellowed Walrus.

"I don't know." Woodpecker emerged from the lectern and again addressed Manny.

"Barkeep! What say you?"

"Uh, what, sir?"

"What say you? Can these poor lads have their grog while we conduct our business?"

Manny appeared perplexed. "Do you mean rum?"

"Dear God, an infidel bartender," cried Woodpecker.

"We withdraw our toast from earlier." Bunny shot the finger at Manny. More shouts.

"Now, now."

"Hang the blackguard!"

Manny blanched, studied the crowd with a doubtful look, then held out a glass. "There's beer."

"Oh, hoorah," cried Coyote. A torrent of cheers followed. "Stout fellow!" "Bravo!" "Knew he was a good man!" "Commission the bastard!" A dozen of them lined up for new glasses.

"Jesus Christ, these guys are loony," John said quietly. He handed his own empty glass to Keith. "We need a couple more, too."

As he waited for access to Manny, Keith noticed that the Toms' disguises were simple Halloween masks that had been altered by enlarging the mouth-holes to facilitate speaking, eating, and drinking. The result was visually disgusting.

As the meeting gathered steam, Keith concluded that the Scalded Toms' business consisted chiefly of non-sensical resolutions, raucous limericks, and testimonials by members about successful "peeping missions" during the preceding year, all done in mock British Sailor accents. The only "weighty" issue they addressed was whether to allow membership to females in the arch-male organization.

Woodpecker: "Now, my friends, be-sotted though ye be--"

"Keel-haul him," toasted Skunk.

"--thank-yew! Avast! Attention to the podium or the grog ration will be significantly curtailed." The din continued.

Coyote was on his feet, his small voice squeaking, "Mr. Chairman, have you tasted the meatballs? I say if the members refuse to shut-up, we have the servants force-feed them these miniature tennis balls of poison." He held one aloft.

Cheers. Applause. "Bravo!" "That's the ticket!"

A loud voice overrode the others: "Those aren't meatballs, they're coyote suppositories."

"Ooh, I say." Coyote sat down.

"Dumb shits," John whispered. "Insult my cooking, will they?"

"Avast, I say!" Woodpecker fought for control. "The fare is quite good, actually. It will do us little profit to insult our hosts. They are cretins who could sully our bloodlines with a single glance!"

"Oooh." Moans. Glances toward the buffet table. John shook a spatula menacingly.

"The issue is, in this age of liberal thought and equality," Woodpecker strode around the lectern, waxing pompous, "--are we to break down those despicable barriers and let in members of the fairer--" Pause for effect. "...SEX?" The last word spoken as a lecherous growl.

Cries of derision. "No!" "Never!"

"Coitainly!" a buck-toothed beaver called.

"Reprehensible!"

A Moose rose. "Can we require them to shave their underarms if they join?' he asked delicately. Howls of laughter.

Skunk stood. "Can we shave their underarms?" Cheers. "Bravo!" "Let 'em in!"

"Admit them." It was Walrus, whose rotund body struck a familiar chord. Of course, Keith thought, most of these guys were probably Sironian businessmen, guys he might know well from contacts at his old job. This could be a priceless opportunity to find out the identity of some of the members of the ultra-secret Toms.

"Admit them," Walrus repeated when the howls died down, "and we will shave them within an inch of their lives!"

Cheers. Manny, who Keith had rarely seen crack a smile, was laughing uproariously. He must be drinking, too, something he never did on duty in the bar.

"Scumbags." John took a sip from his own glass.

"I--mmm--" Gorilla was standing and munching on something which muffled his remark.

"What is it? Quiet lads, Brother Gorilla will speak."

"I move previous question."

"Hear, hear! Previous question!" More toasts.

"Gorilla wants a vote, then," Woodpecker cried, waving for order. "Do we admit those creatures that require--" Pause again for effect...

"Our raging manhood!" cried a Texas Longhorn.

Laughter. Cheers.

"I was going to say, `so much shaving.' But `raging manhood' it is." More cheers.

"A vote then." Woodpecker whipped his cape around. "All in favor of admitting them--"

Coyote popped up. "Wait, it hasn't been seconded." Jeers.

"What is this, the fuckin' Congress?" John sneered and nodded to Keith. "Get me another beer."

"John, you're swaying over the shrimp, as it is." Keith continued stacking empty serving bowls.

"Do you wish to second, Brother Coyote?"

"Yes. I second all that about our raging manhood," he declared in his squeaky voice. Guffaws. More than one Tom fell off of their chairs to laugh.

"All in favor, raise your hands."

"In favor of what?" called Duck.

"In favor of letting the hairy-legs in," snorted Walrus. No hands came up.

"Well, well. Opposed?" Hands went up. No's resounded.

Woodpecker appeared non-plussed. "Not very open-minded, lads. Shall we study the subject more?"

"We'll study the subject through a bathroom window."

"Bravo!" Cheers and stamping of feet.

As if they had been given a secret signal, a new stampede toward the buffet table began. Keith studied their mouths, gestures, movements, anything that might prove familiar. For a moment, a Bear stopped and stared at Keith. The eyes were sharp, unfriendly, unlike the glazed and pleasant headlights of the others. Keith looked away.

"Avast and make way," bellowed Walrus. "Brother Bear, you tarry as usual. Stand clear the devilled eggs!"

Keith thought he detected the Texas Longhorn watching him occasionally. Something familiar there, too. The shape of the body…

Charlie and Jeremy brought down new plates of steaks. "Ready for later?" Charlie asked.

"I guess." Keith loaded his arms with soiled dishes and headed up the steps. "We need utensils and salad. Where the fuck is Larry?"

Charlie shrugged. "I saw him earlier. The bar?"

"*Que pasa*, Alberto?" He paused in the kitchen. Katy had left Cisco's brother in charge of the meat for the first time.

Alberto shrugged. "'s very loud. They drunk?" he asked.

"Getting there. Uh, you staying? Later?"

"*Que*? For the *weetch* hunt?" Of course, he knew all about it.

"Yeah." Keith laughed nervously. If only this stupid night was over. He trotted through the bar. Empty. In the stairs, Ben shook his head.

"I haven't been able to find him, either."

"Goddam it. Didn't you check the puppets?" Keith turned and hurtled upstairs. The spiral steps were even darker at this time of night, but he pressed on. Left alone, Larry was bound to fuck something up. The wooden Indians stood as always, silent, forbidding, alone. The marionettes, though, were gone again. Panic seized him.

262 The Water Company

"Larry," he called loudly. "Get out here. Did you take the puppets?" He waited for a second, hearing only his echo and the faraway rumble of the Toms laughing, banging on tables. "Damn it, Larry, quit playing games or I'll call the whole thing off."

In the kitchen, he retrieved a bowl of macaroni salad from the cooler and trudged back into the basement. The latest Toms assault had left the buffet table an even greater wreck than before.

"No chicken wings," John said. Ben was pouring fresh ice around the cocktail shrimp.

"John, the puppets are gone. Who keeps taking them away?"

"How the fuck do I know? Your weird brother is probably making them have sex. Get some chicken wings." Keith started around the end of the long table. "And bring more french dressing," John called after him.

As the display of rank gluttony wound down, Walrus leaned his substantial mass back and initiated a disgraceful belching match.

"They do it every year." Ben shook his head and started upstairs with dirty hotel trays.

"Disgusting pigs," John pronounced. He sipped his beer, then issued his own prodigious burp which was justly applauded by the other contestants.

Predictably, a food fight ensued. Within minutes, the floor was an unholy mess. Keith could see the ghost hunt turning into an all-night clean-up session.

Woodpecker cried out. "Gentlemen, Lords! Subsist! Defer! And otherwise decease!" He waved his salad-dressing-streaked cape.

Keith slipped through the small hallway to Lionel's room. "Lionel? Larry?" he called in a loud whisper.

The candle burned peacefully in the center, with cushions lined up neatly around the table. He was starting to feel the beer, and leaned against the wall to rest.

His remembered his life as a copywriter. Sleeping alongside Linda every night. He tried to picture her, to want her. Amazing, how life had changed. He sometimes wanted to listen to John and become a chef. The cold concrete, the grease on his hands…things seemed so real here. Especially his co-workers. The phony pretentiousness of the business world, the office politics, such alien concepts to these intense people.

Why couldn't Emily understand? She said nothing, but he knew what she was thinking. A career should not be based on money alone. She had never said it should, but wasn't she thinking it? Perhaps he should tell Ben to produce a waiter's job, or else.

"Gentlemen!" The voice pulled Keith out of his reverie.

"Gentlemen, I present Toms' Playmates of this year past." Woodpecker. Without his garish personage standing before him, that voice sounded oddly familiar. Where had he heard it?

Christ — still no Larry. He pawed his way through the hall and stepped carefully through the refuse. The banquet room was now lit now only by photographic slides being flashed onto a screen. The pictures were clandestine, taken by various Toms during the year.

A shapely blond, clad only in panties, peered into a mirror in what appeared to be her bedroom.

"Bravo!" it was the voice of Coyote.

Ben, smiling, nodded for him to stay. The Wop munched on shrimp, and joined the cheering.

"Hey, bastards," Keith announced up in the kitchen. "You're missing the nudie pictures!" Alberto, Charlie, and the dishwashers hustled toward the cellar entrance. Keith ambled once more through the eerily quiet lounge. It was out of character for Larry to hide this long.

A quick run through the second floor, that storage room, then downstairs again. On the screen, a naked lady strode through her kitchen, a purposeful look on her face.

"*Attencion*," Alberto said to his comrades. Lionel stood and stared, wide-eyed, his chin resting on his broom handle.

The next slide showed a woman caught from the rear. Rat stood, blocking the projector's light, and shook a finger. "For heaven's sake, Jame--I mean, Bunny. Don't you know when to snap a blarsted picture?" Jeers and threats.

"Oh, I say," rejoined the insulted rabbit, "not very sporting, what? There are some bottom-men present, after all." Cheers.

"Yes, sit down, blackguard."

Longhorn sauntered to the table in the dark for food scraps. He looked around furtively. Those eyes were still familiar, even in this light. His light brown hair looked like--

The Scalded Tom leaned over, tugged on his mask, and lifted it up. For an instant, Keith's eyes would not focus. The cheekline, that nose--Larry!

"Hey, bastard-o," Larry whispered and let the mask snap back into place at the same instant that the lights flared on. Though invisible behind the disguise, Keith was sure he felt a sneer of brotherly conquest.

"You ass," Keith hissed. "You never--"

Woodpecker took the lectern again, while the now unkempt animals scrambled for beer refills. "Sit down, my brothers. Hark and be seated. All except for thou, Brother Longhorn." He beckoned Larry to the front.

His brother? A Scalded Tom? Keith reeled. And why were they calling him to the front? Had Woodpecker seen him expose his identity? It would serve the bum right if they drummed him out.

"My Lords," Woodpecker's arms extended. Chairs scraped. Longhorn Larry stood meekly, as if he, too, knew the jig was up.

"--it has been a most officious occasion, what?"

"Hear, hear." A chorus devoid of spirit. The Toms were tired.

"Lords, we must thank our gracious hosts."

A look around. Now John had disappeared. Keith's legs ached from standing so long on the concrete. His food-smeared watch said it was after midnight. God, where had the time gone?

"Huzzah," came the lifeless echo.

"We come to the last order of business for this One Millionth Meeting of the Scalded Toms! I give you Brother Longhorn."

"Bravo!" Scattered applause.

"Good evening, Brothers. We have one more task yet ahead of us, tonight. A great challenge." Longhorn--Larry-- seemed to have perked up. He swelled and strutted.

"Oh, Longhorn, you've got such long horns!" squeaked Coyote. Laughter and jeers.

Larry's eyes were at their most mischievous, his words weighty, building, "This fine assemblage is hereby invited to-- "

Keith felt his stomach falling away. *No. This can't be happening.*

"--a GHOST HUNT!"

Animals leapt to their feet, shoving tables and chairs aside. Quickly, they all stood and formed themselves into ramshackle lines, marching in place.

Larry's eyes twinkled in their mask, so much that Keith could feel the sneer. Longhorn waved his arm forward. "Charge!"

"Charge!" the scoundrels echoed, and began marching, single file up the stairs. Ben stood against the back wall, looking dazed.

"Ghost hunt — Ghost hunt — Ghost hunt — " they chanted. The floor above shook from their cadence.

CHAPTER 42
THE BEAR

"You ass." Keith clenched his fists. Ben bent over, laughing. "You knew about Larry all the time. This was all a set up." He pushed the manager against the wall. "You bastard."

He turned back through the doorway to the cramped hall and stubbed his toe on something. John lay sprawled and snoring in the dankness, his head nestled on one deflated burlap oyster bag, his ample frame and legs filling up most of the supply room.

Thuds and screams resounded from above. "You're no help," he said to the sleeping form, and slogged back into the banquet room. "They're all over the restaurant, bastards." Ben said something under his breath that started Manny cackling. Keith growled. "I know a restaurant manager who might get fired. Let's round these fuckers up before they tear the place apart." Like scolded puppies, Ben and Manny followed him up the stairs, then split up to take different dining rooms.

On the second floor, Keith ran through a skirmish of flying sugar packets being fired by opposing combat teams. Tables had been turned over to provide cover. Broken glass littered the floor in patches. A Tom wearing a tiger mask squatted near the balcony railing, bleeding from his mouth badly enough to smear his mask.

"Damn it, guys," Keith bellowed, and hustled into the alcove. He would find Larry and force the impudent bum to bring this rabble under control.

A variety of animals were actually trying to scale the walls, using the antique farm implements as footholds.

"Get down, you're going to kill yourselves," Keith warned.

"Here, spook. Here, spook," one called. The building reverberated with shrieks and curses. Two Toms tried to pass him, carrying an old tin cola sign. Keith jerked it from their hands.

"Jesus Christ. Are you guys looting the place?"

"Oh, I say," Beaver answered. Keith dragged the artifact down the hall, stashed it in Ben's office.

Hearing shouts high above, Keith plodded up the spiral stairs. On the landing by the Lookout, a battle with breadsticks was in progress. Keith's feet crunched spent projectiles, and he had to smile in spite of his anger. Exactly as Governor Hogg had described, Toms used the Indians for cover, jumping out from them, throwing, then ducking behind.

The fighters--Coyote, a Horse and a Wookie, were grudgingly herded toward the stairs. Keith turned to find he had missed one. Bear, the one with the scary eyes, perched on a wooden railing closed to the air ducting.

"Get down from there," Keith yelled. "That's three stories down, man—"

"Kiss my ass," Bear said, his voice almost a hiss. There had to be one jerk in every crowd, Keith thought.

He reached, trying to keep the idiot from tumbling into the darkness. Bear was more graceful that expected, turned, and leaped down, passing Keith, and ramming into the back of the Wookie.

"Hey--"

Bear shoved his comrades both ways, and disappeared between them down the dark stairs.

Banshee wails boiled up from below, bouncing off the ceilings, echoing eerily against the ducting. Keith tarried. This landing had always seemed a spooky environ. Now, the cries and maniacal laughs made it seem like a corner of Hell, itself.

Where could the puppets have been stashed? The Lookout? He took a deep breath and peered once more through the glass in Thomas's door, wondering – for the hundredth time – if the Chef was at the center of all this weirdness.

The blue numbers on a clock radio were the only thing visible. Wait--a movement! He backed up, stomach tightening--the motion was not inside the Lookout, but a reflection in the glass. He twirled around.

Bear. The masked man held an axe. It was a relic from the wall on the second floor. But this wasn't just another prank. Those hate-filled eyes indicated Bear meant business.

"What the hell--" Keith turned the doorknob. Locked.

"I don't have much time." The mouth moved beneath the mask. "The others will be heading back up here in a minute." Menacingly, he took a step forward.

That voice – now that he heard it clearly – all too familiar. First in the bar, then on the night of the picnic – the eyes –

The young cowboy.

"Ben! Larry!" Keith heard himself scream. "Don't be crazy, man." He felt his pocket through the apron – no knife, nothing he could use as a weapon. Only Ernesto's locket. How could the dead boy help him now?

Another step. He raised the axe.

"Hurry." Keith jerked – a whisper from somewhere – the air ducts? From the corner of his eye, Cochise loomed, like an ally. Bear swung, and Keith launched off the steps, heard the *swoosh* through the air. Behind the big Indian. Another stroke. A *thud*. Then a *grunt*.

The axe lodged in the Indian's base. Bear struggled to free it, and Keith squeezed out from behind and ran for the stairs.

Bear anticipated, blocking his flight. The axe-head glinted, and some instinct told Keith not to lose sight of it. Backing, backing, until he felt the catwalk beneath him.

"Ben! Larry!" Shouts of the revelers below drowned his voice. "Up here. Help!" He waved frantically down to figures moving in the shadows far below his feet.

Bear squared in front of him, blocking one end of the walk. Keith's heart slammed in his chest. "What the hell do you want? Money?"

"Fuck you, man."

Back. Across the shaky bridge, until his hand brushed the storage room curtains. A quick step, and he was through, trying to close them behind him. A thump. Bear was on the catwalk now, and Keith realized its shakiness might give him a second – but then what? Trapped here in the storage room, it would be even harder to make himself heard.

He knew the layout in here and Bear did not, but the room was too tiny for advantage. He wedged behind a box as a shield, groped against the wall for anything he might use as a weapon --

"Move—" Another whisper. Who was it? Keith whipped around, stumbling back between two of the waist-high chip boxes, just in time – a dagger of light slashed in, between the curtains, followed by the flailing axe head.

"Is someone there?" he whispered. "Help me. Quick."

"Fuck." Bear's torso bulged through the opening, a dark hulk against the Lookout light. "You ain't gonna bother any woman I want again." That whiny cowboy voice. The axe poked, twisted. Light flashed from the pulsating curtain, and Keith watched as the psychopath dragged use the axe to drag one box out of the way.

Too late, Keith realized he might have grabbed the axe head, but his right foot skidded on the smooth floor. Another box fell from above. Wrong direction.

"After you're gone, I'm gonna find that girl and screw her. She's mine, you son of a bitch."

The curtains flapped closed. Too dark to see now. Another *whoosh* – right next to his ear! He reached for another box, grasped nothing. Not like this. It couldn't end like this. The pull-string hanging from the overhead bulb tickled his neck like a spider's leg.

Another flash of light – Bear was all the way inside, now. Glint of steel. Another swing. Keith braced against the bricks, snatched for the axe's shaft. Missed.

Bear ripped his mask off. "You yellow coward. Get out here where I can see you." Another thrust.

"Keith..."

"What?" he yelled. "Who's calling me?"

A deep, twisted laugh. Axehead high above now. "Maybe it's your little piece of ass, cook." The axe-head *chinged* against brick. Keith felt a stinging bite on his temple, sank to one knee. The world swam. With a last gasp, he grabbed the edge of a chip box.

"So there you are. Gotcha now." Bear raised the weapon high over his head.

Keith pulled the box. Wondered if he could shove it under, body block the bastard.

But it was caught on something. Things fell from overhead. Dizzy, held his hands up to fend off the inevitable blow. Would it hurt?

That noise – feet stomping. Closer.

"Ben – you coming?" He was embarrassed, his voice sounding that weak –

Holding his arm high – one more chance to dodge him –

Why didn't it happen?

Seconds passed. Hours. He waited.

Screams echoed from below. The party was still on. Somewhere, closer, there was scuffling. Keith pushed back against the bricks, cool at first -- but they gave way!

God, he was falling--*through the wall*? Firm hands grasped him, gripped his shoulders firmly, righted him. Behind, someone screamed.

He blinked his eyes, peering through blackness. Then a mouth pressed against his in a violent kiss, tongue pushing its way in forcefully. His eyes flew open, and he pulled away. The face came into focus.

"Carlotta," he said.

She kissed him again, her lips cold, firm, the inside of her mouth as hot as fire. "Where am I?" he demanded.

Without a word, she embraced him and they spun around together, flying in mid-air! The dark ground passed underneath as they floated toward a large tree limb.

"No." His voice was far away, muffled. Carlotta ignored his protest, and pushed him ahead, into the branches of the tree.

"Goddam, not another tree," he screamed. He thrashed to grab a limb with his free hand, desperately holding onto Carlotta's with the other.

"I'm afraid of heights," he yelled. "Where did he go?"

"Who?" She finally answered him, her voice a soothing hum.

"The bear. The cowboy. Am I dead?"

"Listen to the Great Spirit," Carlotta said simply. He looked at her. She sat easily, side-saddle-style upon the broad branch where they rested. My God, she was still so beautiful.

She reached over and turned his head, directing his gaze toward the ground. At the same instant, the broad light of day exploded onto the scene. Not day, but some time near sunset. Or sunrise, he could not tell. Two men stood on the ground below them. One old, the other perhaps twenty years old, he guessed. They were well-dressed, in the fashion of some time long ago, and the gray-headed one was angry.

"You've failed," the old one's words rose through the branches. Anguish coursed through the younger one's heart. Keith knew this because he could hear the man's thoughts, as clearly as if he had spoken them.

Gray-head used a walking cane, and prodded the young man ahead on a worn path that ran next to the house.

"Give them their orders," Gray-head insisted, indicating a throng of men who looked like field workers, standing attentively outside the back gate of the rather large grounds.

My God, this was the Terrace. He recognized the side of the building, though the fences and layout of the grounds were much changed. A glance around. No street, no Water Company. What sort of illusion was this?

Carlotta slapped Keith's head from behind, making him focus all the harder. The young man shied from the servants, and the old one only vilified him more. How could he not see that each sharp word chipped away at the young one's very soul? That face. Roundish, looking sad. It was the face of Poindexter, young, alive, vibrant, but somewhat lost.

Keith shivered, dared to shake Carlotta's arm. "I'm dead, aren't I? To be able to see such things?"

Light changed. The sun set, maybe. Rose again. Now Poindexter sat on the back balcony of the second floor of the mansion, almost as high as the tree where they were perched.

He looked older, now, sitting forlornly, dressed in a suit. The wood of the balcony looked freshly painted, not old and flaky, the way Keith remembered.

This living version of Poindexter seemed to be simply gazing, out over empty fields, sipping tea from a delicate china cup. As Keith clung desperately to the limb, he could again hear the man's thoughts as they swirled around the visage of a woman, resonating, twisting, turning colors in the air. My god, was that what it looked like to be in love with someone?

The abstract colors grew, blew up like a balloon-cloud, mutated, then faded to gray and black, exploded silently, disappated in the dying light. Something had happened to the subject of Poindexter's fantasies. The image of a woman, hologram-like, danced in the air before him. Danced, twirled, then faded away. A tear traced Poindexter's cheek. Life would not be worth living if he could not have that girl.

"Watch, and learn," Carlotta's voice broke through the bubble that surrounded the scene. "The time of self pity weakens us, then the Children come, and one can never stop them."

At the front of the house, a strange man sat in the driver's seat of an old, covered carriage drawn by horses. Other figures scrambled toward the base of the house, carrying torches. They poured a liquid, then ignited it, trying to set the mansion on fire. The bricks would not burn, but one of the vandals threw his torch through the second story window. Other people came screaming, running up the road that followed the river.

"You have no time," Carlotta said adamantly. Her hand extended, blocking his view of the crime. She drew closer, until her face became clear. So striking. Her beauty seemed to hold up the world. "Act," she said, "or our fates will be yours."

Her eyes grew, until their blackness took up the entire field of vision.

"Who are you? What are you doing to me?" he called into the night. "It's too late. He hit me with the axe. Can't you just leave me alone?" The weight of the nothingness became heavy, until he found himself weeping. A breeze played in the tree, shaking the branch as it blew harder, changing pitch, until it became the familiar grinding of the Water Company air conditioners.

His eyes stung as he opened them to the glare of the bulb over the Lookout. God, was he back here? Close by, someone moaned softly. Shadows shifted, out on the landing. He heard sharp, whispered orders, but could not make them out. The voice — raspy — mutated into a quiet, diabolical laugh that echoed softly, then faded away.

Keith's hand moved to the new bump on his head. Blood? He waved his hand out into space until he found the light's drawstring.

"Oh — " Light blasted through the storeroom, and he fell back against the brick. Above the doorway, high atop the stacked chip boxes, the leprechaun marionette sat, frozen, as if posed that way. His arms stuck straight out, eyes and mouth maddeningly open, strings extending downward from his curled fingers.

Below, at the end of those strings, Poindexter hung in mid-air, arms, legs, and tuxedo tails tangled wildly, his eyes shut, making him look almost peaceful. From his fingers, more strings, continuing downward.

At their end, his face bruised, neck wound around with Poindexter's taut strings, the young cowboy hung suspended in the air. Blue eyes stared vacantly from beneath a shock of blond hair. One booted foot dragged the floor. The other did not quite reach. He was dead.

Voices and heavy footfalls approached.

"Keith! Hey, you in here?" It seemed natural to hear that voice say his name.

Steps on the catwalk. Curtains parted. The harlequin stopped in the doorway, cape flying behind.

"Dear God," Woodpecker said. He leaned over, kicked the axe away, then peered into the young cowboy's face. "I--I didn't know he was that crazy..."

Ben moved through the curtains, flinching as he gathered it all in. He looked piercingly at Keith. "You okay?" He crowded past Woodpecker and the hanging things, and knelt down.

Keith indicated his head. "Don't think it's bleeding much," he heard himself mutter. "I didn't fight him. I didn't do that." He hoped they believed it. He hoped it was true.

In slow motion, Woodpecker pulled his own mask away, revealing Thomas himself. The chef stood, his fingers gliding up the strings, all the way to Poindexter, then he stepped up onto one of the utensil chests, followed the strings all the way up to the leprechaun. The chef's ever-pleasant face was pale, drained.

"We were too slow. I was a fool. They told me he was really a good kid--this is all my fault."

"No," Keith whispered, still out of breath. "You didn't do it, either."

Pounding, stomping, yells of discovery ensued. Rat, Coyote, Penguin, Weasel, and others crowded across the catwalk, their eyes fairly bulging from their masks.

Longhorn Larry shoved through them. "Keith! Good God, are you all right?" Far away and below, other Toms still screeched and laughed.

They helped Keith to his feet, guided him around the hanging corpse, then through the curtains. They dragged him, and he felt the catwalk scraping below his feet.

Strong hands, and yet another voice — was it Walrus? — spoke soothingly.

"I've got him. I've got him..."

CHAPTER 43
SCATTERED PIECES

The policeman sat in the hospital chair for a while, asking his questions with little conviction. Like, maybe he had seen crimes like this before - but that was ridiculous, Keith concluded.

No, Keith answered, fighting the fog in his brain, he was not old friends with the cowboy, had never partied with him, gone to bars with him - other than the Water Company bar - and the man's death was not the result of an argument over a bad drug deal.

TOMS UNMASKED! blared the headlines on the front page. ...*the most appalling scandal in Sironia since the deJune sisters both tried to marry their brother*, one columnist declared.

Keith was diagnosed with yet another concussion, and required a dozen stitches — thankfully, the scar would be hidden by his hairline - as long as the hair grew back.

Rather than cuss Larry out from the hospital bed, the pain drugs had left him thoughtful. "You know those mysterious realms that ghosts supposedly take people to? Maybe they are not other worlds, but other times. You know, like taking you back into the past."

"You bastard." Larry leaned forward, spitting food from the Cupp's burger he had brought for Keith. But food just didn't seem right just now. "Something happened, didn't it?"

Keith closed his eyes, intent on at least a bit of revenge. "Don't get so drunk next time and maybe you'll see it, too."

"Damn it, don't do this to me, Big Brother." Larry got up and paced.

Keith kept talking, gazing at the ceiling. "It's like they're telling me a story. First, they threaten me, then they show me some sort of tale."

Larry slowed. "And? Come on, out with it."

"The janitor." Keith felt like giggling, hearing his own dreamy voice. "He can see them, supposedly. But why me? I'm not a Mexican. I don't have a candle and black tables — "

Larry shook the bed. "What are you talking about? Quit being obtuse."

Thoughts wouldn't come clear. He closed his eyes, breathing rapidly to stop himself from weeping. "I swear to God, Larry, someone else wrapped those strings around his neck. I promise."

Then he was quiet, and his brother wiped the sweat off of his forehead with a cool rag. The smell of hamburger with onions surrounded him, but his stomach was still too tight.

On his first night back, Keith sat, peering out of the bar kitchen, watching with disgust the many people who rose from their tables to gawk and point toward places in the restaurant they thought figured into the crime.

Thomas was exposed, as well as Ben, as members of the infamous fraternity of Scalded Toms. Keith's mother predicted the Water Company would close. The opposite had happened so far; the dining rooms were packed every night.

Most of the staff laughed off Thomas's involvement. Katy, though, was non-plussed. "You know I just love that man to death," she said during set-up. "But I'll never be able to forgive him for gettin' mixed up with that bunch of childish yahoos."

"Lord knows he's got a pretty wife," Nosma added. "Why on earth does he need to be takin' dirty pictures of other women?"

Keith's own spirits bounced from relief to guilt and back again. Life seemed too fragile now. Each time he looked at Emily, striding between her tables, the responsible one, intent on finishing her education and making a life, his breath caught and he closed his eyes.

In the darkness behind his lids, he could almost see a fork in the road. Down one path, he would have to think of himself as crazy, a psychopath who blacked out and strangled people with puppet strings. To take the other path was to live in a world where marionettes could move on their own, hunters who never let up, their relentless pressure sapping the joy out of — even loving Emily. She put beers down in front of an elderly couple, leaned her head back and laughed. No, nothing could really spoil loving her.

Ben convinced him to suck it up and not quit until he found a job. Only an idiot would stay, but then, who would protect Emily? On a couple of mornings, he went to the library and searched through the few books on the history of Sironia, and the owners of the Terrace. Plenty of history, but no pictures. They did confirm, as the River Festival tour guide had said, that the owner had been killed in a fire in the front of the building.

Larry tried to analyze the paranormal aspects of Keith's trip through the air in the heat of the battle. "More *astral-traveling*," he said. "The concussion obviously gave you a temporary power you don't usually have." He sat back from his decimated supper. Mom and Dad had already gone back to the TV room. "Did it ever feel like you crossed one of Heider's *boundary lines?*"

"Hell, I guess it's a boundary when you go through solid brick."

"I would feel better if we both left," Emily suggested, when they finally made love again. "There are plenty of other restaurants in town."

"No. You're too close to the new school year." He kissed her eyes. "And you promised we wouldn't talk about my employment prospects for a while."

She slapped him, perhaps only half in fun, then looked truly sorry, and stretched up to kiss his stitches.

Rather than blow up at her, he heard himself coming clean about the astral vision of Carlotta and Poindexter. "What if the whole thing is a screen to block out the truth? What if I really killed that punk?"

"That's pretty good psychology," Emily said, "but I know it wasn't you." Thankfully, she continued to sneak over to his apartment whenever they both had a few hours. But the pressure loomed in the future. Faculty meetings were scheduled soon, and in a few weeks, school. "My calendar is filling up," she said matter-of-factly when he invited her to go to Dallas on his day off. After she quit the restaurant, where would they be?

Lying in bed at night, Keith couldn't go to sleep without thinking of the young cowboy. Finally, one night he opened his eyes to a bright light. He looked around. He was sitting on a bench in a park somewhere. Many trees, but they did not have the height of the big ones down in River Park. Besides, the ground seemed too flat here. Green grass. He slowly became aware of a form to his side. With slow, deliberate breaths, he turned to look — no, it was not Carlotta or Poindexter sitting next to him — his hands gripped the seat of the bench — it was him!

"Hey," the young man said simply. He looked away, scanning the area as Keith just had, and adjusted the cowboy hat on his head.

"Are you all right?" Keith managed to ask.

A look. A smile. "Sure. Why shouldn't I be?"

Keith groped for words. "This place—" He knew what this place was. The Park, where you came to meet your loved ones after death, was one artifact that almost all of the psychic books agreed upon. "Aren't you—"

The young cowboy shrugged. Actually a nice looking guy. His hard edge was gone. Another smile. "I'm good."

An inner voice seemed to want Keith to go back to sleep. He tried not to think, not muddle up whatever he was witnessing. Instinctively, he knew that thinking would just make the sky tatter and break up the dream. It was nice here. Peaceful. More so, being next to the young man. For the first time, it felt like they could even be friends.

Out on the perimeter, down the smooth paths, near the trees, shadowy figures moved. Keith wanted to study them, but knew it was his turn to speak.

"Where will you go?"

A jolt. The cowboy's hand gripped his arm.

"What's the matter?" Heart pounding.

The cowboy's eyes were wide, looking past Keith, the very picture of terror.

"What — what?" Keith asked, still too frightened to turn to see whatever was behind him.

Now both hands gripped and shook him. The young man's breath came in short, powerful pants. "Help me," he whispered.

Keith twisted, grabbed the bench and reached to take the cowboy's hand, all at the same time – but the dream broke up.

John the Wop delayed his own move until Keith came back to work.

"Damn you, I always miss your fights, you goombah."

"Guess I'm just selfish that way."

"Listen, you shit," John's huge finger stuck in his face. "Take care of that little girl." The burly Italian descended the back steps. "Or I'll come back and kick your ass." He crunched across the gravel and drove away.

Only two days later, Patricio announced that he was going to leave the dishwashing cubicle to work with his brother on a ranch outside Dallas.

"Hmph. You think washin' them pans is hard--wait'll one of those hosses kick you in the haid," Nosma warned him. Patricio winked, and went back to work.

"These things are happening too fast," Keith told Ben. "This was starting to feel like home. Now everyone's leaving."

The manager shrugged. "That's the restaurant business."

"Got a surprise for you," Emily smiled mischievously one night in the bar kitchen.

"What? Did you buy it on one of your shopping sprees?"

"No, silly. Didn't you ask me to spend the night again?"

"Now that I'm healthy? Open invitation."

"How about tonight?"

"What? Are you serious? What about your mother?"

"I'm not sure. Maybe she's mellowing in her old age. Really, though, she's been acting differently since I landed my job. Maybe she realizes I'm really leaving someday."

She stayed that night. Keith woke several times, excited to find her sleeping on his shoulder. At dawn, they made love again.

In quiet moments, their talk always degenerated to future plans and jobs. He found himself defending his low-paying job.

"Keith, I told you. It doesn't matter. Whatever makes you happy is what you have to do."

"Yeah, but I know what you really think."

"I think you're a decent writer. Is that a crime?" She tried to joke. "What about your plans to write for TV? Or write plays? You still haven't finished my poem. How long does it take to write one?"

"Not long, when I don't have the pressure of getting a better job. We're catering two dinners this month. I thought I would give it a chance. I get time-and-a-half for each engagement."

"You're not listening to me." She turned to leave, then broke down crying.

He held her. "Move in with me. I want you to."

She looked up, visibly startled. For a moment, their gazes locked. Finally, she wiped her tears, and turned away to sit on the couch.

"Of course not."

"Emily--"

She stood. "I'm flattered, but I don't have time to explain myself now."

"Then when? Emily, I love you."

She walked toward the door. "I'm sorry. Gotta go. Thanks."

The next morning, she made yet another foray to Dallas with Mary for "schoolteacher clothes." Keith was not invited.

CHAPTER 44
JACK CONRAD

Two glittery ladies approached the bar kitchen the next night. The bored-looking man behind them surveyed the lounge at a distance, then turned around. He was Jack Conrad. The advertising exec thrust his head through the window.

"What the hell? I'll be damned. Keith Simpson!"

"Uh, Clayton," Keith corrected.

"That's right. By God, Marge, you remember Keith--"

She blushed. No one bothered to introduce their friend.

"I remember now, you said you were working over here." Jack shoved his hands in his pockets and rocked on his heels. "Christ, I didn't realize you were cooking."

"Just cooking away."

"I'll be damned! That's the life. Just cooking. Small menu, low stress." Jack switched to a mock-whisper. "You son of a bitch, I'll bet you're working on that screen play, aren't you?" He winked. "Elmer filled me in on you and the rest of his creative types before he folded. Said you were destined for something better than advertising. How far along are you? Found an agent yet?"

"Not exactly."

"You got it made, man. Smart. None of this nine-to-five shit for you." Then to Marge. "Go ahead, girls. Order, order." Keith caught a whiff of bourbon.

Their table in the dining room was ready, so they left. Minutes later, as Keith walked through to deliver Jack's oysters, he caught himself worrying about making the right impression on the man. What the hell for?

He had checked by the Conrad Agency more than once. Earline always waved him away. A few free-lance jobs, sure. Radio copy. Nothing steady.

"Ah, here's our man," Jack said in his boisterous manner. As ever, his hair was perfect. Blown dry, no doubt.

"Oysters on the half shell." Keith bowed ostentatiously.

"Ooh, yum," said their friend.

"My goodness. Red sauce. Oh, that's so spicy. Eunice," Mrs. Conrad shook her poised fork at the other woman, "you'd better not dip them. That sauce is too spicy for your esophagus."

"Oh, to hell with my esophagus." They all laughed.

"Thank you, Keith, my man." Jack handed him a folded five-dollar bill before he could protest.

"Uh, thanks." He shuffled back past the entry way, the question about freelancing still stuck in his throat.

Happy Hour dragged. Certainly, he could have cadged a couple of assignments, with Jack in such a good mood. What had held him back? Pride? Pride, when he was bowing and scraping like a clown? Somehow, piled on top of Emily's rejection, his failure to act pressed in. In this world, you didn't get what you want unless you went after it. Emily would get what she wanted.

A glance at the lounge's side door brought a new shiver. Was that shadowy Larcinter out there, waiting for him in the boat? It was one way out. Either that or cooking school. Without John, though, this profession didn't seem so enjoyable just now. The band was setting up, and Keith started packing up his utensils.

"How about another plate of those oysters?"

The ad exec, himself, loomed over the order window, gulping down the remnants of his cocktail. His tie had been loosened.

"Hi, Jack. Sure." Keith dug a half-dozen oysters from the bag and began popping them under the running tap. "Did the ladies like the first batch?"

"Yeah, the old bags." Jack pulled out the stool under the serving shelf. "I had tc get away from all that gossip for a few minutes. Don't mind, do you?"

"Help yourself."

Jack turned to size up a table of coeds who were growing boisterous. "Good, God, there's a couple o' those I'd like to get friendly with," he muttered.

"Yeah, not bad." Keith chuckled politely.

"What the fuck. Any one of them would probably kill me." His speech was already slurring, but he hailed Andrea and held up his empty glass. "What the hell are you doing here anyway, Keith? Are you really going out to Hollywood, or are you going to shuck these damn things for the rest of your life?"

"Funny you should ask. I was just wondering about that myself." Andrea brought his drink. He gaped at the back of her tights as she walked away.

"Dear God," Jack sighed. "Tell me how I can get in with that little filly, and I'll give you my fucking Agency." He spiked the first oyster with his fork and studied it, exhaling through his nose.

"Maybe we can work something out." Keith played the part, marveling at how consistently offensive the guy was. Perhaps a tiny bit more mellow than he used to be, though.

"You're wasting your talent here. Why don't you come to work for me? I just had a guy move to Dallas. We're doing real good."

"*Well*," Keith corrected him by reflex.

"Huh? Well. We're doing well." Jack chuckled. "See there? A true copywriter. Can't stand to see the language used wrong."

Keith refrained from saying *wrongly*.

"Come on, what do you think?"

Andrea brought him his bill to sign, smiled at Keith, then left. He watched Jack fidget with his credit card on the ledge. Credit cards. That part of his past seemed so long ago.

Jack's eyes kept roving, and the cuff of his jacket slopped through a puddle next to his drink. The last oyster went to its reward.

"Give me a day or two to get back to you."

"No problem. Take forty-eight hours. Say yes, sport. I need to hire soon, and I'd rather have someone with your experience."

Emily finally answered her phone, bushed after her daylong trip. Even so, she said, her mother might take her the other direction--to Austin--in the morning, to see if she could complete her wardrobe.

"I need to talk to you now. I've got a big decision to make and I don't want to do it over the phone."

She hesitated. "It's so late, and I really need some sleep, Keith. Day after tomorrow I'll give you all the time you need. Mom wants to get started early."

"Emily. This is about us."

"Keith, I'm too wrecked to give it the right attention, and I don't have time to talk about any more hallucinations just now, OK? Good night."

Keith reeled. The end could not be far off. She would be smart to cut her losses now. Perhaps she sensed the hopelessness of it all. So what if he did sign on with the Conrad agency, and the infernal dreams followed him there? Larcinter might just keep coming.

He switched the light off and lay, listening to crickets, passing cars, someone's stereo in a far apartment. One hand wandered the night table until it found Ernesto's locket. He held it up in the dark, as if he could see the boy's wan face.

"You never had to fuck around with relationships and career decisions, did you?" he asked aloud. The piece of jewelry jumped out of his fingers, and it took a few moments to find it in the folds of the quilt. He raised it once more, squinting, as if the boy were looking back at him, nodding. As if, even from the prison of his plastic and metal talisman, he had some wisdom to impart.

But relationships and career decisions aren't the real demons, are they Ernesto?

CHAPTER 45
WARNING BY THE RIVER

"I'm sorry, Uncle," Lionel whispered.

Incomplete chants danced through his head at random, memories of Uncle's farm, catalogues of the lines of dust he had swept off into corners, just ahead of the feet of others. Nothing remained in his mind for any length of time. Even calling Carlotta was impossible. And Branwyn only stared at him from lonely corners, too swift for him to catch up with, and he could not find words to say, anyway. Was there any way to put the pieces back together?

"The way to pierce any wall," Uncle said in his memory, "is to begin by confessing that you are ignorant. You may learn everything in this universe, but it will never be enough to ride the wave of the infinite. Only faith will let you do that. Faith is the shadowy backside of knowledge."

He always hated the old magician's riddles.

The candle burned steadily. Ignorant? Yes. *Estupido.* How could he think of assisting Carlotta to re-enter this life, when he was incapable of helping even himself?

He lay back, covered himself with the magic blanket. In the moment when his muscles finally started to relax, a shiver pulsed through the very air, and the flame grew brighter. He stood up, rubbed his eyes, then opened them. He was standing beside the river in broad daylight!

"Surprise is painted on your face," a voice behind him said. "I think it would be easy for that girl to love you at times like this." He turned to see Carlotta, standing easily in the tall grass. "I remember surprise--a wonderful feeling."

"My love." He rushed to embrace her. She allowed it.

"How have you brought me here? I tried to open the gate for you to return to this life, but my will failed me." He buried his face in her luxurious hair. "Oh, *mi amor,* can I have another chance?"

"You are more powerful than ever." Her words were patient, so much more than Uncle's. She stroked his face, and made him look at her. A smile, then she kissed him boldly, took his hand in hers, and led him slowly along the riverbank.

The water flowed, placid yet strong. He was still not used to the nakedness of the hill where the restaurant should be, nor the flat plain across the river, where the city skyline no longer stood. Of course – this was *before,* not the future.

"Tell me." He fell to one knee and kissed her hand. "How can I rescue you now? What spell? What chant can I use?"

"It is fantasy to think I could come back." She pulled away, sat close to the water, and propped her arms on her knees.

"Don't say that, darling. Uncle told me that souls cross over all the time. You came here. This place must be halfway. Give me your hands again. I will hold you when we pass through the doorway back to my world. If I wish hard enough, it may work."

She lowered a finger to close his lips. "I can move now because he gained energy. A powerful burst. He is replenished, and more dangerous than ever."

"So you may go your own way? He won't stop you from coming with me?"

"He does not care about me. For a while. But his appetite is whetted. He and his hell-hound are already hungry again."

He tried to kiss her, but her outstretched finger held him at bay. "You are powerful enough to deal with your fate. Embrace your new love and you can conquer anything. You are emerging from your cocoon, and it is time for your new life to begin."

"No, no. You are my love." He put his hands on both sides of her body. "I can do the spell now, I am sure of it. Can't you feel it? His dirty tension is gone, and a new freedom surrounds you. It will work this time."

"Such a true heart." Carlotta looked away, shaking her head. Never before had she seemed so accessible, so human. It was as if he were talking about daily chores to his sister, if he had ever had one. "It is all my fault. If I had only obeyed, and not told the Gringo to resist, my master would not have grown so desperate. It could have been the same, always the same. Now, though, he grows more like his monster, digesting new energy in huge gulps, licking his lips and looking for more. What you sense is the quiet before the storm."

"Please." He grabbed her arm, and suddenly, the bright blue day went black. A deep heaviness, a sense of fear hung in the sky.

"What's happening?" He gasped, heart racing. A glance across the river revealed that downtown Sironia had reappeared, its dirty brick skyscrapers casting anemic glows from random lighted windows. They were back in the real world, yet she was still with him.

He gripped her arm all the harder, and she rose up on her knees before him, gazing with kind, deep eyes. Sinking into them, he knew her warnings were truth. The fear of her master was something that any sane person must understand, to understand her.

"What can I do? Will he still try to take the Gringo? Will he take me?"

"He will try to take everyone."

She was silent, perhaps letting the words hit their mark. Then she stood, but he could not, even though he tried. It was as if the cold dew on the grass had soaked him, weighing him down. She bent, and put her fingers softly through his bushy hair. His mouth moved, but no words escaped. Frozen in place, he could only watch as she walked away into the grass, lit for a moment by the harsh streetlight across from the restaurant – it made her glow. Yet she cast no shadow.

Life had its sweet parts, but he would give them up, he wanted to yell, if he could follow her into the night. Give them up, pay any price, even face her master on the field of battle.

The river eased by, sliding, shifting, somehow magically immune to the restaurant's oppressive silence. The battle would be here, he thought, were it ever to happen. On the river. Uncle had fought such a battle once. But would he have lost, if he had chosen a river, instead of a fencepost, as the place to make his stand?

CHAPTER 46
THE QUESTION

For a couple of weeks now, Thomas had permitted the repatriation of none other than Chet, the leader of the cowboy trio. On the first night, he came directly up to Keith and apologized, explaining that it was his fault for not realizing that his young protégé had been "bad mean." Then he turned, selected a table, and started nursing a beer along, perhaps more slowly than any teetotaler ever could have. He seemed content to drink the music, the ambiance more.

Each time he ordered something to eat, Chet was overly polite. Against his better judgment, Keith found him affable and intelligent. The rangy character told stories about women, turkey fries, mountain oysters, and often amused Keith by painting speculative pictures about the people who entered the bar. Sometimes, Keith agreed. At other times, they wound up debating human nature.

"I think I'll ask her to move in again." Keith was halfway embarrassed when he realized he was pouring out his troubles to a character he had once despised. "I just have to decide when the right time is to do it."

"Sounds like you're in a bind," Chet mused. "Maybe you oughta rein in and wait for her next feint."

"Sorry I didn't call," Emily said as she breezed by, just arriving for her shift. "Mom and I got back too late last night."

"That's a lot of shopping trips, Lady. Have you spent your first year's salary yet?" Keith asked.

"So what about this big decision of yours?" She pulled her hair and pinned it behind. "When I have a minute, I'll come back. I want to hear."

"Forget it," he said, then instantly regretted his sourness, but it was history. A night of sleeplessness, a phone call to Jack this morning. History. For better or worse.

During a lull, she finally appeared in the little kitchen and gave him a perfunctory kiss, then rushed back out after only small talk. For the next hour or so, dropped by only when he had his hands full of orders.

It's happening. Her attitude had transformed into one identical to Linda's in those weeks before she moved out.

The lounge was packed when Chet appeared and grabbed the last small table opposite Keith's serving window. He carefully laid his Stetson in the chair adjacent. Emily brought his regular beer without even waiting for his order.

The overhead music played while Joe-Ben, Keith's favorite of the musicians who played the lounge, set up his stool and guitar. Rotating between cutting board and deep fat fryer, Keith found himself craning his neck, peering out at the lines of Emily's body, her graceful movements, her smiles for the customers. Pain. His breath came in short bursts while he popped oysters and drilled through fantasies of how the end might come.

Joe-Ben played his first set. The soulful, deep voice that usually soothed Keith's tensions, had the opposite effect tonight. During the break, Emily came into view, and placed soiled glasses up onto the serving shelf while she wiped a table down.

"Hey, we haven't had tiome to talks. I want to see you," Keith said in a stage whisper. A few customers looked up.

"I'm busy. I'm not really in the mood right now," she answered quietly.

Feelings crashed inside. "Look? What's the matter? Can you come over tonight?"

"I don't know." Out came her order pad. A new couple sat down.

While she smiled and scribbled, Keith took a deep breath. His hands shook. Now she moved toward Chet.

"Another round?" Her voice was silky.

He could stand it no longer.

"Emily! What do you mean you don't know?"

Heads turned.

She glared over her shoulder. Cheeks crimson. "Keith. Now is not the time."

"Why don't you know?"

Conversations died.

"This isn't the place--" She picked up Chet's empty mug.

"I don't care if it's the place or not."

She looked up, eyes flashing. He plunged ahead. If it had to be, he would go down fighting. "I'm quitting. Taking an advertising job. I start in two weeks. I'll telling Thomas when he comes in."

Emily's brow furrowed. A long moment. Glasses clinked,

"That's not what this is about," she said.

Another pause. Eyes of the crowd turned toward him, as if this were a tennis match, but Keith was beyond care. If his news meant so little, this really was the end.

Chet wiped his mouth with a plaid sleeve, and stepped into the vacuum. "Young man--" His gray eyes stared evenly from under his heavy brow. Keith wanted to kill the bastard, and didn't care what he had to say. He looked, instead, at Emily, who stared at the floor now, her tray in mid-air, her lip quivering. Chet kept talking, " —I promised you, when we had our little talk, that I wouldn't ever mess with your women folk again, but why don't you cut the shit and go ahead and ask the little girl to marry you?"

The song overhead ended. Bottles, glasses, faces froze in odd poses. Even Jeremy's whining magpie voice ceased behind the bar, and the silence that rushed in blew away what was left of Keith's thought processes.

He exhaled, as if Chet had punched him in the gut. Dozens of stares raked him, but his eyes could not leave Emily. Tears were running down her cheeks.

What would life be like without her? Had this whole Water Company nightmare been for nothing? The silence stretched out, impossible and strange in this den of drunks and wise-asses, but he felt it—all the craziness, the weary hours, the clanging confusion of barked orders, laughter, and cursing in Spanish, felt it shifting and moving like the heavy boxes in the walk-in freezer, settling down at light speed into something that finally made sense. He took a long, slow gulp of fresh air.

"Emily, will you marry me?"

The first note of a new song blasted from the speakers, a college boozer let out a low whistle, and the tennis match faces swiveled back toward the weeping cocktail waitress in the middle of the room.

She wiped tears away with the heels of her hands, and looked up through smeared mascara. "That," she said softly, "is what this is all about.' She rushed to the serving window, stretched her arms, and pulled Keith almost through it. "Yes,' she whispered into his ear. They kissed.

Applause and whistles broke from all corners of the lounge.

"To the newlyweds," someone called. Glasses filled the air.

Keith heard nothing more, but his fingers felt her heart pounding through the back seam of her cocktail dress.

CHAPTER 47
FAREWELLS

The pain of leaving was even worse when Keith looked into Nosma's huge, sad eyes.

"Good for you, hon," the large lady said. "You gonna need a better payin' job if you're getting' married."

"What you talkin' about?" Katy chimed in. "He's blowin' it. Hyar he could just sit back and coast and let Emily bring home most of the bacon. Better think this over, Keith."

"You've got a point there." He laughed with them. "I'm headed back into a stress fatory when I should just stay here with you all."

"Now don't even start," Nosma said. "Ain't no more stress anywhere than Friday and Sat'dy rush. So don't go tellin' all them rich folk they is."

"I won't. Promise." More laughter.

"You go?" Mr. Thieu asked, peering through his coke-bottle glasses.

"Yes, sir. Got a new job."

"Go now?"

"Not today. Few more days."

"When you go?"

"Uh, week from Friday."

The old Vietnamese took off his cap, ran fingers through the few strands of black-gray hair. "No good," he said.

"No good? I make more money."

Still shaking his head. "No good me." He raised a finger, pointed at the freezer. "That monkey house. If you are not here, monkey, he take me into his house." He burst out laughing, and Keith patted him on the shoulder.

"Ehh, you leave." Alberto frowned. Whipping eggs for Hollandaise sauce. It was Saturday brunch already, and Keith had never learned the younger man's knack for making it perfect. "What is your new job?"

"Copywriter. For an advertising agency." The look that returned was not suspicion. Or envy or disgust. More like stupefication. "You know? The guys who make commercials on TV and radio? I'll be writing what they say."

Now it seemed to dawn on him. "You will be rich, *Pendejo*."

Keith shook his head. "I wish. Maybe in twenty years. Maybe thirty. When I start, it's not so much."

It didn't alter Alberto's sneer one iota. He reached up to turn the Mexican radio station louder. "More than minimum wage?"

"Well, yes."

"Ehh, you be rich." An embarrassed silence followed, until Alberto stopped whipping, looked up with an earnest face. "When you make money, you will get a new car, OK?"

Keith laughed. "I promise. And I'll come by and show it to you."

Back in the prep room, Keith put the finishing touches on a pan of refried beans. It was one of the dishes he intended to make at home, as long as Emily put up with them. He felt someone's presence, looked around to see the Intellectual.

"*Como esta?*" Keith asked.

"*Bien.*"

"Did you hear? I'm leaving."

Lionel nodded, leaned on his broom.

"We never did get to talk. Wish we'd had time. There are a dozen things I'd like to ask you."

"I am not the one with answers." The janitor seemed as uncomfortable as Keith felt. He looked around, perhaps to see if anyone else was listening. "You wish to ask the spirits?"

"Spirits?" Enough. Keith was through with all that. How to let the guy down easy?

His mind raced, recounting every interaction with this weirdo, halfway wanting to let him have it for jacking Branwyn around. The poor girl was more of a wreck than ever. Even to Emily. His history in the restaurant loomed in every corner of his brain, though, stopping him from coming out with a smart reply, something to put the freak in his place.

And that wasn't good, he was sure Emily would say, with all her little Freudian answers to things. His mind dodged, every time he evn approached memories of that horrible night. Larry was hardly speaking to him.

But maybe they were both right. There was something here that wasn't settled. A guy had tried to kill him. And died. He took the big spoon off the rack, started scraping through the beans, knocking them off the smooth metal sides, avoiding the processer choppers in the middle. He didn't even concoct his reply – it just came out:

"You mean, like at a séance?"

Lionel didn't even answer the question. Just stood there, glum as ever. "Everybody is leaving now," he said. "Patricio, John, you, Chavo…"

"Chavo? I didn't hear about that."

"Maybe. He has a new job, maybe." There was the slightest hint of embarrassment, whatever that meant.

"Why? He might become a chef here, if he works long enough?"

A shrug. "He is afraid of--" Finger pointing upward. The night of the Toms' Tea had shaken the old building to its foundations, apparently. "He wishes to ask the spirits. He works very hard on a decision."

"That's stupid," Keith said. "You think he's scared of the puppets, but he wants to have a séance."

No reply. Lionel didn't seem happy.

Keith tried to make amends. "I mean, you're going to have a séance anyway? A real one?"

A slight nod.

"Yes, I would be interested. When?"

"Tomorrow. After work. Ben knows we will lock up. You wish to come?"

Keith switched off the chopper, began mixing, looking for hulls. Maybe he had to get all this out of his system. But he'd be damned if he was going to invite Larry.

"Sure. I'll be there. Downstairs." He knew the answer to that. "And it's OK with Ben if we're here late?"

Maybe there was a nod. The janitor just shuffled away.

"*Gracias,*" Keith called after him.

He finished prepping the bar kitchen. They were supposed to have an apprentice for him. The one who would replace him in the bar. Supposedly, Cicso would conjure up a replacement for behind the Line. Tonight, he was still alone. And glad of it.

He thought about Lionel's little tables and candles in the basement. He didn't relish asking questions of any "spirits" in front of Chavo. Besides, there had been no more bad dreams since the incident, and not since Emily said "yes." Was he tempting fate, daring to stir up thoughts about the marionettes again?

Hopefully, Emily would have no objections. Didn't really matter. There were some answers he needed before they both left this place. He doubted Lionel could some up with them, but at least he could leave knowing that he tried. After Friday, it wouldn't matter anymore.

CHAPTER 48
A SÉANCE

Jack asked Keith to come by and pick up an assignment to work on before he actually started.

"It'll help you get your mind back in the right place," the blowhard said. Classic, greasy smile. Perfectly greased hair. What was Keith getting into?

"Ad copy and a radio jingle." Jack swelled around his office, barking curt orders to the underlings who filed in, wanting approval of this or that project. They looked at Keith like sheep welcoming another of their kind to the shearing line.

"Don't have time for this--" He rejected one supplicant, then shoved a folder across the table to Keith. "These are for *La Tapatia*, the new Mexican restaurant opening just down the river from your digs." Smart-ass smile. "Closer to the University. Those kids may just choose to stop there. After all, they can just order chips and salsa to go along with their beer."

Keith shook his head, skimming down the menu. Artwork, very good. Probably Charles Miller, if he still worked here. "Pretty ironic. Working for the competition before I'm even out the door."

"You working tonight?"

"Yeah."

Jack swelled up. "Well, it oughta be pretty quiet tonight, eh? If you have anything written before your shift ends, run it by Thomas. See what he thinks."

This was gall, even for Jack. "I can't tell him I'm advertising for some other restaurant."

"Put a lid on it. Thomas owns *La Tapatia*. You should know that."

"What? Bullshit."

"Oh, sorry." The ad man seemed tickled pink, full of the gloat that egotists get when they're the first to reveal a secret. "I was sure he would have told you by now. Hush-hush. The papers aren't to know yet. That ass, Dillweather, will write a bad review before the doors even open.

"Anyway, this is going to be big. Full page ads, prime time TV, radio, the whole blowout. At least for the Grand Opening.

"I've got Bill Jensen on the television pieces, but he'll be glad to listen to any ideas you have. Don't twist your mouth. He'll listen because I've ordered him to. No petty rivalries in my agency. *Capiche*? Show your ideas to Thomas, for chrissakes. That'd be one way to get the boot in ahead of Bill. Now get out. I'm busy."

This was Emily's last night, and Anna had outdone herself with a fabulous sheet cake. The party after work was impromptu, but Keith was certain most of the staff would stick around.

"Are you gonna make a cake that big for my last night, Anna?" he asked.

"Are you kiddin'? Emily's been here more than two years. You ain't been here six months. I might scrape up a little cupcake, if'n I have time."

Neither Thomas nor Ben seemed in a mood to celebrate anything.

"What's wrong?" Keith asked.

"Oh, it's a bunch of shit," Ben replied. "The fire chief called to say he's coming later to inspect our boiler."

"What boiler?"

"Yeah." Ben took a breath.

"Take care of it," Thomas said, walking toward the entry. "We'll shove people upstairs until it's done."

Ben explained:

"When this was a real water purification plant, they had three big boilers. The last one was built in the Forties, and that's the only one that can even hold water anymore. It's on the river sie of the basement. Walled-off, but there's a little hatch you can go through to get to it."

"I never saw any little hatch."

"In the wall – behind where Manny had the portable bar that night. I didn't point it out to you or Larry, because Thomas's paranoid about anyone screwing around down there. If the Toms had found it, God help us."

"So?"

"So that boiler has to be pressure tested every year or so. Some Civil Defense rule."

"Pressure? What on earth for?"

"It's Homeland Security or something. Goddam government. They know where every big water tank in the country is. If there's a war or a natural disaster or something, I guess the Feds can take them over and use them for – hell, I don't know. They could have commandeered it after the flood, but the goddam thing was under water."

The inspector, Ben went on, had chosen to come late that afternoon, right before the dinner rush. Maybe all the Tom's Tea press had put a black mark on us in City Hall. They would have to pull out the table over the trap door in the middle of everything.

"Pain in the ass." Ben plucked utensils, salt and pepper shakers, napkins off the big table. "To get it up to pressure, we have to light the furnace under it. All that old metal is about to fall apart. Thomas got a bid from Don Crosby to pull the damn thing out of there, but he wants ten thousand dollars. Plus all the red tape.

"By the way, in case you ever go in there, the little hall to the right leads to what's left of the tunnel. That, also, is *verboten*. It's half caved-in, like I told you. So don't get any ideas. Thomas fired the last waiter who got drunk and went snooping around down there. Thomas is convinced someone will die in that tunnel someday, and the lawsuit will wreck the restaurant."

Keith could have guessed the truth would come out someday. But his foundation shook, anyway. He and Larry and Ben had been bosom buddies most of their lives. What did this place have that would make the guy be so evasive – especially about such a juicy thing as a secret tunnel they'd used more than a hundred years ago?

"So what?" Keith played the smart-ass. Ben wasn't the only one with a secret. "He'll have another dining place to retreat to."

The manager paled. "Huh? Did he tell you about it?"

"Didn't have to. I'll be working for the agency who works his goddam account. And thanks very much for being so forthcoming about all this – this --"

"Come on, Keith. I work for Thomas. I gotta follow orders sometimes."

"Yeah? Is it Thomas who keeps hiding the marionettes?"

"Look, Dude, you're obsessed with those damned toys. Some of us have to work for a living. I don't have time to run up there every day to take inventory."

Keith picked up his utensils and started down the hall, partly to keep from socking that sneering countenance right in the nose.

"Hey," Ben said. Voice soft enough to make Keith slow down. "If you're with the Agency, then we'll still be working together. Sort of."

The commotion in the dining room drove more business into the bar. Keith couldn't find a five-minute break to run down and take a look through the hatch. On a trip back to the kitchen , though, he saw the fire chief and his entourage leaving through the back door.

"Thank goodness that's over," Thomas said, loud enough for the whole kitchen to hear. Keith dumped his load right in front of Patricio, and on his way back, overheard the head chef instructing Lionel about how to drain water from the boiler. Intense, nodding. Keith wondered if he would miss the janitor.

The old building was packed, as if the public could always sense which night would be the most inconvenient for them to show up. With lots of orders, the night flew by. News of Thomas' new restaurant plowed through the staff like a tsunami. Every wait person had a plan, already, about how to snag a better position at *La Tapatia*.

Keith delivered a plate of oysters to the main dining room – now in full swing – and Ben yelled at him from the register.

"Why don't you think about staying? I could get you a waiting job over there, for sure."

If Jack Conrad got any more irritating, it might be worth considering.

Nosma pushed her girth through the swinging doors and made her first visit to the bar kitchen since Keith was hired. The good-natured lady had pulled the early shift, as ususal, but had returned for Emily's going away party. She peered through the serving window with a jaded eye.

"Is this all you got to do out here? A little fryin' and listenin' to that awful music? Shit-a-monkey, I'm gonna ask Ben to put me out here. This is a cakewalk."

"Now, Nosma," Keith said as he extracted tortillas – one-by-one – from the deep fat, "it was busier thirty minutes ago. You're here at the wrong time." He constructed a plate of nachos while she watched, shoved it out the window. "Number fifty-three," he yelled.

"You ain't foolin' nobody," she said with a cackle. "You cain't count that high."

Manuel was busy training Humberto, Patricio's replacement in the dishwashing cubicle. Keith thought he would give the wide-eyed hombre a treat early, and brought back a couple of *Shirley Temples* from the bar.

"*Muchisimas gracias*," Humberto said in his booming voice, then gave a slight bow. The new man was as short as Chavo, like a compact brick wall on legs. The other Mexicans teased him for being brought up on a farm. His teeth were jumbled, and big, and Keith had watched over Cisco's shoulder one night when the young mad bit a pork chop bone in half. Humberto's eyes grew huge every time Manuel turned on the conveyor belt.

Keith was sweating and stinking by the time the front doors closed. Anna's sheet cake was brought out, a masterpiece with the words *Good Luck, Emily* written in blue over white icing.

"It's beautiful," Emily squealed. The ladies of the kitchen crowded around. Even Arkie, who had come with Nosma. They began to distribute pieces.

As soon as the party commenced, Chavo disappeared. Near the main entrance, Lionel caught Keith's eye, nodded meaningfully. Keith slid back through the swinging doors, and whispered into Emily's ear.

"A séance?" She was so surprised, icing scattered from her lips.

"Oh, my law," Nosma bellowed. "Let me outta this place, they gonna raise the dead."

Keith laughed. "It's not like that. We're just – Chavo's going to--" But he didn't know how to finish.

Thomas butted in, as if he knew where Keith was going. "Hey, if you see Lionel, ask him if all the water's drained out."

"Water?"

"From the boiler, *Cabrones*." Laughter all around. It was Keith's chance. He took it, trotted to the empty main dining room, past the out-of-place table, and down the steps to the basement.

Lionel had left the lights on. Down the hall on the far side, Keith found them. Black candles were already dripping wax onto the tiny black table. Chavo gave an embarrassed smile, but made no eye contact. Lionel's faded beadspread lay across his lap, and the janitor waved for Keith to sit.

The two cushions were there, as if a white guy couldn't sit on concrete. But before he sat, he whispered Thomas' message to the would-be spirit-talker.

"Water?" The Intellectual frowned. "I think it is broken." He rose, held a hand up to Chavo, and left.

Rather than stay and make the little cook's cheeks grow any redder, Keith followed Lionel down the hall, back to the west wall, toward the river, and watched as the little hatch came open.

Seeming oblivious to Keith's presence, Lionel crawled through. Keith waited a moment, then stuck his head in. A tight, concrete-walled passage led to the right. Cobwebs. A light came from somewhere behind the huge pipes that Lionel carefully scrambled over. Huge metal tanks – like generators in a dam, almost – but Lionel was only concerned with one.

He disappeared around a corner, came back with a flashlight, flashed it along the pipes that lined the wood-beamed ceiling.

By now, Keith was all the way through the hatch. He guessed he was standing right under the register in the front entryway.

"Need help, Lionel?" He was glad he'd lost weight during his months of unemployment. This hole was downright claustrophobic.

"No."

Behind him, back through the hatch, people were laughing. Women.

"Crap. The ladies are coming down the stairs," he yelled at Lionel. As if the man cared.

He stuck his head back through, in time to intercept Katy, Nosma, Mary and Emily. "What's going on?" he yelled. "I don't think Chavo wants this many people at his séance."

"Well, Mr. Supernatural." Katy smiled. "Your fiancée has never seen the basement, and she didn't have a *man* who would show her--"

They laughed, as if it were the funniest joke ever told.

"Oh, quit looking like a disappointed baby, Keith," Emily said. "We all wanted a tour of the place down here. Righ, Nosma?"

"*P –U* !" the big lady replied. "That smell. This place is awful. They oughta just cement it in." She inspected the bare walls. "You all go on. I've seen enough." Headed back to the steps —

"Please, don't leave yet," Mary pleaded, drink in hand. The big cook hesistated, stepped back down.

" Well, you'd better make it quick."

From the side hall, Chavo finally appeared, looking panicky.

"Chavo," Keith yelled. "Please show these ladies what's down that hall, and they'll be on their way."

Puzzled look. Mumbling. *Por favor,*" he said abruptly, bowed, and motioned them down the hall.

"I'll be there in a minute," Keith called after them, and hustled back into the dark passage. Nosma was saying something about not being scared with Chavo along.

"Sorry," he said to Lionel, who was hammered something down by the floor. "Can I help?"

"*Si.*" The Intellectual looked up. A sad look, somehow. "But first, can you please tell the *patron* the mechanism is broken. High pressure. The furnace. Can he fix it? *Por favor?*"

Keith climbed back out, ran to tell Thomas.

In the kitchen, Thomas and Ben ate cake, Charlie was doing impersonations in a circle of waitresses, and Shirley had obviously overdone it on the champagne, because she started punching Thomas' shoulder.

"How does a boy from New York know how to cook Mexican food?" she asked.

"TV dinners," Charlie yelled.

Mouth full, spitting as he talked. "Who the hell said I was cooking Mexican? That's what we have Cisco for." Laughter. By now, Keith was at Thomas's side. He spoke steadily. Clearly.

A shake of the head. "I'm tired of fooling with the damned thing." Thomas slammed his plate down, and poked a finger at Keith's chest. Again. "The valve must be rusted through. Go down there and tell him to look for the bigger valve, up on the wall. Turn off everything, and we'll drain the goddam thing tomorrow morning."

Keith jostled back through the others. Was blocked only by Anna. A strange look in her eyes.

"Keith, hon, would you make sure Nosma's OK? I'm worried about her down there in that hole."

Arkie wiped her mouth delicately. "That gal'll never be able to crawl up out of there," she said. "Might as well cover up the hole and put up a stone."

"Arkie!"

Keith laughed, but someone else grabbed his arm.

"Look--" Julie, one of the other cocktail girls. She pointed toward the icemakers. From beneath, black smoke poured through the wide vents.

"There's a fire downstairs!"

CHAPTER 49
A FIRE

Keith made the dining room first, Ben yelling after him, "Don't go down there – "

But that was exactly – one foot slipped, and he went flying headlong across the click floor. Up again. Around the salad bar – and saw something that buckled his knees:

From the trapdoor, a small figure clambered out, looked over his shoulder, and scampered across the floor, headed for the bar – *the leprechaun!*

Keith fall back, unable to breathe, watching long black strings work the terrible marionette – strings that stretched upward toward the ceiling, three stories above. An impossible nest for a puppeteer. If there was one.

Panting viciously, Keith looked back. Incredibly, no one else had emerged from the kitchen yet.

"Stop that marionette," he yelled. Then, at the smoking hole in the floor, "Emily!"

Taking a deep breath, ducking his head, he plunged downward. On the bottom step, he slipped again, tumbled, came right down, head on concrete. Cool. The smoke wasn't down this low. He groped for the hallway.

"Emily," he called again. Ribbons of fired flashed in lines on the wooden ceiling, through the billowing smoke.

He crouched low, hoping there would still be air near the floor. Why weren't the others coming down to help?

"Emily. Chavo." Lunged through smoke, arms outstretched, groping blindly for a familiar object – the wooden doorway scratched his fingers.

Stepping more surely now. Running out of aird. Was there a pocket of it in the far room? How did the firs spread this fast? Did the women already get out? Did they go the other way? Safe on the front lawn right now?

"Emily. Kary. Is anyone there?"

A wretching cough bent him over, propelled him backward into the banquet room.

"Emily –" repeating all their names, sucking air at the floor before he tried again – "Come out this way. Follow my voice--"

She was in there. Only now did he realize how many fantasies he had concocted these last few weeks. All about her, having sex, making children. Making a life together. At night, it was those images that crowded out the visions of puppets and ancient wagons and boats. So unfair – that he'd seen the leprechaun again, right when their new life was about to begin —

"Go," he commanded himself.

"Keith, come up out of there--" Ben's voice. Or was it John? No, John was gone. Should he believe them?

"Help me," he cried, closed his eyes, and pushed through the doorway again. Eyes pouring. Heat. Blackness. Another step, hands thrust forward -- Nothing.

Had to grab her fast – had to push straight through, not stop this time – hands out, jog – get to the big room at the far end -- A step. A leap –a lungful of smoke sent him right down to the floor again.

Can't stop now. Pushing. Pushing. Crawling.

"Emily – Nosma – Katy--" Voice little more than a whisper.

Suddenly, shadows blotted out the orange glow above him. Strong hands reached under shoulders, picked him up. Dragged him back toward the banquet room

"Ben? Is that you? We have to go the other way."

Good – coughing – he sensed the helper moving away, back down the burning hall. He would get them. "That's right. They're in there--"

The helper stopped making noise. Screams from somewhere – far away – and now little chunks of fire had were raining down from the ceiling. Keith put his lips right to the floor, sucked, hoping it was clean air. Bent his knees. Stood up. The guy wasn't coming back. He had to help.

"Lionel. Is Chavo with you? Bring her out. Hurry."

Something bumped him. A large shadow emerged from the smoke, shrank, coalesced —

"Emily!"

He threw his arms around her. For an instant, it didn't even feel like her. More like stone, unmoving, but she suddenly came alive, as if his touch was all she needed. Squirming, coughing.

"This way--" Holding tight, he pulled her across the floor, hit the bottom step, both of them retching. He pushed her upward, but she resisted –

"Keith – hurry – the others--"

My God, she was right. Nosma would never make it alone. Hands came down from the trap door. He let her go, and stepped back down, and toward the dark corner.

Rains of sparks, strangely like that night with the fireflies – when he reached the hall, more shadows moved.

Katy – then Mary – eased out of the smoke. They stood – no, *drifted* – upright, eyes peacefully closed, until he touched each one of them on the shoulder.

That started the retching and coughing. He pushed them by instinct, puzzled by the broad, tanned hands that had pushed them out of the hallway. Yes, they were both in there, immune to the smoke, doing God's work – but were they quick enough? A large *crash* on the floor above sent a new shower of sparks.

"Chavo. Lionel," he said. But something was wrong – those hands, arms were too massive for either of the employees. He shook his head. A mirage from lack of air.

He heard his own voice, weak, scratchy from smoke. "OK, grab Nosma, then you guys get the hell out." Before the faces of those men came clear, they retreated into the hellish gulf.

Now there was a man at the bottom of the steps – huge coat, strange hat, like something out of a comic book – a fireman. Mary doubled over, choking. He handed both women off to the guy, but only after crossing the floor in slow motion. The orange streaks above them were wide. Something made him turn, and rush back before the fireman could order him up the stairs.

Crack. The ceiling gave way. Blazing timbers smashed against the patched-up wall scar that hid the tunnel to the Terrace.

"Get out," the fireman commanded. He had the ladies halfway up the steps.

"Just one more."

More shadows. A gigantic cocoon – made not of silk or threads, but tightly-wound smoke – bulged out into the center of the room. A gust of air came from somewhere, and the shell came apart. Keith grabbed, felt the weight of the huge lady – Nosma looked like a sleepwalker.

"That's all, guys. Come out of there--"

Sparks rained. Nosma's steps too ponderous.

"Hurry, we gotta get up the steps. Please--"

But the big lady moved like a battleship, and the Mexicans hovered in the smoke behind them. Why didn't they come out? Big coats coming from above – Keith perched her on the bottom step, let go, crossed the room, thrust his hands at the shadows –

Instead of letting themselves be pulled out, weighty hands wrapped around Keith's arms – and pulled.

"No, God, that's the wrong way," he yelled.

They dragged him with a purpose. His head fell back, giving him one last, impossible vision: he could see up through the floor, see the railing on the second floor balcony, all the way up to the attic, all of it ablaze with angry flames, and through a miraculous hole in the roof – stars in a black, smoky sky.

Another jerk from the Mexicans pitched him forward. On the floor, burning embers in a straight, blazing orange line – *one of Heider's boundaries,* he thought. Somehow, this was death. He would never get out of here. Maybe none of them had. All a dream, perhaps – the kind he and Larry had read accounts of, the panicky dreams that mediums supposedly brought back from dead people...But if it were a boundary, he suddenly had no fear, only comtempt.

Lionel's and Chavo's pull was un-resistable, somhow, but Keith wasn't mad at them. He stepped over that glowing line – in a glorious instant, the blazing basement disappeared.

Keith fell headlong into green grass. Looked up, wondering. He knew it was green, because the blazing night had disappeared, replaced by broad daylight.

"Hey – we gotta get out--" he said, and stopped. Did the urge to survive stop here? Wherever this was?

He knew where this was. He scrambled to his feet, not far from the river. This was where the Water Company was built. But not yet. Or maybe never built at all, for the town of Sironia had disappeared across the river.

He looked down at his soot-smudged hands. But of course it was built – he couldn't see it, but he still felt intense heat from somewhere. Or some thing.

The air was very hot, but fresh. No mistake. This was the same world the old wagon driver brought him to before. There it was – the wagon and the old horse, waiting for him on the other side of the river! He wanted to throw up.

Squinting against the sun, he turned to his kitchen buddies – but the two rescuers were not Lionel and Chavo at all.

These men were huge, muscular, wearing skimpy breeches. Dark bronze skin from the waist up.

His gaze met the deep brown eyes of first one, then the other.

"Cochise. Geronimo..." The names flowed out of Keith like a fluid, as if he had met these men in real life a thousand times. He wanted to say more, but the larger Indian's hand jerked, cut the air like a knife. Keith followed the motion.

There, on the river bank near the water, two men were locked in a life-or-death struggle. Lionel!

And there was no mistaking the Old Man. Larcinter. The Leprechaun. Whatever his nightmarish name really was –

In spite of advanced age, the evil dream-master obviously had the upper hand. Shoving, he almost had the janitor's face down into the thick grass. The frightening boat banged against a fallen tree a few yards away. Maybe Lionel had refused to take his ride.

"I'm coming," Keith called out, and ran. Where was this place? Were they both dead? Somehow, the loss of the janitor filled him with more sadness than his own demise — if this was really the afterlife--

But Emily – did she make it?

No time to think – he kept forward motion --

His instant plan was to body block the old wagon driver – but he lost focus, looked to the side – atop a grassy hill, where the Water Company *should* be, Poindexter and Carlotta, both life-size, struggled against their strings. Feet sinking in mud, Keith's gaze followed the strings upward –

The most miraculous vision imaginable. Those strings stretched straight up, into deep blue sky. No clouds for the gods or angels or devils to perch upon – it was as if God himself were making the two puppets – but no, were they really *people*? – dance.

His eyes fell to the woman's. Carlotta's gaze was as black and piercing as ever. But somehow this invulnerable lady was embarrassed – humiliated perhaps that he, once a potential lover, could now easily see her chains.

But that image was also interrupted, because those strings were suddenly swept up in a gust of smoke, collected, gripped in huge teeth -- a dinosaur-sized beast stood on its hind legs only yards behind them. Smoke poured from the beast's long jaws, which seemed twisted in a permanent smile. Why didn't the strings catch fire?

"Rage," the name crossed Keith's lips with no urging. This was a dragon. *The dragon* — "The dragon started the fire." No way to know how, but he felt the certainty in his heart.

A *cry* –

"Gringo, save yourself."

Lionel was outmatched. Somehow that smaller, old man was dragging him toward the boat – the world had gone insane, but Keith knew something instinctively that if Lionel were taken, they would both be lost forever in this strange world.

Keith jumped, lost his footing entirely, slipped down wet grass to the water's edge.

"Run, Gringo--" Lionel said through clenched teeth. Fingers wrapped around the wagon man's arms, but the old one was stronger. The janitor's forehead touched water.

"Let him go--" Keith cried.

Up on his feet, he scrambled up the bank, grabbed one of Larcinter's arms. His weight upset the balance. Twirling, the three of them collapsed in a heap. A long, low *moan* cut the air, and the wind picked up. Rolled over on his back, Keith saw that the hot breeze came purely from the dragon's flapping wings.

Larcinter's hand rose to Keith's throat, gripped it. Face close. The old wrinkles like dirty canyons. In the dimness of the attic, he had never seen this face so clearly, yet every curve, every stain seemed so familiar —

The iron grip squeezed. Searing pain shot up the sides of Keith's his head, all breath stopped, stars and circles filled his vision - until he tried to twist away, and his gaze locked with Carlotta's.

The woman could not speak - she was as terrified of the dragon as Keith was. But her dark eyes told him something. Not love, was it? No—a memory of what she told him from the first - to find a reason to live. It was her doing - bringing him here to the Water Company to find Emily.

But now she was speaking aloud with those eyes. "Help my lover," her thoughts rang out. "For he has tried to help you."

Keith felt a surge. Colors danced before his eyes, but his arms found a grip - an old, rickety body beneath the ancient clothes. He could feel the demon breathing - then not breathing - feel a warm body - then a cold one made of wood. The bones, the flesh, old and frail, then smooth and taughtly tuned as snake.

His foot found a rock that did not move. He pushed against it, grabbed the old man's hand, pulled it away, and drank in the richest air he had ever tasted.

How could he be dead if he could still breathe? Emily – was she only a dream now? A memory?

With uncanny strength, the old man countered, and now both he and the janitor were pressed toward the water –

A roar in the sky, a new wave of heat. Keith blinked, slipping away. Emily. Larry. Mom, Dad ...

This was surely Death – but not the Death he had ever read about. Drowned, so he could be cast into a wooden body that lay on that old wagonbed across the water?

Air. Precious air. He gulped it in. Even if it were too late, he had to make a stand.

"Lionel. Pull."

He dodged one way. The janitor expertly went the other – each of them gripping a powerful arm.

"Cochise. Geronimo," Keith cried out. "Help us if you want to be free."

Lionel had leverage, pointed. "The *Diablo*--"

It was true. Larcinter wriggled like a wet dog, and the giant lizard loomed above them, opened his mouth, dropped the strings and began to move. Carlotta leaped, pulled the tuxedo man with her, and the two Indians took their chance – they snatched up the strings and held them taught across the dragon's path.

Already off balance on the slippery riverbank, the taloned feet couldn't clear the ropes –Rage tripped, fell forward into the river.

"No," Larcinter cried. "My pet."

Flame belched from the giant mouth, and the sound that filled Keith's ears wasn't just that of a huge splash, but the noise that a building makes when it crashes to the ground.

I can still hear the real world, he thought.

"Gringo--" Lionel was loose, gesturing.

Their gazes met.

"Now," Keith called out.

In a single motion, they both grabbed the old man, pushed. It was a lucky aim – he plunged into the boiling water near the dragon's mouth.

Gray hair bobbed up, face crimson red. The old voice, screaming --

"Rage, burn them."

The beast howled, pulled its head from the water, looked back over its shoulder, and breathed –

Geronimo and Cochise fell to the grass, covering their faces. Flame swept over them. Again, as if they had rehearsed all this before, Lionel ran right beside Keith. Together, they made it to the top of the knoll just as the next blast of flame filled the sky. Still moving, he dragged Poindexter down at the same instant Lionel covered Carlotta.

Larcinter's whining, small voice filled the air. "Curse you. Horrid foundling. A curse--"

But the sound twisted, as if it were shrinking in the distance, until it sounded more a munchkin than a demon. On his knees, the tuxedo man behind him, Keith turned back to the river.

Water! – Of course. The water was taking its toll on everything evil: Rage scraped and clawed, but couldn't mount the muddy bank. Larcinter splashed helplessly out in the current.

"He grows small," Lionel cried.

It was true. Even as they watched, the mighty reptile legs shrank, splashes from the massive tail went yards, then only feet. Out in the middle of the current, Larcinter had already shrunk to the size of the leprechaun, a horrible puppet bobbing in the brine, waving his fists.

"God will punish you--" the tiny voice cried. "Rage! Take to the air--"

But something was wrong. Neither monster seemed able to do anything but thrash and splash.

"The water," Keith said. With sparkling, frightened eyes, Lionel nodded.

Gasping for breath, his own clothes smoking, acrid, Keith's held Lionel's gaze. The janitor had his arms wrapped around Carlotta.

"Do you know how this can all be?" was all Keith could ask.

Lionel's large brown eyes turned to the river. The two marionettes thrashed, carried farther and farther away in the river's swift middle, heading south. A tiny voice was rattling on, the words drowned out by the rush of the tide, the lilting of mourning doves, the caws of crows.

This is the way the world always was, Keith thought.

A deep breath. "No," Lionel said. "Only the Great Spirit can know how."

"Very good." Carlotta's voice was calm. Strong. She pushed to her feet, planted a kiss on the janitor's forehead, then looked at Keith. "You both have a gift to see this world. But now you must return to your own."

Keith felt no jealousy that she had chosen the janitor over himself. Yet, he didn't want to stop looking at those deep, dark eyes. Black hair. Sharp, clear face. But when she blinked those long lashes, something forced him to look at the river.

He recognized the geography. Now they were only tiny splashes down by the point, where someday the suspension bridge would conquer the river. Or perhaps this place was not the past before Sironia and civilization, but the future. Maybe this was after everything was gone.

Or maybe this place was always here. A tapestry behind everything humanity could ever build.

But what if the little monster caught a floating log, or sandbar, made it to shore – wouldn't he and his hell-hound start the whole battle over again? Somehow, there was no fear in that – or anything else. He didn't care if this world didn't even exist – somewhere in the back of his mind was the crazy idea, the impossible hope that he was still alive, and might see Emily again.

"But where's the Water Company?" he asked Carlotta. "Can we really get back? How?"

Quietly. "You have true hearts. You both tried to save us, even though our time is gone." For maybe the first time, she smiled. "You did save us."

"Hear, hear." Poindexter stepped forward, reached out, shook hands. First with Keith. Then Lionel. Then he took off his top hat, and bowed.

"Now you must go home."

Keith gasped. "The boundary."

He ran across the grass, looking for the line of fire – could not see it. But the Indians knew. Wearing his sheepish, friendly grin, Cochise took Keith's hand, while Geronimo shepherded the janitor. They pulled them across the hillock, until a puff of smoke came from nowhere – there, a black place in the grass – a flame, leaping, spreading in a straight line.

"Come on, Lionel," he yelled, stepped over it, and into darkness. Hands outstretched in front of his body, he blinked and choked against the terrible smoke, hoping he had the direction right. He bumped into a wall, felt the hot concrete, reached around a corner – the hallway!

Headlong, choking, nowhere to get clear air, hoping Lionel was behind him, but when he looked back, his eyes stung too much to see anything. Shadows – he thought it was the fire-littered banquet room. The steps. He felt. Missed. Hit something square-on. Lip stinging. Taste of iron blood in his teeth. Then, a vision: the trap door above him -- a solid square of flame, but legs, then arms descending through it. Another gasp, and Keith slumped onto the concrete steps. Hit his head again. The world went black.

CHAPTER 50
No llores ninito

No matter how Lionel strained at the valve, it remained frozen. *"Pendejo,"* he said. The night was ruined. There was no way to get his mind back to Chavo's problem. What had Uncle done, when demons got in *his* way?

With one more shove, the flashlight slipped, hit the wall and went black. The only light in this dungeon was from the glowing furnace below. Wait – was that a glow? Carefully dodging the hot metal, he kicked forward, hit the pipe, and stepped over it.

Beyond the furnace – a tunnel. There was even a weak lightbulb burning high up the wall, yards in side it. Why had he never seen it before?

One foot in front of the other, a tight squeeze, and then he was in a musty place. Now he could see an old door, sealed right below that bulb. But how could it be locked? Tiny shafts of light came through the cracks in the door frame around it.

Clawing with his fingernails, he finally pried the ancient, rusted lock loose. Scraping on the dirt and gravel floor, he managed to push the stubborn door half-open. And turned to ice.

There, just inside the room, a short figure stood. But the lightbulb in here was the brightest that could ever be. The short figure wheeled, dodged away ito daylight too bright to make out any features. Lionel blinked. Blinked again – he was in daylight. In the middle of the night. Hands felt eerily numb.

Of course. He had gone into trance without realizing it. Who was this spirit that belonged in the daytime? One of Chavo's ancestors?

He took another step. No – it wasn't a male spirit at all Another, and he was through the doorway, walking on grass, following the figure. He recognized the curve of this woman's hips. Carlotta.

Now she stopped, turned to look at him. Worry wrinkled her forehead.

"How? Where is this place, my love--"

Hands reaching out, but she shook her head, leapt nimbly, gracefully backwards. A shiver. She could leap so because she was suspended on her marionette strings!

"Run away, beloved," she whispered.

He took a step, not knowing what he had planned. A movement stopped him, and he turned around. The tunnel had disappeared, and with it, the entire Water Company.

They were standing on thick grass, full daylight. And they were not alone. The little tuxedo man stood to his right, waving one arm – or, the arm was waving because the string attached to it was jerking up and down.

"Run for your life," the little man said. Eyes black, piercing. The look of raw fear in them echoed Carlotta's gaze.

"No," Lionel cried. He rushed Carlotta, swept her up into his arms, hugged her. "My love, we are together--" he pulled at the strings, peered upward, into the bright sky, could not see what they hung from, "why do you have these?"

"Run away. If you love me, Magician."

"Yes. Magician. That's what he is," a small, old, twisted voice said. "Just the one to join our circus troup-- Welcome, magician."

A shiver raced up Lionel's back, and he whipped around. They were atop a mound of grass by the river. The leprechaun, larger than his marionette self, gray-haired yet stocky, muscular, oozing power, stood below the gathering, a few feet from the boat that bobbed on the flowing water's edge.

"Pay no mind to the lady's complaining." He smiled a very old smile – yet young, like a rattlesnake trying to decide which baby chick to take first. "She does not realize your true power. It will be enough to help me find her twenty more husbands."

He raised his hand, wiped spittle from the old mouth. "You're an amazing young man, letting your rut blind you. She is ungrateful. Perhaps I will allow her *no* more husbands."

His squinting eyes were filled with unholy fire. As if some inner signal told him what he was up against, Lionel shivered, let Carlotta go. She swung away from him on her strings, pointed shoes barely touching the grass.

"My love, don't," she said.

"Cut her strings, Diablo." Lionel took a stance, but the leprechaun waved a hand – rather than rushing the little monster, Lionel felt his gaze seized by a force. He followed that motion, unable to resist, and witnessed the whole landscape.

It was the world Carlotta had brought him to before. This was the riverbank where the gringos had constructed the restaurant, and the older mansion. But they, the road between them, the parkway, the old grain silo to the east, the abandoned shack and junkyard out by the farmland were nowhere to be seen. Neither the streetlights, nor the park gates across the river, nor the train tracks nor the skyscraper, the other stubby downtown buildings. This was the world before all those things. Or the land of the Spirit. The empty place that lies behind the real world.

Uncle had spoken of this world so many times.

"Take me there," Lionel had asked when he was a child.

"You are gifted, *Sobrino*. You will come with me when you are ready."

So now he was ready. But still it seemed impossible. He turned, looking back from where he came. Nothing. Only hillocks of grass. Oak trees.

"No, my friend, it is still there," the leprechaun said, reading his very thoughts. As if the little monsters voice could change reality, a fog started to form where the restaurant would once stand. He waited – no,a fog was all it was. A smudge. If it was once the restaurant, now it was only a shadow.

He stopped squinting at it, because another sight stole his attention: Behind that shimmering shadow, a gray-green beast stood as tall and wide as three or four elephants. Teeth protruded from that dog-like mouth, and the marks on its face confirmed that this was the same creature the elf rode through the air that night in the forest. A wooden gash behind the right eye – the mark Lionel had studied alone many dark nights in the attic. This was Rage, the dragon of the attic.

Before he could move to shield Carlotta, the beast peered down, arched the great long neck, and gushed a fountain of fire down onto the shadow of the restaurant. Like an explosion, flames leaped up. There was nothing there – but something had become a world of burning.

The beast moved like fluid, so much more quickly than an elephant. He stretched his neck again, and snagged the strings of Carlotta and the little Tuxedo man in its teeth. A jerk, and the ropes came clear of whatever up in Heaven was holding them. The beast cocked his head, will-filled reptilian gaze settling on Lionel.

"Run, Magician," the tuxedo man cried. "Run and never look back."

"It will do him no good, my friend." The maddening elf pointed, laughed. "His retreat is cut off." Another wave, and things moved. Even the wind began to blow, seemingly on the little monster's command. And on the wind, a floating boat broke from the current, and nudged up against the shore, not far from him.

"If you want to be with your lover, you must become one of us, after all." A twirl of the gnarled hand. An invitation, like Uncle's gestures from the Old World. Lionel felt his heart beating. With fear. Fear of the finality of all this – his heart might even stop with the next wave of the leprechaun's hand. Was this reality – did he live only with this creature's permission?

"She is mine." Lionel's voice was little more than a whisper, and he had to fight to get the words out. "We are meant to be together."

Taking steps. Climbing the grassy bank. Wide, corrupted smile. The little monster chuckled. "Your fates? The apprentice dares to talk to the master of fates?" Another laugh, only louder.

He spread his arms, a sweeping motion, as if he were presenting Lionel to the others. "This one has audacity. He reminds me of my own youth—

"Yes, Magician." The outspread hands came together, found direction, pointed across the river. "You are meant to be a couple. But only after you become immortal, as we are."

The little demon could indeed beckon things at any distance, because something moved on the far shore. A wagon. The horse pulling it whinnied, twitched his ears, pawed the dirt, and Lionel marveled that he could see such detail this far away.

Something moved in the wagon bed. The river breeze picked up, toyed with the edges of the covering that lay there, but it wasn't the wind that shifted the tarp. A form twisted, turned, and the stained covering fell away. The thing was a person! Sitting up.

Lionel gasped. Not a person – but the shape of one, made of wood. Leather joints. Long, slender fingers. Just as clearly as if he were hovering a few feet above the thing, Lionel could see every curve of the wood, the holes where eyes should be, the sanded, smooth belly, the hint of ribs underneath the skin. Whoever had carved this thing was a consummate artist.

The wooden head turned, as if it were looking at Lionel across the river. Seeking, Lionel realized, for its new soul.

Shivers coursed through him, and his mind was racing as swiftly as his vision had ventured across the river.

His body shook violently – it had never done this since the night they came for Uncle. He remembered crouching in the pigstye – they knew where he was hiding, for townspeople would peek over the old fence, and laugh, or whisper about him in final tones.

He remembered the fire leaping up around the stake the townsmen had buried. The sparks flew into the night sky to join the stars, and Lionel the child wondered what Uncle felt, there in the fire. Wondered what he, himself, would feel when they fed him to it, too.

He remembered when the laughing and singing and praying broke out. When old *Señora Munoz* reached through the gap in the boards and gave him a crust of bread, even though Uncle's wasted body was still smoking, 'slumped down among the railroad ties. And through the smells of creosote and brimstone, he could taste the sweet bread, the crunchy pumpin seeds in its crust. That piece of bread was like Christ's body. Like being born into the world all over again. That rich taste. The singing of birds in the dark country around them.

Another shiver brought him back to this moment. He had already come through the fire, and the only birds singing were angry crows. And this time, his fate had finally been decided. The little man – who knew how old he really was – had chosen Lionel for that wooden tomb. Like the stake they tied Uncle to. Only this wooden post would move, and play, and obey this *monstruo pequeno* forever. Just as he had feared blazing fire then, he now wondered about cold wood.

Shivers. Shudders. Cold hands. But no terror. No anger. Lionel looked into his own spirit for any hope of escape. Found only an empty shell. Had it all led to this? Did he suffer so much as a child, hungry, alone, just to wind up by this river, doomed to the bidding of a demon?

Carlotta had warned him to run away. Perhaps she really meant it.

"Well, Apprentice?" the little voice said. "Your vessel awaits."

Wind blew softly. The wide stream churned. The crows lit in the tall cottonwoods, like little black demons who wanted to watch the transformation. From somewhere, Lionel could hear the great fire still crackling. Even smell smoke. But the devlish little boat bounced on the river's waves, as if it had a soul, too, and was tired of waiting.

At the very instant he was finally ready to surrender a voice came. From the past:

"Father Night will come in his boat on the river," Uncle chanted the strange words one night, leaning back in his rickety chair, framed by the shafts of nighttime lights that pricked through the many holes in his shack's shambled walls.

"If it is your time," he said, "there will be no way to resist him. But it may not be your time. Perhaps he is only shopping for souls. If you feel you still have a hunger for life, tell him to go away."

"But how can I talk back to something so great as Father Night?" Lionel remembered asking.

"You cannot sass him." He could not see the smile on the old man's face, only hear it. "You might as well try to spit on the sun. But the Children of Man have a few resources left." He rocked forward, lay a shaking hand on Lionel's shoulder. "When that day comes, if you still have a taste for life, you must stand your ground, and say these words:"

The chant jumped into Lionel's mind automatically, and poured out of his mouth in a Spanish children's ditty:

> *No llores ninito*
> *Que aqui tengo manzanas dos*
> *Una para la Virgen*
> *Y otra para vos*
>
> *Don't cry little nino*
> *For I have two apples here*
> *One for the Virgin*
> *And the other for you*

He never knew what the apples were until this moment.

A puzzled look washed over the leprechaun's face. Lionel chanted again, heard his own voice echo across the water. Now the questioning turned to anger, and the little ancient man raised his fists. The current grew and thrashed behind him, smacking the boat against the rocks at the shore. A gunshot might have gone off, for the sky seemed to stagger. Lionel had never been in a fight before. Always ran from the town boys. Or just let them beat on him.

But now he felt his own fists grow tight. He started down the riverbank, straight for his enemy.

The leprechaun shook his infernal head. Maybe a flash of fear in those little dark eyes, but that spark flew away, replaced by the arrogant sneer that had always caught Lionel's attention in the attic.

They met where the ground fell away toward water. Under his breath, Lionel's chant continued. All that was left of his determination of only moments before. He wanted to glance back at his love, for inspiration. But he didn't dare look away from this – this thing.

"I am proud of you, young man," the little voice said. "You are every bit as strong as my child said you were."

The smile was fatherly, then like a vice.

" –aqui tengo manzana dos – "

The leprechaun blinked wooden-ish eyes, trying to ignore the only weapon Lionel had left. But the mention of the Virgin obviously nettled him –

"The boat is waiting for you. Your first lesson is never to defy me," the monster said. "Rage!"

The dragon belched, filled the air with fire. A warning shot. Lionel's blood ran fast, and he shoved the elf. So much smaller, but like Uncle's brick oven, the thing did not budge.

"Dios mio! Begone. Leave us alone," Lionel cried, but the little creature snatched at him with sharp fingers and, like some horrible mokey, clambered up his leg, reached for his neck and wrapped one arm around it like a snake writhing up for the kill.

He felt the thing's incredible strength. His neck twisted, until he was sure it would snap. Pain up and down his sides, his legs. He was viewing the world upside down when he saw something impossible: the Gringo, running across the grass.

The elf saw him, too, and flinched. Lionel jerked out of his grip, little claw hands scraping to regain their hold.

"Get his arm," Lionel cried.

The air exploded above them, and the Gringo slipped on the grass, but managed to follow Lionel's order. They each had an arm, and the thing writhed, but Lionel knew there was no hope – the very air was on fire –

Wait – there were more reinforcements on the hill – two men from the restaurant – Cisco? Thomas?

Lionel fell backward to the grass, the other two atop him, the little monster biting his chest – and he realized: those men were the wooden Indians. But they were fighting on his side. One throwing stones at Rage. The rocks caught fire in the air, but the other one grabbed Carlotta's strings.

A *roar*, and fire obscured everything.

They writhed, the three of them, and he saw sweat pouring down the Gringos neck, the leprechaun spitting and twisting when the drops hit him, and Lionel knew what to do.

"Into the river, Gringo," he cried.

Wooden fingers scraped his face.

"Into the boat, weaklings," the elf cried.

"Now." Gringo was on his feet, regained his hold, and Lionel rose, stretching the evil little arm in his own grip.

"One, two--" the Gringo counted.

On *three*, as if both of them had fought the *Diablo* before, they swung the monster back, then flung him, together, into the river.

A great splash echoed the shaking of the earth beneath them. The Dragon was on the move, great talons pounding toward them.

"Rage," the demon cried. "Kill them, and rescue me--" He thrashed violently, his voice twisting into something terrible.

For a moment, Lionel didn't grasp what was happening – of course!

"The water. Gringo--" He pointed. "The water is shrinking the leprechaun.

It was true. Yes, water is the antidote to Evil – but the earth shook again.

Only then did he realize that both he and the Gringo were ankle-deep in the water, themselves.

"Under. Under." The Gringo motioned. He was right. Rage might belch his fire at any second, take revenge for what they had done.

Lionel hesistated. This was the Spirit World, he reminded himself. This river, this water was not water, but Life, itself. For a magician, full submersion might be fatal. Not because he was evil, but because it was life –

When he came back up, would he ever see Carlotta again?

"I can't," he told the Gringo.

"But we'll burn up--"

His innocent friend's eyes shone with fear. The towering lizard was upon them.

"Now. *Now*," the Gringo urged.

A razor pain rippled through Lionel's heart. Uncle had had no choice. He did.

They went under the cold, green surface together. Tumbling, kicking, bracing against the heat that roiled the surface. Opened his eyes, searched for Gringo – nothing but brown murk –

After an eternity, Lionel burst up for air, pawed the slippery rocks, had to duck back down. The great dragon stumbled past him, even closer to the thrashing Gringo. Fire belching, he plunged into the river.

"Rage, no," the frantic leprechaun yelled, his voice that of a little person now.

One thrash of the gigantic tail sent a tidal wave over them. Lionel kicked into high gear, found his feet, and scrambled up the grass.

A loud *hisssssss* sounded under the clouds of smoke.

"Get out of the water, you fool," the little man cried, and Lionel pawed at the smoke, straining to see. It finally parted, and he could see the two demons being swept away by the strong current in the middle of the river. Gringo spat and choked, down by the water, then took a deep breath. A hand touched Lionel's shoulder, and he almost jumped back into the water.

"My love. I thought I had lost you."

He rose, and wrapped his dripping arms around Carlotta.

"Be still, my brave one," she said in a whisper. "I was never yours to lose." She caressed his cheeks, smoothed his hair with her fingers, squeezed the water away.

"Come with me." He squeezed her tighter. "I do not know this world, but we will make a home in it. Your magic and mine will allow it."

Firmly, she took his shoulders and shook him.

"I said be quiet."

Deep, warm eyes sucked in his entire vision. She had never let him get this close before.

"You do have magic, because you have done the impossible." She broke his gaze, and looked out at the river. Gringo trotted up the bank, frantic.

"They're going around the Point. If there's a sandbar there, they might be able to make it out and come for us again."

The beautiful Indian gypsy princess with black hair, full lips, snow-white blouse and blood-red skirt shook her head.

"They are gone. And we are free –" her nod took in the little tuxedo man, and the two great natives. "You have indeed done the impossible. Both of you."

Before Lionel could answer her, she kissed her fingertips, and placed them on Gringo's cheek. Then her lips drew close, and she kissed Lionel's mouth. His lips, his tongue shivered in fire and ice.

"And now, my two lovers, you must *live*."

Her gesture was too quick, the power of the two wooden Indians too strong. The tall one took the Gringo, the broad one Lionel. They rushed them across the grass, and through a bed of smoke, until a line of fire appeared.

"It's the line, Lionel," Gringo said. "Come on."

The crazy cook leaped over the fiery mark on the grass, and disappeared. Lionel fought, but the two Indians were too much for him.

Straining to see her over his shoulder. "My love, don't desert me. It can't end this way."

A great shove, and he stumbled forward, choking and spitting in a dark and fiery hell. Working his way, instinctively, toward the basement steps. Though he didn't want to.

Chapter 51
Survivors

Keith awoke to the sound of a fire truck's grinding engine. A fine mist rained down on him – from firehoses. A flashlight beam searched one eye. Then the other.

"Ow," he said. Head throbbing. He slapped at the offending light, realized he was cradled in Emily's lap. "God. I though I was dead."

"You weren't dead. You saved us, sweet thing." She bent forward and kissed his brow.

"Please, ma'am. I need to see his eyes." A guy in a uniform. Paramedic.

"But I was dead, Emily. Did everyone get out? Nosma? Lionel?"

Emily looked up, left it to the fireman-coat-wearing medic to explain.

"We had you coming up the stairs, and that young lady over there – I mean, the big 'un – slipped out of Jimmy's grip." Keith followed his nod. One ambulance over, Nosma sat atop a gurney, arguing tooth-and-nail with the attendant.

Now Keith's own attendant wore a goofy smile. "Guess her rump landed right on your head. You were out, man." Emily giggled. Flashlight traveling side to side. Keith's head felt like a bomb as ready to go off.

"Now, Darlin'," Katy was consoling Nosma. "They just gonna keep you overnight. The company's payin' for it."

Nosma snorted, and her reply poured out of here almost as hot as dragon's breath. "Don't you darlin' me. I said I was goin' home to my bed, and that's where I'm goin'."
Arkie sat in a wheelchair to one side, wiping her eyes.

A *crash* made them all look up. A brick wall, impossibly aflame, came crumbling down. *Oohs* and *aahs* from the crowd. For the first time, Keith saw it – two-thirds of the ancient building had already collapsed. Above the ruin, streaks of white water poured from ladders, and a universe of fireflies swarmed the sky. *Not insects, but spawns of the devil himself,* Keith thought. Almost said it aloud.

The back parking lot was a mish-mash of workers' cars, fire trucks, ambulances, police cars. Waitresses wore blankets from somewhere. Waiters and bussers standing beside them. All uniforms soiled and wet. Faces marked with ash and soot. Sputtering engines. Diesel fumes.

Keith pulled on Emily's blouse. "Did Lionel make it out?"

Ben arrived, just in time to hear the question. He turned pale, waved Thomas over. The Fire Chief was with him, and was the only one to answer.

"We'll be looking through everything, son. Some of my men are still in danger in there."

Bad answer, Keith wanted to say. Tears had left thick tracks in the soot on Emily's cheeks. Then back to the restaurant's shell. Flames leaped high, higher, as if trying to catch the ladder men off guard. In fits and starts, he described to Ben how the janitor had gone back down the hall – or had he?

"I'll tell them to dig down into that far side, once the fire's out," Ben promised. "Maybe he found a place to hide."

"Now get me down off'uh this thing." Nosma's fat fists threatened all who were near her. "Don't know how you got me up here in the first place--"

Keith wanted to smile. Couldn't.

"They'll find him," Emily said softly.

The fire chief ordered his men back from their forward positions. He barked warnings about the nuisance water tank.

"That water's plenty hot by now. Gotta be a lot of pressure. I don't want my men scalded." He yelled all this at

Thomas, as if the restrateur was the one who started the whole mess about water tanks in the first place.

No sooner did the firemen get back to their trucks than one more great *blast* went through the air like thunder. A cavern-sized hole opened up in the last bit of roof, and then all that was left of the Water Company gave way.

"Good," the fire chief told Thomas. "Less chance it will spread now."

The restaurant owner turned toward Ben with the look of a lost boy.

Emily cried, along with the others. Keith lifted himself up and kissed her.

"You'll never believe who pulled you from those flames," he said.

She grimaced, and buried her face against his shoulder.

"Try me," she said.

"Gotta go, sir." The ambulance attendants were back, but Keith gave them a look, and pointed to a fireman who had to be held up to walk.

"Get him, first."

Then to Emily, "What did you see?"

She whispered. "We were down there, and found this other stairway. Katy said no one had seen it before. It led upwards on the far side of the building, somewhere under the bar, I guess.

"We climbed up. Katy, Mary. All of us. It opened up onto the river. We just stood there, talking about how pretty the water was."

"Did Chavo go with you?"

"No. He was too scared, once we saw the stairs. He's OK." She pointed. "I saw him over there."

A deep breath. She was close to tears again. "Nosma screamed, and we turned around. The whole building was on fire, even though it had only been a few seconds. Then Katy said something about how downtown had vanished, across the river.

"Smoke inhalation, I guess, Keith. I was scared." Her tears came easily as an attendant laid her on a stretcher. Keith reached across and took her hand.

"Two big men came out of the woods." She coughed. "They led us back down the stairs, into the basement. It was them – they, who save us. And you. You did, too." She squeezed his hand.

"Damn," he said. "I hope Lionel's all right."

CHAPTER 52
MALIBU

Keith guided the brand new metallic blue Malibu onto the side street, then up into the gravel lot. Pockets of bluish smoke still oozed from the blackened boards and mounds of the ancient building's ruins. What brick sections still stood were honeycombed with holes, and the trees in the park across the river could be glimpsed. The smell of burnt timbers hung in the air.

"It's a beautiful car," Emily said. "Are you sure metallic blue was the only color they had?"

Even with his pending job, Keith could not have afforded the new care without his father co-signing. He felt proud, nevertheless, every time she pointed out another of its features.

Final paychecks were being handed out today. Ben wanted this to take place at the new restaurant, *La Tapatia*, but its parking lot was being paved this week.

"This is better, anyway," Thomas said with a smile. "We belong here." Keith took his outstretched hand.

Alberto was therte, chatting up a waitress, showing her his Caddy. Emily gave Thomas a hug, then stepped over to Mary, who supervised the cigar box full of checks.

Cisco, his black hair still wet from washing, approached, just as Alberto opened his car door and filled the lot with the thumping Mexican polka beat from his tape deck.

"Cisco, you're looking dapper," Keith said. "Almost as handsome as the *patron*."

Cisco laughed, and poked carefully at Keith's swollen black eye. "Feel better today, Gringo?"

"It's turning a nice purple," Thomas said.

"It's healing. But what's this I hear about you getting a moron to manage the new place?" A sideways sneer at Ben.

"Yep. Old Ben's gonna stick with me a while longer."

"Asshole," the manager said.

Keith turned on Cisco. "And you? Gonna move over with everyone else? Cooking food like your mama's, finally?"

A laugh. "Maybe I just wash dishes. I don't really know how to cook the Mexican food."

Laughs and jeers filled the lot, and for an instant, it felt like they were all back in the kitchen.

"Bullshit," Thomas said. He waved his arms, as if presenting them all with an announcement he'd been waiting to make. "We're going to have the best *guacamole* in the state of Texas."

The crowd splintered again, and the morning river air tasted good, in spite of the wafts of smoke. The little groups chatted separately, though they all shared the same subject: reliving that fateful night. Keith tired, trying to hear snippets of them all.

He turned, and found himself alone with Thomas. This was his last chance to ask.

"You knew, didn't you?"

Foir an instant, the chef looked like he would protest. Then a smile crossed his lips. "I wanted to thank you again, Keith. What you did that night, going down to pull the girls out, that took courage."

"Thomas, don't. You knew the puppets were alive, didn't you? Or possessed, or whatever. You practically lived up in that Lookout. How could you not know?"

Nervous now, Thomas reached his hand into a pocket, pulled out one of his little games. Almost started to play. Thought better of that, too.

"You know my history. Cooking is my life. I used it to survive. Y' know?

"I knew it would give me a living, but I never imagined a person could become this prosperous from it. When I gota that offer from these Sironian businessmen, well…" His gaze rose to Keith's and he took a breath.

"They marionettes were here when I came. Didn't seem that strange. They belonged there, sort of. I never talked with them, like Ben says you did. I told myself it was just my imagination when I did my paperwork there in the Lookout, and I glimpsed the leprechaun looking in my window at me."

Keith felt a shiver, but the chef's eyes grew misty.

"So I did see them. I guess I should have stopped it all, then, no matter how much money I made. I just told myself that things like that were impossible. Lionel paid the price for my cowardice."

His eyes regained their shine. "Things didn't get out of control until about the time you came to work for us."

Keith responded to his smile. "Oh, so it's all my fault. I plead guilty." But he couldn't quite laugh, looking out over the wisps of smoke that hugged the blackened embers.

"So are they still looking for him in all that?"

Thomas shook his head. Took a breath.

"So, I guess the puppets burned up, too," Keith said.

The chef brightened. "Maybe not. I was looking back by the shed – come over here." He led Keith to his pickup truck.

There in the back, caddy-whompus amid piles of soiled linens and a burnt stool, Poindexter lay. Most of his strings appeared burned away. Soot and mud sullied his face and tuxedo coat. Scorched, but something about the wood lacquer, maybe, had kept his face intact.

"How in the hell--" For an instant, the memory of Poindexter on the river bank, in the bar that night he broke up the fight – every time he had seen him – flashed through his brain. Even damaged, he still stared out at the world – or did the fire set him free?

Thomas' voice brought him back. "My best guess is he got blown out through the roof when the tank blew. Don't see how it had that much force, though."

"Carlotta?"

Thomas shook his head. "Gone. I think I'll clean the old bouy up and take him down to the new place. You know, just

for old times' sake. You think that'd be OK?" He looked as if
he really needed Keith's blessing.

"Sure." The very thought produced a shiver, but there
was no denying it was good to see the little guy again. "As
long as it's not the leprechaun, I guess we'll be safe. But the
cops will start asking questions if you just use hime to break
up bar brawls." They laughed.

"Salvage anything else?" Keith asked.

"Just this junk." Thomas moved a box in the truck bec.
"A few bottles of wine made it through. Probably ruined, but
we'll give them a try at the opening party."

He waved across, looking at The Terrace. "Old Crab,
the museum manager over there says he's got a few odds and
ends. Stuff firemen must have carried over in the confusion.
"I'll go look tomorrow."

They rejoined the others. More hugs and goodbyes.
Keith wandered from the cluster to show Alberto the new
wheels.

"*Que pasa*? You get new car?" He sat in the passenger
seat and politely nodded, or said *ahh* as Keith pointed out each
feature on the dashboard.

"Automatic shift – *bien*."

They climbed out, and Alberto passed his hand once
more over the new car's roof, giggling. "It's not too big," he
said, and nodded toward his Caddy in comparison. Cisco
walked over, scowling. He shook his head at Keith. And
smiled.

They took their leave. Keith held his tears, somehow,
but Emily had lost the battle well before. He turned the car out
onto River Drive. Going slowly at first, as if they could drink
in just a little more of what had once been, but when they
reached the far end of The Terrace property, he gunned it.

"Keith. Stop the car," Emily yelled.

"What's the matter? It can handle it--"

She motioned him up onto the gravel shoulder.

"What's the matter? I'll get a ding from these rocks."

Waving. "Get out. There's something in the grass."

She scrambled out, and led him certainly through the wet Johnson grass. They reached the brick fence on the mansion's perimeter, on the side away from the restaurant ruins.

"What the hell?" His gaze followed her finger.

Nestled in the grass lay the gypsy puppet. Face streaked with soot and dirt, just like Poindexter's. Here eyes, too, were wide open.

"Carlotta," he yelled, and knelt down. He tested her legs and arms.

"Still all in one piece." Emily put a hand on his shoulder, and he grabbed it, even as he pulled the puppet up against himself. "How did she get here? My God. She couldn't have been blown this far by the explosion — "

Now Emily was all the way down on a knee, too. "So? You told me they don't have to obey the laws of physics."

He smiled at her. "Don't tell me you're a believer now."

"Doesn't matter. She made it. She didn't burn."

He hugged Carlotta closer, but his gaze was on his new love. "All of this really happened, you know."

A smile. "I didn't always know that." She helped him stand, and cradle Carlotta in his arms. "But when a wooden Indian carries you out of a fire, it's hard to stick with conventional science."

They loaded the gypsy/Indian princess/marionette into the back seat. She lay there eerily, eyes looking up at the ceiling. Keith didn't want to look at her too long, afraid the eyes would blink. They started down the road.

"After I drop you off, I'll come back here," he said. "I'm sure Poindexter will be glad to see her."

Emily laughed. "Do you think they'll get married?"

"Don't know. Something tells me the little tuxedo man's not really her type."

They laughed again, and Keith turned the radio dial until the red bar landed on a Mexican station. A singer crooned mournfully as accordions and bass guitar leapfrogged behind his voice. Violins and horns joined the melee, repeating a catchy melody.

"OK?" he asked.

She squeezed his hand.

CHAPTER 53
MUCHO GUSTO

Kelly Gilles' patience had run out some time ago. If there were much more of this waiting around, she would scream.

Mrs. Hobson had promised that Mr. Crab would be along soon when she left Kelly in charge. Now, more than an hour later, she should be off the clock. The old coot! Probably thought he could take his sweet time at the City Club, since this was Kelly's last day as tour guide at The Terrace. She could almost hear the rotten drunk, "Little Kelly won't mind. She's a good girl. Wouldn't cuss you to save her life--"

Any other day, she would have just left. But it wouldn't do to leave a bad taste in the old geezer's mouth. The Crabs were, after all, on the Debutante Nominating Committee, and good friends of her parents. Even though her mother always said Jolene Crab was a "la-de-da."

Thirty more minutes. No more. Nobody could fault her for leaving then. Every time a car that was not Crab's green Mercury slowed outside the gate, Kelly's heart skipped a beat. This wasn't the best part of town. That new girl, Branwyn, acted like such a kiss-up, volunteerin to stay with her. Oughta leave and let the little hussy have the whole shootin' match.

"Don't hang onto me, little girl, I'm gone," she finally said, when Branwyn's questions just wouldn't stop. "Mrs. Hobson's was the one you need to impress, so ask her all that tomorrow."

The little idiot's mother called just a few minutes before, saying she was coming to pick her up. Then Kelly would be left alone in this drafty old place. Damn that Crab!

Branwyn – now ther was a case, Kelly snickered to herself. Homely and unrefined. And her mother – the poor hag imagined herself some social butterfly. The whole family was trash. Kelly almost pitied the girl as she watched her wander aimlessly through the downstairs study, caressing this or that doo-dad, sighing phony little sighs whenever she thought she might get attention. The wretched thing had no talen for chit-chat, and she knew it. So why did she try? Because no one had ever told her to shut up, likely.

Kelly's mother had already spilled the beans. Little ol' Branwyn had a surprise in store next spring when her mother put her up for coming out. Only fourteen girls would be chosen, as always. Kelly could name the sixteen prime candidates, besides herself, right off the top of her head. Ugly little Branwynwould be lucky if she was even asked to be a greeter at the Debutantes Court!

A red station wagon lingered at the gate, then drove away. Kelly's gaze drifted to the workmen dragging burnt timbers and trash from the shell of the Water Company. What a disaster. A den of sin, Kelly's mother called it, noting the rumors of wild parties and voo-doo. She watched Branwyn run her chalk-white fingers over the ornate wood of the master's desk.

That's all the little hussy might be good for – juicy stories about goings on over there. No, she wouldn't be no harem girl, but maybe she heard tell lots of stuff. Kelly huffed and looked back out the window. It wasn't worth it to stay another hour just to hear any stories from that one.

"Hey, we've probably got a few more minutes," Branwyn said in her squeaky voice. Couldn't the girl stay in a room alone? "You promised me you would show me the basement. How can I answer the tourists' questions if Ive never seen it?"

"Oh, never mind," Kelly said, snapping her fingers for Branwyn to move away from the basement stairs door. "We don't take people down there anyway."

"But Kelly, you're the only one who will let me. I know Mrs. Hobson won't show it to me."

"Well, it's too late. I've got to keep a lookout for Mr. Crab. "Lord, if your momma ain't come by the time he does, then *he'll* be stuck with waiting with you, and then I guess you'll find out who you're working for, Lord help you."

Branwyn didn't look up, but Kelly felt her start to wory. Good. "Besides," she continued, "didn't you hear that rustling down there earlier? The rats got washed out in the flood, but they're probably back now."

"Ooh." Branwyn shivered visibly. "I don't like rats or mice."

Oh, you don't do you? Kelly wanted to say. In that case, maybe I should take you down there all the same. The girls at the club'll love to hear how loud you can scream.

"OK. We'll look around. But just for a minute."

Kelly snatched the key ring off the hook and opened the basement door. River-y mothball-y stench rushed out from the wooden stairway.

"Cool," Branwyn's face was lit up. "We'll just take a minute. You wanna go first?"

"You go on, Dearie. I'll be along directly."

Kelly wondered if the little thing could make it down those stairs without slipping. She'd never see anyone as slow as Branwyn learning the tour script. Even now she stumbled when she had to list the crops they used to grow before the master's death in the fire.

"My God," Kelly mumbled to herself as the footsteps receded. What if Branwyns mother didn't show at all? The hussy might try to wangle a ride home, and what if she turns that in to talk about a sleepover?

No – no – no. Kelly had a good excuse. She had to be fitted for the back-to-school formal. Should she mention it as a pre-emptive strike? Branwyn might not have been asked to it. Might be crestfallen. Of course she should mention it. Kelly had to be honest.

Kelly peered down the stairs. Saw the girl gawking at the stacked furniture, the ruined walls. Ooh, that martyred look on that freckled face! She wasn't the type to look authentic in a hoop skirt.

"Enough. Gotta come back up now," Kelly hollered.

"Sure, sure. But what's in here?" Branwyn strode away from the stairs, right for the old storage room door.

"No, Girly. Get up here like I say--"

But Branwyn jerked the thing open.

Then she screamed.

Kelly jumped, heart booming. "Oh, sweet Jesus, girl, what on earth--"

Branwyn screamed again, and her hands flew to cover her mouth. She stood shaking, staring into the dank old room, then disappeared behind the open door. Whatever scared her was invisible from this angle.

"What the fuck are you doing, girl? Kelly raced down the stairs, and into the room. And froze.

"Lionel. Lionel," was the name the blubbering girl kept repeating. A skinny man with bushy black hair stood there, his arms wrapped around the little hussy. Behind them, two smoke-streaked wooden Indians stared at nothing from their wooden eyes.

"Oh, my God, you scared me to death. Who are you, mister. Branwyn, get away from there. He looks like a criminal--"

But the girl wasn't listening. Instead, she kissed the stranger full on the lips. Again. Harder. Good grief, they were kissing like they'd been dating for a month!

"You awful girl. Who is that Mexican? You get away from him. You can't have boyfriends meet you here on the job."

Still they went at it, so Kelly grabbed Branwyn's sleeve and ripped —

"I said get out of there."

One of the man's arms reached out, as if in greeting. Kelly jumped back, hitting her head on the door.

"Mister, how did those statues get down here? Branwyn, you come on, or I'll call the police--"

They just chewed on each other, but Kelly's heart was coming back down from outer space. She turned up the stairs, stomped across the main floor so the slut would hear her.

The girls won't believe this one," Kelly thought as 9-1-1 number rang. "Hello?" Loud, so they would hear down there. "This is the Terrace mansion. We've got a prowler. Not a prowler, a rapist! Yes, send a patrol car at once--" A hand on her sleeve made her jump a mile.

"It's OK," Branwyn said, a big goofy smile on her face. "He's with me. Lionel, we'll take you home."

As if it were planned that way, a car honked loudly outside. The gangly girl opened the door and led the scroungy-looking man out and down the front steps. Kelly felt to stunned to say anything else. The phone fell from her hand, and she rushed to see if the little tramp was all right.

Incredibly, both of them crawled into the back seat of Branwyn's mother's car. No, this wasn't no set-up. The girl's mother looked as frantic as Kelly felt, waving and puffing, tryin to get the man to leave through the far door.

"Mom--" The girl's voice finally got the upper hand. "This is Lionel. He needs a ride home."

The man finally spoke, in a clear, melodious voice: "Mother of Branwyn. So glad to meet you. *Mucho gusto.* I see now where Branwyn gets her great beauty."

The old lady sputtered some more, then rolled her eyes, and gunned the car down the drive.

"But Branwyn," Kelly called after them. "The police are on their way."

CHAPTER 54
OLD MONEY

Many miles south of Sironia, on the outskirts of another great
State University, Moses Rainey was enjoying the splendid
morning. How brightly the birds were singing. His belly was
full of toast and jelly and coffee, almost as full as the river. The
pain was barely there this morning, and he could feel both of
his feet as he plowed his toes through the gravel on the
driveway. Then back in his shoes. If he had time later, he
would cross Riverside Drive and try his luck at fishing.

Fall was coming. He felt it when he woke up. Moses
couldn't wait. Tired of the heat and the locausts, mowing the
lawn and the bugs. He felt the heat more than most, out in the
open every weekend, tending to his garage sale. His friends
called himself a natural born barterer.

"Damn," he said aloud, as a car rolled up the very
instant he had his display tables situated. Besides the heat, that
was the worst part of this job – lugging this junk in at night
and out in the morning.

He rubbed sparse white stubble on his black head, but
he didn't dare take time to go in for is hat now, because that
woman struggling to get her bulk out of the red Plymouth
wasn't to be trusted. Winona Bristow. The only living soul he
despised doing business with.

Winona owned an antique shop. Whenever she
showed up, she was always first customer of the day, and the
rudest. Sometimes, she jewed him down. On good days, he
jacked her up without mercy. He scored it about even over the
year-and-a-half he'd been in business. Win or lose, it was good
to see the back of her.

"Mornin', Miz Bristow. Mighty nice mornin'. You interested in a typewriter today? Some-a-your clients are bound to like those two old Royals over there." Moses smiled his most beguiling smile, and stuck a foot out toward the card table with the defunct business machines.

"What? Oh, Lord, no." She rushed past him and began digging through the knick knacks. "Those old things have got more dust on them than my whole shop. Why don't you just toss 'em in that dumpster yonder, Moses? I'm getting' tired of lookin' at them every time I pass."

"Why Miz Bristow, how can you say that? You know dang well that these machines would get scooped up in your store in a New York minute. Looky at that old gray one. Ever' key's oiled and slick. A fine antique."

Winona took a second glance, in spite of herself.

"Oh, for land's sakes." She huffed and moved her huge frame to another table, but she was such a sharper observer than most people. Yes, they were still here. She spotted them out of the corner of her eye, not even moving her head. Too bad she never worked for the CIA. Heck, no one else would'a seen 'em in the first place. She was racing by here last afternoon, right when he was puttin' up. Might've stopped then, but she had Mrs. Bain's tea to go to. Didn't want to seem that anxious, anyway. Went home and slept on it. That's what Poppa taught her. "Act like Old Money, and you'll eventually *be* Old Money."

"Some mighty nice clothes there on the rack," Moses said after she finished fingering the old games on the center table. He leaned over, moved his rocking chair to where it faced the street, and sat down. From here, he could still watch every move she made, shakin' his head in little dashes.

Perfect, Winona thought. She sauntered toward the indicated rack. "Lordy, Moses, you don't have to sell me on anything. I know what I want. And what I don't want. Heck, if

I hounded all my customers the way you do, I'd be outta business in a week."

Moses smiled. That was precisely how she treated her customers. Only the insecure, nervous society types had the money and the nerve to darken her door more than once. Some people on this Earth had to be told what to do, and Winona was the kind who would tell them.

"Hmmm..." Winona let out a little sigh of disgust, trying not to be too loud.

Her targets were there. Hanging from the middle of the clothes rack, separating the men's from the women's. Puppets on strings. Thought that's what they were yesterday when she passed. *Of course, Winona. You don't make mistakes.*

Too bad they were a lot dingier than she'd expected. How would Patsy clean them up?

Her niece was in charge of designing the big window displays at Olson's Department Store down on Dallas Street. Patsy often shopped at Winona's place, looking for items to make her windows more authentic. Only Monday, she'd mentioned that she was puttin' one up with a "Pinocchio" theme. Brand new marionettes wouldn't do. They had to be antiques.

Dirty, dirty, dirty. But still they were perfect. Olson's paid top dollar for their windows. With these old dolls, Winona stood to make a couple hundred dollars if she played her cards right.

"Well, Moses, I don't see much I need today."

"Suit yourself." Moses put the old rocking chair into motion. *Then why'd you get out of the car, you old hag?*

"Naw." She hiked her purse up on her shoulder, brushed down her dress. "What'll you take for that ol' card table those typewriters are sittin' on?"

"Naw." Gettin' a little nervous. Fidgetin'. But mayber
– what will you take for that old card table those typewriters
are sittin' on?"

"That thing?" Moses scratched his chin. "That's one of
those ol' things I'm getting' sick of looking at. Ten dollars."

"Oomph." Winona Bristow stared cockeyed at him, as
if he'd said a million dollars. She tarried a moment. Then,
slowly, back to the rack. Moses kept rocking.

"What are these old things anyway?"

"Which ol' things?"

"These – on the strings, you ol' fool. You know,
marionettes."

Bingo. The fish had the bait. Bobber dippin' under the
water. "Man found 'em along the highway. Somebody musta
lost 'em off a truck. That's all I know."

A victory smile of sorts crossed her lips. "Well, I hope
you didn't pay him too much. They're all covered with
gunpowder or soot or somethin'. Don't you clean your
goods?"

Moses let a sigh escape. The price just went up. Rude
people had a knack for just gettin' ruder. "Why, Miz Bristow
you know I launder all these clothes and dust ever' day. If
they's a little dirt left, it's 'cause I didn't want to risk takin' off
some of that lacquer finish with the Lysol."

"Well, they're still dirty. I shouldn't even look at them,
but some of my customers have kids."

"Uh-huh. They ain't nothin' your niece would need for
the department store, is they?"

He might as well have shot off a gun, the way she
jumped. "Oh, Moses, hush." Price just went up, and he choked
down a smile.

"What are they anyway? Punch and Judy, or what?"

He leaned the rocker forward and pointed with his
pen. "Well, now, Miz Bristow, they seem pretty obvious. Fine
woodcarving. Old-time workmanship., though they got
damaged somehow, I'll admit. Maybe a flood or a fire."

"Or both, I'd say." She huffed around a little, and one of her hands left her purse and shook them by the strings.

"As I was sayin' – that big one's a dragon. Can't argue with that. And then there's a leper-corn."

"Leper-corn? Why Moses, you're puttin' on the country dog. I know you talk better than that."

He laughed. She did, too. A little. But he didn't reply. Let her stew in her own juice for a moment. Maybe it worked, 'cause her face got red.

"I'll admit someone did take time with them. But what's my – uh, my customers going to do with a dragon and a leprechaun and a – a—"

"Cowboy. That third one's a little cowboy. Got his hat tied on in the back, see? And look at those boots. That's some fine detail. These days with all the machines makin' things, they don't carve like that anymore."

"Well, they don't even go together. How is she--"

She shut up real fast. Face crimson now, all her pretenses falling away. Poor Miz Bristow. Showing her hand. Caught off guard by something. The price went up again.

"Which she? Your niece down at Olson's?"

"Oh, never mind, Moses. No. I was thinkin' about another niece."

"But Miz Bristow, you told me you only had one niece."

"Hush up, Moses. Then it's somebody else. How can a body think with you yammerin' at them? It's a wonder you ever get a customer." Turned toward him, eyes glarin'. "How much you asking?"

"Twenty-five."

"Twenty-five? Why, how do you plan to stay in business when you jack things up to where nobody can afford 'em? These are for kids--"

She was still blustering, but a blue car started slowing down, like it would stop, and she reached out and pulled the puppets off their hooks, strings and all. For a second, she brushed their faces with a handkerchief from her purse. The blue car paused again, then kept going. Winona stalked over and thrust the puppets into Moses' face. Just held 'em up, twisting there, letting the strings get more tangled than they were already.

"Well, these might be beyond repair. Ain't no way they're worth twenty-five."

Moses was in business because he had the good sense to compromise. But every deal with this lady was a deal with the Devil. He leaned forward, pointing at the puppets with this pen, acting like he was studying them, though he already knew every nook and cranny.

"I'm sorry, Miz Bristow. You might be right for sure, but I just can't get around this fine workmanship. Twenty-five might even bee too little. I might be gyppin' myself--"

She gasped. "Well, just listen to you. I agree somebody took some time with them. But the strings are too short. Just look at that."

"String don't cost much."

"Oh, I know that. But that little leprechaun is smilin' like a fool. And that cowboy – that look on his face – he's – he's--"

"Well, I noticed that, Miz Bristow. Looks like he's scared, don't it? My, my. How a woodcarver can put feelin' into a stick of pine. You wouldn't dream it possible."

"Oh, hush once and for all. You win. Twenty-five dollars." She dumped the things in his lap, and opened her purse.

"Apiece." Moses kept a straight face.

"Apiece?" Winona shrieked. "Man, are you crazy?"

A tan car slowed down, right on cue, and this one was turning in.

Winona looked up. The damned car was full of kids, and her heart was beating. The old fool was right about the workmanship. There were people who could make things look new. She wouldn't ask three hundred. Five was more like it. Maybe eight. Olson's was flush this year.

"Oh, here's your seventy-five." She tossed the bills in his lap, and retrieved the puppet. Not a moment too soon, because one of those little girls started *ooh-ing* and *aah-ing* About them.

"I ain't trying to be unpleasant, Moses. It's just that I got overhead to pay and you don't. Why don't you try to remember that once in a while?"

She cussed under her breath as she stalked toward the car.

"Thank you much, Miz Bristow. Come back soon." Moses let go with his biggest smile. There was no feeling more sublime than the sun on his head and a fat profit.

"Poor man," Winona thought as she pulled out onto Riverside Drive. She glanced over her shoulder at the three new acquisitions. They lay spread out, arms and legs splayed around. The Dragon's mouth was open, showing dingy big teeth. It would take a mathematician to unravel those strings. though. She talked out loud, as if her companions were listening.

"He's gonna have to start gettin' up earlier if he wants to get the best of Winona Bristow. Olson's will pay five hundred for you darlings if they'll pay a dime. She turned onto Fifth Street and shifted the car into third gear. It promptly died.

"Oh, my Lord." She guided it to the curb. Thank God the traffic was light. She turned the key. The engine ground and whined. Ground again. Finally the car kicked into life.

Again, she tossed her voice over her shoulder. "I'd almost wish Mister Bristow was back, but he never was no 'count with cars."

She pulled into the middle lane, free and clear, thinking she might go straight to Olson's. She adjusted the rear-view mirror so that she could glance at her new purchases while she drove.

"What on Earth! --"

Winona jumped in her seat, lost the wheel, regained it just in time to swerve onto the road's shoulder. The car scraped to a halt in a cloud of dust, only a few feet from a mailbox.

She twisted around in her seat. "Why, I don't remember settin' you up there like that--" Incredibly, the leprechaun puppet was sitting upright, like a little kid enoying the ride. The other two still lay in a crumpled mess. "That blamed Moses has got me confused."

She reached back. Tried to separate the cowboy from the dragon on the seat. Gave up. Patsy would just have to get 'em apart.

"Lordy, maybe she'll pay six hundred. We are kin."

After a minute, she finally got back into the middle lane. When she was sure there were no cars on either side, she risked another glance in the mirror.

Another jump. Did that infernal elf thing wink at her? A cold shiver worked up her spine. Had to be the wind, fluttering the wooden eyeball.

"Oh, Winona, you've got to figure out about retirement. Your old eyes are liable to see anything. And dang if she shouldn't have taken Third, instead. Right in front of her, the white and red arms came down, lights flashed, and a freight train crawled across her path. She stopped. Took a breath.

Over her shoulder again: "Sorry, boys. I'm just flustered this mornin'. I've never had anything like you in my store before.

"But five hundred? Could I be lettin' you little darlins' go too cheap? Hmmm. I don't think any of my customers could outbid Olson's. But wait a minute. What about Waite's Gift Shop? They charge highway robbery prices. Wonder if ol' Mr. Waite will think as highly of you as that ol' garage sale shyster?"

Box cars. Container cars rambled past. Empty cattle cars. She chewed on the possibilities. Weren't nobody in this town more knowledgeable about antiques than herself. Why, the smart ones would pay a premium just for her telling them how valuable these relics could be.

"Yep," said back to the puppets. "Olson's is always makin' Patsy bid lowball. Well, this time, they might just be in for a surpise. They don't get you for their window, they gonna see you hanging somewhere even more expensive. Then let that crabby Mrs. Olson feel like a chump."

The rumble contnued, but now the red caboose came into sight. She took the chance to look back, real quick.

"Are you really a leprechaun?" The damned thing's shiny eyes seemed to follow her, somehow. Glint of the sun, likely. "Well, leprechauns are s'posed to be lucky, ain't they? Three wishes, and all?"

Eyes back on the road. The guard arm raised, and she gunned the car.

"Yes, sir. You boys might not be for sale at all, unless the price is right. Imagine that old fool lettin' you go for twenty-five dollars! Winona, this could be your lucky day."

THE END

About the Author...

Bull Marquette is the penname for a Texas native who published his first novel, THE FIFTH PLANE, with Brave New Genre Books in 2008. This was followed in 2009 by his collection of short stories, GOT 8 IF YOU WANT 'EM.

Bull began his writing career as an ad and book jacket writer for Word Books, a religious book publisher, where he was privileged to interview notables like Jeb Magruder – refugee from President Nixon's Watergate scandal, and 1960s hoodlum-turned-civil rights activist Eldridge Cleaver, as well as authors who had come back from the dead.

He worked as an ad agency copywriter, convenience store clerk, high school teacher, construction worker, TV weatherman, radio announcer, apprentice cook under a world-class chef, waiter, bread delivery man, speech writer for a state legislator, branch manager for a national stock brokerage firm and financial advisor. Bull moved to California in 1982 to study parapsychology in the unique masters program at JFK University.

Bull was business editor and columnist for the FRESNO WEEKLY newspaper, and he co-hosted the nationally syndicated WEBMASTER RADIO SHOW, an interview show that featured the giants of the high tech world during the climax of the Dot-Com bubble, from February 2000 to November 2001. He is currently a financial advisor, a columnist for THE FRESNO BEE, and a sometimes announcer for KVPR – national public radio in Fresno.

A paranormal and "alternate history" buff, Bull is working on more short stories and novels, as well as a non-fiction work on the Unified Field Theory.

About the Author...

Bull Marquette is the penname for a Texas native who published his first novel, THE FIFTH PLANE, with Brave New Genre Books in 2008. This was followed in 2009 by his collection of short stories, GOT 8 IF YOU WANT 'EM.

Bull began his writing career as an ad and book jacket writer for Word Books, a religious book publisher, where he was privileged to interview notables like Jeb Magruder –

refugee from President Nixon's Watergate scandal, and 1960s hoodlum-turned-civil rights activist Eldridge Cleaver, as well as authors who had come back from the dead.

He worked as an ad agency copywriter, convenience store clerk, high school teacher, construction worker, TV weatherman, radio announcer, apprentice cook under a world-class chef, waiter, bread delivery man, speech writer for a state legislator, branch manager for a national stock brokerage firm and financial advisor. Bull moved to California in 1982 to study parapsychology in the unique masters program at JFK University.

Bull was business editor and columnist for the FRESNO WEEKLY newspaper, and he co-hosted the nationally syndicated WEBMASTER RADIO SHOW, an interview show that featured the giants of the high tech world during the climax of the Dot-Com bubble, from February 2000 to November 2001. He is currently a financial advisor, a columnist for THE FRESNO BEE, and a sometimes announcer for KVPR – national public radio in Fresno.

A paranormal and "alternate history" buff, Bull is working on more short stories and novels, as well as a non-fiction work on the Unified Field Theory.

www.ingramcontent.com/pod-product-compliance
Lightning Source LLC
Chambersburg PA
CBHW020223180626
46810CB00006B/2023